PUPPET MASTER

DALE BROWN
AND JIM DeFELICE

PUPPET MASTER

WM
WILLIAM MORROW
An Imprint of HarperCollins*Publishers*

PUPPET MASTER. Copyright © 2016 by Air Battle Force, Inc. All rights reserved. Printed in the United States of America. No part of this book may be used or reproduced in any manner whatsoever without written permission except in the case of brief quotations embodied in critical articles and reviews. For information, address HarperCollins Publishers, 195 Broadway, New York, NY 10007.

First William Morrow premium printing: September 2016
First William Morrow hardcover printing: August 2016

ISBN 978–0–06-256709–3

William Morrow® and HarperCollins® are registered trademarks of HarperCollins Publishers.

16 17 18 19 20   RRD 10 9 8 7 6 5 4 3 2 1

PUPPET MASTER

Data sheet

Important people

Louis Massina—scientist and entrepreneur, proprietor of Smart Metal, deeply religious; lost his arm in a motorcycle accident as a young man; never remarried

    Chelsea Goodman—project engineer at Smart Metal; young, genius at math, petite, creative

    Trevor Jenkins—FBI special agent in charge of anti-ATM theft task force; hardworking, always wears a suit; could use a haircut and shave

    Johnny Givens—young, athletic FBI agent on Jenkins's task force

    Gabor Tolevi—first-generation American of Russian and Ukrainian descent, raised mostly in the Ukraine where he served in the army. Now an "entrepreneur" with connections to Russian *mafya,* though not a member of a family; widower and single father

Important places

Boston & suburbs—birthplace of freedom, hardscrabble values, great Italian food

Crimea—peninsula in Black Sea annexed by Russia in 2014 from Ukraine

Donetsk—major city in southeastern Ukraine, center of struggle between Russian-backed separatists and Ukrainian government; under Russian domination

Important tech

Bot—Smart Metal slang for robot that can function to some degree on its own, in contrast to mechs and industrial robots designed for specific, stationary tasks such as welding or chip making; Smart Metal constructs all types

Mech—Smart Metal slang for robots that are preprogrammed for specific tasks but retain more flexibility than industrial robots

Autonomy—ability of bot or other entity to "think" or make decisions without direct commands from operator

ONLY GOD GIVES LIFE

Flash Forward

"I am not in the business of creating supermen." Louis Massina fixed his gaze on Chelsea Goodman, then shook his head. "No. We can't go there."

"You're just going to let him die?" Chelsea touched his arm. "Lou—boss. You can save him."

"I'm not Frankenstein. I don't make supermen."

"That's not what I'm asking."

"It amounts to the same thing. And there's no saying whether any of it will work. The drugs—we've only used them in simulations and on pigs. *Pigs*."

"He dies if you do nothing. You can help him."

"Giving him legs is one thing, even the heart, but the drugs—"

"Without the drugs, Lou, he dies."

Louis Massina turned toward the window, gazing out at Boston Harbor. The wooden remains of a wharf sat in the distance to the right, a sharp contrast to the gleaming pink granite of the unfinished office building just beyond it. Massina liked the incongruity, the mix of old and new. The wharf had last been used close to fifty years before; Massina was sure he'd been on it around that time, a young man taken to work by his father, just a few days before he disappeared. In his lifetime, Massina had seen the white planks turn gray and grow splinters, then gaps. The slow-motion ruin of the wooden pier not only marked time for him; it reminded Massina that life was circumscribed by limits. There were only so many chances, so much time.

"Listen, boss, you have to do something. He was hurt helping us."

"We were helping him," Massina said softly, still gazing out the window. "We were helping the FBI. Not the other way around. This is their person. Their case. Not our problem. Not mine."

"You've saved so many people."

A new heart, two legs, and a batch of untested drugs to take him from the brink of death in a matter of days, if not hours: was Louis Massina a god, that he could give life like that?

Givens was already dead. Really. The doctors all agreed.

"He won't survive the operation," said Massina. "Even with the drug."

"Now you do sound like you're playing God. Or Satan."

Louis Massina did not really think of himself as God. That was sacrilege. But his prosthetics, a sideline of his robotics company, did literally save lives. Was that sacrilege? Or a gift from God that by rights he had to share?

"I don't understand why you're hesitating," added Chelsea.

Massina turned to face her. "The heart is experimental. The spinal attachments are still at a very primitive point. We don't have FDA approval, among other things. And the drugs—"

"You can get all that waived. You know it."

"Just like that." He snapped his fingers.

Chelsea narrowed her green eyes. She was a pixie of a thing, barely five foot, with skin the color of light chocolate; her face glowed like a dusty rose in the fading sun of the late afternoon. He guessed she might weigh ninety pounds, and that was counting the ink on her tattoos and the piercings she occasionally wore in her lip.

"Boss, you know you can do this."

"It may be too far," said Massina, though he had made up his mind. "And we don't know if he'd agree."

"He wanted to be resuscitated," said Chelsea. "His form says, *I want to live*. That's the only agreement you're going to get."

He's hardly old enough to understand what it will mean, thought Massina. Even Chelsea has no idea. Choosing to live—it's a choice for more pain, more suffering. There will be no easy day.

Instead of saying that, he turned back to the window. Chelsea's reflection was there, looming over the old pier. Two large construction cranes stood in the distance; if the light were better, they would have given the illusion of hoisting his employee's face into the sky.

"Arrange it," he told her. "Tell Sister Rose to keep me updated herself. The doctors tend to get lost in the details."

REAL TIME

1

A week earlier—near Boston, Massachusetts
Sunday evening

Louis Massina bent forward and refocused his eyes on the ATM screen.

Account Balance = $0.00

"What?" He tapped the screen to ask for a new transaction, then once again requested his balance.

Account Balance = $0.00

"Impossible."

Massina re-swiped his ATM card and keyed his PIN on the touch screen. There was only one account connected to the card, which he used solely for petty cash. Not only did he know there was money in the account—he had used it on the way to mass this morning—but the sum was $5,437.14.

Massina was *very* good with numbers.

He tapped the screen, then waited. The machine thought about it, then responded exactly as it had earlier:

Account Balance = $0.00

Either the bank's computer network was down, Massina thought, or his accountant had drained it without telling him.

Damn it.

Massina had more patience with computers than with accountants, but only a little. He had considerable experience with both: he ran a robotics and applied AI, or artificial intelligence, firm called Smart Metal, and had in fact been a programmer himself through his early twenties.

That was two decades and three dozen patents ago. In the interim, Massina had built a business worth exponentially more than the amount that should have been in the bank account. But he was not so far removed from a childhood raised by a single mother that he would ignore the disappearance of five thousand dollars, or even five.

He called his accountant as soon as he got back to his car; though it was nearly 11:00 P.M., the phone was answered on the first ring.

"Wasn't me," said the accountant, who was used to getting calls at odd hours and on odd subjects. "I'll check with the bank first thing in the morning." Robert Pesche, now the head of a sizable firm, had first done Massina's taxes in a McDonald's when they were both a year out of school. "It's probably just a computer glitch."

"There are no such things as glitches," said Massina. "Just bad programming."

But this turned out to be neither a glitch nor bad programming: it was theft. The account had been drained an hour before Massina's visit to the ATM—one of two dozen that had similarly been robbed. The bank promised to make good immediately, something Massina was surprised to find it didn't have to do, according to the banking laws.

The felonious transfer both annoyed and intrigued Massina. Not only was his sense of morality and fairness offended—theft, obviously, was a grave sin—but his scientific curiosity was aroused. How did the theft occur? Why was the bank vulnerable in the first place? It was a math problem as well as one of morality.

His accountant couldn't answer any of his questions. Nor could the bank manager, who came out to meet him when he stopped by just before 5:00 P.M. to collect a new ATM card and some cash.

The manager hesitated as she grabbed Massina's hand to shake. Massina was testing a new prosthetic—he had lost his right arm from just above the elbow some thirty years before—and people who knew his hand was artificial sometimes thought he was going to crush their fingers.

Which he could have, if he wanted.

"I'm very sorry about this theft," said the manager. "And your troubles. You are a good customer."

The manager continued on in an overly sympathetic vein until Massina asked how the account might have been drained.

"It was definitely due to an ATM transaction," she said. "There were a large number of simultaneous transfers that were just under the amount our security programs would detect."

"Excuse me—so the ATM system was definitely involved," Massina said. "Interesting. How?"

She suggested that perhaps he had authorized someone else to use his card and been careless with the PIN.

"How would that account for the other thefts that you said happened at the same time?"

"They, uh, just waited." She nodded gravely. "You really have to guard your PIN number as if it were your Social Security number. More so."

"I don't want to get angry with you," Massina answered, "but you sound like you're saying this theft is my fault."

"No, sir. You are our valued customer." She glanced at his hand, somewhat nervously. "We value your business."

Massina resisted the impulse to scoff as he left.

2

Massina's annoyance at being ripped off and then treated like a dunce by the bank had subsided by the time he woke the next morning in his house outside Boston. There were, after all, many other things occupying his mind, most especially the morning's test of a new autonomous bot they were working on.

It was just before five o'clock, and still dark. Winter lingered in the low hills around Boston, fogging Massina's breath as he walked onto the concrete veranda in front of his house. The low-slung, postmodern structure had been situated to take advantage of the view; had it been a little later, Massina might have gazed at the mirror-edged Hancock Tower and the Pru off in the distance. In winter, much of Boston was visible, not just those tall landmarks: you could see the Custom House and even, if the air was clear and the light good, a church spire or two. Thick evergreens obscured things closer to the east and south; the highway, so convenient for his work, was out of sight, as was the industrial area that had first attracted him to the location. If Massina had been more of a dreamer, or rather one who dreamed in a certain way, he might have fantasized that he lived in the middle of untouched land, sufficiently removed from the distant city to be immune from its charms as well as its vices.

But Massina was not that sort of dreamer—no Emerson and certainly no Thoreau; if there was an American he might emulate, it would be Edison or Bell, great thinkers whose thoughts turned to things far more tangible than nature. Though in many respects Massina might be said to be the modern embodiment of the vision Emerson articulated in the essay "Self-Reliance," Massina's world was one of computers and robots, of nanotechnology and forces far beyond Emerson's ken.

The lights at the far end of the winding driveway switched on, announcing the arrival of Chelsea Goodman, who was taking Massina to work today while his car was being serviced. This was a matter of convenience for both of them, since Chelsea didn't own a car and was using one of the company trucks to transport both herself and the subject of the morning's test to the proving grounds south of the city.

The gates at the foot of Massina's property swung open, activated by a coded input from the driver on a small touchpad next to her console. The security system had already read the truck's license plate, comparing it against its database and DMV data; it had also examined an infrared scan of the interior, making sure Chelsea matched the associated profile. Another sensor "sniffed" the air around the truck, analyzing the molecular contrail that had been enhanced by a light stream of vapor flowing from vents at the side of the driveway; had the contrail contained even a few molecules related to explosives, additional barriers would have sprung up just beyond the gate and an alarm would have sounded.

None of that was actually necessary; Massina in fact disliked security measures of any kind and kept as low a profile as possible in any event. But the system was being tested by his company; grounds security seemed like a growth area, and one where the company's expertise in advanced AI systems and robotics might possibly give it an advantage.

As it happened, the driver had worked on a small part of the system a year before and was probably as familiar with it as its owner. Chelsea Goodman had joined Smart Metal as an AI specialist barely two years ago. Since then, she had been promoted three times until, at the tender age of twenty-three, she was now Smart Metal's lead AI developer.

Neither her age nor her rapid advancement was particularly unique, either at the firm or in the industry in general. Even the fact that she was a woman did not make Chelsea Goodman particularly unusual at Smart Metal, which Massina had established as the purest of pure scientific meritocracies from its earliest day. The unique thing about Chelsea was her personality: she practically bubbled when she spoke. Her enthusiasm was infectious, and not just about her field— she could get even a die-hard Red Sox fan, such as Massina, rooting for their longtime nemesis, the New York Yankees, if she wished.

Which made the uncharacteristic frown on her face when she pulled up all the more obvious.

"Problem?" asked Massina, climbing into the Ram 1500 cab.

"We're good," she said, lips barely moving, teeth held close together.

"Coffee," he told her, recognizing the problem.

"I—"

"Starbucks. Go."

"Thanks." Her expression brightened; by the time they reached the street she was more or less back to her usual self, adjusting for the hour.

"Long night?" he asked.

"I didn't sleep. We had some trouble with the secondary logic section." Chelsea said this with the tone of someone describing their stupendous vacation in Barbados. "In optimizing the memory section, Bobby had used a random fill to get around the zero-bit problem. Of course, he hadn't been able to test every last permutation, and wouldn't you know, we hit on a combination that caused a bizarre overload, adding twenty nanoseconds where we should have saved at least sixty-four. . . ."

As Chelsea described the problem and its solution in great detail—in layman's terms, or as close to it as possible, it had to do with what was essentially a trick in utilizing memory more efficiently than the logic chip's cache was designed to do—Massina's thoughts drifted, scattering among some of the other projects his company was working on. While applications for industrial robots were Smart Metal's major moneymakers, the company had projects in a vast array of areas; not all involved AI and robotics. One of his engineers had designed a golf club whose head corrected for imbalances in its user's swing, practically guaranteeing long and accurate drives off the tee.

At least according to its inventor. Massina had never tried it himself. He didn't particularly like golf, and while he had taken a few swings with the club, he could not personally say that it did anything an ordinary driver couldn't. He did, however, like the idea that the pros they'd hired to test it raved about it.

"Want anything?" Chelsea asked, pulling into the lot of a strip mall dominated by Starbucks.

"I don't have any cash," said Massina, suddenly remembering that he hadn't managed to get to the ATM.

"I'll spot you," laughed Chelsea. "Black, no sugar. Tall?"

"Medium. Or small."

"That's tall," said Chelsea, slipping out of the truck. "Twelve shot latte for me."

"Hmmph," he said, mentally calculating the effects of that much caffeine on her small frame.

CHELSEA GOODMAN SHIVERED involuntarily as she stepped from the truck. Despite the fact that she had lived in the Northeast for some six years now—four while studying at MIT, and two with Smart Metal—the San Diego native still had not adjusted to the climate. Winter itself didn't bother her as much as the long wait for spring that characterized the end of March and beginning of April. Mentally done with ice and snow, she wanted flowers and much longer days, or at least days where she could comfortably bike to work without a parka.

Though it was barely past five, the line at the counter snaked around the ground coffee display to the mocha pots at the store entrance. This Starbucks was one of the few in the area that opened before six, which made it an oasis for caffeine-starved early risers.

Chelsea took a step back and did a high lunge, a basic yoga move that stretched her lower body. The man in front of her glanced around, clearly concerned that she might do something more dangerous.

"Just staying warm." She smiled at him, twisting left and right. He rolled his eyes and turned back toward the counter.

Chelsea was excited about the morning test; now that they had solved the memory problem, she felt the bot would easily pass its functional tests. The robot was an offshoot of an earlier design used by the military to retrieve mines and IEDs without exposing soldiers to their dangers. Where the original was operated by remote control, this one was completely autonomous; it could be told to locate ordinance, safe it, and then place it in a robot vehicle for transportation or disposal. While these tasks were relatively straightforward—Smart Metal had a "mech," or programmed robot, that could do all of those things already—the bot's size and production costs were the real innovations. RBT PJT 23.A—more commonly known to the developers as "Peter"—folded itself into a tool-bag-sized case. The AI computing unit and sensors were all off-the-shelf, the former actually centered around a processing unit used for the latest version of the Apple iMac. Pushing an architecture designed to run a home computer into areas ordinarily reserved for the human brain had been, and continued to be, an exhilarating challenge.

Exactly the reason she was here.

A strange scent tickled Chelsea's nose as she moved up in the line. It was an off note, a double-flat in the olfactory symphony of coffee blends and roasts.

Rotten eggs?

It reminded her of the ancient gymnastics studio where she'd spent much of her elementary school afternoons.

Mold?

Natural gas?

THE STARBUCKS BUILDING was in a small strip mall directly across from a row of much older residential buildings; in a few hours the close-in suburb would be clogged with work traffic, but at the moment the streets were nearly deserted. Massina gazed at the row of late-nineteenth- and early-twentieth-century row houses surrounding the plaza. Varying between three and five stories tall, each building housed several apartments, some two or three on each floor.

The inventor had spent much of his childhood in a succession of similar houses. There was nothing to be particularly nostalgic about; his childhood had been far from gilded. And yet he remembered bits and pieces fondly, and knew he had learned a great deal, whether in the hardscrabble streets or the strict Jesuit grammar school where his abilities were first recognized.

Massina had started working at ten, sweeping the floor of a butcher shop several blocks away from here. His boss, a cousin of his mother, had been difficult; work had nonetheless been an oasis compared to his home, where his mother's erratic, alcohol-fueled behavior had filled the small rooms with danger as well as . . .

. . . The building he was looking at suddenly flashed yellow, then red, as fire surged from a dozen points at once. The air filled with glass, wood, and brick. A shock of air yanked the front of Massina's truck upward and back; it slammed down so hard that the air bags exploded.

Dazed, Massina grabbed for the door handle and grappled with the seat belt. He fell out to the pavement, the car alarm blaring. Flames seemed to be everywhere, sucking air so quickly it whistled.

Get Chelsea, Massina told himself, struggling to his feet. *Get Chelsea to safety, damn you, old man!*

His mouth and throat filled with a mist of fine powder from the air bag. Massina began to cough. The air blackened as a furl of soot descended over the buildings; it gave way slowly to a red and yellow glow, the fire pushing away the smoke as it rose. The street looked as if a tornado had cut through a war zone: debris, big and small, littered the road and parking lot.

Legs shaking, Massina steadied himself against his truck, then started toward Starbucks.

He found Chelsea lying on the sidewalk just in front of the building. She had just stepped out when the explosion occurred; knocked backward, she lay on the ground, stunned and surrounded by glass.

Massina bent to her, not sure whether she was dead or alive. He caught a glimpse of people inside the store trying to help each other, moving as if in slow motion.

Chelsea moved her head.

"Up!" Massina barked at her. "We got to get away from the building."

Chelsea's face and clothes were speckled with blood where small bits of stone-shrapnel had peppered her skin. She was in shock.

"Chelsea!" Massina barked. "Get up!"

She blinked, then slowly got to her feet. "My coffee!"

"Come on."

Massina helped her to the side of the Starbucks building, struggling to get his own bearings. The blast had muffled his hearing, and he felt as if he had a helmet over his head.

"Are you bleeding?" he asked.

She waved her hand; she didn't seem to be hearing well either. But she seemed OK, just dazed.

Massina reached his right hand—the artificial one—into his pocket and took out his phone. "Nine-one-one," he told the custom dialing app. "Report fire at this location. And an explosion."

There was already a siren in the distance. People from the buildings across the street came out to see what was going on.

"*People!*" yelled someone. "*There are people inside the building on fire!*"

Chelsea looked at Massina and blinked. Her eyes seemed to focus. In the next moment she was on her feet, running toward the far end of the building.

It took Massina a moment to react, and several more before he realized that, rather than running away to safety, she was running *toward* the fire. "*Wait! Wait!*" he yelled, running after her.

The Starbucks had received barely a glancing blow from the explosion; the only damage was to the windows. The two stores next to it were similarly pockmarked by flying debris and shattered glass; the masonry fronts on both were caved in but still intact. The real damage was to the older building adjacent to them. The explosion had obliterated the front half of the building, a three-story Victorian-era house that had been clad in shingles; the back wall was twisted and shriveling, though its panels had somehow managed to resist the fire. The two row houses that abutted it on the other side had been largely untouched by the explosion, but they were now on fire, as were two more beyond them.

Chelsea stopped in front of the destroyed building, gaping at the twisted wreckage. A woman in a cotton nightgown stood nearby, her face covered with soot.

"Mrs. Stevens! Mrs. Stevens!" shouted the woman.

"Who's Mrs. Stevens?" asked Massina.

"Look!"

Massina saw a shadow in the top window. He guessed it was Mrs. Stevens.

"We have to get her out of there," said Chelsea.

As if on cue, flames flared behind the woman, throwing her silhouette in sharp contrast. She had something in her arms—a child.

Chelsea had stopped a few feet away. She stared up at the house, then started for the front door.

Massina ran to grab her. "*No, no, no!*"

A ball of flames burst through the first-floor façade. Chelsea stopped short.

"Get the bot!" Massina shouted to Chelsea. "Get Peter."

She stood motionless for a moment longer, then twisted around and ran back in the direction of the truck.

"She's going to die," said the woman in the nightgown. "Where are the firemen?"

"We'll help her," said Massina. He looked up at the window. The woman had disappeared.

CHELSEA'S THOUGHTS MOVED in four directions at once; she felt as if her brain were physically bumping against the confines of her skull. She ran in the direction of the truck, or what she thought was the direction of the truck, only to realize that she had gone out to the road; she corrected and darted back toward the rear of the pickup.

The bot's container was in a large box at the back of the truck bed, wedged between two larger boxes that contained monitoring gear and backup controls. Chelsea grabbed the box and, despite its size and weight, hauled it on top of the truck cab; she had to pull over one of the other boxes to get high enough to reach the snap locks at the top of the case.

Come on, come *on,* she mumbled to herself. *Get it out!*

Peter looked a little like a headless horse designed by Picasso. Made primarily of carbon fiber compounds and titanium, the small robot had four legs that articulated from a slim, seven-sided irregular central box; it could stand and move on two or four of any of these legs. The six-fingered claws at the end of each could pick up and hold items as small as a dime. Despite its size— unfolded and standing on four legs, it was only .683 meters tall, or a little over two feet high—it could carry roughly five hundred pounds.

Something exploded in the distance. Chelsea froze, bile creeping into the back of her mouth.

Go, girl, go!

The words were her father's, seemingly implanted at birth. It was his voice she inevitably heard when in trouble, whether on the uneven bars as a five-year-old or a work project now.

Go, girl, go!

His voice was as strong now as it had been in the gym at the state gymnastics championships—embarrassing then, galvanizing now.

Go, girl, go!

THE HEAT OF the fire on Massina's face felt like a sunburn. No more than two or three minutes had passed since the explosion, yet it seemed like an eternity.

Where are those fire trucks? Where is Chelsea with the bot?

"Here we are!" Chelsea dropped to her knees, skidding on the hard concrete. She had RBT PJT 23.A in her arms.

"The control unit!" said Massina. "Go back and get it."

"No time," said Chelsea. "And we don't need it."

She reached under the robot's body and found a small slide; pushing it back revealed a fingerprint reader. Seconds later, the bot stiffened its limbs, signaling that it was powering up.

Massina went down to one knee opposite Chelsea. The bot was between them. He reached underneath, sliding his fingers around until he found the slot where the reader was. The machine, now alive, beeped in recognition.

"Skip diagnostics," he told the robot. "Natural language mode."

It beeped, acknowledging the order.

"Proceed to the four-story building that is on fire. Retrieve woman and child from floor four."

The robot didn't move.

"Go," Massina added. "Take the woman and child to safety one at a time."

The bot still didn't move.

Massina's hasty and frankly vague instructions had to be translated and analyzed before they could be acted on; not only were they fairly generic, at least to a machine, but they also related to a task that the machine had never encountered before. Though it had climbed numerous buildings, and it did know what a woman and a child were, it had never had an exercise anywhere near as complicated as this.

"We're going to have to get the controller," said Massina. "We need to make sure it knows what to do."

Chelsea grabbed him as he got up to run. "Wait. Look."

RBT PJT 23.A beeped and started toward the building.

Massina and Chelsea followed. The heat seemed blast-furnace hot.

But what had happened to the woman? She wasn't at the window.

The robot continued into the flames.

Turning, Massina ran to the truck. The control unit would be the only way to alter the bot's commands at this point, and very possibly the only way to get the small machine out of the building if it got stuck.

If this had happened in six months, even three, the bot could get them out. Now, though . . . there is still so much to do.

Massina grabbed the case and started back to the building. It was a long box, awkward to carry, though not heavy. Firemen were arriving, pulling out hoses, directing a ladder truck. In the confusion no one questioned him; the case made him look as if he belonged.

By the time he reached Chelsea, the woman had reappeared at the window. She was holding her child in one hand and pushing at the glass pane with the other. Someone nearby yelled at her not to open the window, to wait for the firemen to arrive, but even if she could have heard them, the advice would have been difficult to follow, flying against all instinct. She finally succeeded in breaking the glass with the palm of her hand, pulling it back and knocking at the rest of the pane with her elbow. Wind whipped through the opening; the wall at the far end of the room caught fire, flashing red behind her.

"Oh God! She'd better jump," said Chelsea, running toward the building.

Massina left the control unit in its box and followed, thinking they might at least catch the baby. But the flames at the base of the building pushed them back.

More glass shattered above, raining through the fire and smoke.

"Look!" yelled Chelsea.

Peter had bulled its way through a second-story window. Crawling up the frame, it clawed at the shingles, moving up the outer wall like a slow-motion spider.

"Hey! Get back!" Someone grabbed Massina's shoulder, pulling him around. It was a policeman. "The place is going to explode!"

"We have to get that woman out of the building!" yelled Chelsea.

"Let the firemen work!"

The officer began pushing Massina back. Massina raised his right arm, took hold of the officer's uniform, and lifted him backward and out of the way.

Clearly surprised by the strength of the rather short man before him, the officer grabbed at Massina's arm. It was then that he got his second surprise—never much on appearances, Massina hadn't bothered to put the "flesh" covering on today, so the cop gripped several tubes of steel and protective carbon tunnels for the wiring.

A fresh explosion rent the air. Flames shot from the top of the building next to them. Massina released the policeman and turned back, searching for Chelsea through the smoke and dust.

"Chelsea!"

"I have her," yelled Chelsea, emerging from smoke with the baby in her arms.

RBT PJT 23.A followed, moving on three legs; the fourth held the woman it had rescued a foot above the pavement, as if it were an ant retrieving a prize grasshopper for the queen.

3

Standing at the edge of the small crowd that had gathered to watch the fire, Stephan Stratowich felt a surge of relief as the woman was helped to the paramedic van that had just pulled up. It wasn't because he would have felt any guilt over her death; rather, his boss had told him to avoid unnecessary complications. The woman's death would have counted as one.

Stephan had blown up two other similar buildings over the past several years; it was a sideline he didn't particularly like, but the assignments were something he couldn't refuse, especially when they came from Medved and the other associated with the clans that kept him employed. The trick wasn't in making a gas explosion look like an accident; it was in limiting the damage. There was always an unpredictability that the most thorough plan could not eliminate. In this case, the explosion had occurred nearly ten minutes after Stephan had intended, greatly increasing the collateral damage—only the commercial building at the end of the row was supposed to have been destroyed. It was empty; the job was probably part of an insurance scam, though Stephan never knew, or wanted to know, the particulars.

Now that the woman was out of the building, Stephan turned his attention to the odd-looking creature that had retrieved her. It was mechanical, some sort of robot, very unlike anything Stephan had ever seen at a fire.

He had other work to do today, a full agenda. Still, the contraption intrigued him enough that he decided to get a better look, so he edged around the back of the crowd. He took his phone from his pocket and slipped over to the video screen. This was definitely something worth taking a video of.

4

Any other boss would have canceled Peter's tests—surely the bot could not do more to prove itself that day—but any other boss would not have been Louis Massina.

Seeing his frown deepen as he watched the robot climb over a pile of rubble in the test area, Chelsea couldn't help but wonder at the two sides of the man. At work he was demanding and taciturn, eschewing even the tiniest chitchat in favor of a cold stare that seemed borderline autistic. It was a remarkable contrast to the person he was outside the job, one known not only for charity but also for taking a real interest in the people he helped, always anonymously.

"Why is it moving so slow?" demanded Massina as Peter picked its way over the tangle of steel beams and wire placed at the center of the old rail yard they leased for these sorts of tests. "Isn't it receiving the sensor information?"

"It is," said Bobby James, who was watching the bot's "brain" functions on the array of monitors nearby. "It's picking a safe route to the target."

"Hmmmph." Massina folded his arms. RBT PJT 23.A had

been tasked with finding and retrieving a small box that contained gunpowder hidden in the tangle. Besides its own sensors, it was receiving data from a sensor robot stationed nearby. The mech contained a sophisticated "sniffer," which scanned a fifty-meter circle. Peter took the data and mapped chemicals in the air; the sensor had detected the minuscule plume emitted by the stash and provided the data to Peter.

"It's got it," said Chelsea as the robot dug its claw into the pile. "We just have to be patient."

"Patience should not be programmed into the system," snapped Massina. There was still soot from the fire on his pants and a smudge on his face.

"Prudence is," retorted Bobby.

"Where's the line between prudence and negligence?" said Massina.

"We're not near it."

Impatient as he was, Massina generally tolerated a decent amount of back talk—as long as he felt you were dedicated to your job. But his manner of questioning could be cold, and even at times cruel. Any employee who couldn't deal with that—and stand up for themselves and their project—generally left; there were plenty of rivals who would pay handsomely for someone with experience here. Chelsea wondered if Bobby was getting close to that point; he'd recently complained about how much time he was working, something she'd never heard him do before.

"Chelsea?"

Chelsea turned and looked up into the face of Bill "Beefy" Bozzone, the head of Smart Metal's security team. Dressed in a dark blue suit, Beefy looked more like an accountant than a policeman . . . albeit one in very good physical condition.

"A couple of detectives want to talk to you and Mr. Massina about the fire," said Beefy.

"Not really a good time," said Chelsea.

"What?" snapped Massina, turning around.

"Sorry to bother you, Lou." Beefy started to apologize. "But there are some policemen to see you. I didn't know if—"

"I'll handle it." Massina looked at Chelsea. "Finish this, would you?"

MASSINA FOLLOWED BEEFY out past the rows of parked trailers to the whitewashed cement building at the entrance to the yard. He didn't like to be interrupted while working, though at this point there wasn't more he could do with the mech. It had passed all of its tests, albeit a little slower than he wanted.

Two men in ill-fitting suits stood just inside the doorway, shifting nervously. They smelled of cigarette smoke.

"We understand you were at the gas explosion this morning," said the taller of the two men. He withdrew a well-worn leather case from his jacket pocket and let the front flap drop, flashing a Boston Police Department badge; the other man did likewise.

"Yes?"

"Well, if you could give us your thoughts—"

"My thoughts on what?" snapped Massina.

"Run down what happened," said the shorter man. "What you saw."

"I saw a fire."

"And an explosion?" asked the shorter man. "My name's Bill Doyle. This is my partner, Cliff Lycum."

"A flash of light. It was dark. I heard someone say it was gas."

"You wouldn't have had anything recording, did you?" asked Lycum. "Because of your . . . your robot thing? Did you take pictures?"

Massina bristled. Now that the woman and her child were OK, he wanted to avoid giving out any information about the "robot thing" that had been involved.

"No, I'm sorry. We had no photos. We stopped for coffee. We were on our way here. My staff told you I was here?"

"Yes." Doyle nodded. "The explosion came from the right?"

"Yes, as you face Starbucks."

"How did you get the woman and kid out of the building?" asked Lycum.

Massina hesitated.

"We don't want any trade secrets," said Doyle.

"What do you want then?"

"An accurate picture of what happened. So we can figure out where the fire started, why it started. Like that."

"I have no idea when it started or why. There was a blast. My truck was jerked back and the air bags deployed. I got out. A few minutes later, maybe less, we saw the lady at a window."

"And you sent the, uh, machine to get her."

"Yes."

"What is it?"

"A robotic device. That's all."

"It went right through the flames," said Lycum.

"It's designed to deal with worse than that. It's based on a bomb disposal bot, though that's not its function."

"We were wondering if maybe there's a camera attached to it. The images might be useful," said Doyle.

"We have sensor data," said Massina, "but I can tell you it's not going to be of much use."

"Could we see it?"

"I'll have one of my people work through it with you." Massina explained that the data was not video as commonly understood but rather an array of data picked up by a combination of sensors—infrared and sonar as well as optical—that supplied a multidimensional matrix. It needed to be interpreted and translated from its native format; you couldn't just download it to a Windows machine or your TV.

"Wasn't there a surveillance camera on the building?" he asked.

"It was damaged by the fire," said Doyle. "We haven't been able to recover the video."

"Maybe we could help with that," said Beefy. "We have some good technical people."

"We would appreciate it."

"No guarantees," said Massina. "Bill, you can work out the details. Excuse me. I have work."

"Thank you, Mr. Massina," said Doyle. "If there's anything we can do."

"Sure," said Massina, hurrying back to Peter's test.

MANY HOURS LATER, having concluded the day's tests and checked things on a multitude of projects at his office downtown, Louis Massina arrived at Grace Sisters' Hospital. Walking briskly through the front lobby, he aimed for the rehab ward, eyes fixed straight ahead.

A familiar twinge jerked through his shoulder as he neared the oval-shaped threshold of the wing's reception area. It was a mere flash, yet one that pained him greatly. For in that moment, he felt not the stump or the electrodes or the muscle impulses that worked the relays . . . but his missing arm.

What came next was memory: the accident.

More pain, this across his entire body.

He was on his motorcycle, a car suddenly in front of him. He was in the air, flying into blackness.

A truck. The front of a building.

Blackness.

No arm.

That was what he had a memory of. What he couldn't remember, what he had blacked out all these years, was the sensation of his wife clinging to his back behind him.

It was the dark hole he never ventured near.

"It must be Thursday," said the ward's official greeter, wheeling out from behind his desk. "How are you, Mr. Massina?"

"Good, Paul," said Massina. "How are you?"

"Still not scheduled, but I'm hopeful. Then once that's squared away, we go to the prosthetics."

"Hopefully it will be worth the wait," said Massina.

"A step up." Paul laughed.

Massina knew that was supposed to be a joke—people said something similar all the time—but he had never seen any levity in anything relating to injury.

"We have some fresh-baked pastry tonight," said Paul. "Still hot."

"How about coffee?" asked Massina.

"We have cappuccino, you know. Sister's new machine."

"Just coffee."

Paul wheeled himself to the large counter area at the side. Selecting a French Roast from the rainbow of K-Cups, he loaded the single-cup maker. Fresh coffee poured through the coffeemaker at the side of the lounge, its heady, caffeinated scent overwhelming the slightly antiseptic smell of the rest of the hospital.

The lounge was in many ways a pressure lock, a transitional space between the hospital as a whole and the amputee ward. The array of drinks—the automatic espresso maker and coffee machines were well complemented by refrigerators stocked with juices, sodas, and water—was just one of the subtle amenities designed to make the place more welcoming. The ward was unlike any other part of the hospital, and in fact differed greatly from most conventional health-care facilities. The closest parallels could be found at Brooke Army Medical Center in San Antonio or the handful of units sponsored by the VA or military to rehabilitate stricken soldiers.

Like the military hospitals, Grace Sisters' had a large residential facility next door where families, as well as patients not needing bed care, could stay for extended periods. But what truly set the ward apart from other rehab centers was the tight-knit community atmosphere. Patients, loved ones, and staff spent considerable time with each other, as if they were one large, extended family.

That, and Massina's inventions. They were the reason most came here in the first place.

One of the lounge walls was covered with monitoring screens, each of which could be configured to show a different part of the ward. One displayed the exercise pool; another the small lab where

Massina's prosthetics were fine-tuned for patients. Video feeds from the six operating rooms could also be turned on, making it possible for families to follow what was going on.

The ward's ethos was one of openness; information was freely shared between everyone, doctor, patient, friend alike. That extended all the way to Massina's prosthetics, to the great consternation of Smart Metal's corporate counsel, who objected to their lack of trademark protection.

"The goal is to heal," Massina told the lawyer. "If people take my ideas to help others, even better."

There had been other words, none too polite, as well. The lawyer wasn't used to losing many battles and having his advice go unheeded, but it did in this case. He continued to bring the matter up every six months or so for form's sake, though he had long ago conceded this wasn't something he would prevail on. Presumably his annual increases in fees provided some consolation.

Massina had just taken his first sip of coffee when a diminutive woman burst into the lounge from the main hallway, arms pumping as if they were piston rods in an internal combustion engine.

"Louis!" she snapped. "And how are you tonight?"

"Very well, Sister. How are you?"

"Blessed." Sister Rose Marie had given this answer every time Massina had asked, which, given that he had known her for forty-five years, meant he had heard it quite a lot. He'd met her as a boy in grammar school, long before she'd been assigned to the hospital. Sister Rose was the most positive and enthusiastic person he knew when he was seven; she was still that now.

"Come," she told him, "there are some people I'd like you to meet. Bring your coffee—no cappuccino? You really should try that machine. It was a donation."

Massina followed the nun as she reversed course and revved down the corridor. Despite the years, Sister Rose seemed the same age she'd been when they met: ancient. The soles of her thick shoes clicked on the freshly waxed floor as she increased her pace. Massina had trouble keeping up.

The Sisters of Perpetual Grace had given up their thick wool habits and long veils even before Massina had encountered them in grammar school. They wore what even the younger nuns called "civilian clothes"—long dresses that came to midcalf and very modest blouses that neither left anything uncovered nor hugged a body part. All wore necklaces of thick beads that signified their membership in the order, as well as a wedding ring that showed they were "brides of Christ."

Dressed in her typical blue skirt and a slightly darker top, Sister Rose wore one additional item tucked into the side of her waistband that set her apart from some of the others: an old string of rosary beads. These were special to her for many reasons, not least of which was the fact that they had once belonged to her best friend: Massina's aunt, now deceased, with whom she had gone through the novitiate.

"Would you like to look in on young Thomas?" asked the nun.

She veered left toward a clinic room before Massina could answer. Inside, a child of ten was bent over in the middle of the room, pulling new shoelaces through the loops of his shoe. His mother and father beamed behind him.

Tying a shoelace was hardly much of an achievement for a ten-year-old—except that in this case, the fingers he was using were prosthetic. He had lost both of his forearms two years before when a hurricane had taken down his house, crushing them.

More interesting, at least to Massina, was the exact construction of the arm. The "skin" was actually an inflatable membrane of special vinyl that was the most lifelike Massina had ever touched; it was difficult to distinguish it from flesh. Instead of steel rods inside, the internal skeleton was made of flexible tubing inflated like balloons. Small internal pumps gave the arm far more flexibility than normal prosthetics; it could be bent at a ninety-degree angle, for example.

It would take quite some time before the boy could control that ability. For now, he was still learning the very basics, directing the machine with his nerve impulses.

The arm was an outgrowth of Smart Metal's work with so-called soft robots, a cutting-edge area that so far had not produced marketable or even practical items. But the "conversation" between brain and mechanical fingers was already a tested technology. Remarkably, it had been only a theory at the time of the hurricane that claimed the boy's arm.

That was how they worked: fast.

The kid glanced up from his shoe and smiled at Massina. Massina nodded, then watched with quiet contentment as the child finished the bow. The doctor who had helped develop the hands stood at the side of the room, frowning.

The boy's parents applauded as the child finished. Massina nodded to them, then stepped outside. The physician followed.

"Still a bit of a delay in the software," grumbled the physician. "We'll get it." The complaint pleased Massina—he wanted perfectionists working with him. The doctor was one of the best.

"You think it's the flex functions?" Massina asked.

"It would make sense. If it would be possible to have D.J. go over the systematics personally . . ."

"I'm sure he'd welcome the opportunity." D.J. was one of the systems engineers who had helped develop the arm but had recently moved on to another project. "If there's trouble, let me know."

"Thanks, Lou."

Massina decided to drop in on another patient whom he'd met a few weeks earlier. A soldier who had stepped on a mine in Iraq, he had received a custom-made leg a month before but was still confined to a hospital bed because of continuing complications with his lungs.

The doctors who worked with Smart Metal had developed a series of drugs that could greatly speed his recovery, but they were holding off using them because of concerns over the long-term effects. Massina had actually pulled strings and gotten an FDA waiver for them, but they were holding off until and unless they were convinced that he couldn't recover without them.

Massina knocked on the door frame, then took a step inside the room. It was completely empty: no bed, no patient.

"Jason's gone home," said Sister Rose, catching up.

"What?"

"He's with the savior," said Sister Rose.

"Why didn't they use the drugs?"

"You'll have to ask the doctors, Louis."

Damn it. He could have been helped.

"You needn't feel sorry for him, Louis. He was a good Catholic."

Massina's thoughts about religion and the afterlife were considerably more complicated than those the nun preached, but he didn't feel like having that discussion at the moment. He followed her back to the hall, brooding as they walked to another room.

The occupant was a boy who'd had his arm and leg severed in a train accident. He'd been fitted with a prosthetic months before but was back on the ward because of an unrelated flare-up of pneumonia. The boy's face lit up as Massina entered the room—the two were old friends, not least of all because they suffered from the same general injuries. Massina had been very fortunate not to lose his own leg.

They spent a few minutes talking about the video games the boy was playing lately. They were all "shooters," and he had very high scores online—a good sign, since it meant his artificial limb let him keep up with kids who had their original hands.

The boy's father stood in the corner, watching intently as his son chattered on. Finally, Sister Rose broke up the mostly one-sided conversation, explaining that Massina had a meeting upstairs.

"Fist bump!" said the boy.

Their artificial fists clinked against each other. Massina left the room with a smile.

TREVOR JENKINS PULLED the lapels of his suit jacket forward as Louis Massina stepped out into the hallway. Jenkins felt a sudden surge of nervousness but fought through it. "Mr. Massina?"

The scientist jerked his head in Jenkins's direction.

"I'm Trevor Jenkins," said the agent, striding forward. Tall and well-built, he was naturally imposing. The fact that he was black sometimes added to that aura, but it sometimes worked against him. He hoped it was neutral in this case, though racial prejudices were beyond his control. "I don't know if you remember me—"

"Of course. Your daughter has an artificial knee," said Massina, surprising Jenkins by remembering him. It had been two years since they'd last spoken. "How is she?"

"She's fine, she's fine," said Jenkins. "Every day, we thank you."

"We all do what we can." Massina started to turn away.

"Actually, I came here on official business. Semiofficial," added the agent. "You filed a complaint about your bank account. An ATM card."

"Yes?"

"Your office said I would be able to catch you here," explained Jenkins.

"You've caught the thieves?"

"No, but . . ." Jenkins shook his head. "I thought, when I saw your name, I would—that you were owed a real explanation."

"I see."

Jenkins glanced at Sister Rose, who'd just come out of the room. "Maybe we should discuss this somewhere a little more private?"

"Mr. Jenkins," said Sister Rose, belatedly recognizing him. "How is your daughter?"

"Very well, Sister, thank you."

"Business, Louis?" she asked.

"It'll only take a minute," said Jenkins. "Maybe in the lounge, or better yet, downstairs?"

Massina looked at the nun.

"We'll always wait for you, Louis," said Sister Rose. "Go right ahead."

5

Gabor Tolevi walked out onto the platform of Boston South and glanced in the direction of the Amtrak train. Its departure had been delayed forty minutes for unspecified reasons—not unusual for Amtrak.

He hated trains—they reminded him of his early childhood in Europe, Ukraine especially, when his father took him on business trips. He loved his father but hated those trips—far too poor for first class, let alone airplanes, they most often went common or fourth class, which meant jamming aboard the sleeping cars and staying there for the duration of a trip. These cars were traveling dormitories where as many as fifty bunks might be partitioned in. Tolevi and his father would share a bed, which was one thing when Gabor was three and quite another at six; they traveled together until Gabor was nearly thirteen, his father unable to find a suitable sitter after Gabor's mother died. A splurge might buy a *platzkart,* or third-class ticket, which meant a real seat in another car, but that, too, they would have to share, generally as a tag team. The Russian trains were usually cleaner than the Ukrainian, though that was simply a matter of degree, and he'd been on a

Russian train when a fat walrus of a man tried molesting him at age nine. The incident had changed Tolevi, but in his estimation for the better: he had learned how to fight and stand up for himself, and if it was his father who slit the man's throat that night in revenge, it could just as well have been him with the knife.

The Amtrak train was heading for New York City, a destination that Tolevi would have much preferred to have flown to. But he was taking the train, and this train in particular, at the request of Yuri Johansen. Johansen wanted to talk to him, and Tolevi couldn't easily turn down such requests.

Tolevi had met Johansen more than twenty years before, when both had been not only younger but also borderline naive. Tolevi was a young officer in the Ukrainian army, looking to come to America and not particularly concerned about how he got the money to do so; Johansen was a freshly minted CIA officer whose responsibilities included helping people like Tolevi. Johansen had recruited Tolevi following a three-month "courtship"; as these things went, it was rather quick, but it had proved immensely valuable over the years.

The relationship was mutually beneficial. With minimal but strategic assistance from Johansen, Tolevi had exploited his connections in both the Ukraine and Russia to build a thriving import-export business, one that was generally, though not always, aboveboard. American by birth as well as a Ukrainian passport holder, he was now a property owner and a man of some means. The fact that he occasionally worked with the Russian *mafya* was both necessary and a source of endless opportunity, not just for him but for Johansen, too. Johansen had moved up the ranks at the CIA. Even so, he continued to "run" Tolevi personally.

Johansen had once explained to Tolevi that he kept up contact because he "liked to keep a hand in." Tolevi doubted that was true—he suspected that the CIA officer used trips from the Washington area to Boston as a cover for something else, including a mistress—but he was used to Johansen, and in fact would have balked if he had been handed off to someone of lesser importance.

Johansen liked using trains for contact. This was inexplicable to Tolevi. Perhaps it had to do with the CIA officer's ability to scan the tickets and ID passengers; maybe he got some sort of agency discount. It did solve one problem: Tolevi had to be especially careful in Boston, as there were plenty of people around with connections to the Russian mob and, through them, to the intelligence services. Even a chance sighting of him next to a CIA agent would add complications to his life that he preferred not to deal with.

The train was late. He walked back into the station building, circling around toward the eating area between Dunkin' Donuts and the Au Bon Pain. There were no seats, so Gabor satisfied himself with examining faces, trying to decide who in the small crowd might be following him.

No one. No reason for paranoia.

The train was finally called. Tolevi made his way on board, finding a seat in the first car. He took the window seat and left his jacket on the aisle seat, a precaution to ward off a neighbor. The train, though, was relatively empty, and as it turned out, he didn't have to wait long—Johansen got on at Route 128, the second stop after the station, a little less than fifteen minutes after pulling out.

"This seat taken?" asked the CIA officer.

"Go ahead," said Tolevi roughly. He dropped his jacket onto his lap, repositioning his Kindle Fire atop it.

Johansen pulled a laptop from his briefcase before sitting down. Neither man spoke; they never admitted to knowing each other or made any sign of comradery or even bare courtesy during these meetings. They communicated by typing on their devices, pretending to be talking to someone else.

As always, Johansen started the conversation with an inane question.

YOU ARE FLYING?

Tolevi resisted the impulse to reply with something nasty.

PLANE LEAVES TONIGHT.

ARE YOU STOPPING IN CRIMEA?

IF ALL GOES WELL.

COULD YOU PICK UP A PACKAGE?

NOT A GOOD PLACE.

YOU MUST TRY. WE WILL COMPENSATE.

Yes, Tolevi thought. You definitely will compensate. He typed:

I WILL NEED THE RATE APPLIED FOR THE MOSCOW ERRAND.

THAT WAS A ONE-TIME THING.

THIS IS MORE DIFFICULT THAN THAT.

I WILL ARRANGE IT.

I WILL DO MY BEST.

That was the extent of their conversation. Johansen shut down the word-processing program and pulled up the browser; he watched a movie until they reached Westerly, Rhode Island, where he got off.

Always suspicious that Johansen might have left a trail or even some sort of device to watch him, Tolevi waited until he reached New York and was in a cab to make the call.

"Yes?" said Iosif. It was a bare syllable, more a grunt than a word, but it immediately identified him beyond any doubt.

"I'll be out of town for a few days. We have a shipment coming on the ninth."

"Taken care of."

"Good. Anything else?"

"Stratowich stopped by. He wants to talk to you," added Iosif.

Stephan Stratowich was a low-level goon who worked with some of the *mafya* people, Maarav Medved in particular. He obviously had been sent to bug him for either a favor or money.

Probably money. Tolevi owed Medved a payment: a "tax" for the benefit of not being interfered with.

"He was ranting about a robot," added Iosif.

"A robot?"

"You know Stratowich. Always something."

"Was that what he wanted?"

"I don't think so."

"Neither do I. Tell him I'll be back in a few days."

"I did."

"Let me know if anything comes up. I'll check in from Europe."

"Right."

6

According to Trevor Jenkins, Massina was just one of a hundred people who had been victimized in a strain of identity theft involving ATM skimmers.

"The theory is they used a skimmer," said the FBI agent. Massina listened patiently as the agent then explained what a skimmer was—a device that was placed on the ATM, reading the pertinent information.

"There was nothing like that there," said Massina when Jenkins finished.

"They are quite clever," said the agent. He unfolded a sheaf of papers with photos demonstrating how the machines were placed over the ATM's card apparatus. They ranged from crude card readers with a keyboard to a far more sophisticated device that looked like a card slot with a fat lip. "As soon as the PIN is keyed in, the thieves have all the information they need."

"I don't recall seeing anything like these," said Massina. "I think I would have noticed."

"Well, the ATMs seem to be the only link," said Jenkins apologetically. "There have been a rash of these, at different banks."

The incident was one of half a dozen in the area over the past several weeks, explained the agent. The thefts occurred within moments of each other—literally nanoseconds, as computer programs directed transfers over high-speed Internet lines. The transfers would cascade across a number of accounts until finally disappearing somewhere in Eastern Europe, where tracing them became very difficult.

The FBI had dealt with these sorts of devices for years and had a fairly good feel for what they looked like and were capable of. They also knew what sort of fraud pattern they generally corresponded to—quick hits on a number of bank accounts that had only one thing in common: a withdrawal at the compromised ATM. Most skimmer operations were relatively primitive; in most cases, the skimmers had to be recovered for the data to be used. This was more sophisticated; the transfers happened instantly, in small amounts that defeated normal security screening. And it involved transfers rather than cash.

"We have a number of the ATMs under surveillance," added Jenkins. "We'll catch them eventually."

"You're watching every ATM in the city?"

"I wish. Has your bank offered to make good on the money?" asked Jenkins.

"They said they would."

"Then you're ahead of the game. Many banks don't. Technically, they don't have to. If the PIN is used, they claim that you didn't keep it secure."

"That's bull."

"They can say anything they want, right?" The agent laughed nervously. "When I saw your name this morning on the list, I felt I had to tell you what was going on. Twenty-three people were hit last night. They got about ten thousand dollars. Your account was actually one of the bigger ones."

"Must be my lucky day." Massina stood. "I'm sorry, but I really need to go see Sister Rose and her committee."

"Of course." Jenkins took a business card from his pocket. "If I can help—if you have trouble getting your money back—just call. We can put pressure on the bank."

"Thanks," said Massina.

"I'm sorry that I can't be more positive," said Jenkins.

"Give my best to your daughter."

"We think about you every day. You really changed her life."

7

If there was one way to get Louis Massina interested in something, it was by telling him it was impossible. And while Agent Jenkins hadn't used that word exactly, everything he had said about the ATM card thieves made it sound like catching them would be very difficult without some sort of lucky break.

That was a challenge.

Still, Massina never would have pursued the matter had the bank's manager not called him a short while later to tell him that the bank had reversed its decision to reimburse him.

"Why?" Massina asked.

"You must have used your PIN," said the manager apologetically. "The regional office told me that I have to follow the rules."

"This is part of a skimmer operation," said Massina. "I've already spoken to the FBI."

"I'm sorry, but there's no evidence that there was a skimmer. We checked the tapes, and there was no physical alteration at the machine."

"Why would I have used an ATM to make a transfer," said

Massina, not even bothering to make it sound like a question. "And from that account?"

"I can't explain that," said the bank manager.

"If you look at the way that account is used—"

"I've been all through it with my bank's security VP," she said. "If they credit your account, they'll have to credit everyone's."

"As they should."

"You can take it up with regional," said the manager. "My hands are tied."

"You realize I have other accounts with you."

"I told them that. Several times."

He hung up. Chelsea Goodman was standing at his door; she'd heard his side of the conversation.

"The ATM theft?" she asked.

"They think I did it." Massina suppressed a growl. The unfairness angered him. While he could easily afford the loss, the idea of being ripped off annoyed him beyond proportion. Part of Massina realized he should be spending his time on something more productive, but it was overwhelmed by a simmering rage and a desire for revenge, however irrational it might be. He was angry at the thieves, but nearly as mad at the bank; he had to struggle to maintain his outward calm.

"Why don't you just hack into their system and see where the transfer went?" asked Chelsea.

"If I do that, I might just as well reverse the transaction," said Massina.

"That's a thought."

"An illegal one."

"It's your money."

"Tell me how Peter did," he said, changing the subject.

THOUGH MASSINA CUT her off, Chelsea's suggestion started a chain of thoughts that led him to call Jenkins later that day.

Much later. It was a few minutes past midnight.

"I have a proposition," he told the FBI agent. "I'd like to help you and your case."

"Really?"

"We'll do anything short of hacking into the banking system. Though if you want us to—"

"No, no, uh, we, uh, I wouldn't want . . ."

"How can we help?" insisted Massina.

"Uh . . ."

"You don't have the resources to watch every ATM, is that your problem?" asked Massina.

Jenkins didn't answer. Massina finally realized he had woken him up.

Not that it mattered.

"The first thing we have to do is analyze the location of the ATMs that have been hit already," said Massina. "I can supply surveillance equipment to watch a hundred units at a time. Analyze the theft patterns and we'll stake out the likely ones. We can use a remote system. We'll train the computer coordinating it to alert you to suspicious activity. We can then track the suspect, and you take it from there."

"Track them how?"

"We have UAVs," said Massina. "Small ones."

"Drones?" asked Jenkins.

"Depending on the geographical spread, you should only need six or seven."

"Well, I, um," Jenkins stuttered. "B-But . . ."

"What?"

"Well, for five thousand dollars—you'd be going through a lot of trouble."

"You have dozens of cases like this?"

"Over a hundred."

"Do you want to solve this or not?"

"I'll have to talk to my boss."

"Two of my people will be at your office at nine A.M. tomorrow. I'll call them now."

"Um, Mr. Massina, it's after midnight."

"They'll be at work. It's not a problem. What's the address?"

"WHO WERE YOU talking to?" asked Jenkins's wife as he slipped his cell phone back onto the nightstand.

"Mr. Massina."

"Louis Massina? Who helped Deidre? Is he in trouble?"

"No, not exactly."

"Why is he calling this late?"

Jenkins pulled the covers up to his neck, then rolled toward his wife. "He wants to help an investigation I'm involved in."

"Couldn't it have waited?"

"Just be thankful I don't work for him," he said, closing his eyes.

8

Three days later, Trevor Jenkins found himself sitting in the back of an FBI control van, monitoring some fifty ATMs with the help of small video cameras installed on or near the machines. While Jenkins flipped back and forth between different feeds, the real work was being done by a monitoring program hosted on one of Smart Metal's servers down in Boston. The program not only singled out ATMs where there was activity but also looked for images that corresponded to ATM skimmers, as well as tools and other assorted items deemed possibly suspicious, such as briefcases and large bags. There had been five alerts in the three hours since the system had gone live; all had been quickly ruled "benign" by the computer as well as Jenkins.

He still didn't one hundred percent trust the computer—garbage in, garbage out, as his supervisor had warned when he told him of the plan two days before. But it did make things easier to manage. According to the Smart Metal people, the program was an off-the-shelf security program with a few tweaks—none of which Jenkins understood, though it had been laboriously explained to him by one of the program's original authors, Chelsea Goodman.

The vivacious twenty-something had offered to sit with him and his team during the surveillance in case there were bugs; Jenkins had turned her down, citing Bureau rules against civilians in the van, though in reality he was worried she would be too much of a distraction for his unmarried partners, Johnny Givens and David Robinson.

"Bases loaded," said Givens, who was watching a game summary of the Red Sox and Tampa on his phone as they monitored the machines. "Lookin' good."

Jenkins switched through the video feeds, settling on a bank drive-up five miles away. Three cars were queued up—a long line for this particular machine.

The Bureau had tried analyzing the various ATMs that had been targeted but failed to come up with any useful data on why they had been picked. There were no discernible patterns, aside from the fact that they were all within ten miles of downtown Boston. Inside, outside, drive-up, walk-up—it all seemed particularly random.

"Damn," said Givens softly. "Big Poppy struck out. Still no score."

"They always break your heart," said Robinson. Though he'd lived in Boston for a few years, his baseball allegiances were still tied to his hometown, L.A., and the Dodgers.

"Anybody up for coffee?" Givens asked.

"Me," said Robinson. "Assuming I can't get a beer."

"No beer," said Jenkins. "I'll take one, too."

Givens slipped into the cab unit of the van, checked the surroundings, then hopped out. They were parked near a grocery store that anchored a suburban mall; there was a Dunkin' Donuts at the far end.

"Think we'll catch 'em tonight?" asked Robinson.

"Real long shot," said Jenkins. "May not even be a skimmer."

"It has to be a skimmer," said Robinson.

"Yeah, but it bothers me that there's no marks on the machines and no one's ever spotted one—you look at most skimmer cases, eventually someone figures it out."

"That's because the bad guys get greedy. Some of these are damn good."

"I guess."

Givens returned a few minutes later with coffee and a box of doughnuts. The Sox had scored a run while he was gone, prodding him to formulate a theory that the team needed him to be walking so they could score. This of course drew guffaws from Robinson, and the two began trading even more bizarre theories about how the universe intersected with baseball.

That was Givens's real asset on a surveillance team—he tended to lighten the mood. Givens had joined the Bureau after a brief stint in the Army, where he'd qualified as a Ranger but not found a slot in the battalion—a distinction that was lost on Jenkins but apparently mattered a great deal to Givens.

"Time to rotate," said Robinson finally, glancing at his watch. They changed stations every hour to keep a fresh set of eyes on the monitors.

"Don't break anything," Jenkins said, giving up his seat. He was just about to open the van door and get out when Robinson cursed.

"Spilled the coffee," said the agent.

"It's not much," said Jenkins. "Just clean it up."

About a quarter of the cup had sloshed onto the floor. A few drops were on the counter near the keyboard. Robinson carefully daubed them up with a napkin while Givens threw paper towels on the floor. The damage seemed contained until Robinson went to switch the feed. The keyboard didn't respond.

"It froze," said Robinson. "Damn it."

"Man, you have a bad aura," said Givens. "No wonder you like the Dodgers."

"Let me see." Jenkins pushed back into the seat in front of the console. The displays had frozen, and nothing he tried could get them to unfreeze.

"Maybe we should just reboot the system," said Givens, looking over his shoulder. "Hit Alt-Delete-Control."

"I don't think that's a good idea," said Robinson.

"The computer's a PC."

Robinson shrugged. "Your call, boss."

Not knowing what else to do, Jenkins decided it couldn't hurt.

He was wrong, though—instead of a frozen screen, the computer went completely blank. A hard reboot—turning it on and off—changed the color to blue.

"We're screwed," said Robinson. "Great going, Johnny."

"All right, time to call the cavalry," said Jenkins, looking for the paper with Chelsea Goodman's phone number.

FIVE MILES AWAY, at the Smart Metal building in downtown Boston, Chelsea was watching a video of RBT PJT 23.A pick its way across the debris-strewn railyard where it had been tested a few days ago. It got where it had to go, but its movements still weren't smooth enough for the scientist, for whom fluidity of motion was an indication of efficient programming. She was just about to reexamine some of the bot's decision tree when her cell phone began to vibrate.

She took it from her pocket warily. Her ex-boyfriend had called several times over the past week, trying to "talk things out." Tired of the emotional roller coaster he represented, she'd blocked his number; he'd gotten around this by using friends' cells.

Not recognizing the number, she reached her finger to the Ignore tab, then realized it was the FBI agent she'd been assigned to help. She hit the green button and held it to her ear.

"This is Chelsea."

"I need help," said Jenkins without introducing himself. "The computer froze. I tried to reboot—"

"No, you shouldn't do that."

"I know. Now."

"Where are you? I'll get an Uber."

"I'll send someone to get you if you want," said Jenkins.

CHELSEA SPOTTED THE blue Bureau Malibu twenty minutes later. The driver pulled over to the curb and flashed his FBI credentials.

"I'm Johnny," he told her. "You're Chelsea?"

"Yup."

"You need tools?"

"They're right here," said Chelsea, tapping the side of her head as she got into the car. The Red Sox game was on the radio. "What's the score?"

"Four-two. We're up."

"Good."

"You a Boston fan?" Johnny asked.

"Now. But I grew up in San Diego."

"Don't tell me you like the Padres. That's a triple-A team."

"Ouch."

"At least you know something about baseball," said Johnny.

"What's that supposed to mean?"

"Nothing."

"Which do you prefer?" asked Chelsea, deciding to needle him, "defense-adjusted ERA, or defense-neutral ERA."

"Um—"

"The one advantage of defense-adjusted ERA is that it can give you an indirect idea of how good a team's defense really is, since it goes back to NRA."

"I don't really get all that stat stuff," confessed Johnny.

"So you're not really into baseball."

"No. It's just—there's more to baseball than statistics."

"Like?"

"Like hot dogs. What's baseball without hot dogs?"

Chelsea laughed.

"Hamburgers you can do without," said Johnny. He was just

about to expound on his reasoning when the scanner mounted under the dash crackled with a call.

"That's a robbery at an ATM," said Johnny. "It's about ten blocks away."

"Are we going?"

"Yeah, definitely."

JOHNNY PULLED THE car up behind a city police cruiser, angling it so the other vehicle could pull back if it needed to. He flashed on a scene from his childhood—the football field where the varsity team played was only a block and a half away, and he'd spent some of the best days of his youth there. On one particularly glorious afternoon, having completed twenty of twenty-five passes with two touchdowns and no interceptions, he'd run down this very street, shouting, "We're Number 1!" with a pack of friends.

Faded glory now.

"You stay in the car while I see what's going on," he told Chelsea. "Deal?"

"All right."

"They probably don't need us," he added. "But, we're here. So, you know."

"OK. Fine."

He was torn—Jenkins was waiting. On the other hand, maybe this was related. It involved an ATM.

Outside the car, Johnny trotted toward the bank. He waved his creds at an approaching police officer. "I'm with the FBI. What's going on?"

"Two suspects, somewhere in that back alley, we think," said the officer. "Sergeant McLeary's in charge."

"Where's he at?"

"Up over there, behind the car."

McLeary's skeptical glare when Johnny introduced himself told him everything he needed to know: he wasn't needed or wanted. That wasn't atypical—many local departments felt the

Bureau interfered or at best tended to hog the glory when they were involved in a case.

"We've been watching ATMs in the area for a case," Johnny explained. "We'd be interested in talking to your suspects."

"Gotta catch them first," answered McLeary. "We have them in that alley, we think."

"I may be able to get some backup," offered Johnny.

"I have a couple of more cars on the way, and a helicopter with infrared," said McLeary, warming a little.

"I know this street pretty well," said Johnny. "I grew up around here. They could go over the roofs of those houses on Pierce and get out that way."

"Yeah."

"You have somebody there?"

"Not yet."

"I can drive around there for you."

"All right. I'll have a car out there in five minutes, maybe less. I'll tell them to look for you."

IF THERE WAS one thing in the world Chelsea wasn't good at, it was waiting. The police radio made it even worse, tantalizing her with snippets of action that she couldn't be involved in. It was clear from the clipped communiqués that the police believed they had their suspects trapped somewhere in the alley, but it was equally clear that they weren't sure how exactly to get them.

The driver side door suddenly opened. Surprised, she twisted around.

It was Johnny.

"Hang on," he said, pushing the car into reverse. "We're going around the corner to watch the buildings."

JOHNNY SLOWED AS he turned the corner. He scanned the street ahead, then glided into a parking spot across from the buildings.

"They might come out that way," he said, half to himself, half to Chelsea. "Off the roofs."

"Do you know this area?"

"Definitely. There's a high school that way."

"Your school?"

"No. We wanted to steal the mascot one time. We got caught . . . well, chased, actually. We ended up in that alley. And we got out climbing the building."

"Really?"

Johnny laughed. "Good times."

"There's a car down the block with someone in it," said Chelsea. "Is that a cop?"

"What car?"

"Way down near the corner."

"The pickup?" asked Johnny.

"Yeah."

"That's a truck. It's not a cop."

"There's someone in the driver's seat."

"You're sure?" Johnny strained to see.

"Positive."

"Stay here."

CHELSEA FOLDED HER arms across her chest, watching Johnny walk down the street. He reached his right hand behind his hip as he walked.

He's got a gun there, she thought.

Well, duh. He's an FBI agent.

Until that moment, it all had been very theoretical—modifying the program, helping them test it and implement it, then coming out to help them. But now she realized it was something a lot more than a problem to be solved in a laboratory, more than a movie or a video game.

He was really walking down the street, approaching a truck that might be involved in the case.

Or maybe it was just a guy waiting for his wife, or catching a smoke, or . . .

The truck jerked forward.

Chelsea started to climb over the console to the driver's seat. Something flashed behind her—a police car had just turned onto the block.

It took Johnny Givens a few seconds to realize the truck was moving. He started to raise the gun, then realized he had no idea whether the vehicle was involved. He raised his left hand instead.

"Stop!" he yelled. "Police! Police!"

The truck lurched in his direction, accelerating. As he jumped back, he saw something out of the corner of his eye. Then something hard smacked him in the buttocks, and he was dizzy, and everything was black.

9

Boston suburbs—forty-five minutes later

Jenkins stared at the phone in disbelief. "Why was he there?"

"Someone was robbed at the ATM. We went over to help."

"What hospital?"

"Boston Med."

"I'll be there as soon as I can." Jenkins hit the Disconnect button and slumped back from the console. The van seemed to have shrunk in half, everything closing in.

"What's going on?" asked Robinson.

"Johnny was just run over by a truck and a cop car. They don't know if he's going to make it."

"*What?*"

"We're closing down for the night. Shit." He spun the phone in his hand, still in disbelief. Finally he clicked the map program up and queried the location of the hospital.

THE TRAUMA CENTER and Emergency Department at Boston Medical Center was one of the finest Level I trauma centers in the world; the acute-care facility was studied as a model throughout the Northeast. It was a place where miracles occurred. But there were some things that no hospital, no doctor, could do, no matter how skilled, and the face of the first surgeon Jenkins met told him that saving Johnny Givens's life very well might be one of them.

"We're talking very severe injuries," said the doctor. "It's touch and go."

Jenkins bit his lip so hard he could taste blood in his mouth.

It was better than the bile that had been rising from his stomach, and far less painful than the mental anguish turning every thought red. Against all logic, he felt responsible.

He'd never lost a man, not at the FBI, nor the two police departments he'd worked at before joining the Bureau.

God!

"I need to see him," he told the doctor.

"Heavily sedated, but come on."

The physician led him down the hall, past a computer station where patients were tracked. Spare equipment lined the walls below a large clock that ticked off seconds with a staccato beat. About halfway down the hall, they entered a room crowded with doctors, nurses, and other aides, all focused on a man who looked agonizingly small. Wires and tubes rose up from him, connecting to machines and displays that blinked with analytic precision, a sharp contrast to the hushed whispers of the people staring at the injured man.

"No—you're going to have to get out," said one of the doctors through her mask.

"I'm his boss," stuttered Jenkins. "FBI."

"I'm sorry. We're doing what we can. Please."

The surgeon who had led him in apologized and put his hand on Jenkins's arm.

"We're doing our best. His legs are gone."

"His legs?"

"Completely crushed. His spine, his lungs—I don't know that we'll save him."

Jenkins let himself be led out of the room. The voices seemed to get louder once he was in the hall.

"There was a woman with him," said the surgeon. "She's in that room over there."

Chelsea Goodman was sitting in a chair next to an empty bed, her cell phone in one hand and a Styrofoam cup in the other.

"How is he?" she asked, looking up.

"I—I don't . . ."

"I'm so sorry. I saw—"

She stopped. Tears slipped from the corners of her eyes. Jenkins wanted to comfort her but had no idea what to say.

"Maybe we should pray," he told her finally.

"OK. Tell me what to say."

10

Boston—time unspecified

Lying helpless on the bed, Johnny tried to focus.

Blue and red, blue and red—what did any of it mean?

Legs? Where are my legs?

There.

Arms?

Present.

Johnny's heart floated above his head. He could see it pumping, pumping, and pumping. It started to move slowly around the room.

This is what it felt like to be alive: surrounded by pain and a world gone alien.

11

Boston—that same night

It occurred to Jenkins that he was closer to Johnny Givens than anyone else at the Bureau, which very possibly meant that Jenkins was the closest person to Johnny in the Northeast and maybe the world. Johnny wasn't married or involved in a relationship: the girlfriend he'd broken up with had moved to Chicago some months before, something the young agent spent much time grousing about. He was an only child and had no relatives in Massachusetts or the Northeast, for that matter. His mother was dead; his father was in Florida somewhere. He'd listed his father as his next of kin, but the number had been out of service for six months, according to the phone company.

Jenkins wasn't sure what else he could do, aside from stalking up and down the hospital hallway, a reminder to the staff that he was here, damn it, and that someone cared, and that they better do the best they could to save the kid's life. He was angry and he was sad and he was tired, all at the same time, and when his wife, Joyce, called to ask where he was, he didn't even bother to guard his feelings, either from her or anyone nearby.

"I'm in the hospital with Johnny Givens," he told her, his voice a notch too high. "I'm waiting—I don't know what they're doing. He was hit by a car."

"Oh, God," said Joyce. "Are you all right?"

"I wasn't even there. I sent him on an errand, just to fetch someone, and he got—God, I don't know."

"What hospital are you at?"

"Brigham—no, Boston Med." Brigham was where his brother had died.

"I'll be there in ten minutes."

"No, listen, Joyce, there's no—"

Jenkins stopped, realizing she'd already hung up. Folding his arms but still holding his phone in his hand, he walked outside the hospital, circling around in the area where the ambulances waited. It was moments like this, thankfully few and far between, that he wished he smoked; it would have given him an excuse to be here, where he was so obviously out of place.

He thought of calling Joyce back and telling her not to come, claiming that he was on his way home. That would have been a very obvious lie, however, and he decided not to bother.

He wanted her here, in fact. He glanced at his cell phone, mentally calculating how long it would actually take her—twenty minutes, at least—then started patrolling up and down the sidewalk, trying to avoid the temptation of talking to himself. When he calculated fifteen minutes had passed since Joyce hung up, he moved closer to the door, positioning himself so he could see her as she came up the driveway.

Even though he was primed, it was Joyce who spotted him first, approaching from the other side of the street. He saw her as he turned back, just in time to open his arms to meet her hug.

It lasted long enough that it would have embarrassed him under other circumstances.

"Any word?" she asked when finally he eased her back.

"No."

"It reminds you of James, right?"

"Not really."

The fleeting look of disappointment in her grimace told him Joyce hadn't been fooled, but she said nothing. His brother's death was still a difficult subject, even between them.

"There was a girl with him," said Jenkins, eager to change the subject.

"Girlfriend?"

"No, she—she's helping us with the job. She works for Smart Metal, Mr. Massina's company. There was a problem with the computer. She's a techie, and I asked him to get her."

"So it was a car accident?"

Jenkins sighed, then explained the circumstances as he knew them.

"It's not your fault," said Joyce. "I hope you're not blaming yourself. But I know you are."

"I'm not."

"Where's this young woman? Maybe she needs something."

Chelsea was in the same chair where he'd left her; she seemed not to have breathed, let alone moved, in the time since Jenkins had left her. When Jenkins introduced his wife, Chelsea stared at him blankly.

"They said you could go home," Jenkins told her. "Should we call someone?"

Chelsea didn't answer.

"Is your car at your office?" he asked.

"My house is a few blocks away. I don't have a car."

"You want me to drive you?" Jenkins volunteered.

Chelsea rose without speaking.

"I'll take her," said Joyce. "You stay here with Johnny."

"OK—all right with you, Chelsea?"

"I can get Uber."

"It'll be easier and quicker if I drive," said Joyce.

JENKINS WENT BACK to his pacing, adding a loop inside near the nurse's station. The first few times, he stopped and asked whoever was there how Johnny was doing; after that he simply nodded and gave the best smile he could manage.

He was just going out the door when his supervisor strode up. Jenkins was shocked; Perse Lambdin was a tall black man who always dressed impeccably, often in a throwback three-piece suit. Tonight he had on a gray sweatshirt and faded, sagging jeans.

His manner, though, was as imperious as ever.

"What's going on?" Lambdin asked.

"Touch and go," said Jenkins. "I was just coming out for air."

Inside, Lambdin demanded to see the doctor in charge, even after the nursing supervisor explained that he was busy trying to save Givens's life. When it finally became clear to the nurse that Lambdin wasn't budging, she called a resident to talk to him. Jenkins knew that the doctor wasn't directly involved in the case, and he guessed that Lambdin probably knew, too, but the resident was the perfect audience, looking thoughtful and worried and respectful all at the same time. He assured both men that everything was being done for their agent; the head of surgery herself had been called in, and the trauma team was one of the best in the nation.

"Don't bullshit me," said Lambdin. "Just get the job done."

"That's what we're trying to do."

"Good. Good."

The resident clamped his lips together and nodded his head before retreating.

"Now how the hell did this happen?" Lambdin asked Jenkins.

"Wrong place, wrong time," said Jenkins. He repeated what he knew about the incident. They thought the driver of the truck was the ATM thief or an accomplice, but he was still at large.

If the police car hadn't sped down the block . . .

"I want the bastard who hit him caught," said Lambdin.

"The cop car hit him and did most of the damage."

"The other one—the truck," said Lambdin. "I want that bastard hung."

CHELSEA PUSHED HER head back against the headrest of Joyce Jenkins's car. No matter how tight she cinched the seat belt, it still felt loose.

"Turn right on Beacon Street?" Joyce asked.

"Yes." Chelsea couldn't remember telling her where she lived, but the GPS was open, moving an arrow along the map.

"Are you from Boston?" Joyce asked.

"San Diego. I came out for school. MIT and then I stayed."

"You're a computer scientist? There aren't too many women in that field."

"No."

"It's kind of funny to hear Trevor talk about computers," said Joyce. "He can barely get his phone to work. And forget about programming the TV."

Chelsea didn't answer.

"I imagine it must be hard for you to deal with all the men in your field," added Joyce after a few moments of silence. "Are there other women where you work?"

"A few."

Actually, just two dozen, including Massina's personal assistant. The male-to-female ratio in the technical fields was generally abysmal.

"I work in an elementary school," said Joyce. "The girls seem more excited about math than the boys at that age. But they peter out."

"Uh-huh."

"Hormones."

"Huh?"

"I think hormones mess a lot of us up. By the time we recover, we've missed our chance. Girls need encouragement. When they show aptitude. Was there a key? To get you interested?"

"I just was. In math. And stuff."

"Only child?"

"How did you know?"

"I just did." Joyce smiled at her.

"I wish I had stopped him," Chelsea blurted.

"It wasn't your fault, hon."

"I know, but I wish . . ."

JENKINS AND HIS boss were joined by a "comfort team," specialists who worked with the family when an agent went down. Jenkins didn't know them, but he knew their work—a similar team had met him when his brother was shot.

The night passed slowly, like a crippled man crawling up a long staircase. Finally the surgeon he had met hours earlier came out.

Jenkins sprang to his feet and began walking toward him. His heart began pounding in his chest; he could feel his pulse in his neck, a hard roll on a snare drum.

"He's still critical," said the doctor, nodding his head. "We had to take both legs. The next twenty-four hours will be crucial. There's internal bleeding. Did you know that he had a heart defect?"

"No," said Jenkins.

"It's been stressed. There's a hole—I'm very sorry. He needs a transplant, and I don't know."

"Of his legs?"

"No, the heart. Without it, and soon, very soon, he's gone."

12

Boston—early the next morning

Chelsea didn't sleep. She tried, stripping off her pants and curling beneath the blanket, but the accident kept playing in her head. She kept seeing Johnny Givens's face in that last moment when the car hit.

As she thought about it now, logically, carefully, she didn't think that she had seen his face. She'd been too far away, hadn't she? And in the car, and there hadn't been much light.

And yet she saw it in her mind, clearly.

She'd done nothing to stop it.

After a while she gave up even pretending that she could sleep. She was sorry that she had left the hospital. How was he?

Maybe dead by now.

She opened her cell phone's list of calls and found the number for the FBI agent, Jenkins.

"How is he?" she asked when he answered.

"Chelsea?"

"Is he out of surgery?"

"You mean Johnny?"

"Who else would I be talking about?" she demanded. "Damn—is he . . . all right?"

Jenkins's pause told her more than she wanted to know.

"He's alive. Barely." The FBI agent ran down a list of injuries that sounded like the index to a medical encyclopedia. Johnny Givens had already lost two legs; he needed a liver and a new heart—those were the highlights.

"You need to get him to a better hospital," blurted Chelsea.

"Better care?"

"We have . . . Lou has connections. He can help."

"Mr. Massina has already done a lot for us and—"

"I'll call you back," she told him quickly. "I'll call you back."

WATCHED & UNWATCHED

FLASH FORWARD

Massina stared at the FBI agent for a good sixty seconds, not believing at all what he had just been told.

"Mr. Jenkins," he said finally. "You're telling me, in so many words, that after all this work, you're not going to prosecute these bastards?"

The word *bastards* stuck in his mouth; it was very unlike Louis Massina to curse, even mildly, even in private. But there was no other word to describe them.

"These men are responsible for crippling your agent, your friend," added Massina when Jenkins didn't answer. "You're going to let them go."

"It wasn't actually them, as far as we know. The thieves—it's different people, we think."

"You're still letting these people go."

"That's not—that's not exactly what's happening here," said Jenkins. He had the face of a man who'd been punched in the stomach without warning and for no good reason. And yet Massina felt sure he must have expected some reaction from Massina along these lines. How could he not?

"Maybe you should explain what is happening, then," said

Massina. He rose from his desk chair, needing to exercise the adrenaline that was suddenly surging through his body.

"I'm afraid I can't go into the details," said Jenkins. His voice was shaking. "I—there is another agency involved and, it's—I know it doesn't make any sense."

"Well, make it make sense then. You want them to go without any justice?"

"No," said Jenkins quickly. "No—I have to go. I'm sorry. I'm very sorry."

REAL TIME

13

Boston—Tuesday morning

Convinced by Chelsea to help save the FBI agent's life, Louis Massina approached the problem the way he approached any problem: all-out. All of his resources were devoted to the young man. Not only did that mean all of Smart Metal's technical expertise and devices; it also meant all of Massina's considerable contacts. Grace Sisters' Hospital and its experimental operating suite were put at Johnny Givens's disposal, as were its doctors. Drugs that would speed his recovery as well as sustain him through the heart operations—drugs that couldn't be bought at any price—were rushed to the hospital, with the FDA's blessing. Sister Rose Marie saw personally to the young man's care, and even Father O'Gorman, one of the hospital's crusty chaplains, took an interest in the case.

The latter was doubly unusual, in that Johnny Givens was a confirmed Baptist.

It was O'Gorman whom Chelsea met outside the ICU when she came to check on the man she'd helped so much to save.

O'Gorman sighed and shook his head when he saw her. Chelsea was Catholic, but to O'Gorman she represented the grievous future versus the blessed past. For despite working in one of the world's most advanced medical centers, O'Gorman regarded technology as something close to the Devil's plaything.

If not worse.

"Hello, Father," said Chelsea.

O'Gorman shook his head and pointed at Chelsea's iPhone, which she was just turning off.

"I hope you're not thinking of taking a selfie," grumbled the priest.

"I'm just turning the ringer off." Chelsea slipped the phone into her pocket. "I'm surprised, Father."

"What?"

"That you actually know what a selfie is."

"Vanity, young lady, is one of the seven deadly sins. That I know. Book of Proverbs 6:16–19. King Solomon. The phrase is a 'proud look.' And as—"

"How is that vanity?" interrupted Chelsea.

"Just when I thought there was hope," grumbled the priest, stalking away.

"It's vanity because it means to be too proud, which is when God trips us up," said Sister Rose, turning the corner. "But I don't think it's a sin you have to worry about, dear," she added kindly. "It's not wrong to be aware of the gifts God has bestowed on us. As long as we put them to their best use."

"I try."

"You're here for our patient." The nun was practically the only adult Chelsea knew in Boston whom she could regard eye to eye without raising her head. "Come."

Chelsea followed her down the hall to an intensive-care room. Johnny lay sandwiched in the high-tech bed, only his arms visible on the side. His body floated on a mattress of air currents, which bathed him top and bottom with medicated vapor designed to quickly heal his burned skin as well as lessen the pain. Tubes and wires ran from the top of this metal sandwich to an array of machines on both sides of the room.

"We'll have him up by the end of the week," said Sister Rose.

"That soon?"

"He's responded well to the new heart. And we're using an experimental therapy—it is very promising, though it does rely on some nanocompounds. If he hadn't been close to death . . ."

Chelsea did not work on the medical side of the company, and she knew very little about its prosthetics, let alone the more exotic and experimental devices like the artificial heart. But she was well aware of how important those devices were, as well as the huge advances they represented. The heart machine was a perfect example. Made of a proprietary carbon-strand-fiber and microlattice nickel phosphorus, it weighed just under a pound. That was still a little heavier than Johnny's actual heart had weighed, but it was less than half what the leading fully artificial heart weighed.

His new heart was only the headline. Some of his nerve damage had already been repaired by grafts that used a synthetic growth system—the doctor who had pioneered it described it as something like a cancer bath, a miniature tube inside which actual nerve cells were propagated to replace the damaged ones. And Johnny had already been measured for two artificial legs, which were being fashioned to his exact specifications.

Sister Rose stopped Chelsea as she stepped closer to the bed.

"This is as close as we should get," said the Sister. Despite her diminutive size, her grip on Chelsea's arm was remarkably tight. A doctor had warned Chelsea never to arm-wrestle the nun. "You never know what germs we carry."

Chelsea glanced to the floor. Their toes were edging a red line.

"I'm sorry, Sister. I just wanted to see his face."

"Still intact," said Sister Rose. "Barely a blemish. Tell me—is this interest more than professional?"

"No, professional only."

"A white lie is still a lie," said the Sister tartly. "Especially if you tell it to a nun."

TWO HOURS LATER, Chelsea stood in front of a large glass screen in Smart Metal's Number 3 conference room, summarizing the situation for the group Massina had put together to help the FBI on the bank card fraud case. Jenkins, the FBI agent, sat at the far end of the table. Massina was next to him.

"It wasn't a software problem at all that caused the computer in the FBI surveillance van to freeze," she told them. "The operator hit a succession of keys as he tried to clean up the coffee he'd spilled. Two of the keys were shorted, and to the program, this looked like a series of command inputs that overflowed the error buffer. In layman's terms," she added, noticing the perplexed look on Jenkins's face, "the coffee fried the keyboard, so the computer hung. The program did not trap for that kind of error."

"No spilled coffee algorithm?" asked Terrence Sharpe.

Sharpe was the head of the company's programming unit. He was trying to make a joke. As usual, his timing and tact were out of whack.

"I feel terrible about it," said Chelsea.

"We all do," said Sharpe. "But the freeze had nothing to do with what happened to Agent Givens."

"No," agreed Jenkins. "Not at all."

"So, getting back to your situation here, your case," said Sharpe. "Maybe it's not a skimmer."

"How else do they get the data off the ATMs?" asked Jenkins.

"Maybe the ATMs are a red herring. It's just a coincidence that there are transactions being made there with those accounts."

"I think it's way too much coincidence to rule them out."

Chelsea had spent much of the night studying ATM systems and bank security. Even before she started, she knew security on the terminals was a joke. The machines' security features, with four-digit passwords and early DES encryption might have been state of the art when first introduced in the late 1960s, but they were now child's play to crack. Card skimmers could be built and programmed by preteens handy with a screwdriver and willing to spend a few hours searching on the Internet.

"Track the code from the banks," suggested Massina. "There must be a clue there."

"We've been working on that," said Jenkins, "but we've run into a number of technical problems and, frankly, a lack of cooperation from the banks and the processing houses in between."

"Mr. Sharpe and his people will help you," said Massina. "In the meantime, we'll give you hardened laptops. No more worries about spilled anything. You'll use our equipment for your surveillance."

"Nobody is spilling coffee again," said Jenkins. "There will be no coffee in the van. Period."

"I just don't see this as a skimmer operation," said Sharpe. "None have been found at any of the banks. And nobody takes cash from them. You should look in a different direction."

"I have a theory," said Chelsea. "I can't prove it yet, but maybe the coding is on the card."

She suggested—this time solely in layman's terms—that the automated teller machines were being infected by a virus. There wasn't enough "room" on the card's magnetic strip for an actual virus, though; what she proposed was a little more clever. The card directed the machine to go to a bank account where the virus was actually stored; it downloaded instructions to the ATM, then erased itself after a certain period of time.

"Clever, but in that case, all of the machines would have accessed the same account before they were attacked," suggested Jenkins. "And that sort of pattern would have jumped out at us."

"Not if they kept switching those accounts," said Chelsea. "Or if they did use the same account, they could set it up so that it would only activate after a certain period of time or transactions."

"We'll have to look deeper at the pattern," conceded Jenkins.

"Then let's get it done," said Massina, standing to signal that the meeting was over.

14

Johnny Givens ran for all he was worth. He ran and he ran and he ran. His lungs banged at the side of his chest, but still he ran.

The night was deep black, so dark that the landscape had no features. He was in a field or a city or even the woods, it was impossible to tell; he saw only blackness.

Then ahead, on the horizon, a bar of light.

He ran toward it. It gradually grew as he approached, rising up at a slow pace. It was as if a curtain were being lifted, black giving way to pure white.

Run! Run!

15

Chelsea stared out the window as her Uber driver pulled up across the street from a small, one-story mall on Arsenal Street. It was the address Jenkins had given her for the FBI task force's technical crew; it looked like the back side of a 1950s gas station; she'd been expecting something a little more governmental.

"We're here?"

"This is the place," said the driver, reaching for the screen on the iPhone perched on the dashboard holder.

"Thanks," said Chelsea. She got out of the car and rechecked the address against her phone's GPS. It wouldn't have been the first time Uber delivered her to the wrong address.

But the address was right.

She was fifteen minutes early, and rather than going into the building, she began walking down the block, deciding to stretch her legs before going in.

A small wave of paranoia hit her after a block. The neighborhood looked fine, working class but not particularly sketchy.

And yet . . .

She pushed her large bag tight against her ribs, lengthening her stride. Her father began talking to her, warning her to be careful.

More specifically: *Keep your eyes about you, ballerina girl.*

Ballerina girl. He was the only one in the world who could say that to her and get away with it.

Ballerina. Few people would call her that, since even fewer knew that side of her, that ancient ambition. Perhaps another dancer might spot the graceful way she moved, or catch a glimpse of her as she stretched. But there was no chance of a *relevé* or a *saut de basque* in the street, let alone something more interesting and taxing.

The street, her father's voice told her. *Concentrate on the street, ballerina girl. Watch yourself! Eyes about you!*

Chelsea crossed the street to a residential section, passing a row of older houses separated from each other by narrow yards and driveways that looked as if they'd been shoehorned into place. Most of the houses had been divided into two and three apartments; every second one seemed to have something associated with young children—carriages or toys, a bicycle propped haphazardly against a fence.

Crossing to Beacon Street, she realized her decision to take a walk was silly. Yes, she was early, but what if this was the wrong place? How long would it take to find the right one?

Meanwhile, she couldn't shake the paranoia. Apprehension felt like a foggy cloud of steam, clinging to her clothes, accumulating with every step. She suddenly became very aware of her skin color and guessed it was out of place here.

It was absurd paranoia, she knew. And yet, there it was, like a snake slithering up the side of her collar.

Chelsea circled around, heading back toward the building. Though it was already midmorning, traffic was light. Drivers sped along the street. The rush of wind as they passed gave another prod to her paranoia, but this time more understandable.

Chelsea stopped directly across from the building, watching both ways and waiting until there were no cars in sight. Then she sprinted across, careful to lift her toes when she reached the curb on the other side.

Her legs stiffened with the exertion.

God, I'm so out of shape. I have to get back to running at least.

Not even the glass door to the building indicated it was leased by the government, let alone belonged to the FBI. The press-on letters, slightly askew, announced "BI Labs."

Well maybe that means Bureau of Investigation.

Clever.

Chelsea took hold of the large metal door handle and pulled. The door moved an inch or so, then clanged loudly as the dead bolt hit its stop. Chelsea belatedly noticed a placard near the handle.

Enter at back.

Oh.

Feeling a little sheepish, Chelsea walked around the side and made her way down a dilapidated driveway. Two strips of concrete flanked a center island of mud, gravel, and weeds punctuated by the occasional sparkle of broken glass. The back lot was hardly more hospitable; discarded wooden pallets were piled on one end, opposite a row of chained garbage cans and some very rusted metal drums. A solid metal door stood almost in the exact center of the structure, flanked by two barred windows whose glass had been replaced by plywood. The wood was so old the outer layer had peeled and warped. A few graffiti scrawls on the gray blocks looked nearly as old.

A doorbell jutted from the concrete blocks next to the door, protruding on a pair of red wires. Chelsea pressed it.

Nothing seemed to happen. She knocked on the door, but that seemed even more futile. She rang the bell again, then took a step back, scanning the yard. Convinced that she had gotten the address wrong, she was taking out her phone to call Jenkins when the back door popped open.

A short man with a walrus moustache stuck his hand out to her.

"Ms. Goodman, right?" he said.

"Yes."

"Dryfus. Chief, tech section. Agent Jenkins is inside."

"I wasn't sure I had the right place."

"We like to fly under the radar," said Dryfus. "That, and the government is cheap."

He laughed, then led the way through a hallway that connected to the front, where another steel door had been erected just inside the vestibule, in effect cutting off the FBI suite from the front. A computer station showed video covering both exterior doors and the sides of the building; Dryfus had checked the feed before letting her in. Opposite the station was the entrance to an empty room about twenty by thirty; they walked through it to a second room a little bigger than the first. This was the team room, populated with metal desks and stiff-backed chairs. It had the feel of a start-up company—pizza boxes and half-full paper coffee cups were the main decorations—but the computers, all Dells, were primitive, and not just by Chelsea's standards. Equipment cases and bags were piled against the wall, along with coils of wire.

Dryfus introduced Jorge Flores, the tech working at one of the stations. Flores showed Chelsea the list of accounts that had been hit over the course of the past six weeks. It was an impressively long list, filling several computer screens. But it was also incomplete—a number of banks were balking at cooperating with the investigation.

"But you're the FBI," said Chelsea. "Can't you just order them to help?"

"If we could do that, we might have solved the case by now," said Dryfus. "But they seem to think we're part of the problem."

"As long as the case is limited to ATM machines," interrupted Jenkins, who'd come into the room while Chelsea was looking at the computer, "they'll treat it more as a nuisance than a major problem. It's a cost of doing business for them. Besides, they blame it on the customers or the processing houses. Anyone else but themselves."

"A hacker with this kind of access," said Chelsea, "could break into the entire bank, couldn't they?"

"Maybe yes, maybe not," said Dryfus. "They may not be able to do more than issue commands for transfers on accounts they have credentials for."

"They're smart," interrupted Jenkins. "Go too big, and they'll be hard to ignore. This way, they keep getting dribs and drabs, and over the long haul it all adds up."

"Or maybe this is just the first phase," said Dryfus. "Maybe they're planning to do more."

"We've studied the ATM machines and the way traffic is sent," she told them, reaching into her bag for a small USB flash drive, neatly packaged in a clear plastic case. "We have written a small app that will monitor the system and tell you when the data stream is larger than should be expected. It will pinpoint the location of the machine in the network. You can then follow the suspect."

"You're assuming there's no delay mechanism," said Dryfus. "They may insert it, and then nothing happens."

"Possibly. But the simplest way would be to send the commands immediately, and then delay. The information has to be kept somewhere, and the machines don't have enough memory. So if we do this and it doesn't work, then you'll know it's the processing agents in the middle who are compromised."

"We don't think that's true," said Jenkins.

"Then, good. It needs to be installed in the network."

"We can work on that," said Jenkins. "But it's going to take a while. Not everybody is going to cooperate."

Dryfus shook his head. "I can tell you right now, most won't. They don't want us messing with their networks, screwed up as they are."

"We thought of that," said Chelsea. She reached into the bag and took out another case, this one blue. Inside was a flash drive with a different program. "This program can do the same thing if it's inserted into an ATM machine. Even better, it can examine all the coding instantly. So you'll be able to see if a program is being parked inside the ATM."

"Hmmm," said Jenkins.

"Again, getting them to cooperate is going to be tough," said Dryfus.

"That's why we did this." Chelsea removed the last item from her bag. It looked like a paper-thin tongue depressor made of copper, with a gummy black plastic lip.

"What is this?" asked Jenkins, holding it between his fingers.

"Wow, a high-tech card skimmer, right?" said Dryfus.

"That's right." Chelsea was pleased that the tech expert could figure it out, even if it was only an educated guess. Maybe there was hope for the FBI yet. "All the electronics are imprinted in the tongue and the chip that's molded into the faceplate. It goes right inside the card reader. You'll never know it's there. We made a tool to insert it as well."

"I'm not sure I'm understanding," said Jenkins. "This is a skimmer?"

"It's more a monitor," said Chelsea. "It will communicate with another program and just send an alert. The network itself is never broken into."

"Still—"

"We'd need permission from the ATM owners, even if it's just a monitor," said Flores.

"I'm going to have to think about it," said Jenkins. "I may have to run it by the top floor."

"That'll be a 'no' real quick," said Flores. "Even before you go to the banks."

Jenkins glanced at his watch. "I have a conference in a few minutes. Please excuse me."

JENKINS KNEW IT was a lame excuse, but he needed to think.

Boy, did he want a cigarette. It had been two years since he'd smoked—the night of the operation that saved his daughter's life, as a matter of fact—but he still felt the urge at moments like this.

Too often, lately.

He entered his office and shut the door behind him. The space was barely the size of an entry-level worker's cubicle, yet somehow it managed to look massive to him. The bare walls, the empty bookcase, and, most important, the clean desktop.

Who ever heard of a clear desktop during an open investigation?

Jenkins wheeled the desk chair out against the wall and sat down. The sole window in the room was a casement job, the sort installed in a basement, as if the builders really didn't want to let light in here.

The banks that owned the ATM machines *would* cooperate, but only after each was harangued personally. And by that time, these guys would be on to a different city. Or maybe even a different country.

What if the device was inserted by Chelsea? How would something like that play in court?

It wouldn't. No way. The defense would argue that it was akin to a search without a warrant.

Assuming they found out.

Even if she did it? And then did the monitoring and alerted the FBI to a crime?

Maybe she'd be guilty of trespassing—but who would prosecute her?

Not the bank whose money was saved. And not the FBI.

"YOU COULD MAKE some good money with this," said Dryfus, turning the skimmer over in his hand. "The right place in Russia will pay over a million. And in Bitcoin. You won't have to worry about carrying it around."

"Is that where you think these guys are from?" Chelsea asked.

"Hard to say. They could be from anywhere. Czech Republic,

Romania, Bosnia's pretty big with banking scams like this. Most of them are more primitive."

"You've worked on a lot of cases like this?"

"A few. This is the most interesting, though. Most are just tracking down people with skimmers. That's what we thought this was at first."

"It makes it more interesting," said Flores. "But frustrating at the same time."

"So you think you'll get permission to use this?" asked Chelsea, taking back the skimmer she'd invented.

"Oh, it's not about permission," said Dryfus. He glanced over his shoulder. "Jenks is deciding how far to push the envelope."

"What do you mean?"

"We go through channels, it'll be years before we get the OK. Getting permission from the Bureau is hard enough. The banks . . ."

"So what then?"

"Jenks will think of something."

"Let me ask you a question," said Flores, standing up and stretching his legs. "How cooperative was the bank with your boss? Did they give him his money back?"

"No," said Chelsea. "They said they would and then they welched."

"I'm going to guess what actually happened," said Flores. "The local branch was very cooperative. Then somebody above them reversed it. Because there's no obvious sign of fraud. That's why he got involved. And it's not about money, right? It's justice. Or revenge, however you want to slice it."

"The same way it is for Jenks," said Dryfus.

"He was ripped off, too?" asked Chelsea.

"No. His brother," said Flores. "He didn't tell you?"

"No."

"His brother was killed while investigating a similar case a year ago," said Dryfus. "He's convinced it's related."

"Oh."

"I don't think it was," added Dryfus. "The pattern is different. And there we found skimmers. But he's in it until the end now. Once he's on to something, he doesn't quit."

JENKINS WAS STILL feeling the urge to smoke as he walked back into the team room. He decided that was OK, though; get through the afternoon without smoking, and he wouldn't be bothered like this for several weeks at least. It was like being vaccinated.

"I have an idea," he told Chelsea. "Your personnel will have to install the devices and then do the monitoring. Then tip us off. We can be all together, but you'd be the one at the monitor. You or whoever. So we'd be getting the information from you. As a concerned citizen."

The young woman's face blanked. She was a pretty girl, he realized for the first time, very pretty. The glare of the overhead fluorescents shaded her skin so that it looked like the shade of a pale rose, accentuating her eyes. Those eyes narrowed slightly as he stared.

She nodded. "Good," said Chelsea. "When do we start?"

"Tonight."

16

Gabor Tolevi was not a big fan of Grozny Avia, a Russian-owned airline best known for its harrowing flights in and out of places like Chechnya. But Armenia—even Tolevi wouldn't try Chechnya—was the only way to get into Crimea from the West without going to Russia, and Grozny Avia was the only airline, at the moment, connecting it to the recently annexed "free state" of Russian-occupied Crimea.

Getting to Armenia itself wasn't easy; flights from Turkey had recently been canceled, and Tolevi had to fly all the way to Dubai before connecting.

Despite the labyrinthine route, both flights had been way over-booked. In danger of being bumped from the Grozny flight, Tolevi had contemplated bribing the gate clerk, a not-uncommon tactic. He'd ultimately decided against it, deciding it would demonstrate beyond doubt that he was either a spy or a smuggler, and it was always best to leave such issues in doubt. As it turned out, he had kept his seat; he received two large kinks in his neck and shoulder as a reward.

Tolevi exchanged scowls with the steward and left the aircraft, eyes straight ahead as he walked up the jetway. Even before the takeover, flights were routinely monitored by the Russian intelligence agency known by its initials as SVR RF, and Tolevi had no doubt that his arrival was noted by several other intelligence agencies as well. Hiding in plain sight was his only option, and one he was supremely good at; while he had access to phony passports and other IDs, he had left them home for this trip. It was generally safer to do so.

Besides, one could find things of that nature in any country of the world.

Tolevi made his way through the terminal to the taxi stand, where a chaotic jumble of private cars and a few older vans crowded out the two licensed taxis that were trying to reach the queue. Tolevi cut to the back of the mélange, knowing from experience that the easiest way to leave the airport was to find a private car that was just arriving; using Ukrainian, he told the driver in a small, slightly battered Fiat that he was going to Perov, a suburb a few miles south of the airport. The man suggested a price in rubles.

"Fifty euro," answered Tolevi, switching to English and not only bumping the price in the man's favor but offering a currency far surer and more valuable.

It was also a test of sorts, which the driver passed, agreeing in broken English to provide "best service quick trip."

"I don't care about the speed," said Tolevi in Russian.

"*Da,*" said the man. "Yes. We go." He didn't pronounce the words well; clearly it was a second language.

Another test passed.

Tolevi settled back in his seat, observing the man and the car. When they were outside the confines of the airport, Tolevi leaned forward and told the man, in Ukrainian, that he had changed his mind and wanted to go instead to Yalta, on the southern coast.

"Yalta," said the man, feigning surprise, but not very well.

"For two hundred euro," said Tolevi.

The driver considered the offer, then began a long harangue

about how difficult it would be for him to find gasoline for the trip back. Tolevi let him talk, uninterrupted.

"What do you think?" asked the man finally. "Three?"

"Two hundred," said Tolevi. Two hundred euro was an excellent price, and the man should have no problem finding fuel in Yalta.

"Yes, OK, good price," said the driver.

Yalta was roughly an hour and a half away. The first half of the drive was a slog through the mountains. Tolevi's fatigue was no match for the driver's recklessness, the small car spending so much time on the left-hand side of the road that Tolevi began to think the man had learned to drive in England. The second half of the journey paralleled the coast and was considerably calmer, but by then Tolevi was not only wide awake but also brooding on what he would do in Yalta.

He had the driver take him directly to the Embankment, Yalta's fashionable tourist strip on the harbor. After paying the man off, Tolevi went directly into Tak, a popular restaurant that had catered to wealthy Ukrainians from the west and north before "liberation."

The hostess looked first at the bag he was wheeling behind him, then at his jeans, which were fairly new, his sport coat, which was not, and lastly at his face. The puzzled frown she'd worn exploded into a smile; with a burst of laughter she came out from behind the small podium and embraced him.

"Cousin, cousin, what are you doing here?" she said, practically shouting.

"I needed a rest." He hugged her for a long moment, then gently pushed her back. "Anna, you are gaining weight."

"What? What?" She twirled around, as if looking in a mirror.

"No, I'm teasing." It was an old joke between them. Anna weighed ninety pounds, if that. Standing at five-eight without heels, she looked like a toothpick.

"Where is Drovok?" he asked.

"Where is he ever? In the back, as always. Did he know you were coming and didn't tell?"

"No. It's a surprise for him as well. Sshh now, don't ruin it."

Tolevi left his suitcase near the register and went through the restaurant to the kitchen, wending his way past the prep station and the stoves to the alcove at the back, where Jorge Drovok was hunched over a small table. He had two laptops open, and a Microsoft Surface; he clutched a satellite phone to his ear. Tolevi started to tiptoe, but Drovok looked up at the last moment, ruining the surprise.

"Gabe!"

Drovok jumped up to embrace his cousin, then went off to fetch a bottle of vodka. They spent a few minutes catching up on various acquaintances. Then, two drinks down, they got around to business, discussing how and when they would import several shipments of this same liquor. They always spoke of vodka, though most of the shipments included other items. Smuggled caviar and pickled fish were especially lucrative when going west, but the real money came the other way—the European embargo made smuggling food into Russia and its patsy state, Crimea, a very profitable activity. Drovok got a percentage for his work arranging the boats that brought the goods ashore; lately his share had been whittled down because the payoffs were increasing. Where once every fifth or sixth official had a hand out, now it was every other.

"I can talk to my partners, but there are limits," said Tolevi. "They keep talking about Sevastopol, going in through there."

"The bribes there are worse. And there would be no one for you to trust."

"I don't take their side. I'm just saying."

"Another vodka?"

"Just. Then I go."

"How's your daughter?" asked his cousin when Tolevi finished his drink.

"Good, very good."

"I see the photos on Facebook. She looks more like her mother every day."

"Yes." Tolevi felt a sudden wave of emotion. He clasped his hands around his cousin quickly, then went back out into the kitchen, turning down the hall and grabbing a dark workman's coat before exiting into the alley at the back of the building. Walking quickly, he stepped out to the street, then crossed the road and went down a block before going toward the water.

Tolevi might or might not have been followed from the restaurant; it was simply safer to assume that he was. And he didn't want to be followed now.

The Russians and the locals were well aware of the smuggling operations, or at least that part of it involving his cousin; if they weren't, there would have been no need for bribes. But there were other things he needed to do, and those required some measure of privacy. He achieved this in the following manner: After going down the block, he swung into an alley and doffed the workman's coat. He hopped over a fence onto the main street and, two blocks away, entered the Embankment Hotel through the front door.

He slowed as he approached the registration desk, then veered quickly toward the restrooms in the side hall. Tolevi put his hand up to the door, but instead of pushing in, he continued to walk, as if deciding to go somewhere else. At the end of the hall he turned right into another hallway. The pool was here, as was a small gym. There were bathrooms between these two; he went into the men's, where in the last stall he removed his clothes and put on the swimming trunks that he had taken from the work coat. He bundled his clothes, carrying them with him as he went out to the pool and then the boardwalk outside, crossing the cement to a row of lockers. He put the clothes in and carried the key in his hand to the sea on the other side of the boardwalk.

With a dash, he jumped in. Two quick strokes and he dropped the key; two more strokes and he ducked beneath the surface, holding his breath until he was behind one of the boats tied to the nearby wharf.

It would not have been impossible to follow Tolevi from that point on, but it would not have been easy, and when he emerged from the water a half hour later in the backyard of a Russian pensioner, he was reasonably sure no one had followed him. A half hour on, driving the pensioner's car—the man had known his father—he set out for Kerch, another port town on the northeast coast.

Some hours later, he arrived in Kerch. After parking near the town center, he walked across the cement cobblestones in front of the Cathedral of Prophet St. John the Baptist, head bowed slightly as he passed, until he reached the nearby beach. There he found a bench in view of the sea and sat, waiting as the sun set behind him.

Shadows danced across him, extending to the sand as the last few tourists walked to the inns and hotels farther up the street. Tolevi remained, staring at the dark line of the jetty on his left, more park than wharf. A single ship was tied up there: a Russian corvette.

"A warm night," said a voice behind him in Russian.

The heavy Ukrainian accent made it difficult to understand, and it took Tolevi a moment to respond.

"Warm is good," he replied.

"Can I sit?"

Though he had not yet seen the other man, Tolevi raised his hand, gesturing that he had no problem. The man slipped around the other side of the bench, squatting on the edge of the slats. He was much younger than Tolevi, barely out of his teens, and though his voice was even, he was obviously nervous—he jangled his feet around, kicking up a tiny vortex of sand and dust.

"You're Russian?" asked the newcomer.

"My mother was. My father Ukrainian."

"Your Russian is very good."

"My Ukrainian is better," said Tolevi, demonstrating. "I was looking for a good place to eat."

"There are many. You have the numbers?"

They were barely out of the authentication—the switch to

Ukrainian had been meant to seal it—and here the boy wanted to be gone. Tolevi considered—was he merely scared, or was he part of a double cross? Tolevi was particularly vulnerable here, without a weapon or backup. It would be nothing for a group of thugs to appear, drag him a few hundred yards, and throw him in the water.

But if it was a trap, why not just shoot him directly and be done with it? Why play games.

To get the account numbers, of course.

"You have the numbers?" asked the boy again.

"I'm hungry," said Tolevi impulsively.

He got to his feet and began walking. His contact hesitated before trotting after him.

Tolevi stayed near the water, working out how he might proceed. He was sure that he hadn't been followed, but that was all he could be sure of. It was very possible the young man had been, even if he wasn't working for the Russians.

So hard to know. In the end, all Tolevi could do was gamble on trust.

But not yet.

He veered right, walking up toward YugNiro, the solid-looking building on Sverdlov Street that housed the oceanography and fisheries institute. Two blocks farther, he found a small café and went inside; the young man followed.

Tolevi had only been to Kerch two or three times over the past few years, and he couldn't remember being in this particular café. It was nearly deserted—odd, given the hour, though possibly not so strange since the Russian takeover. He asked for a table on the porch. The kid followed.

"I think—do you think this is safe, to spend so much time together?" asked the young man when he sat.

"I wonder if they have beer," said Tolevi.

They did, and while the choices were limited to Russian, Tolevi managed to find a Knightberg Shisha, a good stout.

The kid said he wasn't thirsty.

"Nothing then?" Tolevi asked.

He shook his head.

"How are things in the new republic?"

The boy frowned and shook his head.

Fair enough. The less I know about you the better.

"How do you go back?" Tolevi asked. He had only been to the annexed parts of Ukraine twice since the takeover and was genuinely curious.

"Through Russia; it's easier. I take the ferry. I have an hour."

"Mmmm . . ."

The beer came. The rest of the place remained empty.

I don't trust him, thought Tolevi. *But realistically, this does not look like a trap. And I cannot stay here all night.*

Still, he hesitated, sipping the beer.

"How old are you?" Tolevi finally asked.

"Old?"

"Your age."

"I'm nineteen."

"You go to school?"

"I do many things. I'm not here to play around."

"Mmmmm. . . ."

The brief flash of anger reassured Tolevi. He took a long sip of the beer, then slid back in the chair.

"Here are the numbers. You're ready?"

"Ready."

"I will not repeat them."

"I don't expect you to."

THE NUMBERS WERE accounts in two banks to be used by the resistance fighting the Russians and traitors near Donetsk. This was the only way they were transferred—person to person, with nothing in writing. The equivalent of a half million dollars was in one bank, three times that amount in the other.

How much of that would reach the resistance, Tolevi could

not know. Nor did he want to. He was somewhat ambiguous about the conflict—he had relatives on both sides, after all. His prime interest was in the money he would receive from the CIA for delivering the information.

THE YOUNG MAN closed his eyes, memorizing the numbers. Then he rose.

"You'll pay?" he asked Tolevi.

"Always. One way or the other."

17

Boston, the same day

Borya pedaled slowly toward the bank, watching the traffic with one eye and the curb with the other. It had been cloudy when she left home, threatening rain, but now the sun was out full blast, warming the air with a promise of spring. Buds were starting to peek out of the dead wood of the trees, and already the morning was warm enough that she didn't need the sweatshirt she'd bundled herself in. It was so warm, in fact, that she decided to stop and take it off a block from the bank; she rode up onto the sidewalk, hopping off the bike with a quick, practiced motion. The seat and pedals on the Shimano mountain bike were adjusted so her legs were at full extension, and a careless dismount could hurt. She pulled off her sweatshirt and tied it around her waist, smoothing it against her baggy khaki pants.

She'd decided to skip school at the last minute and in fact was still not entirely comfortable with the decision. Her father was away, which made skipping school more problematic, not less. Any call home about her absence would go to voice mail, where she would intercept it and return it, pretending to be her au pair—a college student who was a serious pain before leaving the family employ two years before. The woman who looked in on her in the evenings—never use the term *babysitter*—was a kindly old dolt who was easy to dodge. But her father had an unfortunate habit of calling the school when he was out of the country, ostensibly checking to see how she was doing; this made skipping more problematic, if not downright dangerous.

Even though he wasn't Roman Catholic, her father had an unworldly and to Borya's thinking inexplicable respect for the nuns who ran the school; a cross word from them always brought swift retribution.

Not that he would hit her—she couldn't remember that he had ever done so, even when she was five or six years old. But his lectures. These were old-school tirades, marathon sessions that varied in volume from hour to hour—and they did last hours. Guilt was a heavy component, as was the sainted memory of her beloved mother, God rest her soul, who would be invoked a minimum of twelve times. Borya hated this mother—not her *real* mother, whom she had only the vaguest memory of, but the sainted, beloved mother her father presented during these speeches.

It was a joke, really. He'd indulged in a series of ho's for as long as she could remember—his various attempts at being discreet had grown pathetic over the years—and Borya was fairly certain that such a practice would have originated before her mom's death. How could you cheat on a person and venerate them at the same time? But he definitely venerated her now. The house was practically a shrine to her, with photos everywhere.

There was a certain resemblance between mother and daughter, as visitors often remarked. Borya focused on the differences—her own raven hair cut short and brushed back, tattoos on both her arms, baggy boy clothes in sharp contrast to the gowns and long skirts her mom wore in most of the photos.

Borya chained her bike against the railing of the Starbucks where she'd stopped, then walked around the side to go into the store. She ordered a venti cappuccino—a two-week-old habit—and gave the clerk a rewards card.

He looked at it suspiciously. Borya's breath caught. The card was bogus, bought online for a fraction of its supposed value.

Did he know it? Was he going to call the cops?

She could get out of the shop easily enough, but it would mean leaving her bicycle behind.

"Your strip's peeling off," said the clerk. "You should get another one."

"I, um." Borya's mouth was dry. "There's still money on it and, uh, it's really my dad's. So—"

"I can transfer it if you want."

"Uh . . . sure."

The clerk tapped his fingers across the cash register, whizzing the card and a new one through the reader on the register. Borya felt frozen, worried that it was a trap.

"Fifty-five dollars and twenty-five cents left," said the clerk, handing her the new card. "Your dad likes his coffee, huh?"

"Lattes," said Borya weakly. Then she had an inspiration. "Can I have the old card?"

"It's worthless now." He had it in his hand, flexing it.

"Yeah, but, my dad—I have to show it to him . . ."

"Control freak, huh?"

"Anal."

He handed it back to her. "Nothing on it now. It's voided out."

"Thanks."

Borya's chest didn't unclench until she was outside the store. Loading cards up with bogus money was a silly game, easily discovered if the chain's security people put their minds to it. Disposing of the evidence was the best strategy.

Transferring balances from card to card—that was something she'd never considered. Did that make it more or less likely she'd be caught?

Borya hung the bike chain around her neck and walked the bike away, coffee in hand. The possibility of getting caught, the rush of having escaped—it was better than any drug, certainly better than the vodka she snuck from the liquor cabinet.

She passed the bank. There was someone at the ATM just outside the lobby door.

Good, thought Borya, spying a bench a short distance away. *I'll drink the cappuccino while I'm waiting.*

It was only after chaining the bike and sitting down that she realized she had forgotten to put any sugar in. She decided she would drink it anyway, as a matter of discipline.

I have to work on keeping my head straight, Borya told herself, taking a bitter sip. *Panicking is the easiest way to get caught.*

18

Chelsea dug into the suitcase and pulled out a case about the size of a cigar box.

"These are small UAVs or drones that can stay aloft for eight hours," she said. "We can use them to trail a suspect."

"They look like birds," offered Jenkins from his spot by the truck. They were in the parking lot of an abandoned warehouse, a spot chosen not so much for its seclusion but for its almost perfect location, equidistant between four of the five ATMs they were going to watch.

"That's the idea. We call them Hums. It's short for *hummingbirds*—not my idea," Chelsea added quickly.

"These can fly?"

"Uh-huh. Once I assemble them."

Chelsea snapped a pair of wings onto the small mech, secured them, then walked a short distance from the van.

"If it comes toward you, duck," she told them.

It was a joke, but they had no way of knowing. Which made it even funnier—to her, at least.

Chelsea tossed the UAV upward. Suddenly the wings flapped to life, and the small robot began to fly in a circle around the lot. It was programmed to move in an ever-widening upward spiral until it reached three thousand feet; there it would await commands from a transmitter Chelsea had also brought along.

About half again as big as a hummingbird, the Hums were propelled by their wings, which moved up and down at a rate that could approach sixty beats a second, depending on wind conditions. That was slower than a hummingbird, but not by much; the flying mech glided more than a bird would, reading the wind current and adjusting as necessary. It wasn't particularly fast—the theoretical limit was twenty knots, though in real-world tests the fastest it had achieved was sixteen.

"It's not quick, so I don't think we can follow a car once it's out of the city," she told the two FBI agents as she walked over to them. "But we can get a good picture of the license plate."

"That'll be enough," said Jenkins.

Chelsea took another from the case. "We only need four to cover the entire area. They'll stay aloft for about eight hours, depending on the wind. I do have to recover them. They're expensive."

"Can I touch it?" Flores asked.

"Of course."

He extended his hand gingerly, as if the Hum had been a real bird.

"It's made out of a carbon fiber compound and a kind of glass," explained Chelsea. "It's stronger than it seems."

Flores held it at arm's length while Chelsea explained some of its features. There was an infrared camera attached in the forward area, about where a bird's chin would be; this supplemented the guidance sensors located in the upper portion of the head. Unlike an autonomous robot like Peter, the Hum relied on a remote control station to direct it; it couldn't make decisions on its own. The control unit had a preprogrammed mode for general maneuvers and unguided transport. In other words, it could be told to fly the

Hum to a specific point at a specific time, hover there for x minutes, then fly to another point; it would cover that on its own. It could also be told to look for certain events and sound an alert, a function of particular value here.

Smart Metal had far more capable robots, but Chelsea had chosen these because they were readily available and she was very familiar with the control unit. They were also commercial models; losing one would not be a big deal, aside from the cost.

Chelsea launched the others in quick succession, then took the control unit into the van and plugged it into the power strip that ran along the bench at the side. While it booted up, she went back to the company pickup truck and took out the antenna assembly, a pair of inside-out umbrellas and whip array that looked a little like the business end of an anorexic devil's pitchfork. Once they were attached to the roof of the van with the help of suction cups and clamps, Chelsea connected a thick cable to their mounts and ran it into the control unit.

"I divided up the watch area into quadrants," she told Jenkins and Flores. "It covers the whole area under surveillance."

"How do we fly them?" Flores asked, pointing at the controller. It looked like a bad marriage between a joystick and a laptop. The seventeen-inch-screen was ultra-high def, in sleek glass, and pretty much looked like something you'd see on any high-end laptop.

The keyboard, though, had four rows of unmarked rectangles running above the joystick, which was flanked by a set of keys arranged in number-pad style. But these had symbols rather than numbers. And aside from an upside-down triangle and an infinity character, the markings bore no relation to anything found on a computer available at Best Buy.

"They fly themselves. But you can give them verbal commands," explained Chelsea.

Flores reached for the keyboard.

"Don't touch," she said quickly. "It's active during the boot up. Once this part of the screen goes green, then we're good. It will take voice commands. I have to get the headset," Chelsea added. "Can I trust you to keep your hands off?"

"We're good," said Jenkins. "No touching the entire time. This is all you."

JENKINS SETTLED ONTO the little bench at the front of the van while Flores checked in with the surveillance teams.

All this whiz-bang high-tech stuff—his head felt like it was spinning. He had trouble working the cable remote.

But this was the way of the future. If it didn't involve a computer screen, it wasn't real.

As kids, Jenkins and his brother solved crimes every day—usually several times. Their obsession began with a board game—Clue—their mom had bought from a garage sale. At the precocious age of seven and eight, respectively, the Jenkins brothers had become the Starsky and Hutch of Danbury, Connecticut. They solved the mystery of the missing cat, the misdelivered newspaper, and countless other crimes, big and small.

And then, both promptly forgot their obsession midway through high school. James found girls; Trevor found football. It was only after college that the younger Jenkins returned to the idea of becoming a detective, and it was in the most roundabout way: joining the Army after a failed collegiate career, he was recruited to CID by a friend from basic who was now a sergeant. CID—the Army Criminal Investigation Command—was the Army's investigative corps. The vast bulk of the unit's work, and certainly everything that Sgt. Trevor Jenkins was involved in, was extremely routine; his most exciting "case" was assisting an investigation into a string of barracks robberies. But the taste excited him, and he soon worked his way to police work, and from there to the FBI, with a brief stint in the Marshals Service in between.

His brother, James, was a bored industrial psychologist when Trevor joined the Bureau. It didn't take long to rekindle his interest; when there was an opening in the Behavioral Science Unit, James took all of thirty seconds to decide to apply. Making the switch to a field agent was more difficult, but a foregone conclusion.

Now he was dead. Trevor Jenkins blamed himself, inevitably.

"We're good to go," Flores told him. "You want me to drop Ms. Goodman off?"

"She has to go alone," said Jenkins, snapping from his reverie. "We watch, and move in if there's trouble."

"Got it."

LUDDITE HE MIGHT be, but the video from the Hums fascinated Jenkins. He'd expected that it would be moving. According to Chelsea and from what he could see on the control screen, the tiny aircraft circled over a set point in what she called an orbit with a five-hundred-meter radius. They were flying slowly, at about five miles an hour, but still, they *were* moving. So why didn't the image?

Chelsea explained that the computer compensated, adjusting the data from the IR sensor in the nose so that the view was always fixed. This was easier for an operator to understand, she explained; more importantly, it provided a set of data quicker for the computer to manipulate.

"Manipulate, how?" asked Jenkins.

"Scan it for significant objects," said Chelsea. "Movement, intensity—it's all a matter of math. Let's say we were using the sensor system to monitor an area for forest fires. We want to be able to discriminate between certain heat sources easily. It's a matrix, really; you want to be able to quickly convert the values, and you want to do everything as efficiently as possible. That's where we get into the architecture of the processing chip—"

"You lost me," said Jenkins.

"It's an arbitrary image," said Chelsea. "A representation of what the computer is actually seeing."

That didn't really help, but Jenkins nodded as if it did. He glanced at Robinson, who was sitting at the side of the van, arms folded, quietly staring at Chelsea, as if he was trying to figure out how to ask her for a date.

An hour passed. Customers came and went, sometimes in bunches, most often in ones and twos. Nothing suspicious occurred. Robinson began talking about baseball and advanced statistics; Chelsea seemed to know at least as much as he did about them, certainly more than Jenkins.

"I'm going to stretch my legs," said Jenkins. "Anybody want anything?"

"Is there a Starbucks near here?" asked Chelsea.

"On every block," said Jenkins.

"I'll come with you."

"You have to watch the monitor."

She took out her cell phone. "It'll beep if there's something up. I can pull up the image."

Jenkins held the door open for her, feeling a little paternal, though he was a good ten years too young to be her father.

"They have a lot of Starbucks in San Diego?" he asked as they waited.

"Every corner."

"I've never been there."

"It's a good place to visit. The weather's always nice."

"So I hear."

They got her coffee—a blonde latte—and one for Robinson, then started back for the van.

"I'm sorry about Johnny," said Chelsea. "But there's hope at least."

"Yeah."

"Do you know who was in that truck?"

"They have a few leads—it's a local matter." Jenkins tried to hide his frustration—while he didn't think the locals would do a bad job, he wanted to be on the case himself. But then he always felt that way.

"I heard the truck was stolen," said Chelsea.

"Yup."

"It didn't seem to be connected to this."

"I don't think so."

They walked a half block more without saying anything. Chelsea broke the silence. "Your daughter has one of our prosthetics."

"That's right," said Jenkins.

"Your wife mentioned it. Mr. Massina will really help Johnny."

"I'm sure he will."

"Can he go back to work with you?"

"Probably not."

In fact, it would be almost impossible for Johnny to return to the Bureau, at least in the sort of job he'd had. But that was something to worry about in the future. Right now, he just had to live.

Jenkins stopped. They were a few feet from the van. He took a long sip from his coffee, thinking of the night when his daughter had been brought into the hospital. It had been a desperate night; he was sure they'd lost her. And then when she'd recovered—seeing her without the leg the first time nearly undid him completely—he'd struggled to try and smile for her even as tears had flowed down the sides of his face.

His wife had been so much stronger.

"Your daughter's away at college?" asked Chelsea.

"Yeah. USC. She wants to go into film. Be a director."

"Nice."

"I think she picked the school because it's on the other side of the country," chuckled Jenkins.

"It's a really good school for film."

"I think it's a tough business," he said, giving the answer he always gave. "But if it makes her happy."

Chelsea's phone beeped.

"I think we got something," she said, reaching for the van door.

THE FIGURE IN the infrared was five-eight and thin, dressed in jeans and a hooded sweatshirt. He'd taken something out of his

backpack at the ATM, a walkup on the outside of a bank building three miles away. The Hum didn't have a good enough angle
to see what he did with it, but his hands were free as he left the
machine.

"Can you get a picture of his face?" Jenkins asked.

"I'm trying." Chelsea slid her fingers around the glass pad at
the center of the control panel. She tapped twice, then pinched her
fingers. The image changed; they were now looking from a feed
focused ahead of the Hum, as if seeing through its eyes.

The figure was about fifty yards ahead of the Hum, walking
quickly. Chelsea directed the drone to circle forward, banking so
that it would come around from the front. But before it reached
him, the suspect ducked into an alley. As Chelsea urged the drone
on, he emerged on a bicycle and began riding back in the direction
of the ATM.

He was fast, very fast—the little UAV couldn't keep up. The
suspect turned left at the end of the block, then rode down a long
hill. He was soon out of sight.

"It's all right," said Jenkins finally.

"I didn't think he'd use a bike," admitted Chelsea. "Or be so
quick. I could have directed the others to help."

"It's fine. Let's go check the ATM. Robinson, you stay with
the van."

Chelsea ordered the Hum to orbit the area, watching in case
the suspect came back.

"I want you to stay in the car while I check the place out," he
told her as they drove. "Just in case."

"In case what?"

"If they're still around."

"The profile on these kinds of criminals is overwhelmingly
nonviolent," said Chelsea.

"Where'd you hear that?"

"I did my homework."

"Even so."

"I can take care of myself," insisted Chelsea.

Jenkins laughed.

"What's so funny?" she said, more a challenge than a question.

He glanced sideways as he drove. Her face was taut with anger far out of proportion with the situation, or so he thought.

"I didn't mean it as an insult. I just, you know, it's a question of common sense. Even I'm cautious."

"I was back in the car when Johnny got hit. If I'd been with him, he wouldn't have been."

"I doubt that. You would have been run over, too."

"I have to go to the bank machine," said Chelsea. "You said that's the way we'd work."

"Once we check it out, fine."

CHELSEA WAITED ANXIOUSLY while Jenkins walked around the ATM. Finally he waved her over.

She hopped out of the car, anxious to see what the suspect had planted. Her heart was pounding.

"It's clean," said Jenkins as she approached. "Nothing."

"Nothing?"

"Nope. Nada."

"Damn."

"Can you tell if the ATM was used?" he asked.

"It didn't trip the monitoring software," she said. "So, if it was used, there was nothing strange about it."

"We'll keep it under surveillance," said Jenkins. "But it doesn't look good."

He sounded as if he'd just lost a million-dollar bet.

19

After delivering the information to the resistance messenger in Kerch, Tolevi headed back south, this time to a village in the center of the peninsula. He was visiting his mother-in-law.

It wasn't a visit in the conventional sense—he wouldn't see her while he was there. This was best for both; neither could stand to be in the other's presence for very long. The old lady blamed him for her daughter's death with a mother's logic: if he hadn't kept her in America, her baby would still be alive.

Forgiveness was impossible. Tolevi naturally resented this and found it impossible not to berate her for the venomous stares she threw his way when they were together.

Still, he felt the obligation, and he left pictures of her grandchild, along with several hundred dollars' worth of Russian rubles, in an envelope just inside the door. He spent the night in the ramshackle barn behind the old woman's tiny house and left in the morning, traveling to Yalta at first light. There he returned the old man's car and spent the day in taverns and bars, picking up gossip; at night he rented a car and drove back to Simferopol, near the airport. He would have liked to check the northern border areas, just to get a firsthand look at what was going on there, but that would have been asking for trouble, or at least complications. He had one more job to do.

Despite the fact that he was helping the Ukrainian side, Tolevi was, in his mind at least, neutral on the matter of the civil war. He recognized the injustice of the Russian interference, despite their lies, but he also knew the rebels who had broken away had real grievances against Kiev and its government. Kiev's corruption and greed could not be easily dismissed—even if he himself benefited from such proclivities. The irony did not make it just, especially as he himself sought no justification.

He spent the day before his evening flight wandering the city, once more listening and gathering light gossip. Immediately after the Russian invasion, a plebiscite had been held in Crimea; over ninety percent of the voters were in favor of their new "status" as a sham independent state under Russian "protection." The results, of course, were phony, but Tolevi had no doubt the result was in line with what the majority felt, if not quite so strongly or unanimously as the announced results suggested.

Russia had a strong pull, historically, culturally. And business, always business. He himself was a businessman.

He got to the airport two hours before his flight. Security had been increased since the Syrian incident, and he stood in line to have his briefcase hand-examined. It was more thorough than the checks at American and European airports, where an X-ray sufficed; here each item was removed and inspected. But it was easier as well; if there was any trouble, Tolevi had no doubt he could buy his way out of it.

The newspapers he'd purchased just before coming to the airport were of no interest to the inspectors, and as they were the only thing in his briefcase, he was passed through without comment. On his way to the gate, he stopped for a coffee; he bought it and sat at a table, stirring it slowly, waiting for his contact and the final task of his trip. He fussed with his briefcase—he'd checked his overnight bag to his final destination in the States—making sure the lock was set properly before leaning it against his leg on the floor.

It was then that he spotted the man watching him several tables away. He was young, no more than twenty-five, wearing jeans and dress shoes. But it was the bad haircut and quick glances away that were easy tip-offs.

Tolevi played with his coffee. If one man was watching him, there were surely others—where the Americans used tech gimmicks, the Russian spy services obsessed with human resources; it was not unusual for the SVR to use upward of a hundred agents when tracking a subject of interest.

There could not be nearly that number here; the terminal halls were fairly empty, and he would surely have spotted someone earlier. But he was sure he had attracted the man's attention.

He's a baby, Tolevi thought, *fresh out of training.*

Tolevi felt a little insulted—surely he was worthy of being tracked by someone with more experience.

Even if the surveillance team amounted to only one—unlikely—it would be difficult to lose the man in the airport; it simply wasn't that big a place, and in any event he had to eventually go to a gate. The SVR had access to the passenger lists and would know where he was headed. A last-minute change could be easily detected.

Am I being paranoid? Surely if they wanted me, they would just pick me up; they've done it before. I am, after all, on their payroll.

But if they *were* following him here—Tolevi started to have some doubts, seeing how inept the young man was with his glances—then they might be waiting for him to make his pickup. This way they would have the incriminating evidence they wanted, as well as his contact.

Tolevi got up and walked in the man's direction. He stared at him, daring him to meet his glare. But the man feigned interest in a woman a few seats away, never turning in Tolevi's direction even as he passed directly in front of him.

Tolevi went into a souvenir shop, then continued down the

hall to a small restaurant. He studied the menu, then went in, taking a seat at a table in the back. When the server came over, he ordered in Russian.

The young man did not follow. Tolevi's seat could not be seen from the hall; he scanned the small room, looking for others on the surveillance team, but there were no likely candidates.

The safest thing to do—the smart thing—would have been to call off the pickup. He could go directly to the gate, board his plane when it was ready, and leave. The SVR might not let him leave, but when they searched him, there would be nothing incriminating.

Not that the Russians ever needed evidence.

Tolevi eyed the kitchen, fantasizing a dramatic escape. It would work for James Bond, but not for him, unless he lucked into an Aston Martin on the apron.

The young man with the bad haircut was nowhere to be seen when Tolevi exited the restaurant, but that only stoked Tolevi's paranoia. Now everyone he passed could be an agent.

Anyone or no one. You're letting your imagination run wild.

Tolevi found the bookshop and went in. Casually lingering near the magazine rack, he checked his watch. Forty-five minutes to boarding, which was when the exchange was supposed to take place.

He bought two magazines. A man, obviously Russian, watched him as he paid. The man was well built, in his thirties—the profile of an SVR supervisor, Tolevi thought.

No. Most supervisors are older, with potbellies and poor grooming.
Still . . .

Magazines in one hand, briefcase in another, Tolevi made his way down the terminal hallway to a gate where a plane was just boarding for Moscow. Glancing over the crowd, he picked out a middle-aged man who did look, in fact, like an SVR supervisor— a dark jacket over black jeans, with a badly wrinkled white shirt. Tolevi slipped through the line, then brushed against him.

The magazines fell from his hand.

"Excuse me," said Tolevi loudly. He handed him the magazines. "I'm sorry."

"These are not mine," protested the man.

Tolevi was already walking briskly away. The man said something else, but Tolevi couldn't hear. He saw a woman darting toward the gate.

An agent? Or someone who had just heard the call to board?

Tolevi's heart was pounding. He crossed to the men's room, found the urinal at the far end, and put down his briefcase as he unzipped his pants. There were three other people in the restroom, all at the urinals.

Four—an Asian-looking gentleman dressed in a business suit came in, pulling a wheeled carry-on and a briefcase identical to Tolevi's. He chose the urinal next to his.

Tolevi fixed his pants, then left, quickly grabbing the briefcase from the floor.

The other man's.

Outside, his plane was being called. Tolevi walked to the gate.

The man with the bad haircut was near the gate, waiting. Tolevi took out his ticket.

He smiled at the man. The man frowned.

Safe. I was just paranoid.

He held the ticket for the gate attendant, who checked off his name on her clipboard, then waved him up the jetway.

Tolevi glanced at his ticket to check where his seat was.

His hand was shaking.

Relax. We're done here.

"Gabor Tolevi!"

His name boomed in the tunnel. Tolevi turned. The woman he had seen earlier was behind him, leading two tall, much younger men.

SVR, all of them.

"Yes?" he said.

"Let me see your briefcase." The woman's voice was just like a man's.

Tolevi hesitated. "Why?"

"Open it."

"Here," he told her, handing the briefcase over.

She grabbed it and clicked open the clasp. The two men stopped behind her, stationing themselves to block off escape.

Stuck here. Better to talk yourself out of it. Call Keisha, the Hound, get him to help.

The handler would never take his call. He was on his own.

The woman pulled out a newspaper, then passed her hand all around the interior of the briefcase. Except for the paper, it was empty.

"You may go," she said, handing it back. "A mistake."

"No need to apologize," said Tolevi. "Have a good day."

20

Cambridge—nearing 9:00 P.M.

The false alarm dampened everyone's spirits but not their appetites.

"I could smell that pizza two blocks away," said Jenkins as they returned to the van.

"I figured you'd all be hungry," said Flores, who'd brought two pies. "Mushrooms and plain."

Chelsea shook off the offer.

"You gotta be hungry," said Jenkins. "Come on."

"Not for pizza," she told them.

"Perfectly balanced food," said Robinson. "Fat, carbs, protein, tomato sauce. Doesn't get any better than this."

She rolled her eyes. Jenkins was right—she really should eat—but not pizza.

She looked at the video console, which showed the ATM they had under surveillance. It was all on the FBI now.

"Nothing going on," said Flores. "Only two people have used it all night."

"We'll keep surveillance on all night," said Jenkins, "but it doesn't look good."

AT PRECISELY FIVE minutes to six, Jenkins's second in command knocked on the door of the van, ready to begin the day shift. With him were two other FBI agents and a young Smart Metal employee, Jason Chi, who worked in the UAV division but had a strong background in AI. It took less than three minutes to brief them; Jenkins checked in with the surveillance teams, who were also being replaced, then walked Chelsea out to her pickup truck.

"See you tomorrow night?" she asked.

"Absolutely."

Riding back to the task force headquarters, he checked his messages. His brother's wife had called twice during the night; both times she'd tried to say something but couldn't get it out. Too tired to call her back, he told himself she'd probably be sleeping. He checked his official e-mail quickly, then left for home.

Two hours after he arrived, Dryfus woke him with a phone call.

"They struck overnight," said the tech supervisor. "I just got a call from Bank of America."

"Son of a bitch. Was it the machine we were watching?"

"No. And none of the ones we staked out," said Dryfus. "But . . ."

"Yeah?"

"It was in the next batch on the list. We just missed it."

Jenkins collapsed back on the pillow, completely defeated.

21

"So as we know, the graph of a hyperbola gets nearly flat as you move from its center. This part is called the asymptote of the hyperbola. And we use these equations to graph . . ."

Borya watched the teacher slash his chalk across the blackboard, dust flying. She liked that—all of the other teachers used smart boards; Mr. Grayson was old school.

$$y = \pm \frac{b}{a}(x - h) + k$$

She saw the graph before he drew it, two slight curves across the x axis, one kissing the y axis, the other, a mirror image, off to the right.

You could flip it:

$$y = \pm \frac{a}{b}(x - h) + k$$

Mr. Grayson continued spewing chalk, almost frenetic as he explained the math behind the graphs and calculations. There was something about calculus that made even boring people, like Mr. Grayson, excited.

Borya loved math—it was the only class she felt any emotion for, good or bad—but she had other things on her mind today. Like collecting the money from last night's haul: the primary reason she'd come to school.

The bell rang. Borya glanced at the board, quickly memorizing the homework assignment, then began filing out.

"Borya, please," said Mr. Grayson, calling her just as she reached the door.

She turned and walked back to the desk. Grayson was a tall, middle-aged man. He had a slight stoop and perpetually smelled of peppermint, which some students thought came from schnapps but Borya knew came from the candies he chain-sucked between classes. Though not handsome like her father, he was not an ugly man, if one disregarded his overgrown nose hair.

"Mint?" asked the teacher, reaching into his drawer for a bag of the candies.

"No, thank you."

"So—asymptotes. Interesting equations, no?"

"Uh-huh." Borya wondered why he had called her back.

"You know, you didn't show your work on your last quiz," he told her, still smiling.

She shrugged. "It was too easy."

He frowned. They'd had this discussion several times. To Mr. Grayson, the steps were always more important than the actual result. Inevitably, he explained, you will reach a point where there will be a mistake, and solving it requires a precise review of steps, and your memory, no matter how good it may be, will fail.

She didn't disagree; there certainly were situations where reviewing steps was absolutely necessary. That just didn't include the questions on most of his quizzes. Or even the tests, for that matter.

"I'll try to remember," she said, taking a step to leave.

"There was something else." Grayson had a habit of bunching

his lips together when he explained a difficult concept in class. He did that now. "Some of the teachers and the principal—it's been noted that you're not doing that well in some of your classes. English, for example."

"ELA? We read stupid stuff."

"What are you reading?"

"*Catcher in the Rye.*"

"Hmmm."

"I really don't give a shit about Holden. He's kind of a jerk. You know what I mean?"

Grayson frowned, but clearly he did know. She could tell.

"Well, be that as it may," he admitted. "But still, you have not been in that class."

"I have this autoimmune issue," she said. "Sometimes it kicks up."

"Yes, I've seen. Well . . . is there something else, something up at home? I only ask because the principal, Sister Josephine, is concerned."

Sister Josephine was always "concerned" about something. Unfortunately, her concern generally expressed itself in the form of detention.

"We're good," said Borya.

"I know your mother isn't, isn't with us anymore," said Grayson quickly. "Very unfortunate."

Borya smiled, nodded, then quickly left, knowing from experience that Grayson would have nothing else to say. Men especially were sweet when they thought about her being dead and all.

A few minutes later, Borya entered study hall, where she got a pass to go to the library. After a few minutes pretending to work on a paper about the odious *Catcher in the Rye,* she opened another window in Microsoft Explorer, tapped a few keys to get past the school's rather pathetic nanny program, then entered the URL of a site that allowed her to roam the so-called black Internet without being traced. Within moments she was looking at a bank account in the Czech Republic.

Eighteen thousand dollars, exactly. Not bad for a night's haul.

The zeroes intrigued her. Theoretically, there was nothing special in the fact that the digits aligned so perfectly, but they appealed to her sense of beauty nonetheless.

She heard the footsteps just in time, completing a small transfer to the account she used for withdrawals before closing the screen.

"Not copying, I hope," said the librarian, peering over her shoulder.

"I don't see why we have to read a book fifty years old," complained Borya, not even bothering to counter the implicit accusation of plagiarism. "Do you?"

"Cite your sources," said the woman, her voice not entirely pleasant.

"I know that."

"J. D. Salinger is a classic," said the librarian as she moved on. "And it's seventy years old. Nearly. Check your sources carefully."

SCHOOL OVER, BORYA walked down the steps and turned the corner slowly, careful not to betray any sense of urgency to the teachers she knew would be monitoring her from inside. Three blocks later, she continued to resist the urge to break into a trot, walking deliberately in the direction of her home. Mr. Grayson's talk was fresh in her mind; she knew the nuns were "worried" about her, which inevitably meant they would be talking to her father when he got back, even if he didn't call himself.

That could mean many things, including a possible grounding; she'd have to prepare for the worst.

Three hundred dollars in cash, rather than the usual two. The machine dispensed the money gladly. She smiled for the camera as the money came out.

Her dad was due back for the weekend. Maybe one more sweep, tomorrow night. Then lay low for a while. She was getting bored of ATMs anyway.

22

By the time he reached Henri Coandă International Airport in Romania, Tolevi was exhausted. The adventure at the Crimea airport was the least of it.

The flight to Armenia had been late, and his connection missed. That left him to fly on TAROM airlines, whose idea of first-class luxury was a worn leather seat in a forty-year-old Ilyushin II-18D. The four-engine Russian airliner was powered by noisy turboprops, and even though he sat toward the front of the aircraft, their drone bulldozed past his Bose noise-canceling headphones until his head felt like splitting apart. Released from the plane, he went straight to the restroom, where he soaked his face in the sink.

He caught a glimpse of himself as he swallowed four Tylenol for his headache. Tolevi looked like a Russian businessman, or maybe a member of the *mafya*—gray suit jacket over a plaid shirt, new leather briefcase hanging from a strap.

His black hair had a few strands of gray. Had those been there before he left the States?

He slicked them down before heading to the food court.

Tolevi's CIA contact was milling around near the popsicle-shaped pop art sculpture by the escalator. Tolevi was surprised—ordinarily a low-level officer, usually fresh from the farm, met him. Instead, it was Yuri Johansen himself.

That couldn't be good.

Tolevi went to the Burger King kiosk and bought a Whopper, along with fries and a shake, then found an empty table. Ordinarily, his contact would wait, confirm his identity, then follow him to the restroom, where they would make the exchange. But Johansen came straight over and asked if he could sit.

Another very bad sign.

Tolevi gestured for him to sit. He played it as if he didn't know the man, not sure what to expect.

"We heard what happened at the airport," said the CIA officer. "We're glad you made it."

I'll bet.

"Did you get it?" added Johansen.

Tolevi glanced up at him. "When exactly have I failed?" he said in Russian.

Johansen smiled. His Russian was very good, but he stuck to English.

"We're very appreciative. There'll be a bonus."

"The man I met in Kerch," said Tolevi. "Very young. The movement—I don't know how long they can last."

He'd debated whether to mention it, deciding he better, in case something went wrong.

"The loyalists are clearly losing ground if they're scraping the bottom of the barrel," he explained. "And that is bad for my business as well. Bad all around."

"I see." Johansen seemed neither concerned nor surprised. But then he never did.

So how had he heard about the problem at the airport? Perhaps the man with the bad haircut worked for him, rather than the Russians.

Tolevi bit into the hamburger. It didn't quite taste like a burger he'd have back in the States. Then again, he rarely if ever ate at a fast-food restaurant; that was only something he did as part of the recognition routine.

Maybe a way for the CIA to torture him, he thought.

"We have something critical coming up we were wondering if you could handle," said Johansen. "We need to get somebody out."

"That's not my usual line," said Tolevi.

"You've done it before."

"That was a onetime deal," said Tolevi, picking up a French fry. "I've been thinking about getting out of the business completely."

"Can you afford that? The rent on your town house is very high. Your car lease, the summer house in Maine? And you owe quite a bit of money to your friends, I understand."

"Easily paid," lied Tolevi. He was, in fact, quite a bit in the hole of late; several deals had not worked out, costing him his principal.

"And then there's college tuition soon."

The reference to his daughter was subtle, but not subtle enough. It was more like something the Russian FGB would say.

"That's not a threat," said Johansen quickly. "I'm just saying compensation will be very good for this. And then maybe that will be the time for a sabbatical. When it's done."

"What exactly are we talking about?"

"In a few days." Johansen rose, then reached across and took the briefcase Tolevi had put on the seat. "Go home and rest. Have a good flight."

23

Boston—the next day

I'm in a room with an aquarium.

I'm in an aquarium.

Who are these people talking?

Why are the lights on?

Johnny Givens opened his eyes. He wasn't exactly sure where he was.

No, he knew he was in a hospital. How he knew that, though, he couldn't say.

A woman was standing over him. She was smiling.

A nurse. She wore a paisley blue top and white pants.

A man stood next to her. Older. Gray hair. He was frowning.

"Doc?" he muttered.

"I'm not your doctor. My name is Louis Massina. I'm responsible for your being here."

"You found me?"

The nurse choked back a laugh.

"No. I had you moved here. You needed a new heart."

"What?"

"Dr. Gleason will be in soon to explain," said the nurse.

"Can I have some water?" Johnny asked.

The nurse left to fetch it. Massina stared at him, his face stone.

"You've lost your legs. Both of them," Massina told him. "We're preparing prosthetics."

"What? My legs? They're here. I feel them." Johnny started to push himself up, but a black wave hit him and slammed his head back to the pillow.

"They're not," said Massina coldly. "It's phantom pain. They've done a lot of work on you. They're going to do more. The sooner you can start rehabilitation, the better."

"What the hell are you talking about?" asked Johnny.

"The heart is designed to last ten years. By then, either you'll be a candidate for a human one, or we'll have a better model. I suspect both. It'll be your choice."

"What?"

"We've given you drugs to speed your recovery. Normally it takes weeks to get stumps. In my day, it was months. Many months. The drugs will make it happen overnight. Literally. Without them you would have died. There are side effects," Massina added, "but we'll get into that when you're well."

"Who the hell are you?"

"I'm sorry you were hurt," said Massina. He turned to leave.

"Wait," demanded Johnny. "My legs—"

"You won't miss them."

"What the hell are you saying? How would you know?"

Massina removed his sport jacket, then slowly rolled up the right-hand sleeve of his sweater. He reached his left hand up to his shoulder below the shirt. Then he removed the arm and held it toward Johnny.

The black wave returned. Johnny felt as if he was going to faint. Massina left without saying another word.

24

Borya threw herself back on the bed, rolling against the twenty-dollar bills she'd sorted into neat piles perpendicular to her pillows. Her home "stash" amounted to just over a thousand dollars, including money from her birthday, her godmother's semi-monthly presents, and her dad's allowance. It was literally more cash than she knew what to do with; it didn't count her "secret" money, or even the bills hidden in an envelope taped to the back of the dresser: two hundred and fifty-seven dollars she had saved from her last enterprise, helping Gordon Heller dispose of two stolen TVs last year.

She shouldn't have done that. Three years older than her, Gordon had practically hypnotized her at the time, though now she couldn't begin to imagine why. He was smelly and not very bright, though obviously smart enough to find someone else to deflect blame when doing something illegal. Two days after she told him she wasn't going to give him a bj—as he called it—he started going out with Cynthia Greiss, and that was that.

Jerk.

But what was she going to do with all this money?

A new computer. Her MSI was starting to seem a little slow, even though it was only six months old. TromboneHackerD had been bragging on Asus lately; maybe she'd check it out.

She didn't have enough for that. She wasn't going to touch the money she'd already hidden in the Austrian bank—the vast bulk of her gleanings from the ATMs. There was a reason to do one more round, then close down.

OK. A goal.

Borya rolled back off the bed, gathered the money back into four separate piles, and hid it away in various places in her room. Then she grabbed a sweatshirt, checked her hair, and went down to get her bike.

When she'd started, the ATM enterprise had been a challenge and a lark, a goof, a little bit of fun and excitement. It didn't hurt anyone, not like Gordon's thefts; the banks made good, from what she heard. She had started by looking into skimmers, then realized that the card machine her father had locked in his office safe gave her possibilities far beyond what a skimmer gang might have. Figuring out how to get the safe open was harder than the coding.

Not really. But the coding wasn't all that hard to do, with the help of a little research on the Internet.

But the excitement had worn off. It was time to try something else.

What exactly?

Borya pondered the possibilities as she unchained her bike from beneath the back porch.

TOLEVI LEANED FORWARD in the backseat as the sedan pulled up the street near his house. As always, he felt a slight touch of nostalgia, remembering how his wife would always be waiting when he returned. That was more than a decade ago, several lifetimes, and a different continent.

As he reached for the door, a figure darted from the driveway of the neighbor's house, one door down. It mounted a bicycle, smoothly gliding down the street.

Was that his daughter, Borya?

It certainly looked like her: slim build, pressing down toward the handlebars exactly the way she rode. The rider passed under a lamppost near the corner; he or she was wearing a gray hoodie.

None of this was exactly verification, but he was sure it was Borya. And he was also sure it was past 8:00 P.M., which was her absolute curfew when he was out of town.

What the hell was she up to?

"Indulge me," Tolevi told the driver. "See if you can follow that girl on the bike. The one who just turned. I want to see where she's going."

"But—"

"It's my daughter," said Tolevi sharply. "I want to see where she's going. She's breaking curfew."

"I don't know, sir."

Tolevi leaned forward and dropped a hundred-dollar bill on the front seat of the limo.

"I have boys myself," said the driver, putting the car in gear. "Much safer."

25

"The problem with the Sox is that they can't get consistent pitch-ing," said Flores. "And they traded away Trey Ball. He was a phenom. Believe me."

"Would have been a phenom. Maybe," said Jenkins.

Chelsea tuned the men out as they continued to argue, gently, about baseball. She checked the gear; they were tapped into twelve teller machines tonight, and would be able to cover another two dozen by the end of the week.

If they hacked into the ATM clearinghouses—something like bus depots for bank transactions—they could cover them all. But even Massina thought that was a bit too far.

For now, anyway.

Jenkins would definitely veto it. Chelsea could tell that he was having second thoughts about what they were doing, even though it had been his idea. He had a line in his head that he wasn't going to cross, though he wasn't very good at explaining exactly where it was.

They had eight UAVs in the air tonight, each doing what the flight engineers called an orbit around their designated air space.

The orbits—slightly elliptical patterns—were designed by the computer for maximum coverage.

Chelsea toggled from Hum to Hum, looking at the infrared feeds. The people walking each starred in a movie she'd come in halfway through, and would leave before it ended. She was a strange kind of voyeur, watching them as if she were sailing above them, an angel from heaven looking for the soul she'd been sent to find.

Or the devil, maybe.

The system blurted an alert.

ATM 4 – unusual activity detected. ATM 4

The UAV in that area tucked its wing and sped in the direction of the machine, a mere three blocks away.

"I have something," said Chelsea.

26

Boston—same time

By the time his daughter turned onto Warren Street in Watertown, Tolevi had decided that he had seen quite enough. He couldn't imagine why she was riding so far from home.

Or to be more precise, he didn't want to imagine. He shut out all possibilities—boyfriends, drugs, worse—and did his best to clamp down on his simmering anger. As they neared Boston Children's Hospital, Tolevi wondered if perhaps Borya was visiting a young friend. While that wouldn't be completely acceptable—she was still out of the house past her assigned curfew—it would still be far better than any of the other possibilities. But she rode past, stopping at a bank machine down the street.

To buy drugs?

"Let me out," Tolevi told the driver. "And wait. Come on, come on!"

The driver pulled across a driveway. Tolevi leapt from the car and ran to the ATM. His daughter was just grabbing her bike.

"Borya! Borya!" he yelled.

"Daddy?" Startled, the girl dropped her bike on the ground.

"What are you doing here?" Tolevi demanded. He felt his

hands trembling; the idea of his daughter as a drug addict or worse was unnerving.

"Daddy—what are *you* doing here?"

"I just came home. Why are you out? What are you doing?"

"Nothing. I was . . ."

Her voice trailed off.

"What's in your hand?"

"Nothing."

Tolevi leaned forward and snatched his daughter's hand. She tried to jerk it away. Though he was surprised at her strength, in the end the young teenager was no match for him. A bank card fluttered from her hand to the pavement.

"What money did you take?" he demanded.

"You hurt me, Daddy."

"No tears, girl. That won't work with me." He was lying— already his daughter's distress was having its effect. His anger weakened. Borya was too precious for Tolevi to be completely unaffected. But this was for her own good. "Where's the money?"

"I didn't take money."

"Empty your pockets!"

He expected defiance, but instead Borya put her hands into her front pockets and turned them inside out. Her cell phone was in her back pocket; she showed it to him, slipping her hand in the other to show it was empty.

"Whose card is this?" he shouted. He glanced at it. "It's not mine." No answer, just averted eyes. "What's the PIN number?" he demanded, holding up the card.

"I'm going home."

"Get in the car," he demanded.

"I'm going home." She picked up her bike and hopped on.

Tolevi started to grab her, then decided to let her go. He turned back to the machine and put the card in.

He hesitated for a moment, his mind blanking as he tried to recall her birthdate. It was the most logical pin.

September 10. 9–10. 09–10

He hit the keys. That didn't work.

Maybe 9–0–1–0? Or was it just the year she was born?

As he started to punch the numbers, a car sped down the street. Hit the brakes hard; the screech filled Tolevi with a dread he hadn't felt since the doctor walked toward him in the hospital the night his wife died.

Borya! Oh no!

Two men jumped from the car. All he could think of was that they had hit her.

It took a few seconds for him to realize that wasn't the case at all. By then, each man was on a knee, aiming a Glock 40 pistol at his chest.

"What is this?"

"Hands up," shouted one of the men.

Tolevi slowly spread his hands. The men were between five and seven meters away, too far for him to try knocking away the weapons.

Had his daughter set him up? Impossible.

Who was behind this? Medved? Sergi?

One of the men was black, and the Russian mob *never* used blacks.

"Keep your hands up," said the closer man.

"Are you robbing me? I have no money," said Tolevi. "I'll give you this bank card. That's all I have."

"Toss it down."

Tolevi's mind jumped to a calmer place. He would talk himself out of this, get close enough to grab one of the guns and then kill them both.

Or just give them his wallet. A cost of doing business. And of seeing his daughter again.

Borya! I didn't meant to yell at you, baby. It's just, you frustrate me sometimes. What were you doing out past curfew?

"Step back to the machine," said the man closest to him.

"It's just business," said Tolevi. "No need for excitement."

"Turn around and face the wall," said the man. His partner rose and scooped up the ATM card.

"I don't think that's a good idea. You get the money, I get away and forget who you are. I'm sure that's a great deal for all of us."

"We're not robbing you, asshole," growled the man who had retrieved the bank card. "We're with the FBI, and you're under arrest."

27

Borya fought back tears as she raced the last block to the house. She was angry with her father, and angry with herself. Why had he come back early? Didn't he trust her?

Why had she insisted on going out one more time? Where was the sense in that?

What was she going to tell him? He had the card. Of course, accessing the account wouldn't tell him anything, certainly not what she was up to.

There was thirty-seven dollars and change in the account. He'd ask where she got it.

That wouldn't be the only question he'd ask. Or the hardest.

How did you set this account up? You're not eighteen.

A friend.

Which friend?

James.

James who?

God, she would never be able to bluff her way through. The account had been set up entirely online.

She could tell him that. Just leave out the details.

I set the account up myself online.

Why?

Why . . . why? Because . . . I wanted to see if I could do it.

Dumb answer. That was practically admitting that she had hacked in.

But she didn't hack in, and she had set up the account online. And lied in doing so, of course, but still, the original setup was legit.

What followed wasn't. Everything that followed.

Should she tell him everything?

Oh, God, no. He'll have a conniption.

Conniption. One of her teachers used that word. It was a good word. It fit.

Borya let her bike drop on the back walkway and ran up the stairs. She'd beaten her father home. Maybe she could pretend she was sleeping.

28

They took the suspect to the FBI Field Office at One Central Plaza, walking him in through the back and up to a suite of interrogation rooms.

The Bureau had assigned an interrogator, Jill Hightower, to the task force. She met Jenkins as they walked in, standing back against the wall as the agents and suspect passed. Letting the others go ahead, Jenkins led her to the small office down the hall.

"He's the guy?" asked Hightower.

"Looks like it."

"He talk?"

"Said nothing."

"Ask for a lawyer?"

"No."

Hightower seemed skeptical but let it pass. "A little older than I expected. Better dressed."

"Yeah." Jenkins thought that, too—he'd expected someone in their twenties, a gofer. This guy looked much farther up the food chain. And he was smart enough to keep quiet.

"Did he have ID?"

"Passport and driver's license." Jenkins showed her the passport. "We're checking it out. There are no local warrants, for what that's worth."

"I hate it when they don't fit the profile," said Hightower. "We going in together, or do you want to hang back?"

"Let's do it together."

"You better get some coffee first. Your eyes are slits."

BACK AT THE van in Cambridge, Chelsea watched as the Hum circled above the black Lexus it had followed from the bank ATM. The driver had gone inside the nearby convenience market.

"Surveillance team is about five minutes away," said Flores. "Any change?"

"Still inside. Oh wait—here he comes."

The driver came out with a large coffee in one hand and a six-pack of something in the other. He went to the rear of the car and popped the trunk.

"Coffee for now, beer later," said Chelsea. "He'd be in the same place if hc skipped both."

"He's not drinking the coffee," said Flores, looking over her shoulder. "Watch."

The driver dumped the coffee out onto the pavement. He had put two cups together, one inside the other; he switched them, so that he had a clean cup on top, then he opened one of the beers and poured it in.

"At least it's a light beer," said Flores.

"Can you get him for DWI?" Chelsea asked.

"Have to call the locals. Not worth it—here are our guys. They'll handle it."

Chelsea watched as two FBI agents walked over to the Uber car. They had already run the plate and found out who the driver was, an Iranian Christian who had come to the U.S. a decade and a half before.

They didn't expect trouble, and they didn't get it. The man

got out of the car without resisting and, after a few moments of conversation, walked meekly back to the agents' vehicle. By then, four other FBI agents had moved in to secure his car; it would be searched and possibly impounded, depending on how cooperative the driver was.

With the driver in custody, Flores visibly relaxed, joking with the surveillance agents and checking baseball scores on his phone. Chelsea flipped back through the Hum video screens, first checking on the two FBI agents watching the ATM, who were waiting for a technical crew and the bank manager to arrive so they could remove it. After that, she flipped over to the other UAV feeds. Their placid scenes were almost shocking to her; how could things anywhere else be calm when there was so much excitement elsewhere?

It was exciting, even just sitting here in the van. More exciting than watching a robot she'd programmed run through its paces.

Or rescuing someone?

That had been different somehow, more immediate, or more dire, or more . . . that was different because it happened so quickly, and she was inside it. This was quick, too, or had been, but she was more distanced, more able to make decisions.

But both experiences were more like dancing than math, more like a sport, adrenaline racing.

And she liked that. It was a part of her that hadn't been used in several years.

"You gonna join us when we wrap up?" Flores asked.

"Don't we have to keep watching?" Chelsea asked.

"Nah. They have it under control now. We'll just wrap it all up. What are you going to do?"

"Go home, I guess."

"Hell, no. We have to celebrate. Ike's."

"Where's that?"

"Downtown. It's great."

"Is it open this late?"

"For us."

TOLEVI SAT RAMROD straight in the chair in the FBI interview room, staring at the two-way mirror across from him.

Did they really think he didn't know he was being watched? Did anyone not know?

The door swung open. The man the others had been deferring to walked in, followed by a short, slightly overweight woman. Neither was dressed particularly well; the man's suit was crumpled at the shoulders, a clear sign that he had bought it at JCPenney or some similar outlet. The woman's slacks were a size too big; her jacket the opposite.

"So, Mr. Tolevi." The man pulled out the chair opposite him. The woman sat down next to him. "You live in Boston?"

Who was going to play good cop? Tolevi wondered. Probably the woman.

"You have my passport," said Tolevi.

"Were you planning to go somewhere?" asked the man, who hadn't introduced himself.

"I just got back."

"And you went to the cash machine rather than going home?"

"I wanted to make sure I still had money in the account."

"No withdrawal?" asked the woman.

They hadn't told her they'd looked in his wallet. Or maybe she was just playing dumb.

"I don't think we've been introduced," he told her.

"Jill Hightower. I'm a senior agent."

Tolevi turned to Jenkins. "And you?"

"Jenkins. Agent in Charge."

"Well, Jenkins, Agent in Charge, why am I here?"

"I think you know."

"No, really I don't. And I believe you're under some sort of obligation to tell me."

"Do you understand your Miranda rights?" asked the woman. "Let's go over them again."

JENKINS STUDIED THE suspect as Hightower went through the pro forma warnings. She was right about him; he was very much more polished than what they had expected.

But his background fit. American of Ukrainian and Russian descent.

Russian mob. Had to be.

"You want a lawyer?" Hightower asked when she was done.

"Not unless I need one," said Tolevi.

"Oh, you definitely need one," said Jenkins. "And a good one."

"Why is that?"

"What were you doing on Warren Street?"

"I think you already know I was at the ATM."

"How did you get there?"

The question took Tolevi by surprise. Why were they asking about the ATM? Surely they were here for something else.

Did they know he had dealings with the SVR? Were they upset about that? But if that was the case, why hadn't Johansen mentioned it—or simply taken him in Bucharest? It could have been easily arranged.

The key now was to stay calm until he figured out what the game was.

"I had a car drive me to the ATM," said Tolevi. "What's the big deal?"

"Who drove you?" asked Jenkins.

He said it so quickly that Tolevi suspected he already knew the answer. There was no sense lying, anyway.

The one thing he wanted to do, however, was leave his daughter out of it. He didn't need the FBI—if these guys were really FBI, not CIA pretenders—scaring the crap out of her.

Though that was tempting, in a way. Whatever the hell she was up to—maybe a little tough love would straighten her out.

No, foolish. They would harm her. Best to leave her out. And yet he wasn't sure exactly how he could do that—lie, and they'd use that to pressure him somehow.

"An Uber car picked me up at the airport. They just started doing that," he added. "I find it useful. Usually a little cheaper than a service."

"And you went straight to the bank machine?"

"No, I was going home and then decided to go there."

"Why?"

"Why do we do anything?" He turned and looked at the woman. She had a sympathetic smile, but of course that was an act.

You have to watch the sweet ones.

"You stopped at home, then went to get money?" she asked.

"We almost stopped. Then, you know—I changed my mind."

"Aren't there more convenient ATMs?" asked Hightower.

"Why are you so interested in my banking?" A strategy started to crystalize. Tolevi would push them a bit.

If they were FBI, they would be looking for a payoff—that would be proof he was working with the Russian spy agency.

They could look for that all they wanted. And ultimately, if—or rather when—he went back to the CIA, he would easily explain that: the only way to get access in Crimea was to deal with them. It was impossible not to.

Surely Johansen knew that, even if he didn't know the extent.

"Tell us about how you skim the ATM machines," said Jenkins.

"Excuse me?" asked Tolevi, taken off guard by the question. It seemed a non sequitur, out of left field.

"Your scam on the ATM machines." Jenkins smirked. "Tell us about it."

Tolevi glanced at Hightower. She had a slightly distressed look on her face; he guessed that meant that the other agent had gone off script.

But what the hell did that question mean?

"I don't know what you're saying," Tolevi told them. "Skim? How?"

"Don't bullshit me," said Jenkins. "Who do you work for? Or do they work for you?"

"You've lost me," said Tolevi. "Explain what you're talking about."

Jenkins reached into his jacket pocket and took out a baggie. Inside was the bank card Tolevi had taken from his daughter. "What's this?"

"An ATM card."

"What about the coding on it?"

Did they think he was passing information with a bank card?

No. This was some sort of ruse or plan to get into his house and unlock his safe, where he had the machine he used to make false IDs, including the credit and bank cards.

Keeping it there hadn't seemed like that big a risk; he wanted to be able to move quickly in case there was trouble, and the CIA knew he used phony identities, so the machine wasn't particularly incriminating.

But they were obviously going to use it as if it were.

Time to call their bluff.

"I know nothing about coding," said Tolevi. "I believe I'm entitled to a phone call, am I not?"

29

Boston—a half hour later

Flores and the others had to secure the van and check in back at the task force headquarters, so Chelsea went alone to the bar, a place on Tremont Street. She'd never been there before—not unusual, since she was hardly a partier.

She'd expected a fairly rowdy place, given the way Flores and the others had talked about it—a sports bar maybe, or a place the Dropkick Murphys would call a second home. But Ike's was far more upscale than that, loungelike, the sort of place you might find on the roof of an upscale hotel, except it was in the basement, and the images that were being projected on the fake windows at the side were just that, images piped directly from video cameras on the roof. The music was cool jazz, late 1950s–early '60s vintage, a very sophisticated vibe that Chelsea never would have associated with the Bureau guys she'd met, and certainly not with Flores.

But they were all here, a dozen of them, all in their late twenties to early thirties. Two were women, which she hadn't realized from the radio transmissions. Only one was black, a tall, football-player type who said he came from Nebraska when they were introduced, then shyly moved away, talking first to the man he'd partnered with, then to the bartender and waitress at the far end.

Most of the agents were not from the Boston area. They had volunteered from different offices across the country, expressing a variety of reasons—boredom, said one outright; the others laughed, though Chelsea guessed they were only surprised at his candor.

Dryfus, the head of the tech team, came in about forty-five minutes after the others. Chelsea was just finishing her beer and was thinking of leaving. He convinced her to stay, asking about where she'd gone to school, what her majors had been.

"And how did you end up in the FBI?" she asked him.

"Ah—I was in the Army, as an E5, which is a sergeant, and I was repairing combat networks. A lot of wires," he laughed. "I left a year after the Gulf War, got my BS at RIT, and . . . here I am. In Miami."

"This doesn't look like Miami," said Chelsea.

"Ssshh, don't tell him," said Flores. "Let him figure it out on his own."

"I'm assigned to Miami. Although I don't think I've spent more than a week there in the last two years." He took a long sip of his drink, a Dewar's on the rocks, then pushed it toward the bartender for a refill. "I got out of Rochester because of the snow. They assigned me to Tulsa first. Took me almost four years to get to Miami, and now look where I am."

"Where the action is, baby," said Flores. He slid his empty beer bottle onto the bar.

He was a little tipsy, but then, so was Chelsea. Not used to drinking, the beer had started to go to her head. It didn't help that she had not eaten dinner.

They ordered some wings. Chelsea had another beer. Somehow she found herself talking to Flores about baseball.

Mostly, she listened, watching his eyes. They were very blue.

"I always thought blue eyes went with blond hair," she blurted.

"Huh?"

"Your eyes. They're blue."

"All my life."

They moved to a table. Another beer appeared in front of her, then another. She felt warm and a little sleepy, as if there were a fire at the far end of the room.

"What do you think?" Flores asked, putting his hand on hers. "Time to go?"

"Where's your apartment?" she asked, surprising herself.

30

"This is his bag," said Jenkins, pointing to the suitcase that had been recovered from the Uber driver.

"Can we look inside?" asked Hightower.

"Not according to the U.S. attorney's office. Not without a warrant. Or his permission."

"But you've already looked, right?"

Jenkins didn't answer. He was starting to like Hightower. A lot.

The office he had borrowed was small, used by two lower-echelon agents. He would have to give it up in a few hours when they came in for work. After that, he'd have to camp out upstairs in one of the empty interrogation rooms.

Or maybe a closet. He didn't want to bring Tolevi to his own headquarters. If the guy was a master hacker, he'd learn too much about the operation just seeing it.

If.

Doubt had started to creep in. Tolevi had some sort of sketchy connection to the Russian mob, but it wasn't at all clear. The phone call he had made was not to an attorney, or a known *mafya* connection for that matter, but to a Virginia-area cell phone. The message he had left—Jenkins had been close enough to "inadvertently" hear—gave nothing away:

I'm being questioned by the FBI in Boston. I have no idea why.

The number belonged to a prepaid cell phone apparently purchased for cash; that certainly fit with a *mafya* or underground connection, but it didn't give Jenkins any real information to work with.

The U.S. attorney wasn't sure they had enough to go on yet for a warrant. And because she was so cautious—anal might be a better word—Jenkins couldn't even examine the ATM without a warrant. They *might* be able to get one, but only by laying out a lot of their theory of the case in court, which would give Tolevi or anyone else involved a map on how to clean up the evidence. Not to mention that he would be opening himself up to potential Fourth Amendment complications, which would throw out everything they'd found.

So he wanted, needed really, Tolevi to voluntarily let them examine it. And once he did that, then by extension they could look at all of its transactions, because what else did looking at the card mean? He'd win without a warrant, and without any worries about using the information in court, let alone tipping their hand or telling the world where they got their information.

Always a dance.

"Did you check on Amsterdam?" Hightower asked. "The hotel he claimed he stayed in?"

"They said he checked out yesterday, which matches his story. They wouldn't give out any other information."

In fact, Jenkins had only gotten that much through subterfuge, claiming to be a friend trying to track him down. The hotel's night manager had rebuffed the FBI's formal request, telling Jenkins's assistant that the request would have to come through channels and be made during the day.

"Just an overnight bag to do business in Europe?" asked Hightower. "I don't know . . . I think I'd take more luggage than that."

"Thin," said Jenkins.

"You have anything else?"

Jenkins shrugged. "Let's play that angle. And ask if we can examine the card. Then Dryfus can analyze it."

TOLEVI FOCUSED HIS attention on his hands, staring at his fingers as if he had never seen them before. It was a technique he had learned in college, from an alleged "mind master," a sort of discipline guru who claimed to have wormed eternal wisdom from a Zen master in Tibet. The man was later unmasked as a fraud, something Tolevi had suspected from the speed at which he bedded female devotees, but the technique itself was a good one. Focus your thoughts so they do not stray—a good strategy in many situations.

His knuckles seemed particularly large and wrinkled. That was where age showed, in the hands. Even the hands of a man such as Tolevi, whose last stint of heavy physical labor dated to a construction job in his early twenties, bore the marks of time.

Breaks as well as wrinkles. A torn ligament. Even now, stiffness that would surely grow as time moved on.

The door to the interrogation room opened and Tolevi's interrogators reentered. Tolevi thought of the airport in Crimea and what might have happened if the SRV agents had understood what to look for—the flash drive embedded in the handle. But these two were even more clueless.

Perhaps. It could easily be an act.

Don't underestimate your enemy.

"So, Mr. Tolevi. You're Russian?" asked Jenkins.

"I'm an American, as you can see from my passport."

"But you're of Russian extraction."

"And Ukrainian," added Tolevi. "What's your background?"

Hightower ignored the question. "Did you visit Russia?"

"Did you visit Russia?" asked Hightower.

"I told you my entire itinerary," answered Tolevi, trying to puzzle out where they were going with their questions.

"A week in the Netherlands," said Hightower. "Nice."

"You've been?" Tolevi asked.

"Yes, as a matter of fact. I rode my bike there."

Tolevi remained silent. She didn't look like the bike-riding type, or a person who exercised fairly regularly at all.

"There are a lot of things to see in the Netherlands," continued the female agent. "And places to go."

"You smoke pot?" asked Jenkins.

"Do I look like someone who smokes pot?"

"What does that look like these days?" said Hightower. "I think just about everyone does."

"I do not."

Tolevi wondered if they were going to set him up—plant marijuana in his bag and hold him on a bogus charge. But wouldn't they have done that at Customs?

Nothing about this was making sense. What exactly were they up to? And where the hell was Johansen?

Maybe behind the glass, gauging his responses.

Tolevi lowered his gaze, looking at his hands again.

"You didn't take much clothes for a week's stay," said Hightower.

"You're detaining me because I didn't pack an extra pair of underwear?"

"Why did you stop at that ATM?" Jenkins's voice was sharp; he was back to playing bad cop.

"Why does anyone stop at an ATM?" asked Tolevi.

"Tell me about that card," said Jenkins.

"It's a bank card."

"What's special about your card?"

"Nothing."

"Would you mind if I had it analyzed?"

"Go ahead."

"Thank you."

There was a knock at the door.

"Come in," said Hightower.

One of the agents poked his head inside the room.

"Mr. Jenkins, you're wanted on the phone."

JENKINS PAUSED INSIDE the observation room to watch Tolevi before picking up the phone. He was a cool one, unshakeable. But it figured that a *mafya* member would be like that. They had no conscience, which made it easy for them to lie.

Still staring at Tolevi through the two-way mirror, he picked up the handset. "Jenkins."

"Agent Jenkins? This is Yuri Johansen. I'm with the Agency."

"What agency?" asked Jenkins. He'd thought it was a call from one of his people back at the Watertown site.

"Central Intelligence Agency, Mr. Jenkins. I understand you're questioning a Gabor Tolevi."

"That's right," said Jenkins.

"What exactly has he done?"

Jenkins hesitated. Was this really a CIA agent on the line? He thought of tracing the call, but there was no one else in the room he could ask to initiate it. And the phone set didn't include a caller ID screen.

"I'm not understanding why it would be your business," said Jenkins.

"The Agency is very interested in everything Mr. Tolevi does," said Johansen matter-of-factly. "So what has he done?"

"We're—he's part of an investigation."

"I gathered that. Into what, exactly?"

Surely this must be a member of Tolevi's *mafya* clan, posing as a spy to try and get him off. That was a good thing—he could get this asshole, too. Surely he'd be easier to break than Tolevi, who right now was staring blankly at the mirror.

"I'm not going to discuss this over the phone," said Jenkins. "If you want to come down and talk about it in person, I'd be happy to share what I can."

"I'm afraid it would be difficult for me to do that. I'm in Europe at the moment."

"Well, I guess that's that, then." Jenkins hung up.

31

Borya woke with a start, disoriented. The sheet and blankets had tied themselves around her so tightly that her right arm was numb.

She stared up at the ceiling of her bedroom, trying to regain her sense of where she was. The tiny LED on the power button of her laptop was blinking next to her, half obscured by the edge of the covers.

Her father must not be home if the laptop was still here. He always turned it off and put it on the desk, generally with a murmured lecture about how expensive it would be to fix when it fell off the bed as she slept.

Not home yet?

Borya raised her head to look at the clock. It was a little past three.

What was he doing?

Whatever it was, it represented only a temporary reprieve, the calm before the storm as her ELA teacher said when discussing *Moby Dick.*

That made her father the whale. But he was more like Captain Ahab, relentless.

Not cruel, though he would definitely yell when he got home. The account. She had to kill the account.

Borya unraveled the covers. Was her father home already? No lights were on in the hallway—he habitually turned them off—but hadn't she done that when she got home, part of the ruse to pretend she was sleeping?

"Daddy?" she heard herself say. "Papa?"

No answer. *Don't push it.*

Borya retrieved her laptop and typed in the password. She hated to kill the account, but there was no other choice. Besides, it was time to move on to the next thing. Maybe she'd write her own video game, something she'd never tried. Or maybe hack an airplane control system. She'd read that it could be done.

Borya typed furiously, her fingers pounding the plastic keys of the laptop. Finally she stopped and stared at the screen, where a cursor blinked in the open program box. There was a long delay between when a command was given and when it was acknowledged as executed, due to the need to traffic the commands through a set of anonymous servers.

Executed

A sudden shiver ran through her. It was cold in the house.

Where was her father?

"Daddy?" she said again, this time louder, though she sensed there would be no answer. "Daddy, where are you?"

32

Boston—around the same time

". . . backward and forward, every which way you can think of and a few I'm sure you can't. There is no special coding on that ATM card. Zilch. It is no different than any other bank card. Including mine."

Jenkins pushed the receiver closer to his ear. "What are you saying, Dryfus? We got the wrong guy?"

"I'm saying there's nothing on this bank card that makes it different than any other bank card."

"But Chelsea Goodman showed you the string of extra commands."

"There's nothing special on the card."

"How can that be?"

"Well . . . maybe the theory was wrong."

"Can you access the account?" asked Jenkins.

"Well . . . Technically, I need a warrant."

"Forget about that. Just access it."

"*Boss.*"

"We have a card used in the commission of a crime. We're investigating the crime."

"The ATM owner hasn't reported any unusual activity. There is no complaint. There's no crime—I can't."

"Just take a look at the account."

"Boss, *really*. I need a warrant. Otherwise I'm hacking into an account. Even if I find something, until there's a complaint—"

"Where are you now?" asked Jenkins.

"Our lab."

"Wait there for me. I'll be over in ten minutes."

"But, Trev—"

"You want coffee? I'll stop at Dunkin' on the way over." Jenkins hung up without even bothering to hear the answer. He looked through the mirror into the interview room. Tolevi was still sitting there, staring at the table. Every so often he flexed his fingers, but otherwise he was a stone Buddha, without emotion or movement.

"So what are we doing?" asked Hightower. She was leaning against the wall next to the door, eyes drooping.

"I'm going to try to figure out a way to access his account," said Jenkins.

"How?"

"Maybe he'll do it for us. He's cooperating. Kind of."

"Maybe because he knows there's nothing there."

He was so close. It was just a matter of time before he came up with something he could use as leverage to break him. If they could only get the god damn search warrant.

"He told me I could examine the card," said Jenkins. "That means I can see if it works."

"You didn't ask specifically if you could look at the account."

"I don't think I have to."

More importantly, thought Jenkins, he hadn't been told he couldn't.

I'll look at the account, then go from there.

"I'll be back in a half hour or so," he told Hightower. "You want something?"

"We can't keep him forever."

"We're not going to."

"He has a kid."

"I realize that. But he left her here in the country, right? She's what? Seventeen?"

"I think fifteen." They'd used a commercial credit-rating database to look up Tolevi's personal details, and they'd filled out more of the information with a simple Google search. The information was not definitive, but a girl with the same last name had been pictured in the newspaper the year before, after being elected to the Honor Society as a freshman.

Borya Tolevi.

"We could be accused of endangering the welfare of a child," added Hightower.

"Come on," said Jenkins. "That's not going to happen. I'll be back."

He stalked from the room, determined to break Tolevi, break this case. And when he did that, when he finally got the scumbag Buddha in there to talk, he was going to find the bastard who had killed his brother.

Jenkins was nearly to the front hall when his cell phone rang. He pulled it from his pocket and saw that the number belonged to Paul Smith, his boss in D.C.

He'd want an update. Jenkins considered putting it off—he had nothing to tell him. But maybe he could suggest a shortcut to getting the warrant. The warrant would make everything much, much easier.

"This is Jenkins," he said, sliding the answer bar on the touch screen.

"What's the status of your suspect?" barked Smith. He wasn't happy.

"We're still working on him."

"What evidence do you have?"

"He was at the ATM when the card was used."

"OK. And the card is definitely tied to the scam?"

"We think so, yes."

"*Think* so?"

Jenkins didn't answer. "It's just a matter of time now."

"Release him," said Smith.

"What?"

"You have nothing to tie him to your case. That's what you're telling me. How can you hold him?"

"I'm just questioning him. He's suspect. And he's cooperating. Voluntarily."

"What's his crime? Using an ATM machine?"

"There was an unusual string of . . . um . . . there was a code in the transaction request that was unusual."

"That ties him to the ATM scams."

"I . . ."

"Did that code say 'Give us all your money'?" Smith was even more sarcastic than usual. "Let him go."

"But—"

"He's a CIA asset, and an important one."

"He's a thief."

"You have no proof. You just told me. You don't even have anything to use a warrant. He could get up and walk out, and you can't stop him."

"Some guy calls and claims to be CIA—that's got to be one of his people, pretending. It's a hoax. These guys are A-1 hackers, these Russians."

"The deputy director of the CIA called Lon personally a half hour ago to say release this guy. You think that's a hoax?"

Lon was Lon Phillips, the executive deputy director for intelligence—two levels above Jenkins's boss.

"That's got to be phony," said Jenkins.

"Believe me, it's not."

"You're telling me the CIA is robbing banks?"

"I'm telling you to release him. Now."

"I think we need to consider—"

"We don't need to consider anything. What was this company Smart Metal's role?"

"Smart Metal?"

"Don't play more games with me, Trev. I know you involved a local company called Smart Metal. They make robots, right? What did they have to do with this?"

"They were robbed, and they were just trying to find their money."

"You didn't have them hacking into accounts, did you?"

"Hell no." Jenkins hesitated, trying to organize his response. It was barely a moment, but it was more than enough of a hint for Smith to jump to conclusions.

Unfortunately.

"They are off, out, not to be involved," said Smith. "You are way out of line. Way out of line."

"I did nothing illegal. They did not hack into accounts."

"We're not having this conversation. Take care of things."

The line died before Jenkins could respond. Which maybe was the best for all concerned.

33

What was the sense of sleeping with someone if you couldn't re-member it?

Chelsea slipped from the bed and tiptoed from the room, snag-ging her clothes along the way. Her head was pounding, her legs were stiff, and her mouth felt gummed up.

Ballerina girl! What are you doing with your life?

She waved her hand, trying to physically block her father's voice from her head. But really, it was a hell of a good question.

Why had she gone home with Flores? If her head hadn't been pounding already, Chelsea would have pounded it a few times against the wall just to knock some sense into it.

She wasn't a prude, but this was absolutely not her style. Hook-ups with strangers were so far out of character that she was sure she wouldn't recognize herself if she looked in a mirror.

Fortunately, there were no mirrors in the small kitchen, where she stopped to get dressed. Pots and dishes were piled in the sink, and the garbage pail, without a top, was overflowing.

Typical guy place.

How many times have I told you . . . ?

"Ssshhhh, Daddy. Please. I know you're right," she whispered.

Chelsea needed to use the bathroom, but as she went to it, she heard Flores starting to stir down the hall. She decided she could hold it for a while and trotted to the front door, jamming on her shoes so quickly that she didn't quite get the heel of her right foot all the way in. No matter. She paused at the door long enough to make sure her wallet and keys were still in her bag—they were— then made her getaway.

It was not yet light out. That was fortunate. Chelsea walked for a block, her head clearing, before she managed to get her bearings. Miraculously, she was six blocks from her apartment.

Maybe that wasn't such a good thing, she thought as she crossed the street. They were close enough that bumping into each other was inevitable.

Then again, even with the arrest, they'd probably have to clean up odds and ends on the project; Flores had alluded to that last night.

Several times. How drunk had he been?

Maybe so drunk he wouldn't remember her being there?

Zero chance of that. And surely he'd been more sober than she was.

Oh well, she thought to herself, angling toward a Starbucks that looked open. There were worse things in life than doing an FBI agent.

Surely there were. She just couldn't think of them at the moment.

34

Johnny Givens struggled to lift his head.

"Are you getting out of bed or what?" demanded the woman.

"Yeah. I'm trying."

"Try harder."

He sat upright. Blood rushed from his head and he felt dizzy.

"Who are you?" he asked.

"Your therapist."

"Right."

"The wheelchair is ready."

"I still have an IV."

"Take it with you."

"How?"

The therapist reached up and unhooked the bag of fluid, then dropped it in his lap.

"My legs," said Johnny. "I don't know."

"You don't have legs. Use your arms."

He edged toward the side of the bed.

"I have to look in on another patient," said the therapist. "I'll be back."

She walked from the room. Johnny took a deep breath, then pushed himself toward the chair parked next to the bed. His arms felt stiff, foreign. It was incredibly difficult to move.

Was this for real? Did the bitch even know he hadn't been out of bed since he got here?

Damn.

He flattened the palms of his hands against the mattress and slid a few more inches.

Why the hell am I being tortured like this?

OUTSIDE AT THE nurse's station, Louis Massina stood with folded arms, watching the monitor playing the video from Johnny Givens's room. He could see the sweat rolling down the crippled man's temple.

"You're really making him work," Massina told the therapist.

"He's going to work a lot harder than this."

Massina nodded. "I have a meeting. I'll look in on him tomorrow."

35

"So we just release him?" Hightower held her palms up.

"Yeah." Jenkins leaned back in the chair. "I guess."

"What does he do for the CIA?"

Jenkins shook his head.

"You know . . ." Hightower's voice trailed off. She put her forefinger to her right temple and rubbed in a circular motion, as if she were turning a wheel there. "I wasn't sure about this guy when you brought him in. But now . . . There has to be some connection with the mob. It makes sense."

"Yeah."

"You have a name, you can flesh out his background, get to work on that."

Jenkins gave her a sardonic smile but kept himself from telling her that he knew how to do his job. It had been a long night for her as well.

It wasn't bad enough that the CIA had ordered Jenkins to let his only suspect go. His boss's decision to forbid him to use Massina was even worse. And he wasn't going to be able to explain it fully to Massina either.

Hey, my boss thinks I was using you to do illegal hacking. We didn't go that far, no way. I was on the right side of the line. I think. But now we have to play by my boss's rules.

Well, to some extent. But I can't get you into trouble. So . . . hasta la vista.

Right. That would be some conversation.

"When are you going to tell him he's free to go?" asked Hightower.

"Would you do it?"

"Me?"

"I'm not sure I can trust myself not to hit him," Jenkins confessed. "Or pound the wall on his way out."

TOLD HE COULD go, Tolevi walked out of the interrogation room and down the hall to the lavatory, moving as deliberately as he could. He guessed that they would still be observing him. This release might even be a trick.

Standing in front of the men's room mirror, he tried to smooth the wrinkles from his jacket. He combed his hair straight back, patting the sides. He was due for a cut.

I look like I have two black eyes.

More than likely Johansen had gotten him released. Though it was possible this whole thing was part of an elaborate plot to pressure him into doing whatever job the CIA officer was pushing.

Whatever that was. It had to be big for Johansen to meet him in person. And not even on a train.

Tolevi's thoughts turned to his daughter. She'd be getting up soon, to go to school. He needed to get home and talk to her before then, find out what the hell she was doing.

Had she stolen an ATM card? He didn't want to jump to conclusions, but there seemed to be no other logical explanation.

What was the punishment for that? Grounding for a year?

What if she just found the card? Or told him that. What would he say?

She'd broken curfew, so the card was irrelevant. That definitely earned her a punishment. A stricter curfew and, better, loss of computer privileges, except for homework.

That was the Achilles' heel—homework. The teachers assigned every damn thing on the Internet. You'd think they never heard of libraries, let alone pencils and paper.

Tolevi continued to brood on what to do about Borya as he collected his suitcase and left the building. The real solution here was to hire a full-time, live-in babysitter; the "nanny" he was using to check on her was clearly ineffectual.

And what would a new babysitter do? Put her in chains?

Maybe that was the best way.

The suitcase bumped along after him as he strode toward the front hall. Tolevi stopped and examined it. One of the wheels was chipped.

I oughta send these idiots a bill.

ONCE, TEN YEARS before, Stephan Stratowich had blown off a speeding ticket in Florida, figuring that by the time the police caught up with him, he would be out of the state, immune to anything they could do.

And he was—until two years later, when he was stopped at a routine DWI checkpoint in Illinois. He'd passed the breathalyzer test easily—Stratowich touched alcohol only on his birthday—but then was detained on a warrant check: the Florida court where his ticket was answerable had filed a bench warrant when he failed to show.

That experience weighed on him now, pushing him to settle the speeding ticket he'd gotten the day before with a quick visit to city court. He was hoping he could plea-bargain the damn thing in person that morning. If that didn't work, then he'd pay the damn thing and be done with it. He couldn't afford to take any chances.

One of his "uncles" could probably get him out of it. But he was already deeply in debt, and he didn't need to add another favor to the fifteen grand.

Stratowich quickened his pace as he neared the FBI building, which happened to be on his way. If he was paranoid about speeding tickets, he was absolutely on alert when it came to the Bureau. Yet it held a certain fascination. You had to know the enemy if you were going to conquer him.

He had just decided to cross the street when he saw the door to the building open. A man was framed in the light behind him.

Gabor Tolevi.

Tolevi?

Stratowich froze. He couldn't imagine what Tolevi might be doing there.

Before he could decide whether to approach him or not, a black Uber car drove up and stopped a few yards from the building. Tolevi—it absolutely had to be him, pulling a suitcase and carrying a briefcase—stepped out into the street, asked the driver a question, then jumped in the back.

Stratowich stepped back into the shadows, shielding his face as the car passed. He caught a bit of the passenger's profile, enough to confirm, at least in his mind, that it was in fact Tolevi. Though he couldn't for the life of him imagine why Tolevi would be talking to the FBI.

His uncle might. Perhaps this might be worth shaving a little interest off the debt.

LEG WORK

FLASH FORWARD

Johnny Givens walked into Louis Massina's office, powered by pride, adrenaline, and a dollop of nervousness.

"Mr. Givens," said Massina cheerfully, rising from his desk to meet him halfway. "So good to see you."

Johnny extended his hand. The two men shook.

It's amazing to think I'm touching a fake hand, thought Johnny. *As artificial as my legs.*

"I'm told you're making excellent progress," said Massina.

"Thank you for your help," said Johnny.

"You've put the effort in. It's all you."

Massina smiled broadly. He was an interesting man—a genius, surely, and a rich one. Yet he was "real," humble in many ways. He didn't talk down to Johnny, as many people did. Nor did he offer bs pep talks.

"Things are moving ahead?" asked Massina.

"Yes. I didn't come to thank you. I came to ask for a job."

"A job? Aren't you—you're still with the FBI?"

"The Bureau isn't going to let me go back to the field. I'm on, uh, a furlough. Unpaid."

"I see."

"I'd like to be part of your security unit," said Johnny. "I've been thinking about your organization, the things you guys are into. You can use people like me."

"You've only been out of the hospital for a few weeks."

"Nearly a month."

A long furrow appeared on Massina's forehead. Johnny's exaggeration was a silly lie.

"I'm not a scientist," said Johnny. He had rehearsed a long speech, but now, faced with giving it in person, he faltered. He'd intended to list his assets as an investigator, wanted to point out how Smart Metal really needed someone like him who could spot trouble, maybe check over security flaws, be *involved* . . .

But the words wouldn't come. His mouth had suddenly dried up. His tongue stuck to the bottom of his mouth.

"We may be able to find a place," said Massina. "But only after your rehabilitation is over."

"I know what you're doing—you're pursuing this investigation into the *mafya* and the bank scams. I can be part of that." Even in Johnny's ears, his voice sounded an octave too high—tinny, almost pleading.

Definitely pleading.

"None of that concerns you," said Massina, suddenly cold. "You go and complete your rehabilitation. Take care of yourself. The recovery period is at least a year. The drugs that have gotten you to this point—"

"I'm ready to work now."

"Come back when rehabilitation is over," said Massina. "Then we'll sit down with my HR people and figure out where you'll fit in. Assuming you don't want to stay with the government."

Anger suddenly welled inside Johnny. Why the hell did he lose his legs? And his heart?

"I'm afraid I have a full slate of appointments today," said Massina, abruptly going back to his desk. "Several people are waiting to talk to me."

"Listen." Johnny trembled. "I need a job."

Damn it to hell! Don't you dismiss me, too!

"I will help," said Massina. "When your rehab is complete. When the doctors say it's complete."

Johnny stood in the middle of the office, unable to move. This had not gone the way he thought it would.

"I can do a lot," he said weakly. "I can help."

"I'm sure. And you will."

Massina looked past him to the door, which had been left open. Johnny turned and saw Chelsea Goodman and two other Smart Metal employees in the doorway, staring.

"You're making a mistake," he told Massina.

The scientist said nothing. Depression, sadness, a sense of utter futility chased away the optimism Johnny had felt only a few moments before.

Johnny knew that he owed Massina a great deal, probably even his life. But he wanted to yell at him, demand to be taken seriously. He was ready to work.

Massina wasn't blowing him off. Yet it felt like he was.

Don't project, he told himself. *Don't turn him into the source of all evil. Keep your head up. Don't beg, and don't betray yourself. Or him. You owe him a lot.*

"I'll be back," Johnny said finally, managing to turn and walk slowly out of the office.

REAL TIME

36

Boston—the next day

Best to face the music quickly.

Chelsea was on her way to the FBI task force's debrief session, knowing she would see Flores there, when her cell phone rang. It was Massina.

"Yeah, boss. What's up?"

"What happened last night?" he asked.

"We got someone." She briefly summarized what had happened. "I'm on my way over to debrief with the task force. I'm not sure whether they're going to need us anymore."

"Jenkins just came in here and told me they've ended their operation and we're out," Massina told her. "What's going on?"

"They ended it?"

"Agent Jenkins interrupted my breakfast meeting to tell me," said her boss. "Why did they close it down?"

"I don't know."

"Find out. Get our equipment back."

Massina hung up. Chelsea knew from his tone that this was far from the end of things. She also knew that she had better come back to the office with at least some explanation, plausible or not.

She arrived at the task force office a few minutes later, not knowing what to expect. No one answered when she buzzed at the back door; she was just taking out her cell phone to call Jenkins when the door opened.

It was Flores.

Awkward.

He waved her in, then followed her into the team room. It was empty.

"Aren't we meeting to debrief?" she asked.

"Jenkins called about an hour ago to tell everyone to take the day off." He shrugged. "I guess he knew we all had hangovers."

"What's going on?" asked Chelsea.

"Have a seat."

Chelsea pulled one of the chairs away from its workstation and sat down. She'd taken a long shower at her apartment; between that, a handful of Tylenol, and two cans of ginger ale, she felt almost refreshed.

Flores, on the other hand, looked like Chelsea had felt a few hours before.

"The guy is hooked into the CIA somehow," said Flores. "They said cease and desist."

"The CIA?"

"It's total bullshit. He's *mafya*. Russian mob. Take a look." Flores led her over to one of the workstations. "You're not seeing this," he announced, dropping his voice to a whisper as he tapped a few keys. A long text document appeared. Chelsea was nearly halfway through when she realized that it was referring not to the suspect, whose name she remembered as Gabor Tolevi, but someone named Medved.

"This is the guy?"

"No, this is a guy we think he may work for. Or with. Or something. Medved is *mafya*. Where the CIA comes in, I have no idea." Flores leaned close to scroll down the screen. He smelled like Dove soap and cheap shampoo; at least he'd showered. "This is a reference to a photo, here, which shows them together."

He tapped the screen and a picture of two men appeared. The faces were in the shadow; Chelsea couldn't tell if either was the man at the ATM last night.

"Tolevi's on the right," said Flores. "He's got some sort of import thing going on. Goes to both sides of Ukraine. Maybe legal; I'd bet not."

"I see."

He was uncomfortably close. She slid to the side and got up.

"The CIA gave you this?" she asked.

"Nah. This is our stuff. The Boston PD has some minor stuff on Medved and his associates. You never get a good picture of these guys, of what they do, unless you get informers. But they're pretty tight around here, as tight as the Sicilians were in the thirties and forties."

Chelsea spotted the coffee carafe and decided she wanted a cup. It was a good excuse to put more distance between them.

Flores followed her across the room.

"I guess I'm unclear what's going on," she said, sipping the coffee. It was pretty bitter, despite being weak. "Are you guys stopping the operation? Was this guy involved?"

"I don't know. They couldn't find anything that would definitely link him to the theft."

"What? We saw the string, the extra coding."

"You saw it; we didn't," said Flores. "When they looked at the card, there wasn't anything special on it."

"You looked at the card?"

"He said we could."

"Did you check the account?"

"We need a warrant to do that."

"Give me the number."

"I can't," he said, glancing at the workstation.

Chelsea didn't need more of a hint. She walked back to the computer. There were several windows open; she moused around until she found a list that showed data inquiries from the compromised machine. Rather than copying them, she sent the page to the printer. Getting up to retrieve them, she bumped into Flores.

He reached to her. For a second she thought he was going to hug her, and she worried what she would say. But he only held his palm out as if to stop her from falling.

"I'm fine," she said, slipping past.

"You don't remember last night, do you?" Flores asked as she retrieved the list.

"Some."

"You fell asleep on the bed. You took off your jeans, and boom. You were out."

"I don't usually drink."

"I collapsed next to you. We didn't do anything."

Chelsea searched his face, not sure if he was telling the whole truth, not sure whether she wanted to ask for more details. He seemed to be trying to smile, but he could only turn up one half of his mouth.

He seemed apologetic. Because they hadn't managed to do anything?

"I just wanted you to know—I just . . ." Flores fumbled with his hands, rubbing them together, as if washing. Finally, he jabbed them beneath his arms, squeezing his chest. "I wouldn't take advantage of you . . . I like you."

"I like you, too, Flores."

Later, back in the lab at Smart Metal, she wondered to herself if she should have kissed him then.

37

Boston—that afternoon

By the time Tolevi got home, Borya had left for school. As angry as he was, he was too exhausted and jet-lagged to go to her school and confront her. He rationalized that little would be gained by pulling her out of class; it was far more sensible to wait until she came home. Still unsure exactly how he would punish her—or even how to find out exactly what she was involved in—he sat down on the couch and flipped on the television. Within moments he was asleep.

GIVEN AN UNEXPECTED reprieve, Borya spent the school day attending all of her classes, uncharacteristically participating in each one, even in a discussion of *Catcher in the Rye,* where her teacher complimented her definition of alienation. While her opinion of the book had not changed—*dreck*—she was now aware of a certain parallel between the main character and her own life. Hers was more interesting and she was smarter, but Holden Caulfield did at least have the right impulses, even if his inventor couldn't express them properly.

Caulfield's escape to New York had a certain appeal, given her father's likely attitude at her breaking curfew and using a "found" ATM card (the explanation she had settled on), but ultimately she decided to go home. She knew from experience that his anger would be short-lived. She also knew, or guessed, that he would be unable to figure out what she was up to, and as long as she supplied a halfway decent story to explain it, the repercussions would be limited.

I found the ATM card on the way home and decided to see if it worked.

A simple story, impossible to refute. She worked on the narrative as she walked home, imagining it unfolding as an interrogation:

Where did you find it?

On the sidewalk.

You didn't look for the owner?

I asked a man I saw. He shook his head.

Where was this?

Around the corner.

No, that was too close. Someone might have seen her, or rather, not seen her.

A block from school, in the gutter. It was wet.

Good touch.

Why did you go out after curfew?

I had to do my homework first.

He'd like that answer. Maybe he wouldn't believe it—she could offer to have him call her teachers, who'd all remember how bright she'd been today.

Curfew was going to be the sticker. She couldn't get away from the basic fact that she had been out late. So she was going to be in trouble for that, no matter what else.

She could say she was sorry about that, right away.

I throw myself on the mercy of the court and I fall on my sword.

He'd ask where she got such expressions. She could mention *Catcher in the Rye,* even though they weren't in there that she recalled. He'd accuse her of changing the subject. She'd say she was simply answering questions.

A thousand variations occurred to her as she neared her home. She needed more time to rehearse—she turned quickly up the block, planning to circle until she felt ready.

TOLEVI LEAPT FROM the couch, caught by surprise.

"Easy," said Yuri Johansen. "Slow down."

Johansen stood in front of him in the living room. Two men, both in black pin-striped suits, stood behind him. Both looked as if they could headline a heavyweight boxing match, even in formal wear. Johansen himself was dressed in tan khakis and a pullover sweater, casual. Tolevi shook his head, trying to wake up. He'd been in the middle of a dream.

His wife was in it, alive. They were in a building somewhere, running, lost . . . He couldn't remember the details.

"What's this ATM scam you're running?" asked Johansen mildly.

"What ATM scam?" asked Tolevi.

"The FBI has you fingered for a bank scam. That's why they picked you up. Luckily for you, I intervened. It wasn't easy. I had to get the deputy director involved." Johansen turned to one of the suits. "Go make him some coffee."

"Why are you here?" Tolevi asked.

"Because you were in trouble." Johansen shook his head, smiling. "You are being a naughtier boy than we thought."

"I don't like games," said Tolevi. He thought of the pistol hidden below the end table, and the other, behind the dresser in his bedroom. It was impossible to reach either, and beyond foolish to use them, yet something about the idea of shooting Johansen appealed to him in a way it never had before.

Kill all of them and be done with them.

Then what? Escape to Mexico with Borya. Or Russia, or Kiev. Neither would do.

"End whatever you are doing with the banks," said Johansen, his tone once more businesslike. "That is over."

"I'm not doing anything with the banks."

"Your mob connections—it's time for you to ease them off. To the extent you can without destroying your contacts."

"I'm not part of the family. You know that. But they are very useful."

"Find another way to get things done."

"Why are you giving me orders?" asked Tolevi. "That's not how I work."

"Have some coffee," said Johansen, nodding at the suit who was approaching with a cup. "You take it black, yes?"

BORYA TROTTED UP the stairs, ready to deal with her father. She pushed through the outside door and walked quickly through the hall. The building had once housed two apartments; when it was remodeled, the exterior stairs to the second floor were retained, along with the opening to the first floor near the rear of the hall. Borya swung her key from its string on her pocket, then saw that the door was ajar.

A sure sign her father was home and awake.

Oh well.

She pushed inside, taking two steps across the foyer before spotting the two men in business suits gaping at her near the open dining area on the other side of the living room. Her father and another man, older, with white hair, were sitting at the table. She didn't recognize any of them, aside from her father.

The man with the white hair turned and looked at her.

"You must be Borya," he said cheerfully. "Hello."

"We're busy," snapped her father. "Go do your homework."

"I get a snack," she said, taken off guard by his tone. "I—"

"Later."

Borya put her head down and headed quickly through the living room to the back hall.

Why were the men here? Were they police?

They must have discovered her ATM scam. She cursed herself for letting it go on too long.

Gluttony. That was the worst sin. The nuns told her that all the time. Why hadn't she listened? They were humorless old farts, but they did know certain things, things that could at least get you out of trouble, or steer you away from it.

She'd damned herself by being too cocky, too confident. She didn't need the money—she'd barely spent any of it. She'd done it for the thrill, and what was that now, now that they were going to send her to jail?

Borya closed her door carefully and threw herself on the bed, completely in despair. She would never get out of this. They would drive her to jail, lock her up until she was an old woman.

My life is over.

She rolled over to her back, staring at the ceiling and trying to hear what the men were saying below. Their voices were too low and muffled to make anything out. Reluctantly, she got up and crept to the door. Still unable to make any sense of the muffled voices, she cracked the door open and put her ear into the opening, holding her breath as she listened.

"We need you there by the end of the week," said one of the men—the white-haired geezer guy.

"That's all you tell me?" That was definitely her father. He was speaking sharply, his tone even harder than he used when the nuns called about a test she had blown off.

The white-haired guy said something too muffled to make out. Then her father again:

"I can't leave my daughter."

"Find a way."

They weren't talking about ATMs and the banks. They weren't here about her at all.

Borya's mood rocketed. She pressed her ear against the open space, leaning out, curious now.

Careful! Curiosity killed the cat.

"Use this phone to contact me tomorrow," said the white-haired guy.

Chairs scraped. Footsteps.

Borya pushed the door closed and tiptoed over to the bed, trying to be quiet.

If they come in, I'll pretend to be asleep.

AS SOON AS Johansen and his goons were gone, Tolevi went to the kitchen and retrieved a bottle of vodka from below the sink. He poured three fingers' worth into a tumbler and downed it all. He refilled it, this time about two fingers' worth, and once more drained the glass. Then he splashed about a finger's worth in and went to sit down on the couch.

You have a name for the contact?

He is the brother of the man we want and he owns a shop. You'll get an address, That's enough.

No, it's not.

If I tell you now, you're a liability, even to yourself.

Is he wanted by the Russian, or the rebels?

Both.

How do I get him out?

Use your skills. I'm confident.

Why do you need him out?

He has information we need. Really, Gabe, you don't need to know anything else. Just get it done.

Tolevi might be a smuggler by trade and an occasional spy, but he was not a killer, let alone the sort of action hero who could dig through the weeds and come out with a prize. That's what they needed here.

Waltz out of Donetsk with some sort of CIA prize? Surely the rebels and the Russians would object. Violently.

Tolevi had killed before, but that was when he was young, and they'd deserved it. Then it was kill or be killed, and such decisions were not really decisions, were they? The species had evolved to make that very decision, to take that action. Kill or be killed.

Going into a place specifically to seek danger—that wasn't him. Profit, yes, and sometimes that involved risk. You could balance that as an equation—it was math: X risk equals Y profit. But this was a little more complicated: risk to X power equals? Profit.

He could make the visit pay—that would be a good idea as a cover in any event. But beyond that . . . was finding some forlorn CIA contact something he wanted to do?

Did he have a choice?

"Daddy?"

"Hey, Sugarbaby." Tolevi put down the glass and went to his daughter. She clutched him tightly, her fists grabbing the back of his shirt. She was getting big, reminding him more and more of her mother, God rest her soul.

"Who were those men?"

"Businesspeople."

"For work?"

"Yeah. Something I need to do. It means more traveling."

"Are you going to do it?"

"I'm afraid I have to."

Tolevi wasn't sure how much his daughter truly knew about his "business" arrangements. And naturally he kept any hint that he was working for the CIA from her.

On the other hand, an array of characters had visited the house over the years, and she'd met even more at various parties father and daughter attended. Borya even knew a number of mobsters' sons and daughters. Though they never spoke about that part of his life, he suspected she had at least an inkling of his connections. It occurred to him that he should discuss that at some point.

But not now.

"I don't like it when you go," said Borya.

"I don't like to leave you either. But you have school."

"The lessons are so boring. They're a waste."

"And what were you doing out last night?" asked Tolevi. "Why were you out after curfew?"

"I found an ATM card," she said.

She'd held on to him all this time; now she let go and sat on the chair across from the couch. He hadn't realized how warm she was until she let go; he almost shivered.

Maybe she had a fever?

"Where did you find this card?"

"I found it near the school. I wanted to try it."

"So you rode your bike all the way across town?"

Borya's expression seemed to say, *Where else would I have gone?* She had a way of doing that—turning a perfectly natural question around as if it were the most bizarre thing in the world to ask.

"Where exactly did you find it?"

"On the sidewalk. Near school."

"You know it was stolen?"

"It was?"

"That's what the police say. It could have gotten you in a lot of trouble."

"Oh."

"You rode your bike pretty far in the dark," Tolevi said, deciding to drop the business about the card. It was only natural that she would try to use it. He couldn't fault her for that.

"It wasn't that far."

"It was after curfew."

"I know I broke curfew." She shook her head. "I know you're going to punish me. I deserve it."

Even though Tolevi knew this was a tactic designed to win leniency, he couldn't help but feel somewhat proud of her for taking responsibility. She really was a good daughter—brilliantly smart, responsible, able to take care of herself. She didn't go running all over town with druggies, and she wasn't throwing herself at boys. She studied, got excellent grades. All the nuns said she could get into MIT. It was just a question of what she wanted as a major.

Probably some computer thing. He'd really prefer a doctor. But she had to follow her own muse.

"I am going to punish you," said Tolevi. "We'll figure out the punishment together."

"Do you have the card?"

"Of course not. Why?"

"I just wondered."

"Do you know whose card it was?"

She shook her head solemnly. Tolevi searched for something to say. He didn't think she'd stolen it herself—Borya wasn't like that—but it was just possible one of her friends had. That Susan Abonfinch or whatever her name was. She was a little sneak.

And the boyfriend last year. He was headed for the penitentiary—though if Tolevi saw him around Borya again, he'd save the state a lot of expense.

"What's my punishment?" asked Borya.

Tolevi felt a pang of sorrow. Her voice sounded so much like her mother's.

"What do you suggest?" he asked.

"No television for a month?"

"That may be too severe," said Tolevi, already weakening. "Two weeks. But—"

"I won't do it again. I promise."

"And not while I'm away, especially. I worry about you."

Borya jumped up from the chair and hugged him again, pushing her face against his chest. She was going to be some heartbreaker, this girl. Worse than her mother.

"You haven't called me Sugarbaby in a long time," she told him.

"I always think it."

"I love you, Papa."

"I love you, too." He pushed her gently from his chest. "Now don't take advantage of that."

"I won't."

"Ha! I'm going to call Mrs. Jordan and see if she can stay with you while I'm gone. *In the house.* So she's here all the time. Do you have much homework?"

"Just science."

"Do it. Then we'll go out for pizza."

"I'd rather sushi."

"Sushi, then. Go."

More and more like her mother every day, Tolevi thought as he looked for Mrs. Jordan's number in his phone's index.

38

Boston—around the same time

Jenkins had no intention of giving up the case. If anything, the fact that the CIA had reached out to pressure him made him all the more determined.

But he had to be careful now, more careful than he'd been. Putting Mr. Massina off was the first step. Staking out Tolevi's home was the second.

The three men who came down the stairs looked a little too polished for mob types, at least not of the Russian variety. The shorter guy might be; he was older, casually dressed, and while he didn't look particularly Russian, he had the swagger Jenkins associated with a street hood.

The other two, though. They might be bodyguard or enforcer types, except for their ties. In Jenkins's experience, Russian mobsters never wore ties, except in court. They preferred open collars beneath their suits.

He took all their pictures anyway.

With no backup, he wasn't in a position to follow them, but he did want to at least get a license plate. He slipped his car into gear and waited for them to get almost to the end of the block before he pulled out.

They turned the corner. Jenkins accelerated, not wanting to lose them. As he came around the corner, a white panel truck cut into his lane. Jenkins hit the brakes so hard the car veered to the right, just missing a Volkswagen parked near the corner.

"Son of a bitch," he shouted.

He laid on the horn, cursing. Then another car hit him from behind, pushing his vehicle into the VW. Jenkins pounded the steering wheel and went to grab the door handle.

Instead he found himself being lifted through the already open door. Before he could react, he was thrown against the hood of his car. His jacket and arms were pulled behind him, and his gun holster twisted back. As two men, each much larger than himself, pinned him against the car, another removed his wallet and his pistol.

"Let him go."

Jenkins shook himself free as he was let up off the car. He turned and saw the man with the white hair who'd come out of the apartment holding his wallet and service pistol. He was grinning.

"Special Agent in Charge, huh?" The man flipped the wallet to him but held on to the gun. "You have to be more alert in Boston, even down here."

"What's it to you?"

"Just some friendly advice." The man flicked the magazine latch on the pistol, dropping the box to the ground. Then he cleared the chamber, making sure the weapon was empty. "The streets can be pretty mean. I know you have a pistol on your leg," he added. "Reaching for it wouldn't be the smartest thing you've ever done."

"I'm going to nail you," said Jenkins.

The man laughed. "You don't even know who I am. Let me give you another piece of advice—don't poke your nose into places where it doesn't belong. The next person who sees it may not be as considerate as I am."

He tossed the gun into Jenkins's chest so quickly that the FBI agent didn't have time to grab it; it bounced through his hands and fell to the ground.

"I'd get the car fixed if I were you," added the man as he started away. "Boston police love to give out tickets for broken taillights."

39

Johnny Givens took a deep breath, then pushed himself forward on the parallel bars.

The legs, newly fitted, felt unsteady.

That was the strange thing—they *felt* unsteady. He really did feel them, even though they were carbon fiber and fancy plastic and wires and circuits—not skin, not blood, not bones or nerves.

Fake legs.

But he could feel them.

Partly this was his brain making things up. His mind was substituting what it knew for the sensations that were tickling the nerve endings in the stumps. But there were real sensations. That was the marvel of the legs Massina and his people had invented for him. They were real legs. Almost.

"Keep going, Mr. Givens," said Dr. Gleason. Gleason was the doctor in charge of his health, the head of a large team of surgeons and other specialists, therapists, scientists, engineers, nurses, and probably a dishwasher or two. Despite his other responsibilities, Gleason spent at least an hour every afternoon with Johnny.

The physical therapist spent three hours each morning, and four in the afternoons. Every moment sucked. Johnny called her Gestapo Bitch.

Not to her face. She looked like she could put him through the wall if he did.

"Use your legs to walk," she commanded from the far end of the bars. "Move!"

"Easy," said Gleason. "I don't want his heart overtaxed."

"He's barely at sixty beats a minute. I've seen nine-year-olds work harder than this." Gestapo Bitch shook her head in disgust. "Move, Givens, move! And put your weight on your legs. They're not going to break!"

Givens put more weight on his left foot, pushing forward. He was a little kid, learning to walk again.

Was he ever going to really walk again?

"You're doing really well, Johnny," said Dr. Gleason. "Keep going."

Johnny felt his hips swinging as he maneuvered down the bars. That was good—he was supposed to use his whole body.

Sweat poured down the sides of his face, down his back, across his neck. It flowed from every pore in his torso, from his arms, from his hands. Gestapo Bitch might think that he was barely working, but he knew better. He could feel the mechanical heart beating away.

It was interesting, though. It did increase its rate, but not nearly as much as a "real" heart would. It was very steady, measured, as if it knew better than the rest of his body what he needed.

As Johnny reached the end of the parallel bars, the sweat from his hands made his palms slippery. He decided to stop and wipe his hands on his shirt, needing to dry them. Steadying himself on his left side, he took his right hand off the bar and ran it down his right rib cage, the driest part of his T-shirt. As he started to switch sides, his left hand slipped. He quickly shoved his right hand toward the bar, but his momentum pitched him to the side.

He tried grabbing the bar, but it was too late; he unceremoniously toppled backward, to the floor.

Son of a bitch!

I am never going to do this! Never!

Why the hell did God screw me like this? Why is he such a bastard?

"Are you all right, Johnny?" asked Dr. Gleason, starting over.

"He's OK," scolded Gestapo Bitch. "Get up and go back. You don't stop until you get to the end. You stop, you do it again."

Johnny didn't move.

"Do you need help?" asked Gleason.

"He doesn't need help," snapped Gestapo Bitch.

Damn you, bitch!

Johnny reached up to the bar. Gestapo Bitch loomed over him and smacked his hand away. "Push yourself up with your legs. Use them or lose them."

"They're not my legs," he told her.

"They sure as hell are. Push yourself up with your legs."

"I hate you."

"Good. Now push yourself up with your legs and stop being a crybaby."

"I'm going to kick your ass when I'm better."

Gestapo Bitch leaned in until her face was an inch from his. "I'm waiting for the day, Sissy Breath." She straightened. "Now get on your feet."

40

Louis Massina was not used to giving up, much less being *told* to give up. There was simply no way that he was not going to pursue the ATM thieves.

On the contrary, it was now his number-one priority. But Massina being Massina, the issue was not simply one of revenge, let alone getting his money back. It had provoked a wide range of thoughts about computer security, national security, and even politics. Petty thievery was one thing; being able to infiltrate and manipulate the banking system, quite another. The FBI's sudden decision to drop the case suggested many things to Massina, not least of which was the possibility that the government could secretly manipulate the banking system for its own purposes. Even if that wasn't what was going on here—more evidence would be needed on that score—the potential surely existed.

Massina had always taken Internet security very seriously; that was a necessity at a firm where IT was critical to its operations. Chinese and Russian hackers, almost surely state-sponsored, constantly tried to break into Smart Metal's systems. And they were only the more notorious—just in the past week, hackers from several Western European countries had tried to breach the company's e-mail systems. Most of Smart Metal's work was done on internal systems that would not allow *any* outside access, from trusted sources or not, but even that system had to be constantly monitored for potential breaches.

Still, Massina had never viewed computer security as a potential business area; he'd been under the impression that there were already plenty of other businesses in that field. But maybe that wasn't true: if the banking system could be so easily compromised, then surely there was room for innovation.

And innovation was what they did. For a profit, of course.

So he had both altruistic and business reasons for pursuing the matter as he walked into Number 2 conference room to meet with Chelsea and his head of security to discuss it.

"The FBI has dropped out. We're pursuing this on our own," he told them as he walked into the room. It was 10:40, five minutes before the time he had specified for the meeting, but both Chelsea and Bozzone had worked at Smart Metal long enough to know they were expected early. "What do we know?"

"We know that sticking our nose into police matters is in general a very bad idea," said Bozzone.

Massina smiled. It was exactly because of remarks like that—speaking his mind even though it was not what Massina wanted to hear—that he valued Bozzone.

Not that he was necessarily swayed by his advice. But the reality check was useful.

"What else do we know?" Massina asked.

"That most likely we're looking at a gang with connections to Eastern Europe," said Bozzone. "Most likely suspects. And that the CIA is involved."

Massina followed Bozzone's gaze over to Chelsea. Number 2 conference room was small, arranged somewhat like a living room with a sofa facing a ring of three chairs and a love seat; there were side tables next to the chairs and at the ends of the couches. It was the only room in the entire building, aside from the restrooms, that did not have hardwired computers. It was something of an oasis.

Chelsea and Bozzone were sitting on opposite ends of the couch, looking slightly uncomfortable; Massina sat in the leather chair at the center of the circle, as was his wont.

"That's what one of the task force members told me," said Chelsea. "The FBI backed off because of that."

All the more reason for us to pursue it, thought Massina.

"I've been thinking about the situation a lot," continued Chelsea. "If it's not on the card, then the command string must come from the accessed account somehow. It nests in the ATM machine for a limited amount of time, then self-erases."

"Not at the processing points?" asked Massina.

"Well, the FBI looked there, so presumably no. Anyway, if I could examine the account that was accessed when that string was sent, it might tell me a great deal."

"Do it," said Massina.

"With the bank's permission or without?"

Massina waved his hand. "However you need to."

Bozzone cleared his throat. "You know, breaking into accounts, whatever the purpose, it's pretty much an illegal act."

"Is it?" asked Massina. He was not speaking theoretically; as he understood the law, stealing something from a bank account was definitely illegal; manipulating something in the account was almost surely illegal; but *looking* at something in an account—that wasn't covered.

"You bet it's illegal," said Bozzone.

"We're not doing anything to the account," said Massina. "I can get a legal opinion if you want."

Bozzone shook his head.

"It's possible the FBI already has the data," said Chelsea.

"Talk to them," said Massina.

"But they don't want our help," said Chelsea.

"Maybe national security is involved," said Bozzone. "We don't know."

"How would that be?" asked Massina.

"I don't know. But if the CIA is involved, there may be a lot of things we just don't know."

"So let's find them out," said Massina.

A long moment passed. "The idea of attacking the account seems pretty sophisticated, but on the other hand, they don't take much money," said Chelsea, interrupting the silence. "I would think if a gang was involved, they'd go for a big kill."

"I agree with that," said Bozzone.

"Maybe that's what they're planning." Massina slid forward on the chair.

"Maybe the FBI has actually already solved this, and they're just waiting for that hit," said Bozzone. "Then they strike. It's possible the CIA is actually helping them."

"I didn't get that impression," said Chelsea.

"Let's stop dealing in the dark," said Massina, springing to his feet. "By the end of the day, I want to know what resources we need, what people, whatever it takes to pursue this. Chelsea, come up with a plan."

MASSINA WAS ALREADY out the door before either Chelsea or Bozzone got up.

"OK," said Chelsea.

"Listen, I don't think this is a good idea at all," said the security chief. "Bad, bad, bad."

"I kinda got that."

"If you are doing anything even borderline illegal, I don't want to know about it. And for the record, I don't think you should do it either."

Chelsea nodded.

"I don't think you should do anything illegal," repeated Bozzone. "Nothing."

"I heard you."

"Is the FBI really out? Or is that a smoke screen to get us to stop being interested?"

"I'm not sure."

"Ask your boyfriend," said Bozzone.

"My boyfriend?" Chelsea felt her face warm.

"Don't you have some sort of connection there?"

Was he just being a bit of a wiseass, or had he somehow seen her? Or had someone else seen her and told him?

"If you hear anything of use from your police friends," Chelsea told him, "let me know."

41

Tolevi was just getting into his car at the parking garage two blocks from his house when a large man in a dark suit approached from the shadows. This was not entirely unexpected; if it had been, Tolevi would have stepped on the gas and run him down.

Actually, he was sorely tempted to do just that now, even though he knew the man well. Or more accurately, *because* he knew the man quite well.

Instead, he held his temper and rolled his window down.

"What are you doing, Stratowich?"

"Looking for you. Medved wants to talk to you."

"What a coincidence. I want to talk to him."

Stratowich snorted. He didn't believe him, though it was in fact true.

"Get in," Tolevi told him.

"That's not how this works. I drive you."

"I'm not getting out of my car. You can get in, or you can follow. Your choice."

Stratowich thought about it for a moment, then went around

to the passenger side. Once again, Tolevi suppressed the urge to hit the gas.

"Nice car," said Stratowich as he closed the door. "New?"

"Six months."

"You could have used this to pay your debt."

"I need a car."

In truth, though expensive, the Mercedes E63 S wouldn't come close. And it was leased.

Tolevi played with a bit of its twin turbo V–8 power as he raced the light. The big brakes worked pretty well, too; they kept him from crashing into the side of a Nissan Altima that pulled out in front of him just ahead of the intersection.

"Jeez, take it easy," croaked Stratowich.

Tolevi grinned. "I will if you put the pistol away."

"It's in my pocket."

"Then take your hand out of your pocket. You're likely to blow your nuts off and mess up the leather."

Tolevi drove at an easier pace for the next half hour, skirting the airport and heading north along Route 1A, heading for a bar Medved owned not far from the Boston Yacht Club; how he had managed to get the zoning changed to permit the conversion of two former family homes to commercial was a mystery only to those naive enough to believe in the Tooth Fairy. The Russian *mafya* was not particularly large in the Boston area, at least not when compared to places like New York and L.A., but what it lacked in absolute size it made up for in connections, with both the legitimate power structures and the illegal underground, still largely dominated by the Irish and the Italians, respectively.

Maarav Medved was not the top Russian in the local network. Not only did Tolevi not know who the chief was—the *"pa khan"* had no business contact with anyone below his generals— but Medved's exact position was murky as well. Maybe he was a general, or maybe he was just a colonel; Tolevi couldn't tell. And obviously he would never ask.

Like many other Russian *mafya* organizations around the

world, activities in Boston were decentralized and malleable; your position often depended as much on your ability to bully and persuade as it did on the size of your army and the number of your guns. Tolevi had to deal with Medved because he needed his dock connections to unload his items without problems; from that arrangement, others flowed. Tolevi cut him percentages of certain deals that were of interest, and sometimes carried messages back to Russian and other Eastern European countries for him. He'd also borrowed a fair sum, which had come due with interest, undoubtedly the subject of tonight's meeting.

Medved welcomed Tolevi with a bear hug when he walked into the club. One reason was that, business aside, he seemed to like Tolevi, who was easy to talk to and smarter than most of the goons Medved surrounded himself with. The other was that he liked to personally make sure his visitors were unarmed.

"Beautiful night," said Medved. He nodded to Statowich, who went off to sulk by the bar. "Nice and warm. Should we sit outside?"

"Fine with me."

Tolevi followed him outside. They chatted in Russian for a while, Medved asking about his daughter; Tolevi inquiring about the health of Medved's mother, who had recently had a heart attack.

"You were in Russia last week?"

"No," said Tolevi. "Crimea."

"That's Russia. Now." Medved raise his glass. "Putin, he is a bold one, no?"

Tolevi shrugged. "Obama's a pansy. Anyone could have taken it."

"What were you doing in Crimea?"

"For one thing, seeing my mother-in-law."

"Your mother-in-law?" Medved laughed. "And she didn't shoot you?"

"She would if she could. I had some other business. When the arrangements are finalized, of course we'll make the appropriate requests."

"Very good." Medved reached across the table for the vodka bottle. Tolevi caught the strong scent of sweat. It was not a warm night; there was no reason for Medved to sweat as if he'd been out running a marathon.

Medved filled Tolevi's glass, then his own.

"So what did your friends want?" Medved asked.

Tolevi heard the door opening behind him and immediately went on his guard. He shifted his weight in the chair, calculating what he would do if grabbed from behind.

If it was Stratowich, kick him in the shin—the bone there had been broken barely a year before and was still tender. Anyone else, though . . .

"Which friends do you mean?" asked Tolevi. "My cousin?"

"Your friends at Center Plaza." Medved slapped his glass on the table.

As if that's going to intimidate me, you fat frog.

"The FBI?"

"So Stratowich was right."

"Like a broken clock," said Tolevi. "They seem to think I'm a spy."

"Are you?"

"Not as far as I know." Tolevi pushed his glass forward, staring into Medved's eyes. After a few moments, Medved frowned, then refilled both glasses.

"They followed me there from the airport," Tolevi told him. "They made some sort of bullshit excuse. You know something about it?"

"I know that you don't want to talk to the FBI under any circumstances."

"No shit."

That was the moment, Tolevi thought, when Medved would signal whoever was behind Tolevi.

He waited, trying to keep his muscles as relaxed as possible. He'd need to push into whoever attacked, catching them off guard before he kicked for the groin.

Would it work?

Probably not. But it was better than simply giving up.

"Why are they following you?" Medved asked.

"I'm wondering the same thing," said Tolevi. "They followed me to the ATM and accused me of being involved in some sort of scam they didn't explain. Maybe you can find out why. You have contacts."

"Why did they release you?"

"I called a friend." Tolevi had to be careful not to give too much away about that—mentioning that he worked with the CIA would be even worse than the FBI. "An attorney. I have rights."

Medved smirked.

"They were asking about ATM cards, something I don't deal with," added Tolevi quickly. "Is that something I should be worrying about?"

Medved shrugged—which convinced Tolevi that he had an ATM scam operating.

Great. But why did they come after me?

A subject for another time—Medved will tell you nothing you can trust.

"In any event," said Tolevi, "I assume they were looking to make me into some sort of spy. But they failed."

Medved studied his drink. "You owe me a lot of money."

"I'm about to conclude a deal that will pay you in full."

"With the FBI's help?"

"You think I've lost my head?"

"I think you need money."

"I do need money. You know I'm good for it. I've owed you more in the past. I always pay."

"You see, Gabor, this is why we are friends." Medved downed his drink and poured another. "Because we understand each other. We're family. But. Debts must be paid. And talking to the FBI, to the *federal'nyy d'yavol*—that would be something my friends would not like. And I would not like."

Tolevi's Russian was not perfect, but Medved's was worse. Still, the meaning—"federal devils"—was pretty clear.

"I can't stop them from harassing me. I think this whole business is them thinking I'm a spy. So if you have influence—"

"I think this is a personal matter for you," said Medved lightly.

"Fine. I do need your help. I need some travel documents to go to Donetsk."

"Why there?"

"You want your money, right?"

"You can talk to Demyan." Medved shrugged. "But make it clear it is not my business."

"Unless there is a profit."

Medved smiled.

Tolevi downed the rest of the vodka, then got up to leave.

"By the end of the month, but no more," warned Medved. "And talking to the Americans, never a good idea."

"I'm not so foolish," said Tolevi.

42

"The bank refuses to cooperate without a warrant," Dryfus told Jenkins. "We're not looking at that account. Or any other without the paper. They did say there's been no reported theft in any of their accounts during the past forty-eight hours."

"None?"

"No." Dryfus shook his head. "We must have scared him into shutting down."

"Or laying low."

"It's not that they're being uncooperative," said Dryfus. "They're just sticking to procedure. Covering their asses. . . . How's Johnny?"

"He, uh, he's doing a lot better."

"Without his legs?"

"He's got, uh, prosthetics."

"Like the blade runner things?"

"No, these are, they look like real legs."

"I've been meaning to go over there."

Jenkins understood. He'd had to force himself this last visit: it was tough seeing Johnny, even if the doctors said he was recovering at a remarkable pace.

"We have to figure out a way to get this guy," Jenkins said. "For Johnny."

"Sure."

The look on Dryfus's face suggested just the opposite of what his response implied—the incident that had claimed Johnny's legs was not connected. Boston PD had already made an arrest.

And his brother, James?

This isn't a personal thing. This isn't a personal thing. And you have no evidence tying them together.

I'll get it, god damn it. I'll get it.

"Boss?" Dryfus had a concerned look on his face.

"Just thinking," confessed Jenkins.

"We can't get a subpoena?"

Not without saying who it's aimed at, Jenkins thought. And that will kill it. Even assuming they could get it, which was a stretch.

"We need more evidence," said Jenkins. "We have to just keep plugging away. We'll dig into this Tolevi character, see who his connections are, what he does with the mob, everything. Something will come up."

"He's got a kid," said Dryfus. "Raising her himself. His wife died of cancer when she was like three or something."

"That's nice. I'll nominate him for father of the year. Right after we put him in jail."

THE INFORMATION THAT Tolevi had a daughter—and Jenkins's flip remark—haunted him later in the day. Not because he didn't think a father could be a criminal: there were plenty of examples of that.

What bothered him was the fact that he kept thinking of different ways he might use the girl to get information on her father. And even for him that ought to be out of bounds.

Jenkins had worked for the Bureau for some sixteen years. Like just about every other newly minted agent, he'd started out as a strict by-the-book guy, unstintingly self-righteous—so much so that if he could go back in time and confront his younger self, he would slap him across the face, then throttle some sense into him.

Experience had erased both the self-righteousness and his approach to solving crimes. But that was not to say that he believed that the end justified the means. If he had long ago stopped being an Eliot Ness wannabe, still he believed in observing the broad rules of justice and procedure. He wouldn't plant evidence, for example. And he wouldn't harass children.

Yet since he took this case—no, since his brother died—reality had appeared starker than ever. The guys in the white suits were losing the fight to the guys in the black suits. Why? Because they had to follow procedures that made no sense.

The best among them—his brother, Johnny Givens—followed their impulses to do good. Where did that leave them? Dead or crippled.

And yet . . . if there were no rules, where did that leave anyone? Where did that leave society? There were too few people like Massina, altruistic do-gooders who acted generously, righteously, under any circumstances.

I need to solve this case somehow, Jenkins told himself.

I'll talk to the girl, but I'll be careful about it.

43

Boston—that morning

Tolevi had told Medved about the trip not only because he needed travel documents but also because he figured that it would be far easier to get in and out of the Donetsk area if the Russian secret services thought he was helping the rebel government. Which meant that he had to contact someone he knew in Moscow, and word of that would inevitably filter back. It was even possible that Medved would start the information chain himself, since scoring points with the various services was always useful.

Tolevi had nothing against helping the rebels at the same time he was hurting them, especially if this brought a little extra profit. As it was, the sum Johansen promised would barely cover what he owed Medved. Making a little money on the side was only prudent business.

Smuggling guns into the contested area would have been foolish and barely profitable; not only were the Russians already supplying plenty but the rebels had raided Ukrainian armories and had enough guns and ammunition to supply a force several times their own. What they didn't have was medicine and related supplies. Even aspirin would get a pretty good markup. A truckload of baby diapers would double or triple its investment.

In theory, of course, shipping such items into the contested area of Donetsk was strictly regulated, if not forbidden. But Tolevi knew he could work around that. The question was how. He wouldn't bring the items now, of course; instead, he would make arrangements with buyers and shippers, setting things in motion. It was a bit like the opening sequence in a chess game—you thought some twenty moves ahead, preparing the board for the final onslaught.

He pondered the details and pitfalls as he drove to Quincy to see Demyan Kasakawitz for the paperwork he needed to enter Russia. Kasakawitz was a Pole who worked out of an electronics distributorship not far from Quincy's business district. Ostensibly the distributor's bookkeeper, he had the thick glasses and meticulous manner of a careful forger. His documents were known to be top rate, and among other things he had supplied Tolevi with the title to his last car, which he had traded in as a down payment on the AMG's lease.

Short and round, Kasakawitz was a friendly man, the sort who always had some sort of sweets on his desk and could be counted on for an off-color joke or two before getting down to business. Today, however, was different: when Tolevi went into the back where his office was, a tall, thin man hovered behind him, staring with unblinking eyes at Tolevi as he greeted the forger. Kasakawitz answered with a low grunt, and Tolevi told him he would come back.

"No, I have the package for you," said Kasakawitz, still not smiling.

"Where is it?" asked Tolevi.

"First, tell me about these robots," said the other man.

"What robots?"

Kasakawitz got up, clearly not wanting to be included in the conversation. "I am going for a cigarette."

Tolevi folded his arms and waited until they were alone. "What exactly is it you want?"

"Stratowich told you about a robot and sent you a video."

"Stratowich." Tolevi shook his head. "He's a dunce."

"He erased the video. But he sent you a copy."

Tolevi took out his phone and checked the messages. "Looks like I erased it, too."

"Show me."

"I don't think so." He wasn't lying, exactly: Once read, the file would no longer appear on his phone, though it was easily recovered from the server. But he was reluctant to hand over his phone.

"You are going to Russia. You need friends there."

"I have friends there."

"Give me your phone."

"I need it."

"Let me make sure that you don't have the video."

Tolevi handed it over. "Do you own this robot, or what?"

"No. We want it. Can you get it?"

Now, that was a business proposition if ever Tolevi had heard one. Unfortunately, he was already busy.

"Maybe when I get back. I'll need more details. You have my documents?"

The man stared at him for a few moments more, then pointed to a large manila envelope on the corner of the desktop.

"When you return, we will talk."

Tolevi rolled his eyes and reached for the envelope. The tall man grabbed his hands just as his fingers touched it.

"You live a dangerous life, Gabor Tolevi," said the man. "Do not cross us."

Ordinarily, Tolevi would have acted on impulse, breaking the man's grip and then teaching him that there were limits to what he might stand for. But there was so much venom in the man's voice—and his grip was so strong—that Tolevi decided to be cautious.

"I wouldn't dream of it," he said. "Now let me go before I break your nose."

A smile flickered across the man's face, as if he would like to see Tolevi try. But he released him all the same.

44

Finding the account from the inquiry string that her program had captured was not difficult once Chelsea understood the protocol.

What was baffling, though, was the fact that the account didn't seem to exist.

To make sure she understood the protocol and was therefore getting everything right, she canvassed the cafeteria for anyone who had an account at the same bank. She recorded a query with the card—that morning Massina had leased an ATM machine for the lobby, for research as well as his employees' convenience— then replayed everything with the account information.

Nothing. Nada. The account didn't exist.

Which a bank manager confirmed for her in person when she went to inquire about it, asking about a check supposedly written on it.

It had to have been erased. There were ways to get the information back—looking at backup files would be the easiest, but she'd need the bank's cooperation. And if they weren't going to cooperate with the FBI, they surely wouldn't work with her. She didn't bother asking.

Not sure what to do next, she went back to the lab and re-played the drone footage. It had taken the drone about ninety seconds to get over the site after receiving the command.

Which wasn't all that much time, but it was certainly after the card had been used.

So why was the suspect facing in the direction of the ATM when the drone arrived?

At the time, they thought it was because he'd heard the boy on the bike behind him, but the more she considered it, the more Chelsea wondered. She went back to the drone's video and zoomed in, looking at the scratchy images from the distance. The earliest image showed the suspect on the sidewalk alone, walking toward the ATM. It wasn't until several frames later that the bike appeared.

Maybe nothing.

Or maybe they had gotten the wrong person.

THE PERSON ON the bike was a girl. The drone had gotten a decent facial image, good enough to use for a search.

The computer system went to work, testing the image against a series of commercial identity databases, starting with anyone ever charged with a crime in Massachusetts—police mug shots had recently been declared public information. After the criminal databases turned up nothing, it began trolling through Facebook, Twitter, Instagram, paging through a mountain of selfies.

But it wasn't until a full five minutes had passed—an eternity considering the computer resources Chelsea had at her command—that it found a hit on a picture that had appeared in a school newsletter the year before.

The girl's name was Borya Tolevi.

Gabor Tolevi's daughter.

Chelsea replayed the drone's image, looking at the confrontation between the two. There was no sound, but it was clear that the two were having an argument.

What about, Chelsea wondered. But it wasn't hard to guess.

45

Grace Sisters' Hospital, Boston—same time

Time for a run.

Johnny Givens stood at the end of the field, surveying the track. It was an old cinder-and-dirt affair, exactly a quarter mile, dating from the days that the grounds had belonged to a Catholic school. Never quite abandoned, it had recently been adopted by a local track club, whose members had smoothed out a decade's worth of ruts and re-topped it with extremely fine gravel, donated by an area mining operation. It was even but hardly perfect, but that was fine as far as Johnny was concerned; he could run here without being bothered, and there would even be less shock to his stumps than on a "real" track.

Stumps. He was just getting used to the word.

"You don't really think you're going to be able to run this," snarled Gestapo Bitch. She'd seen him in the hall and followed him out.

"I'll walk it if I have to," he told her.

"Are you trying to prove something?" she retorted. "You're barely off the IV."

Damn straight he was trying to prove something. Johnny took a breath, then leaned forward.

Suddenly he was running.

Not very fast, or very steadily. But with Gestapo Bitch watching him, he sure as hell wasn't giving up.

The doctors were feeding him with some serious medicine, steroid concoctions, and a shelf full of vitamins. He was their guinea pig. But that was fine by him.

His heart pounded as he took the first turn. The weight on the side of his head grew. His arms weren't keeping up with his legs.

The left one gave way. Johnny collapsed to the ground, face-first.

Damn! Damn!

Why does God hate me? Why is he doing this to me? Why?

Johnny pounded the ground. Tears rolled down his face.

Why?!

"I told you," snickered Gestapo Bitch.

He slipped again getting up. Tiny stones were embedded in the palms of his hands. The front of his shirt was covered with dirt.

Run. Run!

Unsteady, he took a step to find his balance, then began running again.

More a trot, but he *had* to move.

Why is God doing this to me?

46

Boston—later that afternoon

"Nice bike."

Borya looked across at a short black woman. She had her own bike, a Trek Silque with custom red fade paint on a gray frame.

"So's yours," Borya said, tightening the strap on her backpack. She tried to puzzle out who the woman was.

Not a mom; more an older-sister type.

"What are you doing?" asked the woman.

"Riding home."

"Want some company?"

Weird.

"Free country. I guess."

"I'm Chelsea. Chelsea Goodman." The woman stuck out her hand.

"You a lesbian?" asked Borya.

"No." Chelsea laughed. "Why?"

Borya shrugged.

"I have a question for you," said Chelsea, sliding her bike parallel to Borya's. "What do you know about ATMs?"

Borya stabbed at the bike pedal, launching into a sprint. She charged down the block, wind whipping back her hair. She sped across the intersection, barely dodging a turning car, then crossed back and turned the corner.

She looked up. Chelsea was pedaling alongside.

"Nice bike," she said again. "You change gears a little too much. You can pedal a little longer before shifting for better speed."

Borya put her head down and pedaled furiously. Her legs were starting to tire, and as she felt the burn growing in the top of her thighs, she realized she would never be able to outrun the woman, who was still alongside her.

You're an old suck. You should be tired!

Borya dropped to her usual pace. She thought of leading the woman across the city but decided she'd have a hard time losing her. Besides, her father had given her strict orders to check in with him from the house phone when she got home.

She narrowed her eyes as she rode the last block and a half to the house, practicing the glare she would greet the woman's inevitable questions with. She felt as if she was putting on a costume, becoming someone else—a superhero tough girl, impervious to attack.

Pedaling around to the back, Borya hopped off the bike as she glided toward the back porch. She picked up the bike in one motion and carried it up the steps without stopping. The front wheel was still spinning when she began wrapping the chain through the frame to secure it.

"You're still here?" she said nonchalantly, as if noticing for the first time that Chelsea was parked at the base of the steps.

"You never answered my question," said Chelsea. "What do you know about ATMs?"

"They give you money."

Borya turned to go inside, deciding it would be easiest simply to avoid talking to the woman. But Chelsea was quick, and prepared: she hopped off her bike and was at the door in a flash, pushing it closed as Borya reached her hand in with the key.

"Are you a cop?" asked Borya.

"No. I'm not a cop."

"Why are you here?"

"I know what you did. I'm interested," added Chelsea.

"In what?"

"In how you do it. You're good with computers. I'll bet you're great in math, too. And also bored in school."

"Maybe."

Borya sensed—knew—that the woman was just pretending to be nice so she could get what she wanted. Still, the attention was flattering.

"If you show me how you did it, I'll show you some cool stuff," offered Chelsea. "Computers, robots, and other cool stuff."

"Yeah, right—like you're going to offer me candy next," snapped Borya. "You're going to break the door."

"I work for a pretty interesting company," she said. "We need more smart people to work there. Women especially."

"You're hurting me."

Borya faked tears. It was a lousy try, but it worked. The woman let go of the door.

"See ya," said Borya, slipping in the key and unlocking the door. She expected Chelsea would try to stop her, but she didn't. Borya squeezed past her and fled into the house.

CHELSEA STOOD ON the back porch for a moment, considering what to do. She sensed that she had aroused the girl's curiosity but at the same time had somehow made a misstep, either coming on too strong or not being enticing enough.

I should have mentioned money. That's probably what motivated her in the first place.

Money? Here? Unlikely.

Should have been clearer about not being a cop.

Threatened to turn her in if she didn't come with me.

That's kidnapping.

She stood on the porch for a few moments, until she was convinced that Borya wasn't coming back out. Then she went down to her bike. But she wasn't going home—she walked around to the front and went up on the stoop. She rang the bell. When there was no answer, she sat down on the steps.

One of the teachers had told her a little bit about Borya when she was waiting. Most of it she could have guessed: smart girl, somewhat rebellious, good at math.

The fact that she had lost her mother when she was young and that her father hadn't remarried—that was unexpected. If not for that, the girl would have been very similar to her.

Maybe. Had Chelsea been that rebellious?

You were a handful, she heard her father say.

She laughed.

Maybe I was.

BORYA LOCKED THE door and raced upstairs, checking to make sure she hadn't missed her father's call.

No calls.

She ran to her room and woke her computer from sleep mode. She checked Facebook and her e-mail, then looked quickly at her father's account—if school or the police were trying to contact him, she wanted to know.

A lot of spam, nothing official.

She'd just backed out of the account when the phone rang. She grabbed it without looking at the caller ID, then belatedly realized it might be the police. She held it to her ear, listening.

"Borya, what are you doing?" demanded her father. "Talk."

"I'm about to do my homework," she said. "I just got home."

"How much homework do you have?"

"Not much," she answered without thinking. The truth was, she had done it all in school already, at least the homework that she cared to do. But an ambiguous answer gave her room to maneuver.

"I'm on my way home. Do we need milk?"

"Um . . . let me check."

As she trotted down the stairs, she noticed the woman sitting on the steps at the front of the house.

That's no good. How do I get rid of her?

"Yeah, I guess, um, we do need milk," Chelsea told her father after picking up the downstairs phone.

"Anything else?"

"Wait . . ." Chelsea walked to the refrigerator and opened it. It was well stocked—and in fact there was a nearly full gallon of milk right in the front. "No, nothing. Snacks, maybe."

"You don't need any more potato chips. They'll give you zits. I'll be home in a bit."

He hung up. Chelsea put the phone down and went back to the refrigerator for the milk. She drained the jug into the sink, leaving only a finger's worth at the bottom, then ran the water to remove any trace.

The woman was still there. This was *not* going to do. Her father was already past the ATM situation. A question or two from this Chelsea, and she was back in trouble, big time.

The phone upstairs began playing a message that it was off the hook. Borya trotted up and turned it off, then traded her uniform skirt and blouse for jeans and a sweatshirt.

Still there. What happens when Dad comes home?

Borya *had* to get rid of her somehow. She stood at the top of the steps, hoping for an answer.

Nothing occurred to her.

There was something near the door. She slipped down quietly and picked up a business card.

Smart Metal
AI, Bots, et al
Chelsea Goodman
Chief AI engineer

Not a cop. OK. What was Smart Metal?

AI and Bots . . . artificial intelligence and robots?

Huh?

Borya put the card on the table, then paced back and forth, trying to decide what to do.

The doorbell rang. She turned. It was Chelsea.

Open it or not?

She undid the latch and yanked the door open.

"What do you want?" Borya demanded.

"I want you to come with me and see my lab. I want to give you a tour."

"Then what?"

"Then nothing."

"You'll leave me alone?"

"Yes."

"I'm not going in a car."

"I don't have a car."

Borya peered out to the street. The woman was alone. "You'll let me go home when we're done?"

"Absolutely."

"I have to be home because my dad will have a shit fit."

"Of course."

"You're not lying. You're not the cops?"

"I'm not the cops. I know what you did." Chelsea's voice became a little less sweet. "I'm interested in it. But I'm not turning you in. I would love to know how you did it."

"I don't know what you're talking about."

"That's fine. Come on, let's go."

"Wait. I need to tell my father where I'm going," said Borya, who was already thinking of an excuse—the library or a friend's, nothing related to this woman.

"I'll wait out here."

47

Jenkins slowed the car as he approached Tolevi's house. There was someone out front with a bike, waiting by the driveway, back to him.

A girl, but not Borya.

There was Borya, coming up the driveway with her own bicycle. She hopped on. The other girl started riding as well.

Is that Chelsea Goodman?

Jenkins got a good side view as he passed. It *was* Chelsea. What the hell was she doing with Borya?

He turned at the next corner, then accelerated away. He had to think about this.

48

Chelsea took a step back, watching Borya as she stared in awe at the tiny flying machine. She had told the airborne bot to fly into the 3-D maze and retrieve a tulip; the UAV was now wending its way around a string of Plexiglas baffles, buzzing up and down as it looked for its target. It passed a decoy lily, then a bunch of daisies, and finally hovered above the tulip. It circled twice, measuring the stem, then dove down and plucked the flower near its base. Moments later it hovered above Borya's hand, waiting for her to take its prize.

"It's for you," prompted Chelsea.

"Wow."

"Bot B, go home and close down," commanded Chelsea. The small aircraft climbed a few feet, then zipped across the lab to the bench where its "nest," or launching pad, was kept. It plopped down on the pad and promptly shut itself off.

"Is this some sort of trick?" asked Borya.

Chelsea laughed. "No, but sometimes it does seem like magic. Come here. I'll show you the coding."

She walked over to a sixty-inch computer screen powered by a workstation at the side of the room. Chelsea tapped the command key and had it display one of the subroutines the on-board computer used to pick out the flower by comparing it to its on-board records.

As impressive as the demonstration was to the uninitiated, the bot had actually done nothing that wasn't being demonstrated in the MIT robotics lab three or four years before. The truly innovative thing was its size and autonomy. The processors used a carbon nanotube architecture (licensed from IBM for experimental purposes only) that made the small aircraft's brain as powerful as a 1990s-era mainframe. The nanotubes replaced silicon, allowing the transistors on the chip—essentially the on-off switches that made everything work—to be about a twentieth the size of the smallest possible in silicon, roughly 7 nanometers. They were thinner than strands of DNA.

Borya gaped at the coding. It was a proprietary language, presented here without notes and explanations.

"It's not C++," said the girl. "But this sets up an array, right?" She pointed to the screen.

"Very good," said Chelsea. She tapped the keyboard. The screen began scrolling quickly. "I just want you to see how long this is."

"Wow," said Borya as the characters rolled off the screen.

"This is just one subroutine. There were five thousand six hundred and thirty-two involved in that test we just ran."

"Really?"

"When we started, there were almost twice that many. We had to find a way to tighten it up. We're still working on that."

"How long did it take you to write this?"

Chelsea laughed. "I'd love to take credit for writing the whole thing," she said, "but I had a lot of help."

"How many people?"

"I can't tell you that." It was, in fact, proprietary information, as were the tools they had used to help construct it. "But I can say that it wasn't just people. Automated tools are very important. They're like computer writing assistants."

"I've heard of that," said Borya.

"Smart Metal is a pretty cool place, huh?"

"It's all right."

"Hungry? We can get something to eat. There's a café upstairs."

"I should go home," said Borya. "My dad will be wondering where I am."

"No soda?" Chelsea asked. "We have Coke, root beer—"

"Do you have potato chips?"

"We do. Come on."

Borya followed her to the elevator. The doors in the hallway were to other labs, where different scientists and engineers were working. A few wore white clean-room-style suits, but most were dressed in jeans and casual shirts. There were computers and sensors and wires everywhere. When they'd come in, Chelsea had walked Borya through a display area of artificial limbs. It was like a museum exhibit, starting with peg legs and moving up to a sleek arm and hand with thin metal tubes and wires, which, Chelsea told Borya, connected to a person's nervous system.

She wanted one. Not that she would trade her actual arm for it, though.

"Who's this?" asked a short, white-haired man as they stepped off the elevator on the top floor.

"Mr. Massina, this a friend of mine. Borya." Chelsea put her hand on Borya's back and pushed her gently toward Massina. "She's a high school student. She's very good at math."

"Hmmmm."

Borya stuck out her hand. Massina shook it. He had a firm handshake, though not quite as crushing as her father's.

"Keep studying," he said as he let go. Then he stepped around her and entered the elevator, frowning until the doors closed.

"He's a bit of a sourpuss," said Borya.

"He owns the company," said Chelsea. "A lot of the things you're looking at, he invented."

"Really?"

"Yup. He's pretty much a genius."

Chelsea got the girl some chips and a soda, then led her out to the terrace. It was a beautiful early spring day, nearly eighty degrees; the large windows at the side were open, letting in the gentle breeze.

Borya had clearly been impressed, but that was all. Chelsea had imagined that the visit would open her up. She'd ask a few questions and find out everything there was to know about the ATM scam—like, had her father put her up to it? Was she involved? Had she even done the coding, possibly with the help of some scripts off the Internet? Just how precocious was this girl?

But Borya hadn't opened up. And sitting down at the table overlooking the harbor and skyline, Chelsea felt as if she was back in middle school, trying to make friends with one of the cool girls.

That had never gone well.

"Have you thought about college?" asked Chelsea. As soon as the words left her mouth, she regretted them; they were something a parent would say.

"No."

"College is a good thing."

God, I'm hopeless.

"Uh-huh." Borya ripped open the bag of chips with her teeth and began eating.

Don't ask her about a boyfriend. Or anything else about school.

What, then?

"So—what did you do with the ATM card?" There was nothing else to talk about, Chelsea decided. She might as well just cut to the quick.

"The ATM card?"

"The other night. One of my drones, a Hum, saw you at the machine."

Borya shrugged.

"I know you have a way of stealing money from the accounts. I'm not going to turn you in. I just want to see how you do it.

It's pretty clever." Chelsea's mind flailed, trying to come up with some strategy that would work. "Did you write it in C++?"

"You have to use coding that the bank systems understand," said Borya.

"And how'd you learn that?"

"The machine at the bank uses one language, then it gets translated. You don't know that?"

"I don't know anything," fudged Chelsea. "I don't work on those systems. Did you have to revise the program every time you hit a different bank?"

"I have to go." Borya jumped to her feet.

"It's at the intermediary," said Chelsea, finally realizing that she had been mistaken about how the thefts were arranged. The code in the bank account that was queried went there, which then issued other commands. Otherwise it'd be too cumbersome.

"I have to go. My father is going to be looking for me."

"Sure," said Chelsea as nonchalantly as she could. "Come on. I'll get you a ride."

"I have my bike."

"Sure you don't want a ride?"

"No."

"When do you want to come back?" Chelsea asked as they waited for the elevator.

"Come back?"

"You haven't seen half of the awesome stuff we have. There's plenty more."

"I don't know."

Borya said nothing until they got to the lobby. Chelsea walked her to the security desk, where they retrieved her phone.

"You're not coming with me, are you?" asked Borya. She seemed worried.

"I have to work."

"OK."

"Here," said Chelsea, holding up her phone. "Here's my number. Text me when you want to come back."

Reluctantly, Borya pressed the key combination to allow the phones to exchange information.

"Anytime," said Chelsea at the door to the lobby.

She watched Borya spring to her bike, chained at the rack in the vestibule. She mounted it and rode it through the door, clearly impatient to be gone.

"THAT WAS OUR thief?" Massina stared at Chelsea from behind his desk.

"Apparently. I'm not sure whether her father put her up to it or not."

"Hmmmph," said Massina. Finding out a teenaged girl was responsible for a string of thefts that had the FBI twisted in knots—that wasn't exactly what he'd thought they would find.

On the other hand, if a *kid* could do this, then the field was wide open for improvements.

"We should think about taking her on as an intern," suggested Chelsea.

"What? Reward a hacker?"

"She's fifteen. She's smart enough to figure this out—maybe with some help, maybe a lot of help, but still. She's got potential. The kind of person who ought to be working with us."

Massina pressed his lips together. No way was he hiring the girl, under any circumstances, even if she wasn't a thief, and even if her father wasn't part of the Russian mob.

"I was wrong about how it works," said Chelsea. "She gave me a hint. I have to work on it."

"Commercial applications?" asked Massina.

"I think so. If you want to branch out into banking systems and security."

"Keep working on it," he said, turning back to his computer.

49

Boston—a half hour later

Needing to perfect an excuse for her father, Borya stopped briefly at Mary Lang's house on the way home. Mary, an awkward, wall-flowery kid at school, was overjoyed to see her, eagerly inviting Borya in and asking if she wanted to stay for dinner.

Borya ignored both invitations, asking instead about a social studies assignment she had finished at school. Lang ran and got the handout with the question, copying it out for her in a neat script. Handing her the paper, she offered to help with it; Borya managed a polite smile, then told her that she had to get home.

"Did my dad call your house?" she asked, stepping back from the door. Mary shook her head. "If he does, I was here all afternoon. Right?"

"Oh, yes." A bright smile broke out on Mary's face. She practically salivated at the idea of being in on a conspiracy. "The whole afternoon. Doing social studies."

"Not the whole afternoon," coached Borya. "Just from like, three. Until now."

"Until now."

"Gotta go."

"See you tomorrow," said Mary Lang.

"Oh yeah."

Borya flew home on her bike, confident that her cover story would stand any scrutiny her father threw at it. Skidding to a stop behind the back porch, she hoisted the bike on her shoulder and hustled up the steps, chaining it quickly and heading inside, barely catching her breath.

Her father was standing in the kitchen.

"What is Smart Metal?" he asked.

The question drained the blood from her head. How had he found out where she had gone?

He must really be a spy, she thought. *He must have put a bug in my clothes.*

Her father held a business card out to her. "Smart Metal?" he asked again. "Chelsea Goodman?"

"Oh." Borya struggled to come up with an explanation. She had completely forgotten about the card; it must have been in the front hall. "My, uh, she's my friend's older sister. They do computer stuff. And robots."

That wasn't enough explanation. Borya struggled to find the line between just enough information to satisfy him and not enough to get her into trouble. Part of her wanted to tell him about the place—it had been the coolest thing she'd ever seen, awesome beyond awesome. But opening that door would expose her to many more questions.

"Uh, she, they want to hire more girls to be in, uh, like STEM stuff," said Borya, stitching in information from a school assembly they'd had a few weeks back. STEM was big, especially for girls.

Study your math!

Ppppp.

But finally an assembly had proved good for something.

"What STEM?" asked her dad.

"STEM, you know. Like, science, technology, engineering, and mom."

"Mom?"

"I mean math."

The unintentional slip caught them both by surprise. Borya felt as if she had lost all the air in her chest. Her father looked the same way.

"I . . . I don't know why I said that." She felt tears starting to well in her eyes.

"It's OK, baby," said her father softly. His eyes were heavy as well.

TOLEVI WORKED SILENTLY in the kitchen, making his daughter's favorite dinner, soft tacos with extra cheese. Technically, it was only her third or fourth favorite—pizza was number one, and her aunt Tricia's pot roast was number two—but it was the only one of her favorites that he could actually cook himself.

Borya didn't know her mother's cooking. If she did, those would surely be her favorites.

Tolevi pushed his sadness away, concentrating on the meat cooking in the pan. He stirred it around, working it until no pink remained. He drained the oil into the sink, then put the pan back on the stove and began adding sauce and spices.

I need to ask about this friend's sister, he thought as he stirred. *Get us off the topic of missing mom.*

"Borya, set the table," he called.

"Already done."

He turned around, surprised to find his daughter already at the table. He wondered if she had somehow heard what he was thinking.

"Good day at school?" he asked, getting the taco shells out of the warming tray.

"OK day."

"A lot of homework?"

"I'm on it. I told you I did most of it."

"You did?" He didn't quite succeed in making that sound like a statement rather than a question.

They ate in silence, Tolevi dreading the fact that he had to tell her that Mrs. Jordan had bailed on him and he was substituting a former au pair, Mary Martyak. Borya hated Martyak, and he wasn't particularly fond of her himself, but she was the best he could do on short notice.

"Can I be excused?" Borya asked, her plate clean.

"I have to travel again."

"You told me."

"I'm going to be gone for a week. Maybe more. I don't know. The business—there are a lot of loose ends. It may be less time," he said, trying to sound optimistic. "But Mary Martyak is coming to stay with you, starting tomorrow."

"I thought Mrs. Jordan!"

"She can't. But Mary was very excited. She really likes you."

"Ugh. Is she still doing that history stuff?"

"Anthropology."

"Whatever. She thinks she's a psychiatrist."

"You mean psychologist."

"And a know-it-all. And bossy."

"She's in charge."

"Phew." Borya got up from the table with her plate. "I'm old enough to stay by myself."

"And break curfew like the other night?"

"I won't do that again."

"Maybe next time. Break curfew or give Mary a hard time, and I'll sell you to the nuns," he told her, softening what had started as a threat into a joke. His daughter came and hugged him around the neck. "I mean it."

"I know."

"Where were you this afternoon?"

"Mary Lang's, studying. You said I could study with friends. That's always been a rule. If their parents are home."

It was a rule. Though she should have told him.

She had texted, though, hadn't she? He was so distracted with everything else now that he couldn't remember.

Focus on your daughter. She's all you have.

"Mary Lang is the little fat one?" he asked.

"No, you're thinking of Georgina. She's kind of skinny, with kinked-up hair."

"You know if anything ever happened to me, you would go and live with Uncle Bob and Aunt Lisa, right?"

"What?" Borya practically crossed her eyes as she stared at him.

"I'm not saying something is going to happen," he added quickly. "But you know them and like them."

"Yeah."

Bob and Lisa weren't actually related to Borya or her father, but were such close friends that they fully earned the title of uncle and aunt. As long as Borya could remember, she had spent at least a week with them every summer in upstate New York, where Uncle Bob owned a radio station and Aunt Lisa had the world's biggest collection of nail polish, always gladly shared. Their three daughters and son were a few years older than Borya, and all were out of the house now.

"But nothing's going to happen to me," added Tolevi. "That I promise."

50

Boston—two days later

Johnny Givens took a deep breath, then lowered himself on his haunches in a squat. He put his two hands on the bar, closed his eyes briefly, then lifted.

The bar with its plates weighed only twenty-five kilos, not a lot of weight; before his injury he was doing military presses with eighty easily.

But this was different.

He came up out of the squat slowly. So much of this was done with your legs, yet he felt nothing there, only a very slight strain in his shoulders.

Hardly any strain.

Up. Up!

He cleaned the bar, pulling it from his waist to his chest with a quick jerk. Too quick a jerk, really; bad form, but he had it and this was no time to critique technique. He paused a moment, then pushed up slowly, shoulders doing the work.

Easy.

He felt a slight tremor at his back, the muscle weak. He fought against it, remembering what the doctor had said about how it would feel. This was all very strange. It was his body and yet it wasn't his body.

I'm still who I am. Still me. Still Johnny Givens.

But who was Johnny Givens? An FBI agent? No—the Bureau had already put him on permanent disability, the bastards. The one time the bureaucracy actually worked expeditiously, and it was to screw him out of a job.

"Oh don't worry," said the idiot HR person, "you're on full disability. Losing your legs does that."

He wanted to scream at her. But some inbred courtesy kicked in, and all he did was hang up—gently.

His mother would have been proud; he'd controlled his temper.

But, Mom, you just don't understand. Being polite, being reasonable—that's not always the best way to do things. Sometimes if you don't yell at people, they think what they're doing or saying is OK.

The world is not a reasonable place. If you're reasonable, you're at a disadvantage.

Johnny lowered the weight to his shoulders. He took a deep breath, then slowly lowered himself. He could feel the strain in his thighs.

Really? Strain in your thighs?

You have no thighs! You have no legs! You're metal and carbon and wires and digital crap and fake stuff. You don't exist from a few inches below the waist.

He knew he had nothing there, and yet he felt it. He was sure he felt it.

He let go of the weights and stood straight up, head swimming.

"You're not supposed to be in here!" said Gestapo Bitch.

He glanced up and saw her in the mirror at the side of the room. She had her arms crossed and was staring at him with a look of disgust.

"Who says?" he snapped. He didn't bother to look at her.

"It's not on your rehab program. Weights—no."

"Yeah, well, here I am." Johnny squatted back down, grabbing the bar.

Up, up up!

He held the bar straight overhead, then lowered it slowly to his shoulders, then pushed back up.

Six reps.

Six—you can do it.

Six.

"Your form sucks," said Gestapo Bitch as he returned the bar to the ground. "Your tush is too far out. You're going to strain your back. Then what are you going to do?"

"Bench presses."

Straightening, he walked over to the dumbbell rack, still refusing to look in her direction.

"You hate me, don't you?" she asked as he selected a pair of dumbbells.

"Bet your ass."

"Good."

Johnny made a fist and slammed his right hand down on the twenty-kilo barbell.

"What turned you into such a bitch?" he shouted, turning to confront her.

But she was gone.

51

The Mercure Arbat was a well-regarded hotel in central Moscow used by many tourists and a decent number of businessmen, including those who had appointments at the nearby Ministry of Foreign Affairs. Gabor Tolevi booked a room there not because he liked the hotel—he did, in fact, but that was beside the point. He needed a place not only convenient to the Ministry of Foreign Affairs but also one that would make it seem that he was doing nothing to hide his trip from any of the intelligence agencies that might be involved in Donetsk, including and especially SVR.

Which meant that he would be followed whenever he left the hotel. He decided to test this with a walk immediately after arriving. Not bothering to change his clothes—he wanted it to be as easy as possible—he left his bag in the room and went out, strolling casually, as if taking in the sights.

A young man in a blue sport coat and faded black jeans followed him out of the lobby. Tolevi wandered a few blocks, then went toward the metro, curious. Ordinarily the Russians used teams to trail anyone of real interest, and their usual procedure would call for a handoff at fairly regular intervals. But his shadow didn't change, even inside the station; either Tolevi was considered of low value, or he was being followed by a Western service, probably the Americans, who didn't have the manpower to waste on large teams.

For someone used to the T in Boston, walking into a Moscow metro station was almost always disorienting. The stations, or at least those in the central part of the city, were works of art, temples even, as if the trains running through them were mythical gods. Walking into Smolenskaya metro station, which was hardly the fanciest, was like walking into a nineteenth-century monument. Arched glass fronts welcomed passengers, huge stone blocks made up the walls, and the platform could have been a dance hall at Versailles.

The architectural flourishes and the artwork made it easy to feign interest while checking around, but Tolevi still couldn't spot anyone tracking him except the man in the blue sport coat. He hesitated when the train came in, almost deciding to turn around and go up in the crowd, which would force the man to show that he was trailing him. But there was no point in that. He wasn't trying to lose the trail, just make it seem as if he was taking precautions. And so he got on, rode two stops to Aleksandrovsky Sad, and walked to the Russian State Library; he mingled briefly inside, then came out and returned to the subway, heading back to the ministry.

The man in the blue jacket had disappeared, but Tolevi couldn't figure out if he had been handed off or not. As a final touch, he hailed a cab—more a whim, as he saw one nearby—and had it take him to the ministry.

Even with all of his travel across Moscow, he was still nearly an hour ahead of his appointment. And this being Russia, it was another two and a half hours before an assistant to the deputy he'd been assigned to meet had him ushered in. The man's name was different from that of the person he'd been told to meet, which was not unusual.

Tolevi could complain about none of this. He sat as patiently as he could, trying not to squirm as the bureaucrat fumbled through some papers on a desk that looked as if it were a receiving station for a recycling operation. Files and loose papers were piled everywhere in the office, including on top of the computer at the side.

"You are wanting to import household items," said the clerk, fumbling with the paperwork.

"No," said Tolevi. "Common medicines—aspirin, cough syrup, bandages."

"Not Russian?" said the man, looking up.

"These items are going to our friends in Donetsk," said Tolevi. "There are needs."

He handed the man the paperwork. The man frowned, then slowly read through it.

When Tolevi first started out in the import business, he'd made the mistake of offering a bribe to a Russian official. Fortunately, he did this subtly enough that he could back out with some amount of grace—and, more importantly, avoid arrest. It was not that all Russian officials were scrupulously honest; they were probably no more honest, on average, than the officials in other developed countries. But corruption here took place at a different level than it did, say, in Azerbaijan. One did not bribe the men responsible for looking over the paperwork. If a bribe were to be required, it would be presented elsewhere, and always as a fee related to some function. It was very civilized.

He'd already paid that fee. This should just be a formality.

The clerk read through the paperwork, carefully checking each line against some mysterious page on his desk. Tolevi had no idea what he might be doing—the paperwork was very straightforward at this stage—but he knew better than to question the man.

Finally, the man reached down and opened a bottom drawer. He took out a stamp and crashed it down on Tolevi's documents until each was marked.

ОТКЛОНИЛ

Tolevi stared at the red characters in disbelief. The word—in Western letters, it was o-t-k-l-o-n-i-l—meant "rejected."

"Excuse me, sir," he said, trying to maintain his temper. "Why is this rejected?"

"You're a foreigner."

"Yes, but I have the proper forms. I was told I had approval."

The clerk launched into a long explanation, speaking very quickly. Tolevi spoke excellent Russian—he had done so since he was a child—but he couldn't understand half the words, let alone the logic.

"How can I appeal?" he asked when the man finally paused to take a breath.

"Appeal?" The clerk could not have looked more confused had they been speaking Greek. "There is no appeal."

"There is always a process," said Tolevi. "I have been in business now for—"

"I am sorry. I have another appointment."

"No. I want to see your supervisor."

The man rose. Tolevi debated; he could stay, which might bring out a supervisor, or it might result in a call to security. Once security was involved, anything could happen, including jail on whatever charge happened to be popular that day.

"Really, there is no way?" said Tolevi, rising.

The man shook his head.

"Here." Tolevi took out a business card. "I am staying at the Mercure. Uh, if maybe something changes?"

"It won't."

"Take my card anyway," said Tolevi, knowing he sounded more than a little desperate. "If it does."

The man wouldn't even look at it. Tolevi placed the card on the corner of the desk and left.

Was he being held up for another "tax"? But in such a case, it was unlikely that the clerk would have stamped the papers. The ministry could always issue new papers, but that required steps that others might see; it was unusual.

He was walking back to the hotel to have a drink and puzzle out the situation when he realized that the man in the blue sport coat was following him again.

Part of him wanted to confront the bastard and see if he had anything to do with the rejection. But good sense prevailed; Tolevi simply continued to the hotel and made his way to the bar. He ordered a vodka and tonic, then took a seat across the room.

The man in the blue jacket hadn't followed him inside. Tolevi looked over the rest of the room, but if his shadow had an accomplice, he couldn't pick him or her out.

He could go on to Donetsk without the permit and complete the CIA portion of his trip. But it would dent his cover story and, more importantly, prevent him from doing any real business, as the contacts would want the assurance that he could deliver the promised goods.

More importantly, it might mean that the Russians he dealt with no longer wanted him doing business in their territory. That was a problem of potentially catastrophic proportions.

Had he angered someone in the trade ministry?

Maybe Medved had somehow. But that seemed unlikely.

The drink was weak, the vodka not the best. Tolevi decided he would go upstairs to his room and rest a bit before having lunch.

Heading for the elevator, he spotted a restroom and ducked in. He was washing his hands when two other men came in, both Russians, both dressed like workers. Barely noticing them, he dried his hands and started for the door. It swung open just as he reached for it, smacking his right hand; as he jerked back, both of his arms were grabbed and he was pulled backward to the far side of the sinks. Three more men entered, two dressed as the others were, in T-shirts and black trousers. The third wore a tracksuit that would have been high fashion in the U.S. around 1980.

"What the hell?" Tolevi sputtered in Russian.

"Gabor Tolevi, welcome to Moscow," said the man in the tracksuit. "State your business."

"I was washing my hands."

The man holding his left arm jerked it upward, pressuring Tolevi's joints. The man in the tracksuit shook his head, though Tolevi wasn't sure whether it was at him or the goon holding him.

"You're in Moscow for business," said the man in the tracksuit.

"I don't talk to people when I'm being bullied."

"Are we not gentle?" Tracksuit laughed, but then he waved his hands and the men behind Tolevi let him go. "We'll use English," he added. "So you're more comfortable. And your accent is very bad."

"I hang around with the wrong crowd."

"You are here to sell medicine to the rebels. That is not a good thing."

Rebels.

Until now, Tolevi had guessed the men were SVR or otherwise Russians. But the word *rebel* marked him as a Ukrainian.

Or did it?

"Medicine is medicine," responded Tolevi.

"Yes, the medicine is one thing. Who it helps is another."

"Aspirin helps everyone."

"And that's what you're selling?"

"I don't have the right permit," said Tolevi. "So I'm not selling anything."

"That is a shame. So you have no reason to go into the rebel lands, then?"

The man didn't look particularly Ukrainian. Was he SVR posing as Ukrainian to test his loyalties? Or maybe *mafya.*

The only way to find out was to play along.

"Maybe I can find some reason to go there," said Tolevi.

"Give me the papers you brought to the ministry."

Tolevi hesitated. One of the men behind him—the one on the left, obviously an overachiever—moved close, reaching for his arm again.

"Work with us, and things will go well," said tracksuit. "Hesitate, and—what is the saying, 'All is lost'?"

Tolevi took the papers out of his sport coat pocket and handed them to the man.

"In the morning, there'll be an envelope under your door," said tracksuit. "Go about your business. We will contact you when we need you."

He waved his head at the others, who shoved Tolevi as they walked to the door. Tracksuit paused.

"We know you spoke to partisans in Crimea," he said. "That would not be a good thing to do again."

And then, with a frown, he left.

52

Chelsea had forgotten she had a date with Flores until he texted her that afternoon, asking what kind of food she liked.

Japanese, she answered, taken off guard.

SUSHI OR HIBACHI?

Neither.
But that wasn't a good answer.

SUSHI, OF COURSE. I DON'T LIKE TO HANG OUT WITH PEOPLE
WHO THROW FOOD AND KNIVES AROUND.

Flores met her at Sushi Z, a trendy place not far from downtown that served all-you-can-eat plates of sushi for twenty-eight bucks a pop. The menu consisted of two pieces of paper, on which you marked what you wanted; the one caveat was that you had to finish all you ordered, or be charged for it. Flores ordered a pair of dragon rolls and spiced crab sushi; Chelsea, not impressed by the frenetic pace of the waitresses, ordered tuna sashimi.

The warm sake Flores recommended was good, and very easy going down—too easy, thought Chelsea after her first few sips, and she resolved to go more slowly.

She wasn't sure about Flores. He wasn't the sort of guy she had gone out with before. She couldn't decide whether the fact that he worked for the FBI made him more or less interesting.

He was white, but that wasn't necessarily a big hang-up; she'd gone out with white guys before. And her father was white— though anyone seeing her just automatically checked the black box.

They talked about movies and then their food, light chatter without commitment or pressure. She was feeling good—partly a function of the sake—until their plates were cleared.

"So what's the daughter like?" asked Flores out of the blue.

"Daughter?"

"Tolevi. You met his daughter, right?"

"The ATM guy?"

"Yeah. I heard you made friends with her."

"How'd you hear that?"

"Just heard it."

Chelsea refilled her sake cup without commenting.

"You know, if you guys are still working on that, we could possibly trade information," said Flores.

"How so?"

"I don't know. It might be useful. If you talk to the daughter, maybe she can tell us about her father. What he's up to."

Oh, so he's pumping me for information. This isn't a date.

She felt both relief and disappointment—mild disappointment. This was business, not romance.

Trade information. But what?

"Do you know how the scam worked?" he asked.

"Do you?"

"We haven't been able to find the key," he confessed. "The code—there's nothing there."

"Your boss told my boss to drop everything," said Chelsea.

"My boss says a lot of things. That doesn't mean you and I can't work on it."

Chelsea finished her sake. "I don't know."

"Well, think about it." Flores looked up as the waiter approached with the check. "I got it," he said, holding out his hand.

JENKINS WAS JUST leaving the task force headquarters when Flores called him on his cell phone.

"How did it go?" he asked Flores.

"She didn't really say much about the girl."

"Nothing? They totally dropped it?"

"She only said you told her boss to back off. That was pretty much all I could get out of her."

"Keep at it."

"This isn't really the kind of thing I'm comfortable with."

"I know Massina. He's not going to drop this. If one of his people is talking to the girl, they're definitely working on it."

"You're the boss."

"That's right."

53

Moscow—later

For hours, Tolevi drifted between sleep and wakefulness. Every time he started to slip off, his mind threw up something that spiked his attention just enough to keep him from drifting off: possible problems at the border, possible trouble getting into Donetsk, how to get out of the country if the airport was suddenly closed.

And the identity of the people who had stopped him in the restroom. Clearly they were Russian, aiming to help the rebels even though they'd tried to provoke him with the clumsy reference.

SVR, then. He had contacts, he could check.

Not wise.

He tried moving his mind away from those thoughts, but nothing was safe: thinking of home, he began fretting about Borya, worrying how she was getting on with the babysitter. Nothing was safe: he thought of a baseball game between the Red Sox and the hated Yankees he'd been to recently . . .

For some reason it triggered a memory of the goons who had trapped him in the restroom.

Yankees fans, no doubt.

Around 3:00 A.M. he heard a noise at the door. He rolled out of bed, grabbing for the piece of iron he'd put on the nightstand to use as a weapon. Twenty-four inches long, the flat bar was part of his suitcase frame, specially installed to be used as a last-resort weapon in places like Moscow, where obtaining a real weapon was either not worth the effort or too dangerous. It was solid and heavy, more than enough to disable someone temporarily, if not break their neck—something he had done some years before in Brazil, of all places.

Bar in hand, he slipped to the side of the wall and waited, expecting someone to come in. Within moments he realized that wasn't going to be the case; a clerk had only walked by and slipped in the bill.

And another envelope, just as the goons had promised.

Tolevi stood by the door, listening. The only thing he could hear was his own breathing. Finally he bent and took the envelopes, then tiptoed back to his bed. He used the small light on his keychain to open the envelope. His import papers had been perfectly duplicated, with two exceptions—the stamp now indicated that the import had been approved, and two zerocs had been added to the number of tractor trailers he was authorized to import.

Two hundred containers' worth of aspirin and cough medicine? The profits would be considerable—but so was the up-front cost. And that was if he could make the necessary arrangements, both to buy and to sell.

But his new "partners" had probably taken care of at least one half of that equation. The question was how to avoid getting stuck with the bill, since a shipment this size would require hefty deposits.

Opening the other envelope, he saw that his bill had been paid, undoubtedly by his new "partners." There was a note attached with a Post-it.

G sends his regards.

One of his SVR contacts. So at least he was sure about whom he was dealing with.

DESPITE THE FACT that Russia and the Ukraine were fighting a war in all but name, trains and airplanes still traveled regularly between Moscow and Kiev. Getting to Donetsk was a little more complicated—all airplane flights were officially canceled, though it was still possible to charter something if you had the right connections. The train took some twenty-one hours and traveled across three borders, if one counted the rebel area; while Tolevi had the requisite papers, driving was far faster and at least arguably more reliable.

This was not without its own complications. Tolevi left the hotel at five for Moscow airport; he boarded a plane three hours later for Rostov-on-Don in the south. There he had arranged to meet a driver he trusted because of prior arrangements. But when he got to the bus station where they'd agreed to meet, neither the driver nor the car was there. Though this was uncharacteristic, Russians in general were not exactly known as paragons of timeliness. Tolevi stood near the curb at the corner of the building, not far from the closed ticket window, waiting in the cold. After half an hour, he concluded that his driver was not going to show. He was just walking toward the terminal door, intending to call a taxi so he could get to a rental car, when a Mercedes C class sedan drove up alongside him.

"Mr. T?" asked the driver as the window rolled down. He spoke in broken English. "So sorry late. Needed petrol."

Tolevi didn't recognize the man—or the car, for that matter.

"Who are you?" he asked in Russian.

"Boris send me." The man stuck to English. "His wife have baby."

Boris was not a young man, sixty at least, and Tolevi couldn't imagine him being married to someone young enough to still be fertile.

"I don't need a driver, thanks," said Tolevi.

"Boris told me you go over border, need guide," added the man. "I know how to get around."

"Yeah?"

"Вам потрібен гід," said the man, suddenly speaking Ukrainian. *Vam potriben hid.*"

It meant "You need a guide."

"Mozhlyvo," replied Tolevi. "Perhaps."

"Call me Dan." This in English.

"Where do you come from, Dan?"

"Do you wish to know too much?" asked the man rhetorically.

"You have papers?"

"I can get wherever you need to go. Your Ukrainian is not bad," Dan added. "But you will immediately be spotted as a foreigner. Maybe Russian, maybe not."

"What's Boris's wife's name?" asked Tolevi.

"Anas, after Anastasia, and she is young enough to be his granddaughter, I think. How the old devil does it, I don't know. You are to pay me half in advance."

"Good," said Tolevi, opening the car door.

IN TOLEVI'S EXPERIENCE, there were two kinds of drivers—ones who said absolutely nothing as they drove, and ones who said far too much.

Dan was one of the latter. Despite his earlier hints about Tolevi not knowing too much, he told his entire life story within their first half hour. He was a native of Temyruk, a tiny town not far from Donetsk; like many in the region, he was of Russian extraction and had been visiting friends in Rostov when the civil war began. Twenty-eight years old and a trained architect who had never worked as an architect, he was at least nominally on the side of the rebels who now controlled Donetsk, though Tolevi suspected what he said about the rebellion was more calculated to win his trust than to express his true opinions.

Whatever. Dan had clearly found a way to make the rebellion profitable; he was practiced at going back and forth across the border, something that became clear as they approached it. Rather than going through Vyselky, the town that sat on the highway they were taking, he detoured two miles east, driving across a succession of dirt farm roads in a crazy pattern of Zs. After about a half hour of this, they emerged on a paved road, driving north for another fifteen minutes before seeing even a single rooftop in the distance.

"We have about an hour to go," Dan announced. "We can stop in Amvrosiivka for something to eat if you are hungry."

Tolevi took that as a hint. Dan drove to a small café a few blocks off the highway; the recommended *pirozhki*—meat pastries—were excellent.

"How long will you need me for in Donetsk?" asked Dan as they finished.

"I don't need you there," Tolevi told him. "You can go after you drop me off."

"Boris thought you would need a guide. I can stay for two days."

"And did Boris tell you what I was doing there?"

"Only that you have business. I assume you bring items into the country."

"Something like that."

Tolevi nursed his beer. He didn't trust Dan, of course, and was more than half convinced he was in the employ of the men he'd met in Moscow. But if that was the case, he might be useful, and in any event wouldn't be so easy to get rid of. Tolevi decided to keep him where he could see him.

"I might find having a car and driver useful," he told him. "If the price is right."

"Another ten thousand euros would cover it. And my expenses."

It was far too much, but the response was reassuring—it made it more likely he was on his own. Tolevi bargained him down to five, with expenses and gas. He might have gone further, but

Dan was still smiling; Tolevi had learned long ago better to leave everyone happy than to scrape shins fighting over a few dollars.

Donetsk was a strange mixture of calm and violent destruction. Though it was close to the front line held by regular Ukrainian troops, a cease-fire had been in place for several months. This meant that residents could go about their business with some degree of normality, except for the periods when both sides exchanged artillery or rocket fire. These exchanges took place on almost a daily basis and followed a predictable pattern: one side would fire first, then the other would answer. The exchanges would last no more than five minutes; always the side that initiated the gunfire would stop first.

There were two unpredictable things: one, when the gunfire would begin, and two, where the shells would land. Damage was neither limited to military areas nor reliably repaired. An otherwise normal-looking city block was punctuated by blackened, burned-out façades; another featured row after row of bricks so neatly piled up that they looked as if they were for a new construction project, rather than salvaged from the buildings that had once occupied the craters behind them.

More than a year before, a railroad bridge over one of the main highways into town had been destroyed, temporarily blocking passage on the road. The rail cars had been removed, and much of the track and its overpass torn down, but the ends of the tracks on either side were still there, jutting above the road like fingers trying to close. Debris—ironwork, mostly, along with large chunks of concrete—sat scattered at the sides of the road. Tolevi couldn't help but think they would make the perfect cover for an ambush as they passed.

The city was much as he remembered it, though there were noticeable gaps and plenty of burned-out buildings. The Donbass Hotel, one of the grandes dames of Ukrainian hospitality, stood untouched at the corner of Artyoma Street. Tolevi hadn't bothered to make a reservation; he had guessed, correctly, that there would be no problem getting a room.

The hotel, which only a few years before was regularly filled with tourists and businessmen, was now mostly empty, operating out of sheer will. Only a single car, marked with prominent UN signs on the sides, hood, and trunk, sat out front.

A mustachioed clerk snapped to attention as Tolevi and Dan came in. Rooms were quickly found—fourth floor, back side; you didn't want to face the street if you didn't have to. Tolevi gave Dan a hundred-euro down payment and told him to take the rest of the night off.

"Won't you need a guide?" asked the young man.

"I can get around for a while. We'll meet for breakfast. Seven A.M."

"That early?"

"Arrange a wake-up call."

Tolevi checked the room. He assumed that he was being watched by the local intelligence network, whatever that might be; while he couldn't be sure there was a direct connection between the rebels who were now in charge and the SVR, he had to assume that there was. Nonetheless, it didn't look as if he was being followed when he left the hotel for a stroll.

Despite the presence of Ukrainian troops to the west and north, the city appeared calm, and there were no signs of rebel fighters, or Russians for that matter, in the area near the hotel. Tolevi walked several blocks without seeing so much as a policeman, let alone a military vehicle. Cars and trucks, mostly Western, passed; there was less traffic than he remembered since his last visit, but more than two years before. People passed with shopping bags slung from their shoulders; the handful of luxury shops near the hotel all looked open for business.

Tolevi found a café and went in, ordering a coffee; if anyone thought he was out of place, they didn't stare or make any overt sign. He paid with Russian rubles—it had been declared the official currency a year before—but the waiter didn't seem to care, nor did he say anything to the woman who paid in hryvnia, the official Ukrainian currency.

Reasonably sure that he wasn't followed into the café, Tolevi left and continued walking, heading toward a small park a few blocks from the hotel. He found a bench near some children playing on a swing, and once again scanned the area for a tail. Still not seeing one, he walked a few more blocks to a store that sold prepaid telephones. He bought one, then summoned a taxi.

Twenty minutes later, Tolevi arrived at an early-Soviet-era apartment building. After the cab turned the corner, he walked around the block, turned left, and went into a gray four-story building that smelled of simmering cabbage. He walked up a flight, paused one last time to make sure he wasn't being followed, then went up to the top floor and knocked on the door of an apartment at the far end of the hall.

The man who answered the door nearly dropped the cigarette from his mouth when he saw Tolevi. He grabbed it, then spread his arms wide to embrace him.

"What? What are you doing here?" asked the man, ushering him inside.

"Business, Grandpa. Business."

Denyx Fodor was not Tolevi's real grandfather, but he had known Tolevi as a baby, and the families had once been close enough to earn that sort of endearment. They had not seen each other since Tolevi's last visit to Donetsk, and Fodor cataloged the changes with some relish over a bottle of French wine. The old man still had a store of bottles left over from the days when he imported it; that business had crashed during Ukraine's depression, which had preceded the revolution and then been deepened by it. Now he was semiretired, with small interests in two shops in town; the proceeds paid his rent but not much more.

Tolevi waited patiently through Fodor's stories, mostly of rebel and Russian outrages, then explained the outlines of the deal he had come to make, carefully leaving out the business in the restroom, as well as the CIA mission.

"We can get medicine at the pharmacies," said Fodor. "But not reliably. And the quality—I think it is Chinese."

"This will be from the West," said Tolevi.

"You can get past the embargo?"

Tolevi shrugged. "There are ways."

"And what do you need of me?"

A ride to a place where using the cell phone would not be a problem either for Fodor or anyone else, and a set of eyes to watch for anyone following. Fodor was more than game.

They finished the wine while waiting for the sun to go down, then went out to Fodor's car, a ten-year-old Lexus. A half hour later they stopped near a railroad siding that had not been used since before the civil war.

Tolevi walked down the tracks for five minutes before making the call to the number Johansen had given him. There was no answer.

He was walking back, considering what to do, when a text arrived with an address and the words "butcher shop" in Ukrainian.

Right. Pick up some meat. Ironic and yet fitting at the same time.

"I need another stop, please," he told Fodor when he got back to the car. "And go over the river so I can throw the phone away."

54

Gestapo Bitch's real name was Joyce Kilmer, "like the lady who wrote about the tree." She had been a CPA with a running fetish until she'd broken her leg.

Learning how to properly rehab after the injury had taken her quite a while, until she'd found the right specialist. It had convinced her she could do better.

"What did you learn from the Marines?" asked Johnny Givens as they warmed down after his Saturday morning run. Kilmer had surprised him by joining him.

More of a surprise was the fact that she didn't bark at him, only laugh.

"Let's just say she pushed me," said Kilmer. "Then I met Mr. Massina."

"You work for him, not the hospital?"

"That's right. Keep walking. We need two circuits. Then we'll work on some core exercises."

They completed the walk, then began doing some exercises. Sweat flowed from Johnny's pores.

"All right," she announced suddenly. "You're done."

"Really?"

"Until five o'clock, yes. Kale smoothie for lunch. Don't forget your medicine."

"I can't forget that."

"It's important. Your body has been through enormous trauma. You've come a long way very fast—too fast, probably. But there's no going back. Just stick with the program."

They walked back to the building in silence.

"I didn't know you worked Saturdays," he told her as they reached the door.

"I don't. But you're my prize pupil." She smiled.

"Is that why you're being so nice?" he asked as the door flew open.

"Don't worry. I'll keep kicking your ass. But . . ." She paused. "They're going to release you this week. I wanted to make sure you're OK with that."

"Really?"

"Technically, there's no reason for you to be in the hospital. The amount of recovery you've done, the stage you're at—it would be, well, two months at least. But physically, you're there. So, a hospital being a hospital, they're ready to let you go."

"Wow."

"But you have to keep up with the program."

"I will. There's no doubt about that."

"Good."

"Are you going to still work with me?" Johnny asked.

"You'll be assigned a new therapist. Two, probably. The post-release team likes to work in pairs."

"But I was just starting not to hate you."

"Time for you to fly, little bird. Fly, fly, fly." She patted him on the back. "You're on your own."

DESPITE WHAT HE told her, Johnny didn't feel ready. He didn't think he'd ever be ready. So when he saw Sister Rose Marie waiting in his room when he got back, Johnny felt something close to panic.

"How are you?" asked the diminutive nun.

"Good."

"You've come a long way. How do your legs feel?"

"Strange." He laughed. "Very strange, still. But—I guess this is how life is going to be."

"It is."

"You guys have treated me really well."

"It's what we do," said the nun sweetly. "We're thinking of releasing you."

"Ms. Kilmer told me."

"How do you feel about that?"

"I don't know."

The nun nodded solemnly. "We'll continue to see you on an outpatient basis. We have a therapist I'd like you to work with."

"Ms. Kilmer has been pretty good. I'd like to keep working with her." Johnny sat on the edge of the bed.

"The therapist I was talking about is a psychologist. Because there are issues."

"Like what?"

"He'll talk to you about that. There are adjustments. But physically . . . Johnny, you've done more in two weeks than a lot of our patients do in six months. Partly, it's the drugs and the legs themselves—Mr. Massina's work is quite incredible. But most of it is due to you. Even so . . . you do have adjustments you have to make. Mentally."

"Sure."

"Are you a religious man, Johnny?"

"I'm not Catholic, Sister."

"I'm not trying to convert you," she said gently, "but I do believe that faith can be a powerful component of healing."

Johnny didn't know how to answer that.

"You're still angry with God, I would imagine, for doing this to you," said the nun. It was as if she read his mind. But maybe that wasn't so hard to figure out.

"It is what it is," he said.

"God only gives us what He knows we can handle," she told him.

"I guess."

"Nurse Abramowitz will be in to help with out-processing Monday," said the nun. "She's Jewish, by the way."

"Does that make a difference?"

"To her, I would suspect." She smiled. "If you ever need anything, I'm always here."

55

Donetsk, occupied Ukraine

Tolevi had Fodor drop him off several blocks from the address he'd been given. The old man was dubious; it was not a good part of town, even before the war, and aside from that it was a frequent target of the government's mortaring. But Tolevi insisted, and in the end the old man reluctantly let him go.

"I'll see you before I leave Donetsk," Tolevi assured him. "And we will solve the world's problems."

"That will take more wine than I own," said Fodor sadly. "Take care, young man. Take care."

The streets were dark, lit only by the dim light cast from nearby windows. There wasn't much of that: more than half of the buildings Tolevi passed were gone.

Tolevi walked to the south first, away from the address, always on guard against being followed. The air felt damp and cold; a storm must be coming on, he thought. With so many buildings gone, he had to guess at the block segment where the butcher shop would be. He came around two blocks east, walking with a quick, businesslike pace toward his destination.

He was very conscious of the fact that he had no weapon to

defend himself with. Ukraine was not known for crime; if anything, before the war Donetsk was far safer than Boston, itself a
relatively safe city. But war and deprivation made people desperate.

I can take care of myself.

The butcher's shop was dark. The storefront, which had probably been plate glass not too long ago, was covered in plywood,
but the door at the side was glass and intact. Tolevi knocked on
it, pushing his head to the glass and trying to see if there was any
light inside. But the place appeared empty.

He stepped back to look at the apartments above. No light
came from any of the windows. The sky was overcast, and without
light from anywhere nearby, it was difficult to see, but to Tolevi it
looked as if the right corner of the top floor appeared jagged, torn
off by some prehistoric monster—or, more likely, a mortar shell
from government lines.

He knocked again, this time much louder. Still nothing.

All right, then. I'll come back in the day.

Tolevi cupped his hands over his face and peered inside, trying
to see if the place was simply abandoned. But he saw only shadows, and even these weren't more than indiscriminate clouds.

He stepped back, reluctant to leave. Finally he turned in the
direction Fodor had taken bringing him here.

Tolevi was a long way from the hotel, but there was no alternative to walking. He turned his collar up against the cold and
hunched forward, hands in pockets.

"You! Stop!" shouted a voice in Ukrainian behind him.

Tolevi kept walking.

"I said stop!" repeated the voice. It was deep, masculine, at
least middle-aged, maybe older.

No. Stopping is never a good idea, Tolevi thought. *Stop and be
killed, or robbed at least. Walk and at worst they think you crazy, and who
messes with a crazy man in a war zone?*

He pushed his hands deeper into his pockets, hoping it looked
like he had a gun.

"I said halt!" This time the man behind him used English.

Surprised, Tolevi stopped. The man flipped on a flashlight, casting a long oval ahead that silhouetted Tolevi on the street.

"Turn around or I shoot," said the man.

Tolevi turned. Three men were standing a few meters away. The one in the middle had a Kalashnikov.

"Show your hands," said the man, still in English.

"What are you saying?" asked Tolevi in Ukrainian, though of course he understood. "I speak Ukrainian and Russian. Take your pick."

"Hands up," repeated the man in Ukrainian.

The man on his right walked up to Tolevi. He was a few inches shorter, and much thinner. Pointing at Tolevi's sides, he indicated he was going to frisk him; Tolevi widened his stance and submitted.

"What were you doing at the shop?" asked the man with the rifle when the search was over. He played the flashlight's beam across Tolevi's face.

"Looking for meat."

"At this hour?"

"I was looking to make some stew," said Tolevi.

Still holding the rifle, his inquisitor handed the flashlight to the man on his left, then took out a cell phone. He looked at the face of the phone for a moment.

Give me the answer, thought Tolevi. *Ask me who is it for.*

But instead, the man asked again why he would go to a butcher shop in the middle of the night.

"I heard sometimes it is open," answered Tolevi. "If you want meat."

"You don't look familiar."

"I'm a visitor. Trying to find food for a friend."

"You will come with us," said the man. He slipped the phone back into his pocket.

"I don't want any trouble," said Tolevi.

"You will come with us." He pointed the gun at Tolevi's face. "Now."

56

Johnny Givens stopped at the foot of the steps to his house on St. Charles Street and took a deep breath.

"I'm home," he said to no one in particular. "Home."

He put his hand on the rail and went awkwardly up the steps. There were so many things he had to get used to—his new legs, his mechanical heart, his new status as a "medically furloughed/ soon to be retired on full disability" former government worker.

The last would be the hardest, he was sure.

Givens's home was a duplex in Fields Corner West, an area described by the real estate brokers as "up and coming," though some of the residents might take issue. It certainly had the requisite mixed population—Vietnamese as well as Hispanic, black, and younger white. But it was also the neighborhood where Guinness had first been served, which made it quintessential old-school Boston. Had Givens been in a different kind of mood, he might have gone to the very bar, the Blarney Stone, which was only a short walk from, or a longish crawl to, his house.

But he wasn't in a drinking mood. Stepping into his apartment was like stepping into a different life—an old one that he had left not a week but eons ago.

It wasn't just that the place smelled stuffy, or that here and there a fine layer of dust had settled. The dimensions of the rooms seemed to have changed. The walls looked darker than he remembered, the furniture shabbier. His bed, unmade since the morning he left, looked different, smaller and angled in the room in a way that was unfamiliar. Nothing was exactly the same, and when he went from the hallway between the bedroom to the kitchen, he tripped over the wooden threshold. He caught himself on the doorway, but even as he righted himself he felt sheer panic, his emotions free-falling.

What if I fall here and can't get up? What if my heart stops? What if the legs become unattached or stop working?

What what what . . .

Irrational fears, all of them. If anything, he was stronger than he'd been—he'd always had a flawed heart, even if he hadn't known it; now he had one that was perfect, as the doctor who'd plugged into its magnetic sensors had told him with some glee before his release.

His artificial legs were several times stronger than flesh and bone. The drugs had pumped his muscles to a peak he hadn't experienced since high school, and maybe not even then. He was a bionic man, better than before.

Yet, not complete. Missing. A man missing who he was, who he had been.

Johnny straightened himself and walked to the refrigerator to take stock. The milk was bad, but there was an unopened bottle of cola on the top shelf. He took it out and, in a sudden fit of tidiness, poured it into a glass before sitting down at the kitchen table to drink it.

He'd only taken a single sip when his cell phone began to buzz. It was in his pocket, set to vibrate—which in itself was weird, because he had no way of feeling it.

Everything was different in this world.

It was a Boston number. He didn't recognize it, but decided to answer anyway. Maybe it was a doctor—or the hospital calling to tell him there had been a mistake; he wasn't supposed to go home.

"Hello? Johnny?"

"Who is this?"

"Chelsea Goodman. I stopped by to see you. They told me you were released."

"I was. I am."

"Oh. That's great."

Johnny felt as if he should say something, but he wasn't quite sure what.

"You should come to the office," said Chelsea. "Everyone would love to meet you."

"I'd like that," said Johnny. "When?"

"Whenever you want."

"How about now?"

"Well, it's Saturday, but . . . sure. A lot of people are here. Including the boss."

"Maybe I'll be there in a while, then," he said. "What's the address?"

THE OUTSIDE OF the Smart Metal building was very nineteenth century. Brick interrupted by steel cross beams, large windows that caught the sun and reflected the nearby harbor, a shiny metal roof with thick standing seams and snow guards.

Inside, Smart Metal was the future, and beyond.

While the shell of the old factory building had been restored, the interior had been gutted and completely rebuilt. It was now a building within a building, sleeker than anything Johnny had ever seen. The entrance lobby rose five stories above street level. Thick panels covered with granite rose to the ceiling; steel and glass walkways ran the length of the interior. Behind the panels on the first four floors were labs; there were offices on the fifth. Thick glass pipes ran across the top of each hallway, a ceiling of conduit, optic fiber, and HVAC trunks.

For all its high-tech look, cooling the building was a major problem, Chelsea told Johnny as she led him through; though the most powerful computers were confined to the basement "processing farm," there were workstations and even mainframes scattered throughout.

"It got so bad last year Mr. Massina assigned me to write an algorithm that would take into account how much the computers were being used," she said, pausing at the elevator on the first floor. "Since then it's been better. Everyone sets their lab at a different temperature, though, which drives the maintenance people batty."

The elevator arrived. Like everything else in the place, it was cutting edge, both in appearance and in function. There were no buttons anywhere on the exotic wood paneling; you spoke the floor where you were going. There was a security benefit to that—the elevator would not take you to a floor if you weren't authorized to go there, explained Chelsea.

"Can't you just take the stairs?" asked Johnny.

"Doors won't open, except in an emergency. If you weren't with me, you couldn't get out of the visitors' area on the first floor. That's why you don't need a pass."

"You're my pass."

"That's right."

"I better not let you out of my sight."

Chelsea led him out into another hallway, this one on the fourth floor. So far, they had seen labs where mechanical birds flew through mazes and an electric piano was hooked up to a computer that was composing its own music—melodic but somewhat boring.

"This is the biomechanical lab," said Chelsea. "This where your next heart will be grown."

"Grown?"

Chelsea smiled, then waved him through the door.

Full-spectrum fluorescents bathed the interior of the building with light so intense that Johnny had to shut his eyes so they could adjust. When he blinked them open, he found himself standing at the edge of a long row of what looked like oversized aquarium tanks, the sort a fish farm might use when breeding small fish. The interior of the room was very humid, and the place had a sweet smell unlike the rest of the building.

"Nutrient baths," said Chelsea, stepping over to one of the large tanks. "Think of them as large, artificial wombs."

Johnny followed her. The tank, a good three meters long and another meter wide, looked empty, except for a pair of marbles nestled in what looked like rubber material at the bottom.

They weren't marbles.

"Eyes," said Chelsea. "They're grown from pig cells. The difficult thing is the interface."

"Human eyes?" asked Johnny.

"They will be. Eventually. We have a lot of work to do."

She continued down the tanks. Two lab technicians were working at the far end, running a series of tests on handheld instruments whose wires snaked into one of the tanks. Chelsea waved at them but didn't interrupt. She led Johnny around the tanks to a bench where a set of large flat screens, each roughly eighty inches diagonally, were lined up in front of keyboards. Screen savers played on the screens, creating multi-stringed parabolas that morphed from red to green to blue and back. They looked like webs made by spiders tripping on LSD.

Chelsea tapped one of the keyboards. The screen behind it blanked. She bent over and began typing rapidly.

That girl has a beautiful shape, Johnny thought. He'd noticed it before, but something about the way she leaned forward now made lust erupt in him.

It scared him a little. He wasn't sure he could act on that impulse anymore. It was the one area he hadn't talked about with the doctors—an oversight born of shyness and fear.

But she was beautiful.

"This is what your mechanical heart looks like," said Chelsea as a three-dimensional image rotated on the screen. "And this is what the next generation will look like."

The device on the left side of the screen looked like a pair of inverted and intertwined trumpet mouthpieces made of white plastic. The bottom openings were fitted with corded plastic tubes; the tops looked not unlike the fittings on home plumbing. Between these two carbon and fiber constructs was a plastic-covered collection of circuitry, artificial nerves that not only governed the pump but were also grafted to Johnny's nervous system and a set of leads that could be used to test and monitor the unit externally.

His was handmade, fitted, and programmed specifically to his needs. All of them were, adapted from a basic but flexible blueprint.

On the right side of the screen was something that looked exactly like a "real" heart except for the wires and the nubbed fitting on the bottom.

"How long before that's ready?" Johnny asked.

"Mmmmm . . . Hard to say. The growing techniques are still in their infancy."

"Is this what you do?"

"No. My field is AI—artificial intelligence. I work primarily with the robots. But I do a little of everything. That's what I love about working here."

"I want to work here," Johnny told her. He felt he was gushing almost—he was intrigued and excited by everything he saw, and it was hard to hold his emotions in check. "I want to be part of this. How do I join?"

"As scientist?"

"As—security or something like that. Are you still working on the ATM case?"

"Well . . ."

"You are," said Johnny. "I can help on that."

"We're working on it, but not with the Bureau. Not officially," she told him. "Your boss didn't want us involved."

"Well, I can work with you on that. I can be involved. You're

not an investigator, but I am. Who do I talk to?" Johnny asked.
"Mr. Massina?"

"I don't know that there are openings."

"He told me if I wanted anything, to see him. Is he in?"

"Isn't it kind of soon for a job?"

"Take me to him. Please."

57

The air inside the building smelled like pulverized brick, as if the façade had been ground into tiny particles and was now being sent through the ventilating system: an impossibility, given not only the lack of such a system in the structure, but anything resembling a roof. There was no electricity either, and nothing that it could have powered; Tolevi followed the path of his captor's flashlight as he was marched to a crate at the back corner of a building a block from the butcher's. The nearby floor was littered with rags and shoes. He kicked one as he walked, and something rolled out from under the pile; it was a syringe.

It took him a few moments to realize the building had been used as a makeshift hospital.

"What is your name?" asked the man with the gun when Tolevi sat down. So far the men had done nothing physical to him, barely even threatening him, really.

No doubt that wasn't going to last.

"Gabor Tolevi."

"Why were you at the butcher's?" asked the man with the gun again.

"Stew meat," said Tolevi.

Against all logic, he hoped for the reply that would show the man was his contact. Instead he got a slap across the face.

"Why are you here?"

"I am in the import business," said Tolevi. "I sell things at wholesale and—"

Another slap, but this one was with the butt of the AK. Tolevi tumbled to the floor, jaw broken.

"You will tell me why you are here, Russian," demanded the man. "No more games!"

Before Tolevi could think of an answer, the room exploded. He felt himself being thrown backward into an abyss, the world vanishing beneath him.

BLASPHEMY

FLASH FORWARD

Louis Massina was on top of the world, and he was falling, sliding, unable to stop, unable to save himself.

God, he prayed, *if it's your will to let me die . . .*

The prayer died on his lips.

If it's God's will, the nuns all taught, so be it.

So be it.

No way. No.

The bastard's going to kill me, and there's so much more I have to do. I cannot die now. No. I am not going to die.

"God," he said aloud, voice trembling, "if it's your will that I die, screw it, because I'm not going, not without a fight."

REAL TIME

58

Donetsk—moments later

Tolevi rolled on the floor as the room exploded, covering his head with his arms. The flash of light had left him temporarily blinded; the loud boom made him deaf.

He thought about Borya back home. He was supposed to call her tonight at 5:00 P.M. her time.

Not going to make that.

He tried to crawl out of the confusion, unsure where he was going but believing movement would save him. Air rushed past and the ground rumbled; he heard something in the distance, a metallic rattle, then a softer but stranger sound, a thin sheet of aluminum foil being torn in two. Grit slammed into his face. He started to cough and pushed harder, dragging his legs across rubble, knowing that he had to get away, knowing that he would get away, but not sure what he had to get through to escape.

Then he was lifted, flying in the air.

Tolevi's eyes felt glued shut. He started to cough again. The gunfire became louder. He became aware of the sides of his head pressing against the soft parts of his brain. He could feel his skull from the inside, could feel the bones as if they were a helmet pressing around his entire being.

I'm flying.

He moved his hands to pry his eyes open, but the lids wouldn't budge.

A rush of cold air against his face. He opened his mouth and gulped. It smelled of the night, damp, thick with exhaust.

Someone called to him from the distance. Lights were moving nearby.

A car?

He fell onto something hard. The side of his face brushed along metal.

He was in a car or a truck, on the floor. They were moving. A voice floated over him in a language he couldn't make out.

"You're lucky they didn't kill you."

Russian. It was Russian.

"Da," he mumbled, answering his own thought, not the voice. It continued, strengthening in tone, starting to become coherent. It was asking him questions, asking him why he had gone in there, what the wolves had wanted.

Volki. Wolves.

Not a question about whether he was OK.

Which should tell him something, should identify who he was with, but it didn't.

Other voices, speaking Russian.

Two hands took hold of Tolevi from the back and hauled him upward, pushing him around so that he was sitting back to the wall of the vehicle. Water slopped over his face. Shaking his head, Tolevi reached his hands to his eyes and rubbed them.

He blinked; a flashlight shone on his face.

"Why were you with the criminals?" asked the voice. It belonged to a man in a black combat uniform, kneeling next to him. He was wearing a black watch cap with a ninja-style mask that covered his face.

They were in the back of a cargo van. Besides the man talking to him, there was another nearby, to his right. He, too, was wearing a mask. He was also holding an assault rifle—not an old Kalashnikov, like the man who'd stopped him on the street, but something newer, an AK-74 maybe, though Tolevi wasn't sure. There were two men in the front of the truck; he could see their heads.

"Why are you in the People's Republic?" asked the man next to him.

"Business," mumbled Tolevi.

"With the criminal government?"

Tolevi struggled to clear his head. The man's Russian had an accent that he couldn't quite pick out, but he wasn't Ukrainian.

Special operations troops helping the rebels. Spetsnaz.

Or not. They could be anyone, on any side.

You'll never see Borya again.

"Where did you get these papers?" asked the man, holding them out.

"Checkpoint," said one of the men in front.

The man who'd been questioning him stopped talking and moved to the other side of the van. But clearly they weren't worried about being stopped: they slowed, the driver opened the window, and then they sped past.

A few minutes later they stopped at the rear of a large house. Tolevi was led out of the truck, not gently but not roughly either, and walked to the back door. Other vans pulled up as they walked, driving past to a barnlike building fifty or so meters away.

Inside, his escort pointed to a chair in the hallway and told him to wait. Tolevi sat down, scanning his surroundings. Oil paintings lined the walls, and the two lights he saw were small chandeliers, their chiseled crystals reflecting kaleidoscopically with a shimmer of bright white and tiny rainbow triangles.

There were more people inside, many of them.

I can probably walk out of here without anyone noticing, Tolevi thought. *But where would I go?*

Best to play along and see where this leads.

It was impossible to be in Tolevi's business and not encounter difficult situations. He'd dealt with police and customs agents in Russia, the Ukraine, Poland, and Georgia; South America and Mexico. Most were surprisingly civil, more businesslike and less aggressive than the average traffic cop in the States. And these men, though clearly military, were far to the professional side of the spectrum. They weren't treating him like a prisoner, really— no harsh pushes, no gruff language.

Yet, anyway. So hopefully things would go well here.

If not . . .

If not, I'll take what comes.

59

Borya glanced at the clock on the kitchen wall. She was pretending to work on an essay on *King Lear*, her last remaining homework for the weekend. Martyak was inside talking on her cell phone to some dweeb; thank God for that, Borya thought, because otherwise she would be hovering over her at the table. The babysitter was making an effort to be friendly; she had even offered the night before to help her with her homework. But her help was worse than useless; she had an impossible interpretation of *King Lear*: a metaphoric statement about why war is hard on families. And even Borya could tell her spelling was atrocious.

Borya's father always called at certain intervals when he was gone, generally at 5:00 P.M. He was due to call tonight, but the hour had passed without a call.

That wasn't necessarily unusual, but Borya found herself missing him, and anxious to hear his voice. That was the strange thing about their relationship: when he was here, she couldn't stand the way he was on her, always around, snooping, checking up on her. But when he was gone, she missed him dearly. She thought of things they might do, like getting ice cream, or maybe going to the movies.

Not that he knew much about movies. But at least most times he would let her pick them. So it wouldn't matter if he fell asleep in the theater, which he often did.

"How's it going in there?" asked Martyak from the den.

"Slow."

"Has your father checked in yet?"

"No."

"No text?"

"He doesn't usually text when he's away. He calls."

"Did he call?"

"No."

"He said he would. Tonight." Martyak came into the kitchen. Her jeans were at least two sizes too small, a look that did nothing for her. Her lumpy sweatshirt was something an old lady would wear. The guy she was dating must be half blind.

"You think he's OK?" asked Martyak.

"My dad is always OK," shot Borya.

"I'm just saying, he forgot to call. Maybe you should call him."

"I don't have his number."

That was a lie so blatant that Borya couldn't imagine why she had even said it. But the words were out there, and she couldn't take them back.

"Well I have it," said Martyak. She went back inside and got her cell phone.

"Here, I'll call," said Borya, picking up her own.

"Are you calling his overseas phone, or his domestic?" asked Martyak.

Domestic *is such a weird word.*

"Whichever one he answers," said Borya.

"I'm calling his sat phone." Martyak already had it dialed in.

Go ahead, thought Borya. Her father never answered that line; his regular phone nearly always worked in whatever country he was in.

Borya called the cell. But it went to voice mail after four rings.

"Hey, Daddy," she said. "The babysitter is getting nervous because you haven't called. I told her everything is fine. But, you know how girls are. I love you."

She hung up.

"It says leave a message." Martyak held up the phone, as if to show her.

"So? Leave one."

"Mr. Tolevi, we were just checking in," said Martyak. "Everything is fine here. We're working on an essay on *King Lear*."

Borya rolled her eyes.

"Hope to talk to you soon," said Martyak, hanging up.

Borya and her father had a code—if she called on the sat phone, he would realize she *really* needed to talk to him, and he would call her right back from his cell. She figured the code would hold up even if it was the babysitter who called. She went over to the refrigerator, phone in hand, and got out some soda.

"I'm sure he's fine," said Martyak.

"That's what I said."

"Still working on *Lear*?"

"Uh-huh."

"Want help?"

"Nope."

"Goneril is my favorite character."

She would be, thought Borya, staring at the computer screen.

Ten minutes passed. Fifteen. A half hour.

Really, Dad, what are you doing that's more important than me?

60

Boston—about the same time

"I hear you turned Johnny Givens down for a job," said Chelsea, greeting Louis Massina when he walked into her office. "How come?"

"I didn't turn him down. I told him there'd be a job for him when he got better. He still has a long way to go."

"He didn't hear that part," said Chelsea. "The only part he heard was *no*."

"That's not my fault."

"You know, Lou, you can be kind of, well, deaf sometimes. To other people's emotions."

Massina frowned. "Best to be direct in the long run," he told her. "People appreciate you being honest."

"Honest and blunt are different."

"I wasn't blunt." Massina brushed his hand, tired of the argument. "What's new with our ATM project?"

"It was an application layer attack on the local machines," said Chelsea. "The solution isn't difficult—it's just fixing old code. But that'll still be patchwork. I have a better system. I just need to test it."

"Marketable?"

"Absolutely. The whole ATM system is ridiculous," continued Chelsea. "It's 1970s tech. I mean like, forget it."

"Put together a task line and get ready to hand it off. I want you back on Peter. Las Vegas is coming up, and we need him ready."

"You're going to demonstrate him at a consumer show?"

"Why not?"

"You want to go into mass production?"

"Eventually." Massina's real goal was to kick a little sand into the eyes of a competitor who had just pulled out of the show. The bot was at least a year from any sort of regular production and even then it would be far too expensive for anyone but the most deep-pocketed company or the government to buy. But some wows from the media would look good in the marketing material.

"I talked to Flores, at the FBI, last night," Chelsea added as he was about to leave. "He was trying to pump me for information on the girl."

"Last night?"

"He made it look like a date."

There was a wistful note in her voice.

Hmmmm, thought Massina. "What did he ask?"

"Nothing specific. But they're definitely still working on the case, no matter what they told you."

"If they want to cooperate, they should just come out and say that," Massina told her. "You see? It's best to be direct."

"Should I tell Agent Jenkins that?"

"No. Let them come to us. Or me. You're sure this girl is responsible?"

"No. But she's smart enough. Maybe we should hire her."

"You're going to be running my HR department soon."

CHELSEA WATCHED HER boss leave. She wasn't kidding about getting Borya Tolevi to work there. Not as a full-fledged employee:

she needed to go to college and get more formal training. But the girl needed something to push her in the right direction. She was a smart kid, interested and intrigued—there was huge potential there if she just got the right chance.

She needed someone like Chelsea's dad to push her. She didn't have that.

That was the difference between them.

Maybe. Borya was far more rebellious. Chelsea would never have broken into an ATM network.

Not that she couldn't have.

No, Borya was already a thief and a black hat hacker. If anything, she should be locked up in jail—and she would be if Chelsea told Jenkins what she knew.

Give her a job here? Ha!

Maybe it would steer her in the right direction. And Johnny Givens?

He was cute.

And incredibly strong. Mentally. It was impossible that he was out walking around. His face was still covered with scabs, his arms red with flash burns—and yet there he was, walking on artificial limbs Massina had invented.

Other people, too, but Massina mostly. The prosthetics were an obsession.

Chelsea rose from her workstation. Borya did remind her of herself, or a self she could have been under different circumstances.

How am I going to save her?

MASSINA HEADED HOME to change, then drove to the Antiquarian Club, where he had promised to put in an appearance at a fundraiser. He didn't particularly like playing VIP, but it was a favor to a member of his board of directors.

It meant putting on a tie as well as a suit. He fiddled with it in his bathroom, trying to get the knot centered perfectly. It wasn't easy, and he was too distracted, thinking about a million things: ramping up production on a new bot line, repurposing an older generation of chips for handheld devices, the possibility of revamping ATM networks, Chelsea's dalliance—or not—with the FBI agent.

And that little girl hacker.

Give the girl a job? Throw her in jail first. What's wrong with parents today?

Thirty minutes later, tie still slightly askew, Massina walked into the lounge at the Antiquarian Club. The club's name was not meant ironically—it was devoted to preserving the past, raising funds for the city's museums and historical sites. He shook hands with the VIP host, then nodded his way to the bar, where he had just obtained a four-finger bourbon when a familiar voice scolded him.

"Now Louis, remember you have to give a speech," said Sister Rose.

"Sister Rose Marie. Night off?"

"They cut the ball and chain for special events," said the nun.

"I don't have to say more than five words. That's in my contract. What are you drinking?"

"Seltzer, please."

"Not white wine?"

"Too early. I might tell some of the politicians what I think of them, and things would be awkward for the rest of the evening."

"Sister, I don't think you've ever offended anyone in your life. Even your insults are a blessing."

"Don't butter the bun on both sides, Louis. It's likely to fall."

Massina got her the drink.

"Your young man made remarkable progress," she told him, sipping the seltzer daintily. "The drug regime is very, very good. And, of course, God was with him."

"He came by and asked me for a job today."

"Really?"

"I told him he has months to go. But he has the right attitude."

"You can't let him go back to work yet. He needs time."

"I don't intend to. Down the road, maybe."

"Make it a long road, Louis. This is very fast."

"If you're thinking of poaching him, Sister, you're welcome to take first shot. Half the people on my payroll work for you as it is. Or they think they do."

"I'm worried about the effects as the drugs taper off."

The mayor's wife greeted Sister Rose, interrupting the conversation. Massina excused himself; spotting his board member, he went over and said hello. He soon found himself talking to a Harvard history professor who was an expert on the Revolutionary War and was working with an archaeologist planning to excavate a site near the harbor. The site was not that far from his laboratories.

Dinner passed quickly. Massina gave his very brief speech commending the organization with a slogan his PR director had suggested—*The future needs the past to get ahead*—and made his getaway as the session broke up.

Out front, he gave his car's ticket to the valet and waited for the vehicle to arrive. Different projects flicked through his mind, problems, solutions.

Will Peter be ready to demonstrate?

How much of a test should it be given?

His car pulled up. He reached for his wallet to get a tip for the attendant.

At that same moment, someone behind him shoved a cloth bag over his head. Before he could react, something slammed into the back of his head. A curse died on his lips as he fell, unconscious.

61

Near Donetsk—about two hours later

Tolevi's wife watched him run through the deserted streets. Somehow she kept up with him, even though she wasn't moving. Dark clouds passed overhead. He looked up and saw they were airplanes, jet bombers. As he stared, they fell to earth, landing on legs that sprouted from their wings.

Robots.

He was surrounded. Their black metal smelled like coal dust and iron, pulverized grit.

He began to choke. He glanced up and his wife was looking at him, concerned.

"How are you here?" he asked her.

"You are dreaming," she said. "You fell asleep."

TOLEVI WOKE WITH a hard shudder, disoriented. It took a moment to remember where he was: on the bench in the house near Donetsk.

People were moving around upstairs and inside. He seemed to have been forgotten.

Maybe I should just leave.

He got up, a little unsteady.

"So you're back with us?" asked a bearded man at the end of the hallway.

Tolevi wasn't sure he was speaking to him. "Me?"

"Come in here."

Tolevi got up and walked down the hall, flexing the stiff muscles in his legs. He rubbed his shoulders; the house felt cold.

The bearded man sat behind a desk. The room looked like a den. There were stuffed animals on the shelves, and large animal heads on the wall: a lynx, an elk, a moose. The rug was striped; it took a moment for Tolevi to realize it was a leopard's skin. Various small birds lined the shelves, the taxidermist having posed them in perfect gestures suggesting flight.

"Gabor Tolevi," said the man. "Tell me why you shouldn't be executed as a spy."

"A spy?"

"And a smuggler."

"I'm just a businessman."

"Moscow likes you," said the man behind the desk. He was speaking Russian, though his accent indicated he might be Ukrainian. More likely he was a Russian native but had spent considerable time in the republic before the war. "Yes, Moscow likes you, but I'm not sure."

The man leaned back in his chair and folded his arms, revealing a tattoo on his right biceps. Most of it was obscured, but the bottom looked like a set of crossed swords at the base of a skull. "Your papers give you the right to import medicine," he told Tolevi.

"Yes. It's much needed."

The man opened his desk drawer and took out a lighter. Picking up the papers on the desktop before him, he flicked, igniting the flame.

Tolevi debated whether to say anything. It didn't seem worthwhile—what could he say to make the man stop?

Your people in Moscow asked me to do this?

That clearly had no weight.

The paper flared. The bearded man held on to it as the flames engulfed his hand, then he dropped the black curl to the desk.

"You'll go back to America," said the man. "You're not needed here. I don't care what Moscow says. We have plenty of black marketeers. All of them more honest than you and your masters in Moscow."

"OK."

The man laughed. "No argument?"

Tolevi shrugged. "What can I say?"

"Why did you go into that end of town?"

"I was looking for a place to store the goods."

"Why would you need a storehouse?"

"If things went well, I wouldn't. But in this sort of business—anything can happen."

"Yes. You might lose your papers. You might go home empty-handed. And be lucky to get there."

"I agree."

The bearded man pushed his hand across the desk, removing the ashes that had fallen.

"One of my men will drive you to the city. Wait outside."

Tolevi started to leave.

"I would not stay in Donetsk for very much longer," added the bearded man. "It is not a safe place. Too many recidivists and anti-democrats marching around. You never know what may happen."

62

Massina regained consciousness in a grungy room with a view of the Charles River. His hands were tied behind his back, and his feet were chained to the leg of the couch he'd been deposited on. He knew it had to be past midnight, though his watch had been taken, along with his wallet and phone.

While he was well off, Massina had never considered himself a prime target for kidnapping or even robbery. The company's security forces were focused on the plant and IP, not his own person. So he looked at the situation the way he looked at everything unexpected: with great intellectual curiosity. What did these thugs think they were going to get, and why? How were they going about it? What were their assumptions and their motivations?

Money would be a good guess as to the latter.

Standing, he found he could move a few feet from the couch before being held back by the chain. He stretched as best he could, then tried to figure out where exactly he was by staring out the window at the darkened river.

Lights were scattered along the far shore. He thought he could see the outline of the bridge to his right, but the window wasn't clean enough for him to get a good view of what was outside.

West maybe of Arsenal Street or Route 20.

He strained to see if there was traffic on the bridge—a lot of traffic would make it the highway, but he couldn't tell from where he was standing.

"Awake, good!"

Massina jerked around. A man leaned up against the corner of the room. Massina hadn't even realized he was there.

"You're pretty rich, huh?" said the man.

"Who are you? What do you want?"

"Just to make sure you were OK. I apologize for the rough handling. It was a mistake. The people responsible have been punished."

His face was obscured by the shadows, but Massina guessed that he was in his thirties. He spoke English with a heavy accent, Russian or German.

"Is this a kidnapping?"

"A kidnapping, no? Not even a robbery. Your wallet and phone are in the outside room." The man stepped forward. His face was covered by a ski mask. Massina tried to guess his size— over six feet, but by how much?

"Here's the key," said the man, turning as he reached the door. He threw a small ball of tape at Massina, hitting him in the chest. The ball dropped to the floor near the couch. "You may go when you free yourself."

"Who are you?"

"Friends. You may do well to take on investors," added the man. "As insurance in the future."

"What are you talking about?" demanded Massina, but the man left the room without answering.

63

Donetsk, early morning

Two burly men in civilian clothes drove Tolevi back to the city. They were quiet the whole way, but it didn't take much to guess that they were Russians. The fact that they weren't hiding their faces was a good sign, he thought: it meant they felt he had been sufficiently cowed not to be of further trouble.

It might also mean that they were going to kill him. He tried not to think about that possibility.

Whatever they were thinking, the less they knew about him, the better. The hotel key card was generic enough that it might not have been recognized; even if it had, a little misdirection might be useful. So he told the men to take him to the Ramada, which was on Shevchenka Boulevard near the reservoir. They dropped him there and took off quickly, not even bothering to wait until he entered the building.

Aside from the fact that the hotel was in eastern Ukraine—or the Donetsk People's Republic—it was similar to every other Ramada on the planet. Tolevi went inside, nodded at the sleepy desk clerk, then walked over to the large coffeepot set up at the far end of the lobby. He filled a cup, then went out to the patio near the pool to sit, as if he were waiting for someone. He was surprised to find that his jaw, although painful as hell, was working. Maybe it wasn't broken after all.

What he was really doing was sorting himself out. He'd lost his prepaid phone; he'd need a new one. Using either the sat phone or his regular cell, which were both back at the hotel, was now out of the question while he was in the city. The Russians used scanning technology just like the Americans; they might not be quite as sophisticated, but even they could figure out how to snag his number, location, and even conversations.

Without the documents permitting him to bring the drugs in, there was no sense contacting the men he'd planned to deal with. He'd only be putting them in danger, and at best he'd be cutting off the possibility of future deals. So that part of his trip was over.

SVR would not be happy. But they could take that up with the bearded Spetsnaz general.

More likely a colonel. Tolevi decided he would think of him as a colonel, though the man had not made his rank clear.

Were the Russians following him? The two men who'd dropped him off seemed not to care very much about him, but that could easily be a ruse.

Maybe they knew everything.

It was easy to get too paranoid, to let fear freeze you.

On the other hand, he had narrowly escaped death. The Russian operation against the loyalists had saved him.

But was that an accident? Or was that even part of a plan?

Too much thinking. Stop.

The coffee was terrible. Tolevi rose and dumped it on the concrete. He walked through the lobby and back out to the street, where he checked his watch.

Five past five.

Too early to see Fodor.

He decided he would get something to eat, then collect his luggage and ask the old man for a ride to the border. Surely he knew a way across.

Get home and regroup. He'd come up with something else for Medved.

It was a decent walk to the Donbass Hotel, a bit over twenty minutes. The air was still damp, but the predawn sky showed the clouds were breaking up; Tolevi guessed it would be a decent spring day once the sun came up. He imagined himself showing Borya Ukraine—not this Ukraine but the Ukraine of his youth.

An improbable dream now, but these idiots couldn't stay at war forever; remove Putin and the conflict would likely evaporate. And Putin wasn't as secure as the West believed.

Yes, but he would die before giving up power willingly? What Russian would?

Tolevi was lost in his thoughts as he neared the hotel. It was the fatigue and the calmness that came with having a plan. In a place like Donetsk—in any place really, given his profession—it was very dangerous, and he realized it as soon as he entered the lobby and saw Dan rising from a couch to confront him.

"You're up," said Tolevi in Russian, as matter-of-factly as he could muster. "I thought we weren't meeting for another hour and a half."

"Where have you been?"

"Just a walk," said Tolevi. "Have you had breakfast?"

The other man glared at him. He had the look of someone who thought he'd been cheated, or about to be cheated.

"Come on," added Tolevi. "Let's get coffee and food."

"Where?" demanded Dan.

"There's a good place across the street," said Tolevi. "Come."

THE CAFÉ WHERE he'd stopped the afternoon before was not yet open, but another shop farther along the block was. The owner was clearly a morning person; he greeted the two men warmly and struck up a conversation with Tolevi about how difficult it was to find good coffee anymore.

As the man went on with his complaints, Tolevi slyly eyed

Dan. The driver's anger had started to dissipate, but his body language said he didn't trust Tolevi. That wasn't particularly surprising, and in a way it was reassuring—he wasn't trying to hide his feelings, which told Tolevi that he wasn't working for the Russians at least, or probably anyone else.

But it didn't mean Tolevi could trust him either.

He wouldn't turn on him as long as he was expecting to be paid, Tolevi decided. After that, though . . .

Another customer came into the shop, and the owner ended the conversation.

"He talks a lot," said Dan.

"Everyone has a story."

"For all his complaints, you would think his coffee would be better."

"It's about what I had in Russia."

"No. Russian coffee is better."

Tolevi stirred his cup. The coffee wasn't particularly good.

An opportunity?

"You know, driving a few suitcases of coffee over the border might be a good idea for you," he suggested to the Russian. "You might be able to pick up some extra money."

"Too risky."

"No riskier than driving me across. Less."

Dan shrugged.

"What if you had a permit?" asked Tolevi.

"Where would I get that?"

"Do you go across the borders a lot?"

"Enough."

"Do you go west?"

"Into Ukraine? Of course."

Just then a pair of twenty-something women entered the shop and came toward their table. Tolevi changed the subject, commenting on how pretty they looked. Dan glanced at them, then said they were nothing special.

"Maybe you're right." Tolevi pretended to agree. "I'm just deprived."

"The beautiful women are in Crimea," said Dan. "That's the place to see them."

"I agree with that."

"You've been to Crimea recently?"

"A few weeks ago."

Their breakfast came: rolls with mystery meat. It had a strong taste that hinted of sour anchovies; Tolevi ate anyway. He'd missed dinner and was operating on no sleep, something that always made him hungry. He hoped he wouldn't pay for it later.

If the taste bothered Dan, it wasn't obvious. He cleaned his plate in two gulps.

"I can get you to Crimea if you want," offered the driver.

"It's a long way," said Tolevi.

"We can go directly. A few hours."

Before the war, driving from Donetsk to the isthmus would have taken at least six hours. Now, assuming one could get across the two borders and make it through the potentially dangerous area in between, Tolevi reckoned it would be at least ten.

"How?" he asked Dan.

"I have a friend with a boat."

"Where?"

"If you are serious, then we'll talk about it," said Dan. "You don't need details. And you will have to pay."

"No, I don't need details. You're right."

"You want to leave today?"

Tolevi took a final sip of his coffee, working the small grinds that had been at the bottom of the cup around his tongue. Was the driver's offer a trap?

"I have some things to do," he told Dan, pulling out some rubles to pay. "Let's see how the day goes before we decide."

64

Boston

The police were professional.

That was the best and the worst Massina could say. They went through the building with him, checking for any overt sign of his captors; naturally there was none. They didn't bother checking for fingerprints, let alone DNA.

"That's *CSI* stuff," said the lieutenant in charge. "It looks great on TV, and everyone thinks it's a miracle drug, like aspirin, fixes everything, solves every crime. But look at this place."

He swept his hand around the empty room. It was the top floor of a five-story office building that had not been occupied in more than a year. Its previous owners had leased it to a video game company that had gone bankrupt; since that time, it had been vacant, used mostly by vagrants and homeless drifters, except for a two-week stint a month before, when a film company rented out the floor.

"We wouldn't know where to begin with DNA," said the lieutenant apologetically. "There's so much potential for things being around, for contamination—"

"Can't you tell what's fresh?" asked Massina.

The lieutenant's sigh was the sort an exasperated parent might make when explaining to a three-year-old that the world was round for the five hundredth time.

Just because, kid. Don't you get it?

They weren't completely without leads: Massina's Cadillac could be swept, though even there the police thought they'd find little. And they would look for video surveillance cameras at the club and on the route to the building. They had Massina sit with an artist, who tried to get a composite sketch of the man who'd spoken to him. But since he hadn't seen the man's actual face, they ended up with only the most generic description: roughly six foot, average build, foreign accent.

"I narrowed it down to maybe a tenth of Boston's population," said Massina sardonically when they were done.

"It's a start," said the artist.

I oughta nominate you for optimist of the year, Massina thought as he left.

BOZZONE, SMART METAL'S head of security, was more sympathetic than the police, but he, too, offered little hope when he picked Massina up at the police station.

"The theory is, they made a mistake. They found out who you were and backed off," said Bozzone after ushering his boss into one of the company cars, a GMC Jimmy. "That's the only thing that makes sense."

"Who were they looking for?" asked Massina.

"That's the sixty-four-thousand-dollar question. There are plenty of possibilities. There are a bunch of people who have cars like yours."

"Could this be related to the ATM scam?"

"They're looking into that," said Bozzone. "You might mention it to Jenkins. But from what they said to you, it doesn't quite match. And Chelsea said that was a kid, right?"

"True."

Bozzone walked through Massina's house with him, carefully checking for signs of an intrusion even though the security system indicated there had been none.

"Put a hold on all your credit cards," suggested Beefy after they were done. "And get new ones."

"What a pain." Massina walked to the kitchen.

"Better safe than sorry."

"Would you like some coffee?"

"I'd like to get back to sleep, if it's all right."

"Go on."

The security director hesitated.

"What?" asked Massina.

"About that business with the ATMs."

"You think it's connected?"

"No. But I think you went over the line."

Massina opened the cupboard and retrieved a box of green tea. He wasn't particularly concerned about caffeine content; it was only a few hours to dawn, and he'd already decided he wasn't going to get any meaningful sleep.

"I'm not trying to lecture you," added Bozzone. "But once you start going down this road, you open yourself up to all sorts of things."

"Noted. Are you sure you don't want something to drink?"

"I'm good."

"Why don't you go home, then?" Massina suggested. "I'm sure Tricia's wondering what's keeping you."

"She could sleep through a hurricane," said Beefy. "Thanks. I'll see you Monday."

TWO HOURS LATER, having showered and done some yoga to loosen up, Massina headed in to his office. He loved coming to work, and Saturdays were his favorite days to be there; while the place was far from empty, his calendar was generally free, allowing him to roam at will. He liked to plant himself at the back of a lab and watch what was going on; he loved listening to conversations among engineers and scientists as they puzzled over problems. True, his presence often made such exchanges stilted, or cut them off prematurely, but he relished even the snippets of true creative endeavor and the conflict it sometimes brought. The words *fail forward* were more than a slogan to him. Wandering around his building kept him close to the hidden energy of the place.

Smart Metal's vast array of projects was both an asset and a detriment from a business point of view—an asset because it continually presented fresh areas of commercialization, and a detriment because it divided the attention not just of Massina but his staff as well. If the company had been publically traded, it would have had to stop and focus on one area or another— probably robotics, as that was not only its most profitable area but also the one with the best growth potential. But that was one of the reasons Massina kept the business private: he wanted Smart Metal to do what he wanted it to do, which was varied and full of possibilities.

Massina went down to what they called "Underground Arena One," a very large workspace under the back of the building. It had been excavated during World War II for some reason no longer remembered, then covered by a two-story addition to the building. During his renovation, Massina had had the floors above the basement gutted so that the space was just under fifty feet high, and completely open; some municipal convention centers were smaller.

Peter—RBT PJT 23.A to Massina—was undergoing new tests this morning on "his" intuition system, the AI component that was supposed to let the robot spontaneously make decisions. The tests were open ended, as the engineers did not know exactly what the machine would do—more or less the point, after all, of the whole spontaneity concept. Massina came in when the robot was surveying a row of cages occupied by puppies. The dogs, curious about the roving mechanical creature, barked wildly as it approached. Massina went over and stood by Chelsea, who was in charge of the AI section and had designed the test.

"What's going to happen?" Massina asked as the robot paused in front of a rather rambunctious Dalmatian.

"I'm not sure."

"What are you going to do if it decides to kill them because they're so loud?"

Chelsea held up the unit's remote. There was only one command showing on the touch screen: STOP.

Massina smirked.

Peter peered in the cage, taking a series of measurements. Then it moved on to the next. Massina went to one of the monitoring units and saw that the bot was primarily interested in the dogs' heartbeats and body temperatures. It worked its way down the row, then came back to the Dalmatian.

The bot reached one of its arms toward the cage. The Dalmatian, which had been barking loudly, quieted, then moved back. Haunches up, it prepared to spring. Massina heard a distinct warning growl above the yip and yap of the other dogs.

Peter withdrew its hand, snapped the lock on the cage, and pulled the door open. Then it backed out.

The bot had decided to free the dogs.

Confused, the Dalmatian hesitated before bolting from its pen. The robot, meanwhile, freed the shepherd mix next to it.

"You better turn it off," Massina told Chelsea, suppressing a laugh. "We'll never round them all up."

Peter managed to free two more dogs before Chelsea pressed the Stop button. The animals took a victory lap around the caged area, then went over and sniffed their savior, perhaps wondering if there was a way they could return the favor. The support team went to work trying to corral them, moving in with treats and leashes.

"I'll bet it thought they were in distress," said Chelsea.

"A good theory," said Massina. "I want to talk to you about something. Maybe upstairs, where things are a little quieter."

"TELL ME WHERE we are with the ATM project," said Massina as he pulled out his desk chair to sit.

"I have to pull together a proposal," said Chelsea. "I didn't get to it—I needed to make sure Peter was ready for the test so we stay on track."

"You have a reasonable idea of what happened with the ATMs, though?"

"Reasonable, yes."

"And it involved the girl?"

"Yes."

"I was wrong." Massina put his elbows on the desk and leaned forward. "I should have told you not to look at the accounts."

"I didn't go into the accounts or the banking system," said Chelsea. "I looked at the video."

"You didn't hack into the systems?"

"No, Lou. Not at all."

"Good. Good on you." He sat back in the chair. "I got carried away about working with the FBI. I should have been more thoughtful."

"OK."

There was a faraway look in his eyes, as if he'd already started thinking about something else.

"The girl," said Chelsea.

"What about her?"

"She's worth saving."

"I'm sure the FBI—"

"They'll throw her in jail," interrupted Chelsea.

"That's not where she belongs?"

"Hell no. And I'm not completely sure it was her," added Chelsea. "Without hacking into the account—"

"Which you're not going to do."

"Check. So I don't know with one hundred percent certainty that it was her."

"But you strongly suspect her."

"Yes."

"Then we have to tell Jenkins that."

"I agree. But I'd like to do it my way. And yes, I think she can be saved. She's not evil. She's just . . . a girl."

65

Boston, an hour later

Borya answered her cell phone as soon as it started to ring.

"Daddy?"

"Borya? This is Chelsea Goodman, from Smart Metal."

"Oh. . . . Hello."

"I was wondering if you'd like to continue your tour today."

"Of your labs? Sure." Borya glanced at Mary Martyak, who was sitting across from her at the kitchen table, finishing her lunch.

Always eating, the fat slob.

"Great," said Chelsea. "I'm just driving up your block."

"You are?"

"Can you come now?"

"Um . . ." Borya searched her mind for an excuse to give Martyak. "Wait a minute."

"What's going on?" asked the babysitter.

"A friend, um . . ."

Martyak looked at her. Borya couldn't find the right words for a plausible lie.

Tell her the truth. Why not?

"A friend of mine wants to give me a tour of this cool lab where they make robots." The words gushed from Borya's mouth.

"Oh?"

"Want to come?" Borya asked.

"Where is it?"

"It's here in Boston."

"We were going to that movie."

"This is way cooler. Let me ask her."

CHELSEA'S PLAN HADN'T included a "friend," but it was obvious that she was more babysitter than friend. As soon as Chelsea determined that Borya's father wasn't around, she decided the babysitter would do, at least temporarily.

Chelsea led them to the SUV. Twenty minutes later, they were sitting in Underground Arena One at Smart Metal, watching as Peter selected one of the dogs—Dusty, a collie-shepherd mix— to go for a walk. The dog pulled eagerly at its leash, venturing around the massive work area in search of interesting smells.

"You don't have to control it?" asked Martyak.

"Only in the most general sense," said Chelsea, trying to keep her explanation to the simplest terms. "It's the same as if I asked a person to take the dog for a walk."

"But you programmed it to do that," said Borya.

"No, we programmed it to learn. It picked up the routine on its own. And it has taught itself how to deal with dogs based on trial and error."

It might not sound like much to a layman, Chelsea continued, but for a computer system, it was extremely advanced. It wouldn't be long before commercial versions of "home assistants" would be available, and capable of much more complicated tasks. A robotic home assistant could stay with a bedridden patient, fetching medicine and common items, even making the bed and cooking a simple meal.

"It's kind of creepy," said Martyak.

"I think it's cool," insisted Borya.

Chelsea let the robot run through its paces for a while longer, then suggested they go upstairs to her lab to look at some of the coding. When they got there, she asked if either of them wanted something to drink.

"I'll take a root beer," said Borya.

"Me, too," said Martyak. "But uh, first—can I use the restroom?"

"It's right down the hall on the left," said Chelsea. She waited until Martyak was out of the room, then tapped her computer screen. "Take a look at this, Borya," she said as a page of coding filled the screen.

The girl leaned in and began examining the program. She squinted, then began to pale.

"I know what you did," said Chelsea. "With the ATM machines? I got the coding off the dark net myself, just as you did."

"I . . ."

"You're going to get in a lot of trouble. But I have a way out for you. We need to talk to your dad."

"You're going to tell him?"

"You should tell him. Can you give the money back?"

Borya didn't say anything.

"You've stolen quite a lot," said Chelsea. "This is very serious. The FBI—"

"I can give it back," blurted Borya. "But my dad—he's missing! He was supposed to call me and he hasn't. And he hasn't answered our code. He must be in big trouble."

She started to cry.

66

Donetsk, that day

The day did not go well.

Clearly no longer trusting him, Dan didn't want to let Tolevi out of his sight. Tolevi accordingly changed plans, deciding that he would take up Dan's offer to drive him to Crimea; he could fly from there or, if things seemed to be going south, call on contacts for help. It was a better option than inadvertently leading Dan to Denyx Fodor.

He put off telling Dan, deciding to get a better idea of what was going on in the city, since they wouldn't leave until night in any event. They visited several cafés and coffee shops that morning; Tolevi began asking about coffee, warming to the idea of importing the commodity. In the afternoon, he went into a few pharmacies, checking their stocks. Coffee and aspirin would be big moneymakers here, he decided; too bad the bearded colonel had declared him persona non gratis.

Maybe that could be reversed.

Tolevi watched Dan's reactions as he chatted up the shopkeepers. He was curious, a hustler himself no doubt, smart enough to be quiet.

Maybe it would make sense to partner up. If Dan got him to Crimea: That would be the first test.

By mid-afternoon, Tolevi wanted—needed—a nap. Dan insisted on staying in the room as he slept. That was more than a little awkward, but Dan couldn't be talked out of it, so Tolevi caught a fitful hour and a half of sleep, ending up feeling more tired than when he lay down.

They had dinner at the hotel. Tolevi felt Dan's eyes on him as if they were a physical thing, rubbing against his temples, scratching at his throat.

"Let's go for a walk," he suggested when they were done.

Two blocks later, he asked Dan what it would cost to get him to Crimea.

"Round trip, two thousand euros."

"I can get you five hundred, for one way," said Tolevi. "When we get there."

"One thousand five hundred, all in advance."

Tolevi laughed. "I'm not so stupid that I would pay anyone for that trip in advance, not even my own brother. And I don't have the money, besides."

"Then pay me now for the trip here, and we're done."

"We can do that," said Tolevi.

They continued walking, still heading away from the hotel. After a block, Dan stopped him.

"I would consider taking the money when we got to Crimea," he said, "if you pay me the money you already owe me now."

"You have papers if we're stopped at the border?" Tolevi asked.

"We won't be stopped. I know several ways."

"I'll tell you what. I'll give five hundred euros before we leave, and two thousand in Crimea when I arrive. But first we have to do one thing."

"Name it."

"I need to get a gun. I'm not going near the border with no defense."

BUYING A GUN in Donetsk was harder than Tolevi would have guessed. There were several gun stores in the city, including one not far from the hotel, but all had been closed since the beginning of the war. Dan claimed not to know of anyone who would sell one, and Tolevi finally decided he would have to use one of his business contacts to get the weapon. Using Dan's phone, he called him, and after buttering him up with talk about importing medicine and coffee, he found him willing to help. In fact, the man was so cheerful about it, telling him not only where to go but also saying he could use his name, that Tolevi felt a little guilty. If the Russians were listening in, they would roll the shopkeeper up by the end of the week.

The gun dealer worked out of a club on the eastern side of the city. The area had become something of an unlikely hot spot in the past few months, with young Donetskers flocking there after hours to hear dance music and lose themselves in alcohol and whatever drugs they could find. Even at this early hour, the district streets were full, which seemed to throw Dan as he hunted for a place to park.

"Just drop me and wait," Tolevi told him as he went around the block.

"I'm coming in."

"These things are better done alone."

"I'm coming in."

"You've been in this place before?"

"Never."

"Try the next block. Let's not get too close."

Even three blocks away, it was hard to find a spot. Dan locked the car, checked the door twice to make sure, then ran to catch up to Tolevi, who had assumed his jaunty, no-one-better-screw-with-me step. Tolevi glanced at Dan's face as he caught up; he had the look of a worried younger brother.

Under other circumstances, Tolevi might have been amused, but at the moment any sign of vulnerability was potentially a fatal liability. He whirled on Dan. "Hike up your game."

"What?" stuttered Dan.

"You walk like a scared rabbit. Go in confident, or stay here."

"I don't know what you're talking about."

"Pretend you're a gangster," Tolevi told him. "And walk like it. Or we're dead meat."

The quizzical look on Dan's face made it clear he still didn't understand. Tolevi gave up, charging toward the club.

It was barely midafternoon, way early for a place like this, but two bouncers looked over anyone who wanted to enter.

"I have business with Mr. Ivan," Tolevi told the one with the more intelligent face.

The bouncer looked at Dan.

"He's with me." Tolevi brushed past, walking with the swift determination of a veteran party crasher. The door led to a wide ramp that made an L turn after twenty feet; there was another bouncer stationed there, though all he did was glare as Tolevi passed. A set of double doors separated the hallway from a large dance area that vibrated with Euro electric pop. It was Western music circa 1995, an odd choice for Donetsk, but then there was no telling what sort of psychological undercurrents ran through the population, especially the younger crowd that frequented the place.

The dance floor was surprisingly crowded. Women in skirts that barely covered their butt cracks gyrated around and between men wearing jeans so tight they could only be eunuchs. Colored lights throbbed from above in no discernible pattern; a five-year-old playing with a light switch would have produced roughly the same effect.

Tolevi angled through the dancers to the bar area on the right. It was an odd contraption. A third of it was wrapped in black leather with Christmas lights stapled into the fabric; another third was a pressboard frame, unfinished except for the cherry bar top. The final third extended the same bar top on sawhorses. The bar was standing room only, and not much of that. Tolevi squeezed in, ordered himself a vodka, and asked the bartender where Mr. Ivan might be.

The bartender thumbed toward the back. Tolevi took his

drink and set off in that direction, expecting to find either rooms or, maybe, a table. But though a shade darker because of the way the lights were fixed, there were neither tables nor rooms back there, just more dancers and would-be dancers, milling around in time to the beat. Tolevi resorted to asking people if they knew where Mr. Ivan was; this got him a few blank stares, but mostly he was ignored or unheard.

After a few minutes of this, he lost his patience. He went back to the bar and found the man who had served him. Holding up a hundred-euro note, he lured the man to him—it was a miracle the way cash got someone's attention.

Grinning, the bartender leaned toward him.

Tolevi lurched forward, grabbing the bartender by the throat. "Take me to Mr. Ivan. *Now.*"

The bartender started to object. Tolevi tightened his grip, then shoved the man to the right, where the bar section turned into a sawhorse. He reached under and hauled the man out. Then, with a push, he set him in motion, his fist holding the back of the bartender's shirt.

Mr. Ivan turned out to be a young man in a print silk shirt staring at a pair of women who were dancing a few feet away.

Tolevi pushed the bartender aside.

"Ivan, a friend sent me." Tolevi spoke to him in Ukrainian. "We need to talk."

"Who are you?"

"I need to make a purchase."

"You are Russian?"

"Don't worry about who I am," said Tolevi. "Doneski sent me."

Ivan nodded, then began walking directly through the crowd. Tolevi followed, ignoring the bartender's complaints about the hundred-euro note.

You're lucky I don't throttle you. I am normally a peaceful man, but when I am pushed, it is too much. And I have been pushed for too many days now.

Mr. Ivan went out the front door and headed around the block to a black BMW 7 series that had to be nearly twenty years old. He popped open the trunk, revealing three large suitcases. He opened each, setting up a display in the back of the car, oblivious to the people who were passing.

"How much for the Sig?" Tolevi asked, pointing to the P226. The .40 caliber weapon looked to be the best of the bunch, which included a pair of 9mm Berettas and two Russian pistols Tolevi wouldn't even consider. The Sig was a bit too large to be easily hidden, which was a drawback, but Tolevi thought its other advantages—the rounds it fired, as well as the fact that it could pack twelve of them—made it the obvious choice.

"Two thousand euros," replied Mr. Ivan.

"A hundred," said Tolevi.

It was a ridiculously low offer, insulting even. Mr. Ivan batted it away with a wave of his hand. "Two thousand."

"Five hundred."

This time the gun dealer shook his head. Tolevi said nothing. Two thousand euros was about two and a half times what the gun would go for in the States. But even if it was a reasonable price for a quality gun in Donetsk, it represented just about all the cash Tolevi had, in euros at least.

When Tolevi didn't make a counteroffer, Mr. Ivan reached back into the trunk and began closing the cases, starting with the case that held the Russian weapons.

"Wait," said Tolevi. "Seven-fifty. Let me see it."

"Two thousand," insisted Mr. Ivan.

The impatience Tolevi had felt a little while earlier returned. He leaned closer to the man. "A thousand cash," he snarled in a low voice, "with six magazines and bullets."

Mr. Ivan glanced over the back of the car at a large man in a black T-shirt. The thug leaned forward, as if ready to pounce, but stopped as the dealer shook his head ever so slightly.

"Two magazines," said Mr. Ivan. "With the bullets. One thousand. Now, and be gone."

"Let me see the gun," said Tolevi.

Mr. Ivan dropped the mag and cleared the chamber, making sure it wasn't loaded, before handing it to Tolevi.

At least he's not stupid.

The weapon sat heavy in his hand, a reassuring feeling. It looked clean and, if not brand-new, only very gently used. The trigger was light. There was no way to fire it here, though; he had to trust that Mr. Ivan valued his reputation.

Ha.

Tolevi slid the gun into his waistband and fished out a thousand euros. Mr. Ivan handed over the loaded magazines and they were done. Tolevi quickly darted across the street, earning a hail of horns. He trotted around the corner, spotting Dan and the car coming from the opposite direction. He ran across traffic again as Dan pulled the car to the curb. Tolevi jumped in.

"I thought you got lost," Tolevi told Dan, pulling on his seat belt. "Let's go back to the hotel and get our stuff. I'm done here."

Tolevi, busy loading the pistol and familiarizing himself with its feel, didn't recognize where they were until he saw the storefront.

"Where are you going?" he demanded, jerking the gun toward Dan.

"Relax, and don't point that thing at me," said Dan, speaking in English. He slowed as they passed the butcher shop, but he didn't stop.

"Who are you?" Tolevi switched to English as well. "Who are you *really?*"

"A friend of a friend. You missed your connection last night," added Dan. "Luckily, the Russians missed the brother."

As they turned the corner, a short, thin man, barely five-four, stepped from the shadows and walked toward the curb.

"Don't stop," said Tolevi.

"If we don't, I suspect the man on the roof at the end of the block will shoot us both," said Dan. "Put the gun away. It'll make them nervous."

67

Boston—about the same time

Trevor Jenkins wasn't sure what he expected when Massina asked him to come to the office late Saturday afternoon, but it absolutely wasn't an attorney, let alone one with a proffer already filled out.

"There's no way I can go along with this," the FBI special agent protested as he finished reading the legal document.

"It's very straightforward," said the attorney. "Restitution guaranteed by Mr. Massina personally, and an explanation of the technique, in exchange for a guarantee of no prosecution. You do it all the time."

"No, we don't."

"I can call the U.S. attorney myself if you want," said the lawyer. His name was Jasper Lloyd; he was one of the top criminal lawyers in the state. "I'm sure he won't mind."

"You don't understand how complicated this is," said Jenkins.

"We're making it uncomplicated."

"I already have a suspect."

"As far as we know, you have the wrong suspect," said the attorney. "And here we can not only solve a crime but prevent future ones as well."

"You're withholding evidence in a federal investigation," said Jenkins.

Lloyd made the slightest of shrugs, as if what Jenkins said was beside the point.

Jenkins turned to Massina, who was sitting across from him at the large conference room table. Chelsea Goodman was next to him.

"No," Jenkins repeated. "I'm not letting him off."

"You have the wrong person," said Lloyd.

Massina rose. "Let's you and I go in the other room for a minute."

Jenkins followed him through the door that led to Massina's office. The building was an amazing mix of architecture, from the nineteenth-century brick exterior shell to the sleek surfaces of the interior walls and floor. The furniture on the upper floor was all exotic wood and looked as if it had just come from a showroom. But Jenkins wasn't here to admire the decorating job.

"You're not going to prosecute a fifteen-year-old girl," said Massina as soon as the door was closed.

"What are you talking about?"

"You haven't solved the case, have you?" said Massina.

"Like hell. As soon as Gabor Tolevi comes back to the States, we move in. We already worked that out."

"First of all, he's missing," said Massina. "And second of all, he's not the one who did this."

"What do you mean?"

"Maybe you should go back inside and call the U.S. attorney. Agree to the terms, sign on the dotted line, and then we'll explain. Everything will work out, I guarantee."

"You guarantee?"

Was this the same man who had sat with Jenkins and his wife all day when their daughter was being operated on and then fitted with the prosthetic? He had seemed so kind then, and understanding. Jenkins knew that Massina was no fool; not only was he a Boston native but no one could do business on the scale he did without a good helping of street sense. Still, his tone and the sharp-elbow approach didn't quite jibe with the man Jenkins thought he knew.

"Do you trust me, Trevor?" asked Massina, sounding for just a moment like the kind man who had helped give Jenkins's daughter a new lease on life. The words were exactly those he had used when they'd hesitated about the operations.

Do you trust me?

He'd nodded. What choice had he had? To see his daughter walk again, he'd have done anything.

And now?

What choice did he have, really?

"Let me call my boss," he told Massina.

BORYA LOOKED UP as Chelsea came into the room.

"We need you now," she said. "Are you ready?"

"Did you find my dad?"

"We're working on that," Chelsea told her. "That's going to take a little time."

"Where is he?" asked Martyak. "He really should be involved. It's his decision."

"This is what's best for Borya," Chelsea told her. "And he can choose to ratify it or not. But otherwise, she's going to jail. And for a long time. These are serious crimes."

Borya lowered her head. If her father hadn't been missing, all of this would have been different. She'd have been able to tough it out.

But losing him was too much. She felt as if she'd been stabbed with a knife a hundred times.

God, please, get him back. Make them help me! Get him back.

Borya glanced over at Beefy Bozzone, who'd been keeping them company, playing cards and telling her stories about dogs he'd owned. He seemed to have had nearly a hundred of them, with a particular fondness for pugs, " 'cause you just about keep 'em in your pocket."

His pocket, maybe. He was big.

"Are you going to come with me?" she asked him.

"No one's gonna hurt you," he told her.

"I know, but—"

"Yeah, I'll come," said Beefy. "And you guys owe me twenty cents and fifty-five," pointing first to Borya, then to Martyak. "Don't forget."

"What?" asked Chelsea.

"Card game," he explained. "A debt's a debt."

68

Tolevi brooded silently as they drove, angry with himself for not figuring out that Dan was a plant. It was the sort of mistake that could have gotten him killed—and still might.

The butcher's brother sat behind him in the car. Aside from answering Tolevi's question—"Are you the brother?"—in the affirmative, he'd said only one thing since getting in the car: "*Starobeshevskaya.*"

It turned out that Starobeshevskaya was a small city centered around a power plant some forty-five minutes south of Donetsk. The power plant and city were separated from the surrounding area on the north and west by a wide lake and reservoir. Security was intense; they were stopped at a checkpoint a mile from the only bridge on that side of the water, and nothing Dan said about "urgent business" could convince the poorly dressed rebel guard to let them through. His gun was persuasive, but the two cars parked across the approach made it clear this was not going to be the way into town.

They drove back about three kilometers and turned south, circling around the lake to approach the area from the east. There was another checkpoint; this time Tolevi handled it.

"I have business with the mayor," he said in dismissive Russian, leaning across Dan as he rolled down the window. "We're late."

The man asked for their identity papers.

"We're Russian, you idiot," said Tolevi.

He grabbed Dan's ID before he could give it to the guard. "Drive!" he demanded.

Flustered, Dan threw the car into gear and drove ahead.

"Awful ballsy," he said when they were clear.

"Sometimes you just have to play the part," said Tolevi.

"He'll probably call ahead," said the brother from the back. He spoke in Ukrainian, while Dan and Tolevi had used Russian.

"That'll be fine," said Tolevi.

"Where do we go?" asked Dan.

"To the prison." Tolevi turned around. "Tell me about your brother. Tell me everything you know."

THE BUTCHER—OLAK URUM—had been a member of the rebellion until a few months before. But he had fallen out with the leadership over two issues: first, he had opposed Russian "assistance" in the revolution, believing it would not only taint the movement but also lead to annexation, something he didn't want. And second, he had become disillusioned over the amount of corruption in the newly installed "People's Government." Apparently he had made the mistake of protesting this to the head of the Donetsk People's Army Council—the rebel leadership, of which he was a member—and had subsequently been arrested on trumped-up corruption charges. The butcher owned the shop; the brother was just a helper.

"The charges, they could make them because we always had meat," said the butcher's brother. He hadn't bothered to give his first name. Tolevi decided that was fine; the less he knew, the better. "Even in the worst time, with the blockade, our shop was open."

"And how did you manage that?" asked Tolevi.

"I don't know. My brother handled the business always."

Tolevi was skeptical—chickens were one thing, but only someone very well connected would be able to bring in large quantities of good beef.

"The people at the prison, did they know your brother before he was arrested?" Tolevi asked.

"I don't think so."

"Your brother wants to be saved?"

"He wants to liberate all of Ukraine," said the brother. "He has information to expose the rebels. They are very corrupt. A reunion with the west is the only way."

It wasn't the most heartfelt declaration, Tolevi thought, but he wasn't here to judge where the man's ultimate loyalties lay. He was just here to get him the hell out of Donetsk.

The Starobeshevskaya power plant was a massive installation. It burned coal; despite claims that it was one of the "greenest" plants in Eastern Europe, a heavy smog hung over the region as they drove toward the town that supported it.

If the brother's story was true, freeing the butcher would be relatively easy, so long as Tolevi could come up with the money. Dan's presence convinced him that wouldn't be a problem; he suspected that Johansen simply wanted a bit of distance between the Agency and the rebels if things went wrong. But before he could start spending the CIA's money, he needed to get a feel for the situation. Who was the highest authority? Was the "mayor" beholden to the rebels who guarded the prison, or vice versa? Where were the Russians in all this?

Hopefully far away.

He also wanted to find out about the prison itself. If, as with many Ukrainian facilities, the prison was old and ill maintained, it might be easiest to bribe a few guards and skip the mayor or warden completely.

The first order of business was gathering information, and the best place to do that was in the local bars. Tolevi assigned Dan and the brother a job: find a good place to stay in town, the nearer city hall, the better. And then he went to drink in some gossip.

69

Many things about Johnny Givens's new "condition" were strange, but the weirdest were the shoes.

The feet on his prosthetic legs had been designed to replicate his "original" feet, so that as much as possible walking felt like it always had been. And it did. Except when it came to putting on the shoes.

While Johnny had considerable control over his "feet" and could even wiggle his toes, the prosthetics could not be manipulated to quite the same degree as his "original" feet. This made it hard to get his old shoes on without a shoehorn. Even with a shoehorn it could be difficult; it was far easier to put the shoes on the feet when they were off his body. But though physically easier, mentally it was very difficult—there was no more obvious example that he was now literally half the man he had been.

And it was just strange, like dressing a mannequin. Only he was the mannequin.

Johnny adjusted the shoes and then began strapping the legs to his stumps. Unlike "conventional" prosthetic legs, Massina's version used feedback via the nerve endings in what remained of his upper thighs to communicate with his brain, interfacing through a series of contacts implanted in the stumps. The arrangement didn't fool his brain into thinking that he still had his original legs, but the feeling was close, as if he'd put on a heavy snowsuit and clunky boots.

Eventually, it might all feel very familiar, and even comfortable. Eventually.

In the meantime, there was enough flex, as well as support, in the prosthetics to allow him not only to walk but also to run fairly well. In fact, he could run faster and with far less fatigue, thanks to actuators in the leg that literally put a spring into his step. He suspected that he might do extremely well in next year's marathon, assuming he was in shape to enter.

Which meant a lot of running in the meantime. And for want of something better to do, he decided to start training that evening.

One leg at a time, just like always.

Gestapo Bitch's joke. He liked her now, admired the way she had goaded him into working harder and harder. She was the perfect bitch, as good as the drugs he was taking, maybe even better.

Johnny strapped on his legs and connected the electrodes. He pulled on his pants, making sure the Velcro straps at the bottom were secure; the pants had always been a tiny bit big.

They were *very* big at the waist now. Amazing how much weight he'd lost.

Don't need to stretch these babies. Just grab the phone, some backup dough, and rock 'n' roll.

Johnny slipped his wallet clip—which held his FBI creds, a credit card, and a few bucks in cash—into his pocket, next to the phone, and hit the road.

70

Starobeshevskaya village—after midnight

The mayor was, by all accounts, a man of extremely sober reputation, completely incorruptible.

The deputy mayor, on the other hand, was open to all offers, intending to make as much as he possibly could before he was fifty, then cash in and move to Crete. Crete was not only the most beautiful place in the world but it was also the home of the world's most beautiful women, and when he was rich, the deputy mayor was going to bed them all, one by one. This was his God-given right, and anyone who stood in his way would answer for it.

Tolevi heard all of this from the deputy mayor himself, who held forth at кінської голови—Kins' koyi Holovy, or Horse Head, a bar two blocks from town hall. The man weighed three hundred and fifty pounds if he weighed an ounce, and however he had managed to get his job, his fellow citizens, at least those in the bar, gave him a wide berth. He had a volatile temper, which he hinted at as he spoke, gesticulating wildly even when making a mild point. Three times as he and Tolevi spoke about the power plant and the local coal that fed it—the most benign subject Tolevi could imagine, short of the weather—the deputy mayor balled his fist up and slammed it on the table.

Tolevi could not have wished for a better person to deal with, temper or no. After most of the bar's patrons had cleared out for the night, he suggested that they move to a table near the back.

"Why?" asked the deputy mayor.

"Maybe we can do business," said Tolevi nonchalantly.

"What business?" The tone could not have been less pleasant if Tolevi had threatened to rape the man's daughter. "What business with you, Russian?"

"I am actually from America," said Tolevi. "And my business is bringing things to Ukraine, where my family was born."

"What things?"

"Aspirin, cough medicine. And real coffee."

"You can import these things to my town?"

"Let's get a bottle and talk."

THE DEPUTY MAYOR was fond of single malt scotch whisky, expensive under any conditions but outrageously priced here. Tolevi put down three hundred euro for a bottle of Macallan 12-year, which represented a markup approaching ten times what the original would have cost at the distillery.

He brought the bottle back to the table and poured the deputy mayor a drink, three fingers of scotch *neat,* no ice, no chaser.

The Ukrainian took the glass in hand, toasted the room, guzzled the liquor, and slid the glass back for a refill.

"Where's yours?" he asked Tolevi as he took back the glass.

"I don't like scotch."

"I don't drink alone."

Sociable devil, aren't you?

Tolevi reluctantly went to the bar for a glass and some ice. By the time he came back, the deputy mayor had drunk about a quarter of the bottle.

"So what is your business?" asked the deputy mayor.

"As I said, I bring things across the border," said Tolevi. "My business is mainly in Crimea, but I'm looking to branch out."

"Why here?"

"Because there is money to be made," said Tolevi.

"We have our suppliers."

"The shelves are bare in the pharmacies. No aspirin. And many other things."

The deputy mayor shrugged. Clearly the man was a dolt.

"Band-Aids," continued Tolevi. "Cough medicine—"

"We have many such items in town with the plant. They can get us anything we want. We are richer than Donetsk by far. Richer than Kiev. Even than Moscow."

"How's your coffee?" asked Tolevi.

It was the magic word. The deputy mayor lowered his drink.

"Tell me more about your business project," he said. "How exactly does it work?"

71

Massina watched the girl as she described what she had done. Much of it was simply adapting program code she had found on so-called black sites on the dark Web—an illegal area used by hackers and other miscreants for various illegal purposes. She had a good understanding of how the different systems worked, and she knew how to look for "holes" or problems inherent in the programming.

She was creative. She was young. She was smart.

The question: Was she inherently evil? Or just a kid who needed guidance?

Chelsea was convinced it was the latter. But Massina could tell by looking at her face that she had some doubts as well.

Not that she would admit them to him.

Giving back the money was the first step. The girl hadn't spent much; by the FBI's accounting, less than five thousand. He'd agreed to guarantee a full recovery, which meant he'd be out that.

An investment? Or just a good deed?

What would Sister Rose Marie say?

Kiss it up to God, Louis.

Easy for a nun to say. They kissed everything up to God.

Jenkins and the U.S. attorney had gone home, as had his attorney. Massina, Chelsea, Borya, and her babysitter, who looked as if she'd been hit by a car, were the only ones in the conference room adjoining his office. Together, they'd finished off nearly two pizzas—one thing he could say for the kid, she could eat. The remains of the second pizza were in the box at the far end of the table.

He cleared his throat. "This is what I think," he told her. "When your father comes home, he will review the arrangement my lawyer has worked out. You will give all of the money back."

The girl nodded.

"The money that you've spent, you'll pay off," Massina continued, "by working here. Assuming your father is OK with that."

"How much will I get paid?" she asked.

"We pay our interns fifteen dollars an hour." It was a made-up figure—they had no interns. "You will work directly under Ms. Goodman's supervision. If there is any hint of illegal activity, you will be fired. You understand that?"

Borya nodded.

"If your schoolwork slips, you will be laid off."

She nodded again.

"You are a very lucky girl," added Massina. "Ms. Goodman believes in you. As for me—the jury is out."

"What does that mean?" asked Borya.

"It means that you have to prove yourself," said Chelsea. "You have to be on your best behavior."

"And you'll find my dad?"

"We're working on that," said Massina.

CHELSEA WASN'T SURE whether it was the fatigue or the reality of what she had agreed to do. Whichever, she felt as if an immense weight of iron had settled onto her shoulders.

Borya was clearly worried about her father. When he turned out to be fine—which Jenkins said was surely the case, after checking with his superiors—how would Borya react? Would she renege on the whole deal?

Then she'd go to jail. Juvenile probably, according to the lawyer, though there was always a chance she could be prosecuted as an adult.

That would be a tremendous waste.

"Mr. Bozzone will drive you home," Massina told Borya and Martyak. "He or someone on his staff will stay at your house until your father comes home."

"I think we'll be OK," said Martyak.

"No. I want someone there," said Massina. He got up. "We're done here. Chelsea, can I see you for a moment in my office?"

Chelsea started to say good-bye to Borya. The girl hugged her, pressing tight against her chest.

"It'll be all right," Chelsea told her. "I promise."

Don't make promises you can't keep!

She walked out with them to the hallway, where Beefy was waiting. Then she went to Massina's office and knocked on the door.

"Come," he said from inside.

He was sitting at his desk, thinking about something, hand supporting his chin.

"I know I have a lot to do," Chelsea started. "I'll make up for it tomorrow."

"No one works on Sunday," he said. "And relax. Peter is on schedule. I was impressed with the demonstration today. The bot will be fine for the demos."

"Thank you."

"You'll have to get the ATM proposals into shape for a new team to take over," he told her. "Make that your priority Monday."

"Right, boss."

He frowned. "So you trust her?"

"I think so."

"I suppose I should ask you what your confidence level is," he said. There was the slightest hint of wryness in his voice—the term was one they used when assessing the likely outcome of an experiment. "Have a good night."

72

Starobeshevskaya village—first light

The hotel Dan and the butcher's brother found in Starobeshevskaya was a scurvy place, filled with rats and smelling of stale cigarette smoke. Tolevi managed a few hours of sleep on sheets that looked as if they hadn't been washed in months. Between that and the aftereffects of the scotch he'd had to consume with the deputy mayor, he felt as if he'd been dragged through a field at the back of a bulldozer, then run over a few times.

But there was work to be done. And now with the lay of the land exposed, he felt energized. He went downstairs and found Dan and the butcher's brother sitting in the hotel's small dining area, waiting for food.

"We're getting eggs," said Dan in his accented Ukrainian.

The kitchen was through a door to the left. Tolevi could see an old woman working at a stove. She was wearing a housedress; her gray hair was tied in a long braid that reached halfway down her back.

"I wouldn't trust it," Tolevi told them. "How's the coffee?"

"Terrible."

At that, he smiled.

The old woman walked out, wiping her hands on a towel. "For breakfast?"

"I'll have some coffee," he told her.

"Yes, yes. And what else?"

"Just that."

"You must eat. You are skin and bones."

"Just coffee. Where do you get your coffee?" he asked.

"Ahhh. Our troubles! We once had the finest coffee in the world. Now look at us. Nowhere can we find any that is good. We buy from Russia."

She spit, shook her head, then went back to the kitchen.

"She's right," said the butcher's brother. "This is terrible."

"Opportunity knocks," said Tolevi. "In the meantime, a full agenda today. Tell her I'll take a rain check."

"What are we doing?" asked Dan, starting to rise.

"You, not a thing. I have to talk to some people."

"You need backup."

"No, I don't," Tolevi told him. "Let me do what I do."

TEN MINUTES LATER, Tolevi pushed a business card across the desk of the young man sitting at the entrance to the deputy mayor's office. Though he was already losing his hair, the young man couldn't have been a day past twenty-one. His face was a blotch of pimples, which ranged in color from bright pink to crusty red, and in size from microdots to a jagged mass about the size of an American dime. The latter had the misfortune of sitting on the young man's forehead and was a great distraction as Tolevi explained that he had come to talk business with the kid's boss.

"You're far too early," he said, studying Tolevi's card. "He is never here before noon."

"He told me eight."

"Ha. You can never trust what he says after five."

Five drinks or five o'clock? Tolevi wondered.

"We were going to the prison to visit the warden," he told the young man. "Can you arrange that?"

"I am not sure."

"Try. It has to do with a business deal the warden may be interested in."

"It wouldn't have been the warden. The warden is in Donetsk."

"Who would it be then?"

The young man simply frowned and picked up the phone. Tolevi listened as he spoke to his counterpart at the prison.

"Olga Uvenski will see you in a half hour," announced the aide. "If you leave now, you may get there in time. Security takes a while."

It did, though not because it was thorough, which it was. The problem was that Tolevi had to run through the gamut of pat downs and metal detectors three different times, and more importantly had to be escorted from each by different guards, each of whom could be summoned only after a successful search. The guards took their time coming, responding from somewhere deep inside the complex—a cave perhaps, as they looked like Neanderthals and smelled not a little like sewage.

The prison was relatively new, with thick cement block walls, heavy steel gates, and generous rolls of razor wire even in the interior hallways. You couldn't run in a straight line for more than twenty meters due to either barriers or the wire; there was even one twist-back on the large main stairway that led to the administrative section. Dozens of guards were scattered around, armed with long riot batons. Most were dressed in ill-fitting uniforms, and Tolevi got the sense that they were here more as a make-work project than out of any real need for security. A few joked, many listened to music on their phones, and nearly all were smoking cigarettes when he passed.

"You're late," said Olga Uvenski's assistant when Tolevi finally arrived. The assistant was about the same age as the deputy mayor's, but that was all they had in common. His skin was clear; tall and trim, he could have passed as a model.

"I apologize," said Tolevi. "Is Ms. Uvenski in?"

"Wait."

Tolevi sat in a leather seat at the side and folded his arms. The office was a few ticks above what he had expected, the furniture on par with what you'd find in the waiting room of a prosperous law firm in Boston.

That was a good sign.

Even better was the spring in Olga Uvenski's step as she came out to meet him.

"A friend of Victor's is a friend of mine," she said, ushering himself inside.

Her office was decked out in enough fresh flowers to make a florist weep for joy. The furniture was even more impressive than what was in the waiting room. Her desk's front featured an eagle head inlaid in cherry and oak, so highly polished that Tolevi could see a reflection of his shoes.

This was definitely his world, a place that knew no nationalities, where greed and weakness made anything possible. They were the counter to power, the remedy to the brutal Darwinian way of the universe, and even to the laws of physics. If you had money and wiles, you could escape any tyranny, or at least turn it to your advantage.

"And so, why did Victor send you?" Uvenski asked after her assistant brought them a tray of fresh tea.

"I notice that you offer tea rather than coffee," said Tolevi, holding up his cup.

"You prefer coffee?"

"I suspect that you would, too, if the coffee were good."

"Possibly."

"Let me be frank. The deputy mayor and I are working on an arrangement that would provide coffee, among other things, to the area," said Tolevi, launching into his pitch. "Good coffee, from South America. He is, well, I think of him as a franchisee.

I import different things to parts of the world where they are sometimes not available. As you can tell from my accent, I am American, in a way."

"You speak well. Your accent led me to believe you were Russian."

"I have family there and in what is now west Ukraine, as well as the Donetsk People's Republic." He stepped lightly here, moving quickly. "A facility such as yours must need many items. I can supply them. I need to be able to bring things in bulk," he added as an explanation. "To cover my costs. Unfortunately, they are significant, as you might guess."

"What items would we need here?"

"Perhaps you would tell me."

Uvenski, until now very neutral, leaned forward and, with a few words, showed why she ruled this domain. "I purchase items for the prison and the plant," she told him with a sharp edge. "All items. Luxuries such as coffee are not needed here."

"Ah well then, I guess my friend was simply making conversation." Tolevi rose. "I'm sorry to have wasted your time."

"Sit down, Mr. Tolevi. And let's talk business. Meat. Beef. And yes, coffee. Fifty percent to me."

"That's a heavy percentage."

"Half in goods, half cash."

"Still. I have so many expenses. If those are taken into account—"

"Sit. Drink some more tea. Forty percent in cash, the rest in goods."

"At that price, then I would need favors," said Tolevi. "Another way for me to earn money, perhaps in a way you can't. Some old employees are kept here. They would save me costs if they were on my payroll."

"I do not think that is possible."

"What if their parole were purchased? As part of the payment, one or two thrown in, for good will."

"My good will or yours?"

"I have many high expenses. Forty percent—I doubt I can get a contract worth enough if the Russians oversee it. And without them, importation is too dangerous."

"They don't oversee anything. My budget comes from the Republic's government, and with the power plant, we have a lot of leeway. I can guarantee the goods will arrive."

"Forty percent then, and a dozen men."

"Who?"

"I'll supply a list."

"If I wanted to make money that way, their families could pay me directly," said Uvenski.

"Until one complained. Then you would find yourself accused of blackmail. Whereas if I did it, I am to blame."

"Forty percent. I give you ten prisoners. You pay ten thousand euros per prisoner up front. I pick them."

"You'll pick people who can't pay. I make the list. That's a deal breaker. And you have to come down in price. My margins are very slim."

Johansen would consider ten thousand euros to bail out the butcher a bargain. But one had to bargain.

"That's my final offer."

"Forget the prisoners," he told her. "I don't really know that business anyway. It was Victor who mentioned it, as a possible way of paying for the arrangements. I don't need complications."

"So, we have a deal?"

"I can't afford it, even at forty percent. I'm sorry." Tolevi rose to go. "Maybe some small shipments, something easy like aspirin or Band-Aids. But beyond that, to get coffee. I only get the best, because I drink it, and so it's absurdly expensive. Everyone holds you up. So many payoffs just getting it on the ship."

"Sit, Mr. Tolevi. Certainly we can work this out."

BY THE TIME Tolevi emerged from the office, he had a tentative deal to supply the prison with medicine, coffee, and cigarettes at regular intervals for the next six months. To seal the deal, he would provide an up-front payment of ten thousand euros, to be transferred by wire to an account in Crete by the end of the week. In return, he would receive two prisoners, both of whom she said he could choose.

She then gave him a few suggestions, along with an idea of what he could probably get for them.

The butcher was not on her list, a minor matter—or so he hoped.

Tolevi got a tour of the facility on the way out. His guide— Uvenski's assistant—walked him across a bridge that ran on the border of the exercise yard into an older brick building used as a storehouse for supplies. There was no direct connection between the building and the outside world; supplies had to be hand-carried past the outer wall and the rows of razor wire.

The aide was quite proud of this. Tolevi suppressed his disappointment.

Worse was the isolated building at the back end of the compound. This was a small, cubelike structure surrounded by a barbed-wire-topped fence and numerous warning signs indicating that the ground was mined on both sides of the fence.

"What's in there?" Tolevi asked.

"Traitors."

Back at municipal hall, the deputy mayor had not yet reported for work.

"You might have better luck looking for him where you found him last night," suggested the young man.

"I'll give that a try," said Tolevi, anxious to close the deal.

73

Even the most insanely dedicated Smart Metal worker—and the description would apply to just about everyone—did not work on Sundays. That was an unbreakable rule set by Massina himself, and often enforced by a personal walkthrough shortly after midnight. As hard as he pushed his people, he thought the day off was critical for creativity—as well as religious observance, though this was unstated in his company's policies.

He also liked having the building entirely to himself for a few hours.

The no-work policy was well known and absolute, so when he heard what sounded like footsteps below as he walked through the third-floor hallway, he dismissed the sound at first, thinking it just ambient echo of his own steps. But then the noise grew louder, and he thought he heard a whisper.

"Who is that?" he said aloud. "What's going on?"

There was no answer.

Foolish. Massina walked to the security station near the elevator and tapped the screen. Everyone's tag was coded, and the system kept track of everyone in the building. So it was a simple matter of typing a command to identify who was here.

It was him. With two guests.

"But I'm on the third floor, and they're on the first," Massina told the machine.

He clicked the rescan command, unsure whether he had typed a wrong command. But the system repeated the information. It was showing two Louis Massinas were in the building.

Which ought to have been an impossibility.

Massina lost himself in the problem for a moment. He was sure duplicate employees would set off an alarm within the system; both sets of IDs would be locked down and an alert would be sounded. But his ID superseded the system: he could go anywhere at any time, without being blocked.

The error must have to do with the way that part of the program was written—my ID overrides everything. And it has never been tested for two Louis Massinas.

The simplest things were always what tripped you up.

Massina got hold of himself. The first thing to do was to turn off his own transponder. That could only be done from one of the two master stations—one at the security control downstairs, and the other in his office.

Upstairs. Quickly.

"SOMEONE IS UPSTAIRS," Stratowich told his two accomplices. "I thought the place was empty Sundays. Didn't that article make a deal of that? The one Medved gave us?"

Neither man answered. Medved had supplied both men and the IDs, along with the schematic and information on the place's layouts and security procedures. Clearly the intelligence had its limitations.

"Go take care of whoever it is," Stratowich told the men. "I'll get the robot thing."

FEARING THAT THE elevator would give him away, Massina decided to take the stairs to his office, moving as quickly as he dared without resorting to running, fearing it would make too much noise.

The door to the stairwell slipped from his hands as he went to shut it; it wasn't a slam, but to him it sounded almost as loud as a firecracker.

It was too late to do anything about it. He bolted up the stairs, two at a time, running now for all he was worth until he reached the final landing. Nearly out of breath, he put his hand on the door and pulled it open, trying as hard as he could to be quiet. He squeezed out into the hall and this time held the door as it closed, holding it back so it wouldn't slam.

The elevator was moving upward.

Massina let go of the door handle and bolted toward his office.

He heard the elevator opening behind him as he reached the outer door. He took his ID from his pocket and tapped it against the reader.

"Hey!" yelled one of the men who'd been in the elevator. "Hey!"

The door opened. Massina threw himself inside, then reached to hit the auto-close switch.

Something whizzed past as the door closed.

A bullet.

Jesus.

He ran to his office and shut the door. This was just a regular door, with an old-fashioned lock—something he guessed wouldn't withstand a bullet.

How long would the outer door hold? Or the glass front of the office?

STRATOWICH CURSED AS soon as he heard the gunshots. His simple job was suddenly extremely complicated.

Get the robot thing and get the hell out!

He tapped the card on the door reader, but the door didn't open. Instead, an alarm began to sound in the building.

What the hell?

"Shots fired, floor four," said a mechanical voice. "Lockdown in effect."

"Fan-fucking-tastic," he cursed. "Where the hell are the damn stairs?"

ONCE IT DETECTED the gunshots through audio analysis, the security system was designed to shut all of the doors and contact the police. The labs were locked as a precaution. These could not be opened except by coded overrides; simply swatting the card reader wouldn't do—a PIN number had to be spoken and the voice recognized. The elevator also shut down, and an alarm periodically rang through the building.

But any temptation to believe he was safe inside his office died in the fusillade of bullets that flew through the door at chest level. Massina's insistence that his employees be able to see him was now a serious liability—the glass at the front of the office was thick, but not so thick that it couldn't be shattered, as the two thugs in the hall were working to demonstrate.

Massina felt trapped by his own errors—the glass at the front of his office, the security flaw—who to blame for those but himself?

Kick yourself in the butt later. Right now, you need a way out.

74

Boston—around the same time

Johnny Givens ran for about an hour, until finally he had had enough. Not that he was tired—in fact, he felt strong, ridiculously strong. He just didn't feel like running anymore.

But he didn't feel like going home either, so he started walking instead. He walked around the Common and Faneuil Hall, though it was closed. He walked to the Aquarium—also closed. He walked to the North End, where the Italian restaurants were still doing a decent business. Though dressed in his tracksuit, he knew he could be served at Lou's Basement, a small place generally skipped by tourists and run by a man friendly to cops; the hostess got Johnny a place at the bar and he sat for a while, eating homemade ravioli and watching the end of the Red Sox game, a victory in Seattle. By the time the game was over, the place was ready to close. Johnny left a good tip and went out walking again, this time with more purpose—he was going home to bed.

All this energy was a by-product of the drugs he'd been given. The therapist and the doctors had made it clear what to expect. Throttle back, they said, or eventually you're going to crash.

So it was time to go home, even though he didn't feel like sleeping.

Though by now it was close to 1:00 A.M., this part of the city was still lively, and as he wound his way in the direction of the T—no sense walking *all* the way home—he found himself in the middle of a small crowd. He started listening to the different conversations. A couple was talking about parents coming for a visit; another sounded desperate to have children. A feeling of estrangement fell over him; the people were talking about things he had always wanted—marriage, family—but now thought he could never have.

The doctors claimed there was no physical reason he couldn't have children, let alone a girlfriend or wife. But who would want a cripple? Who would want a man with mechanical legs, no matter how good they were? They might look real in the street; they might even carry him farther and faster than his "originals"— the marathon might be an interesting test—but he took them off when he got into bed.

He began feeling sorry for himself. That was a bad trap, something he knew he had to avoid, yet he couldn't help it. It was as if a cloud settled on his head, blocking out the positive feelings he'd felt earlier. Maybe it was the drugs wearing down—he ought to have taken his nightly dosage by now.

Or maybe it was reality.

People say, Hey, you're doing fantastic. You're really something! You're an inspiration.

What they don't know is what it feels like inside. They don't know how much it sucks, truly sucks, not to have real legs. Not to be a full person, to be only half.

And yet, he was stronger, wasn't he? His upper body had responded to the medicine as well—he could bench-press twice his body weight, something he'd never been able to do before. Sure, rehab helped, but the drugs were like supersteroids.

This is really a new life. What are you going to do with it? Wallow in your shit? Or be somebody?

Johnny began to run. It was a trot, slow at first, barely above a walk, but gradually he picked up speed. He passed the entrance to the T.

Closed. He'd dawdled too long.

Have to go home by foot.

He pushed himself, running, and hoping that by running he could escape the cloud and its despair.

HE'D BEEN RUNNING for only a few minutes when he heard sirens nearby. Instincts took over—he began running in their direction, heading with them near the harbor. He took a turn and found himself two blocks from the Smart Metal building. A police car, lights flashing, was blocking the street nearby.

Johnny ran up to one of the officers, who was waving away traffic.

"John Givens," he said, pulling out his wallet clip for his FBI credentials. "What's up?"

"Got a call of an intruder up the street."

"Where?"

"Number ten."

"Damn," said Johnny. "Backup coming?"

"Yeah," said the officer, but Johnny barely heard—he was already sprinting in the direction of the building.

75

Boston—around the same time

Chelsea rolled over in her bed, drifting from consciousness as the cell phone rang.

Who's calling me in the middle of the night?

Crawling to the edge of the bed, she grabbed the phone.

"Hello?"

"What are you doing?"

"Who is this?"

"It's Beefy. Can you go over and stay with Borya? I just left. One of my security guys is with her and the babysitter, but I can tell they're nervous."

"What's going on?"

"We have an intruder alert at the building. I have to check it out. I just want someone the girl knows. Not a big deal. I didn't wake you, right?"

"Shit."

"Oh—I'm sorry."

"I'm on my way."

STRATOWICH REACHED THE top floor just in time to see one of Medved's goons charge at the glass wall. He fell, twisting on the floor.

"What the hell are you doing?" Stratowich demanded.

"There's someone inside," said the man, whom Stratowich knew only as Tomas.

Stratowich examined the glass. It was cracked, but it hadn't shattered.

"All right," he said, kicking at the crack. He kicked a few times, and a large piece caved in. Two more kicks and he had an actual hole.

"I hear sirens," said Paul, the other man.

Stratowich pressed his hand to his head, trying to think.

"We'll take him prisoner," he said finally. "He'll know a way out, or we'll use him as a hostage."

A GUSH OF wind hit Massina in the face as he climbed through the window onto the small ledge outside his office.

It was humiliating to be running from some low-level burglar in his own building, but preservation was more important than dignity.

There were sirens outside—at least the police would be here soon.

His left foot slipped as he moved along the ledge. The space was about two feet wide, with a two-foot double rail that ran around the outside. The railing was sturdy—during the reconstruction, it had anchored the workers' scaffolds. But it was low, and Massina was worried about falling if he leaned against it and then lost his balance.

If he could get to the corner, he could climb up on the roof and wait.

Like a cat running from a dog.

And he hated cats.

THE POLICE HAD cordoned off the building and were waiting for the head of Smart Metal's security unit before going in. They had to wait—the front door was locked.

Johnny walked around the side of the building. From the outside, at least, it looked as if nothing was wrong. The place looked like everything else downtown; quiet, buttoned up.

Then he saw someone walking along the top floor.

What the hell?

He stared at the top floor, trying to make sense of what he was seeing. A torso popped out of the window a few yards from the figure.

He had a gun.

I have to do something.

"Are there sharpshooters?" he yelled to one of the policemen nearby.

"What?"

"People are climbing around the side of the building."

One of the officers came over with a pair of binoculars and scanned the building.

"Can I see those?" Johnny asked. "FBI," he added, taking out his wallet to show his creds.

The cop handed over the binos.

The second guy definitely had a gun. He was yelling something at the man who'd gone out first. He was still moving along the side of the building, albeit slowly.

Massina. That's Mr. Massina!

MASSINA CONTINUED TOWARD the corner as the man at the window yelled at him to come back or he'd shoot.

The one thing I'm not doing is going back, thought Massina. *Though I'd rather not fall either.*

The roof pitched at the end closest to the river. Massina calculated that he could climb up if he could get a few feet farther. The man behind him was threatening to shoot, but he was far more concerned about keeping his footing than getting shot.

Massina's artificial arm had a very strong grip. He reached up, digging its fingers against the bricks.

Something flew past. He heard the dull echo of a gun.

Bastard is trying to kill me.

Don't help him by slipping.

STRATOWICH TUCKED THE gun back into the holster. The idiot who'd gone out the window was trying to climb up onto the roof.

"You're going to kill yourself, you shithead," he yelled.

He might also get away. Which would give Stratowich exactly zero leverage with the police.

A small part of him knew he should go back inside and give up. But his adrenaline was flowing, and the idea of someone actually getting away from him filled him with rage. So he hauled himself up on the ledge and began to follow.

When I see Medved, probably in ten years, I'm going to break every bone in his body. His, and the bastards he's working with. They sent me here with crappy information. "Easy money" my ass.

Stratowich glanced to his left. He was up at least seventy-five feet, more. It wouldn't be a pleasant fall. He pushed himself against the ledge and worked his way toward the side of the building.

The man he'd been chasing was just climbing up onto the roof. *Damn it.*

There wasn't supposed to have been anyone inside. Medved had assured him of that—easy in with the purloined ID, grab the little robot thing, and leave.

Simple.

Stratowich reached up and put his hand on the roof, feeling around to make sure he had a good grip. It was tar or something similar; in any event, it didn't feel like it was going to give way. He reached up with his other hand.

Something kicked his right hand, mashing his fingers. He pulled back, then remembered where he was.

"Damn you!" he yelled in Russian. He tucked back down, huddling against the wall. "I'll get you, mother fucker!"

MASSINA SLID TO his right, expecting the man to try again, this time closer to the edge, where he wouldn't have to climb up so high. Sure enough, a hand appeared there. Massina kicked at it. This time the hand grabbed at his shoe and pulled. Massina kicked violently—the shoe flew off; the hand disappeared.

A moment later, a head popped up farther to the left. He was a big man.

"I'm going to throw you off the roof," growled the man.

Massina backed up. The roof's pitch was gentle, but otherwise it offered nothing to him—no cover, and no way down. The nearest building was a good fifty feet across the side street—no way he was jumping to that roof, even if it hadn't been two stories higher.

One shoe on, one off, Massina calculated how he might fight the man. Most likely they would both roll off.

The man rose unsteadily at the edge of the roof. "I'm going to kill you," he growled.

"Do it then," said Massina. He lowered himself slightly, ready to shift his weight—if the man charged, he would slide out to the side, kick him in the face.

And pray.

"Arrrrrr!" yelled the man, as if he'd been a Viking berserker. He jerked forward, then fell flat on his face.

Massina hesitated a moment, unsure, then started forward to kick his antagonist in the face as he struggled to stay on the roof. Massina was still a few feet away when he realized someone else was behind the man, punching him in the back from the edge of the roof.

Johnny Givens.

SOMETHING INSIDE JOHNNY exploded as his fist hit the man's back. All of his frustration, all of his anger, flew into his muscles. He was a nor'easter, a monster, Godzilla come to life—the bastard who'd pursued Massina had no chance. As Johnny pounded the side of the man's ribs, he felt them give way. More punches—it was like beating down cardboard for the recycling bin, and with as little conscience as that.

Terrible sounds came from the man—a howl first, then a groan, then a wheeze, then something like a plea, followed by a whimper.

What are you doing?

What are you doing?

Johnny heard his own voice echoing in the hollow of his head, coming from a long distance.

The man's life was in his hands. He could throw him to the ground. He wanted to.

That's not who I am.

He delivered one more punch, then pushed the bloodied, beaten man to the side. Behind him and below, a fire truck's ladder was being quickly cranked upward. Police were shouting.

"Mr. Massina?" yelled Johnny. "Are you all right?"

"I'm here," yelled Massina, farther up the roof. "I'm here."

CHELSEA HAD LEFT Massina alone at the office, and when she couldn't get him on his cell phone, she decided he must still be there and was in trouble. She rode her bike to Borya's house, dropped it at the stoop, and ran up the steps to find the girl and the babysitter sitting in the living room with the security guard Beefy had left. No one there looked very comfortable.

But they were safe.

"I'm going over to the building," she told them. "I think Mr. Massina's there. I want to make sure he's OK."

"I'm going with you," said Borya.

"That's a really bad idea."

"I am going. I'm part of the company."

"Then we're all going."

Chelsea managed to convince the security officer to take them. Piling Chelsea's bike into the back of the Jimmy, they drove over in time to find a pair of fire trucks maneuvering near the far end of the building.

Beefy was standing in a cluster of police officers, watching the trucks.

"What's going on?" Chelsea asked. "Was there a fire, too?"

"Lou climbed up on the roof," Bozzone told her. "He just about kicked one of the burglars down. Someone stopped him, though."

"Who?"

"I don't know."

"God, it's Johnny Givens," said Chelsea, spotting him as he came down the ladder. "Our Johnny Givens."

"The FBI guy?"

"Yeah, look. There's Lou."

Johnny waited for Massina as he came down off the fire truck. The police were lowering the intruder, who'd been handcuffed, on the other truck.

Chelsea ran to Massina and hugged him. "What were you doing on the roof, Lou?"

"I'm thinking of adding a patio," said Massina.

Chelsea turned to Johnny. His shirt was smeared with sweat, black tar, and long streaks of blood.

"What were you doing?" she asked.

"Job interview," said Johnny.

76

As his assistant had predicted, the deputy mayor was holding down his corner at the tavern where Tolevi had first found him. He was neither surprised to see Tolevi nor apologetic that he hadn't met him at his office as planned.

"I talked to Olga at the prison," Tolevi told him, sipping a vodka. "We have an arrangement. But her price is very high."

"How much?"

"Forty percent."

"Outrageous!"

"Yes. Half of it is in merchandise, at least. But I have to pay her ten thousand euros up front."

"You should have waited for me. I could have driven a much better bargain."

Tolevi shrugged. "If you can cut a better deal, it will go to your share. In the meantime, she will give us two prisoners we can charge for release. This way, I can recoup a little of my investment."

"Ah, excellent idea. Which ones?"

"I have a man in mind. You can name the other."

"Who is your man?"

"Olak Urum."

The deputy mayor straightened, suddenly sober.

"Why do you want him?"

"I can get a good price. And he did me a favor before the war. Several, actually."

"Olak Urum? He was involved in the rebellion. They won't give you him."

"I would think that's a reason they would. He was one of theirs."

"No. He betrayed the cause."

"How?"

The deputy mayor shook his head.

"He will owe me and be of use then," said Tolevi.

"You told Olga this?"

"Not yet."

"She won't agree. I guarantee."

"Just get me another name. Someone who will pay at least fifteen thousand euros."

"Fifteen thousand? Impossible. No one is worth that much. Not even your Olak."

"Then name a friend if you want, someone who will owe us and be useful. There's too much to do to haggle. We have real money to be made here."

"HOW INFAMOUS IS your brother?" Tolevi asked when they were all back in the car, heading toward Donetsk.

"He's not."

"Why is it that the deputy mayor doesn't think I can get him out?"

"There was a falling out in the committee. Some people hate him. Some don't."

"What does the prison director, the deputy warden or whatever she is—what does she think?"

"I have no idea."

Tolevi pondered this. "He's in the most secure part of the prison."

The brother scoffed. "The house? They have real beds there. Not like the rest."

"How does he rate a bed?"

"Some of the guards like him."

"Have you thought about bribing them yourself?"

"They may arrest me, too. For being his brother."

Back in Donetsk two hours later, Tolevi bought three more phones. He realized now it was going to cost more than ten thousand euros to free Olak, but Tolevi had no doubt from his conversation with the warden that greed would win in the end. The only problem would be making the suitable connections and then ensuring follow-through.

Don't trust too much. This is always the stage where things are most vulnerable. You get overly optimistic and forget to be suspicious. Paranoia is not a bad thing.

Paranoia did serve him well, but so did optimism. At the moment, Tolevi was feeling almost invincible. He knew he had to guard against overconfidence, but on the other hand, wasn't confidence necessary for victory?

The de facto partition had made it difficult to get money transfers into Donetsk from anywhere but Russia. Tolevi called a man in Moscow who he knew would lend him the ten thousand euros he needed to satisfy the prison administrator, with another forty on call just in case.

The only problem was his interest rate—one hundred percent, compounded weekly.

The CIA was good for it. Tolevi hoped. If not, it would come out of the butcher's bounty.

Agroros Bank had recently opened a branch in Donetsk. Tolevi spent an hour and a half establishing an account there, using his Russian papers. The bank official was friendly until they got to the final set of forms, which asked what business the account holder was in.

"Importing," said Tolevi. "Medicines, mostly."

"From?"

"South America."

"This is what you do?"

"Yes."

The man picked up the papers and went into the back. It wasn't clear what the objection might be. As the minutes ticked by, Tolevi considered whether he might be better off just leaving. But that would mean he'd have to give up getting Olak, give up on the million dollars the Agency was going to pay him for getting him out.

The money or your life?

It's not going to come to that.

Tolevi sat for nearly twenty minutes before the clerk emerged with another man, whom he introduced as the branch president.

"You are an importer?" asked the president.

"I have arrangements with friends in Moscow," Tolevi told him. "We have papers from the trade ministry."

"Can I see them?"

"They're at the hotel."

"You ship medicine?"

"Aspirin, things like that."

"Nothing else?"

"Coffee."

The branch president stuck out his hand. "Thank you very much for using us."

77

Smart Metal Headquarters, Boston—morning

It was Jenkins, called to the scene by Bozzone and Johnny Givens, who connected the attack on Massina with the forged entry at the building. The men who'd kidnapped him had been after his ID card; they'd copied it and returned it, along with everything else in the wallet. Massina had stopped his credit cards but hadn't given the ID a thought. Its embedded data has been copied and used to get in.

"Basic mistake on my part," said Bozzone as they debriefed what had happened. "I should have had the entire system reprogrammed."

"We need to update our security," said Massina. "I'll take the blame. We'll fix it."

"And we need people in the building on Sundays," said Bozzone. "The automated systems aren't enough."

Massina frowned. But Bozzone was right; having people in the loop did help deal with the unforeseen.

Sometimes.

"We'll talk about it Monday," he said. "Right now, I have to get to mass."

JENKINS LEFT THE Smart Metal building feeling like he was rocket propelled. They had Stratowich on more than a dozen charges, from attempted murder down to breaking and entering. They could probably find a jaywalking charge in there, too.

Stratowich, a quick check showed, had definite connections to the Russian *mafya*.

And among his "possible associates" was Gabor Tolevi.

Bingo.

With all due respect to Massina, he'd obviously been taken in by the girl's story. Tolevi undoubtedly had put her up to it, right before vamoosing. She might even know where he was; Jenkins recognized crocodile tears when he saw them.

Maybe he wouldn't be able to touch Tolevi ultimately. But he'd be able to pressure him, and besides, Stratowich wouldn't know that—he could tell him that Tolevi had caved. So Stratowich would have all the reason in the world to give up every SOB in the Russian mob to him.

Including the SOB who had killed his brother.

That was the real goal—not the ATMs, not even the *mafya*.

Burglary was a local crime, and Stratowich was taken to Boston police headquarters for questioning; he'd be processed from there. Jenkins woke the Bureau's Boston PD liaison up and had her clear the way so he could question him before arraignment. That was a coup on her part, since the locals were always suspicious that the Feds would swoop in and grab their case from them.

They certainly had a lot of firepower on it: Jenkins counted three different lieutenants in the hallway outside the interrogation room, and the DA himself was inside making sure all the legal niceties were observed.

It was because of Massina. He was well liked, well respected . . . and rich. A trifecta when it came to police concern.

Jenkins made a beeline for Bill Grady, the homicide lieutenant in charge. Grady was a forty-something veteran whom Jenkins had met at a St. Patrick's Day celebration some years before; their paths had crossed a few times since.

"I'm not here to steal your case," Jenkins told him. "Your suspect is involved in something I'm working on, and I'd love to piggyback if I can. All credit to you."

"I heard your guy was the one who made the actual grab on the roof," said Grady.

"That's right. He was talking about what a great job Boston PD did surrounding the building and getting him down."

"We can share."

"I appreciate that."

"Just remember, it's a two-way street," said Grady.

"Absolutely."

Grady clearly wanted something, and not something small. Payback would undoubtedly hurt. But Jenkins would worry about that down the road.

Jenkins watched the interrogation via a closed-circuit camera. Stratowich had invoked his constitutional right and didn't look particularly worried, sitting silently, arms crossed, refusing to talk.

Maybe that's why they don't mind me being here, Jenkins thought. *They're not getting anything out of him anyway.*

"Let me try a bit," he told Grady. "Maybe I can loosen him up."

"We're not offering him a deal," said the DA.

"I wasn't going to suggest that. Just that he might be able to make things easier on himself if he talked."

"We're *not* offering a deal."

"If you could roll up the entire Russian mob in Boston," said Jenkins, "you wouldn't offer him a deal?"

"Well . . ."

"But who would get the credit?" said Grady. "The Feds."

"There would be enough credit on something like that to go around," said Jenkins. "A lot of credit."

"Only if the Boston PD was the lead agency."

"And the prosecutions were local," added the DA.

"Look, I don't know the politics of it," said Jenkins. "But I do know that this guy is connected to the guy I've been pursuing on an ATM case. And that he is in deep with the Russian mob."

"We know that," said Grady.

"So—you're talking, what, at least two dozen other indictments. And you got the guy on attempted murder." Jenkins shrugged. "You have a triple already. Why not go for a grand slam?"

78

Starobeshevskaya village—the next morning

A small bit of Tolevi's paranoia had returned—enough to make him cautious when they saw the van parked outside the bar where he had arranged to meet the deputy mayor.

"Drive us around the block," he told Dan.

"Why?"

"Just do it." Tolevi reached beneath the seat, making sure his pistol was still in place.

"What's going on?" asked the butcher's brother from the back.

"I've seen that van before," said Tolevi. It was similar to the one he'd been thrown into the other night. It might even be the same one.

Thousands of trucks like that. Even here.

They circled the block without seeing anything particularly exceptional. Starobeshevskaya was a sleepy village no matter what time of day it was.

But that van . . . surely it was the same one the Russian Spetsnaz had used.

"Go down by the power plant, then take me near the prison," he told Dan.

"What's going on?"

"I don't know. I just have a feeling."

"A feeling?"

"If you don't want to know the answer, why do you ask the question?"

Nothing exceptional was going on at either the jail or the power plant that Tolevi could tell; the guards looked half asleep, just as they had the other day. The Starobeshevskaya municipal building looked almost deserted—also the way it had looked the other day.

I'm really letting my emotions get the better of me. I have to relax. I'm so close to pulling this off that I see devils in every shadow.

He had Dan drop him off two blocks from the bar. The stroll calmed his slight case of nerves—as did the pistol, which he'd slipped under his jacket.

The bar was open, but the only patrons were two old crones sitting in a corner playing some sort of card game. A young woman was behind the bar, slowly drying glasses and setting them on the counter. She shrugged when Tolevi asked if she'd seen the deputy mayor.

"I just got here," she told him. "Maybe he was here, maybe not."

"Doesn't he come in every day?"

"Have you tried his office?"

"That's where I'm going next."

The van was gone. Tolevi went inside to look for the pimple-faced assistant, but he wasn't in. Neither was the deputy mayor. In fact, he had a hard time finding anyone in the building, on any of its floors; it wasn't until he reached the third floor that he found someone, and he was a maintenance man.

"Say, I'm looking for the deputy mayor," Tolevi said.

The man barely looked up from his mop.

"The deputy mayor," repeated Tolevi. "Would you happen to know if he or his assistant is in?"

The man made as if he didn't understand, even though Tolevi

was speaking Ukrainian. He tried again. This time the man shook his head and pointed to his ears.

"You're deaf?" asked Tolevi.

The man pointed again, then nodded.

No wonder you got the job, Tolevi thought as he went back downstairs.

He was just coming out of the building when the first Gaz drove up. Four Russian special forces troops, dressed in black uniforms with no insignias, hustled from the vehicle and began running to block off the street.

Tolevi backtracked quickly, going through the door and then running down the hall to the nearest trash can. He dumped his pistol there, then ran to the entrance on the west side of the building, hoping to get out there without being noticed.

The way was clear. He put his head down and went out, walking briskly toward the sidewalk and then turning to the left. As he did, a second Gaz sped down the road in his direction, stopping at the intersection behind him.

Tolevi slowed his pace slightly—he didn't want to seem as if he was in a hurry to get away—and crossed the street. He could hear boots scraping and some instructions being barked, but no one accosted him as he reached the next corner and turned. Curious about what exactly was going on, he considered turning around and going back, but that was foolish; the Russians would not like bystanders. So instead he walked two more blocks, then turned to the south and made his way back to where he had left Dan and the butcher's brother with the car.

Dan wasn't there.

Damn it.

They had arranged to meet a few blocks away if there was trouble. Tolevi turned around and headed in that direction, but he saw another Russian military vehicle parked in the intersection a few yards from where Dan would have been. So he went back to the bar, figuring it was the best place to pick up gossip and hoping that he might find the deputy mayor there. But the bar was now empty; even the bartender was gone.

He decided to help himself to a drink while he considered what to do. Leaving two five-hundred ruble notes on the bar— about twenty dollars U.S.—he took a half-full bottle of vodka and a glass and sat down at a nearby table. He was just pouring himself a drink when a pair of Russian soldiers, all in black and wearing balaclavas covering their faces, rushed in. They looked over the place quickly, then came to him, pointing their AK-74 assault rifles at his face.

"Just having a drink," he told them in Russian.

"On the floor," barked one of the men.

He started to get up but was apparently moving too slowly for the men. One of them grabbed him and threw him to the ground. He started to protest, but a sharp kick in the small of his back knocked the wind out of him. He felt his wallet and identity papers being lifted from his pocket.

Another man came into the room.

"Let him up," said the man after a few moments.

Tolevi got to his knees, still trying to catch his breath.

"Mr. Tolevi, again," said the bearded Russian colonel standing behind him. It was the same man who had questioned him after the raid on the butcher's shop. "When I told you to leave Donetsk, I had something much farther in mind."

"I was never very good at geography," said Tolevi.

The remark earned him a swift kick in the stomach. His reaction—to grab the colonel's boot and twist him to the ground— earned him a nozzle strike to the temple, dropping him to the floor, unconscious.

Puppet Master

FLASH FORWARD

Massina looked up from the computer screens and scanned the small room he had created.

Is this what my work has come to? he asked himself. *Is this what I want to do?*

But there was no time for introspection, especially on such complicated questions. People's lives were at stake—including, and especially, his people, people he had put here.

So the only question to ask was: *How do I help them?*

REAL TIME

79

Starobeshevskaya village—a short time later

Tolevi woke up on a cement floor in a dark basement. He knew he'd made a huge mistake—very possibly a fatal one.

Never be a wiseass. First rule of business.

He turned over to his chest. His hands and feet were free.

Good sign or bad? He had no idea.

Managing to sit, he looked around, eyes slowly adjusting to the dimness. The wall nearby was laid-up stone. There were pipes and a very dirty casement window across from him.

Two red eyes stared at him from a short distance away. A rat.

Lovely.

He stomped his foot. The eyes didn't move.

"You're a brave little thing, huh?"

Tolevi took several steps before it scooted to the far corner.

An overhead light flicked on before Tolevi could reach the window. He shielded his eyes as a pair of boots came down the steps. He turned toward them, unsure what to expect.

A man—dressed in black, one of the Russians—came about halfway down and leaned over the staircase.

"Who are you?" Tolevi asked.

The man turned and went back up without answering. The light flicked off; the door at the top closed with a slam.

"Let me out!" yelled Tolevi in Russian. He went to the stairs and started up, not sure exactly what he was going to do.

The door opened as he got to the second step. It was the bearded colonel.

"You want more, Tolevi?" he snarled. "You think because some jackass at SVR has use for you that you are free to do what you please? You are *mafya shit*."

"What's your name and rank?" Tolevi demanded.

"What difference would that make to you?" The Russian stepped back and called to someone. "Bring him up here. Watch it—he fights like a girl, dirty."

You're the one who kicked me, thought Tolevi, but he said nothing, not even when the Spetsnaz soldier grabbed his arm and yanked him up the stairs. He was led to the kitchen—they were in a small house still in Starobeshevskaya, on the opposite side of the village from the power plant and prison.

The Russian who had kicked him was talking on the phone. The soldier pushed him into a chair. Tolevi sat, trying to make out the conversation, but the Russian was mostly listening.

"What's your rank?" asked Tolevi when the man hung up.

"Higher than yours." The Russian laughed. "Donetsk is without corruption, unlike Kiev. They don't need smugglers like you. And your friends in Moscow."

Tolevi said nothing.

"The deputy mayor has been arrested," added the Russian. "The prison is now under Russian control. Volunteer control."

"You're Spetsnaz. I know. So what's your beef with SVR—with Moscow? We'll cut a deal. I know how these things work."

"You know many things. Do you know to keep your mouth shut?"

Tolevi glared at him.

"Good. You are learning. I would arrest you, but I'm sure your friends in Moscow would raise a stink. That is where they draw the line. So here is what I am going to do. I am going to send you back to them. And you know what you are going to do?"

Tolevi shook his head.

"You will tell them that the volunteers don't need their interference here. We don't like mobsters, especially ones who are working with the West. Do you understand that?"

"You can tell them that yourself."

"You don't take me seriously, do you?" The Russian's face flushed. "I'll fix that."

One of the soldiers behind Tolevi grabbed his arms. As Tolevi struggled, the Russian took something from his side and lunged toward Tolevi. As Tolevi struggled to get away, he felt something sharp and cold against the side of his head. Pain followed, then weakness that hollowed the center of his stomach and made him collapse.

The Russian threw something down on the floor. It was the bottom third of his ear.

"Deliver that to your friends in Moscow."

80

Louis Massina stared out the window. Hard to believe that less than twenty-four hours ago, he'd climbed out the small opening and made his way along the ledge to the roof.

A ledge that now looked incredibly, harrowingly small in the daylight. And very slippery.

Lunacy. Or survival instinct.

That wasn't going to happen again. He was never going to feel unsafe in his own building, let alone his office.

He'd already decided that he was going to keep the glass wall. The engineers had assured him they could replace the front with glass thick enough to be bullet- and shatterproof. Anything less would be giving in.

People working on Sunday. He would discourage it for most.

"Mr. Givens is ready," said his assistant on the intercom.

"Send him in."

Johnny Givens strode into the office, a big grin on his face. It would have been difficult for anyone who didn't know him to realize that he was walking on two artificial legs.

"I finished all the paperwork," said Givens.

"Have a seat." Massina watched him fold himself into the chair. Simply recovering from his accident in such a short time was remarkable; there was much more here, much more.

Not Superman, not Frankenstein, but . . .

If you can do this with someone from a car accident, what else can you do? It is godlike, however blasphemous that may be.

"You're not tired from last night?" Massina asked.

"A little, maybe. Because I didn't have much sleep."

"I talked to Jenkins and your personnel office at the FBI," Massina told him. "They may be willing to keep you on at the Bureau, at your old job."

"I don't want that. I just did all the paperwork to work here."

"A federal job does have its benefits."

"So does this one. And it pays better. I've seen some of what you do," said Givens. "I want to be involved. And this heart and legs—this is pretty special."

"It is. There are downsides."

"I know that."

"The job is boring," warned Massina. "Mostly, you'll be a guard."

"Are you rescinding your offer?" asked Givens.

"I just want to make sure you know what you're getting into," said Massina.

"Mr. Bozzone and I talked about it. I'm sure I'll do fine."

"Good, then." Massina went around the desk and extended his hand. "Welcome aboard."

"Roger"—Test Robt RG/65-A—was a small bot constructed to look something like a miniature spaceman. His "hands" could manipulate objects and had optical sensors that were ten times as powerful as human eyes. But his function at Smart Metal was to test different AI learning routines and their relationship to chip design; in other words, help the scientists discover what processor and memory architectures were the best for learning.

Chelsea, who was leading the programming team, had invited Borya, their new intern, to witness the afternoon's test.

"What we're going to do now is a variation of the Three Kings test," Chelsea told Borya as she finished going over the robot's vital signs. "Do you know what the test is?"

Borya shook her head.

"It's kind of a classic induction logic test. It comes from this story: There are three wise men or kings. Each is given a hat, either black or white. They can't talk to each other, but they have to figure out what color hat they are wearing. They can't see their hats, but they're told that there is at least one of each color. So you ask the first king what color hat he is wearing. If he says he doesn't know, then the next king should be able to answer, right?"

"Because he saw black and white, right?"

"Exactly."

"That's not much of a test."

"Not for you. But let's see what the robot does."

Chelsea had placed three white balls in three boxes in front of the robot.

"Roger, wake up," she said, walking to the bot.

The robot raised itself on its four legs.

"I have placed a black or white ball in the boxes in front of you," she told it. "Open two boxes, and determine the color of the third ball. There is at least one ball of each color."

The robot immediately moved to the first box.

"Chelsea," hissed Borya. "You made a mistake in the instructions."

Chelsea put her finger to her mouth, shushing her.

The robot opened the box, examined the white ball, then moved to the second.

"The third ball is black," it declared.

"Why do you say that?" asked Chelsea.

"By logic. One ball must be black. Two white balls have been discovered."

"Open the third box."

Roger moved to the box and opened it.

"I have been mis-instructed," said the robot. "This ball is white."

Chelsea brought out three more boxes and set them down.

"Roger, same instructions as before."

The robot opened two boxes, then stopped. "I do not know what color the third ball is."

"Why?" asked Chelsea.

"Because the instructions may be faulty, as they were before."

"Good. Roger, sleep mode."

The robot settled down onto all fours.

"Did it pass the test?" asked Borya.

"So far."

"Was the idea to see if it would use logic?"

"Partly it was to see if it would use the results of what it had learned to draw a conclusion and act on it a second time," said Chelsea. "As it did that—and for us this was the important part—we recorded what was going on in its processing chips. We'll compare all of that to a different version of its brain. Because we want to see what the best construction of the brain is. Is it just size?"

"The bigger the computer, right?"

"Well, humans don't have the biggest brains on the planet, but they're the smartest mammal."

"Some are pretty dumb," said Borya.

Chelsea laughed.

"So what's next?" asked Borya.

"What's next for you is homework," said Chelsea. "Which means it's time for you to go home."

"Come on. This was just getting good."

"Those are the rules. I'll walk you out."

"My dad still hasn't called," said Borya as they waited for the elevator. "The FBI guy told Beefy there's nothing new."

"Are you worried?" asked Chelsea.

"A little . . . A lot."

"Mr. Jenkins is trying to get him to call," Chelsea told her. "I'm sure he's OK."

"He doesn't like him."

"Jenkins? Why do you say that?"

"I can tell. He has that look."

"So, that's it, though, we just watch the kid?" Johnny asked Bozzone. "Were there threats?"

"No. But Lou's worried, since there was a *mafya* connection. And the father has missed his calls to her. Two and two, right."

"Sucks for the kid."

"Yeah, well, just remember she was smart enough to run the ATM scam. I have it in four-hour shifts. Watch her. She's, uh, a free spirit."

"I saw."

"Chelsea's waiting with her in the lobby. When you get her home, don't let her take her bike out. You'll never keep up."

Actually, Johnny thought he could. "Are we walking?"

"Take our pickup." Bozzone pointed to the keys on the board at the side of the room. "You can drive, right?"

"Sure."

Or at least I could before, thought Johnny as he headed for the elevator.

Borya recognized the security guy—Johnny Givens, from last night—as soon as he came down the stairs.

He was frowning. But his eyes widened when he saw Chelsea. *Ha! He likes her.*

"I'm Johnny Givens," he said, holding out his hand. "I'll be with you for the next four hours."

"What if I have to go to the bathroom?" Borya asked playfully.

"There's one right there. I'll stay outside the door."

"It was a hypothetical." Borya looked at Chelsea. "Think he could pass the Three Kings test?"

"I'm sure he'd ace it. I'll see you Wednesday."

"Got it."

"We're going to go this way," said Johnny. "I need to find the pickup truck."

"I have my bike. I can just ride it home."

"Is it a tandem?"

"What's that?"

"A bicycle built for two."

"Just one."

"Then we'll take the truck and put it in the back."

"Why don't we walk?"

"I'll tell you what. If I'm with you later in the week, I'll get a bike and we'll bike together, all right? Unless you jog."

"Jog?"

"You know, run. Like, exercise."

"I could do that. But I'd rather bike."

"All right."

"You have a bike?"

"No."

"You need one if you're going to ride."

"No shit."

Borya laughed. "I know where you can get a good one."

"Then we'll go there the next time we work together."

"Work?"

"I'm working. And you're supposed to be doing your homework, right?"

"Don't go dad on me. You were doing so well."

"Here's the elevator."

None of the security guys were particularly friendly. This one, at least, seemed like he wasn't a complete jerk.

"You have bionic legs, right?" she asked as they walked to the back hall and the entrance to the parking lot.

"They're not bionic."

"Can I see them?"

"Maybe later."

"Just your legs," she said quickly. "Not—you know."

Johnny laughed. He stopped and pulled up his pants leg. "There."

"It looks real."

"That's how they made it."

"Does it hurt?"

"Not as much as it did at first. But, sometimes. Yes."

"Can I touch it?" asked Borya.

"I guess."

Borya dropped to her knee and touched the exposed calf. It didn't quite feel real, but the skin was soft, not hard, as she'd expected.

"Do you like it better?" she asked, rising as he pulled his pants leg back down.

"Better, no. But it may be pretty cool."

"You're a real hero," said Borya.

"Come on, let's get going," said Johnny, in what Borya knew was a pretend-tough voice. "You have to do that homework, or they're going to be on my ass."

81

John F. Kennedy Airport, three days later

Shoved on a plane to Moscow by the SVR in Donetsk, Tolevi was met at Domodedovo International Airport by a mousy woman holding up a sign with his name on it. He considered just walking by, but realized that was foolish; the Russians could grab him any time they wanted. The woman looked at his ear, shook her head, then walked him to a car in the terminal's no parking area, all without a word. They drove about fifteen minutes before arriving at a clinic; patched up by an elderly doctor whose Far Eastern Russian was difficult to decipher, Tolevi emerged to find an envelope with his name on it at the receptionist's desk. Inside was his ticket, a baggage check claim for his luggage, and a stamped visa that expired three hours after the flight boarded.

He knew better than to dawdle, let alone ask questions. His ride was gone, but a cab to the airport easily arranged. It turned out that the visa's timing was prescient; they sat at the gate for exactly two hours and fifty-five minutes past boarding time for reasons never announced; then they spent another half hour on the tarmac due to "air traffic controller problems."

Flying coach nonstop from Moscow to New York—if it wasn't

the worst flight Tolevi had ever taken, it certainly ranked close. The plane itself wasn't horrible—Aeroflot used an Airbus 330 for long-distance flights—but he was stuck in a middle seat with a snorer on his right and a woman who prayed to herself the entire time she wasn't eating.

But when he landed, he was in the States, finally.

The first order of business after collecting his bag would be to find a pay phone. He hadn't been able to call Borya the whole time he'd been gone. She'd be worried, as would Martyak.

Assuming Borya hadn't killed Martyak by now. A definite possibility.

"Gabor Tolevi?"

Tolevi turned to see a tall, middle-aged man in a suit standing next to the rope at the gate exit.

He looked familiar.

"You'll come with us," said the man, flashing an ID. "Trevor Jenkins. FBI. We met in Boston. Come along with us."

Another man in a suit rose from a chair at the front of the gate. Tolevi spotted two more men in suits rising at the edge of the waiting area.

"I have to call my daughter," he said.

"You can do that from the car."

"I don't have a car."

"We're going to drive you," said Jenkins. "We'll take care of the luggage."

THE BIGGEST SURPRISE was waiting in the car, actually a large SUV with three rows of seats: Yuri Johansen.

"Good evening, Gabe," said Johansen, sitting in the first row behind the driver. "Have a good flight?"

"The flight was terrible." Tolevi had no option but to slide next to him. "My stay was worse."

"You didn't get our guy," said Johansen.

Outside the truck, Jenkins shouted to some men boarding a

vehicle behind them. Another vehicle pulled up in front. It was a regular caravan.

"I'm lucky I got out with my life," Tolevi told Johansen. "One of the Russians in charge down there decided he liked me so much he cut off part of my ear as souvenir."

Tolevi turned his head toward his CIA handler.

"I bet that hurts."

"Jenkins said I could call my daughter. Is he FBI, or is he with you?"

"Bureau. Use his phone when he gets in."

"I met Dan," said Tolevi. "If you were going to have people there, you should have had more."

"If we had access to more," said Johansen, "do you think we would have sent you?"

JENKINS TAPPED THE back of the driver's seat and they pulled out, a three-vehicle parade to Boston. He didn't particularly like the CIA officer, Johansen, let alone the arrangement the bosses had come to, but "make the best of it" was now the clear order of the day.

National interest and all that.

They were at the precipice of a huge bust, breaking not only the back of the Russian mob in Boston and New England but also some of its connections back to Russia and the Ukraine. Even if Tolevi didn't cooperate and the CIA chose to keep him off limits, major criminals were going down. This meant cybercrime, prostitution, drugs, cigarette and vodka smuggling.

But the big prize was the Russian intelligence service connection.

Stratowich wasn't talking yet, but he would. It was just a matter of time. They'd already gotten information from his apartment, his phone records, even his girlfriend.

The day before he broke into Smart Metal, he'd met with Maarav Medved, a known *mafya* chieftain; from him he'd re-

ceived instructions on how to get into Smart Metal. Twenty minutes before that meeting, which had taken place at a restaurant in
downtown Boston, two members of the Russian SVR had gone
into the restaurant and sat with Medved—something the FBI
knew from routine surveillance, and now a security video from a
store just across the street.

How much they could make of the connection remained to
be seen. The U.S. attorney had asked for a wiretap warrant on
Medved; thus far the most interesting tidbit was information about
which Russian prostitutes were the best in bed. But it was early
days; Jenkins had no doubt they would end up with considerably more dirt, and undoubtedly have enough hard evidence to
expose SVR operations. A serious win for him, even though his
task group hadn't been assigned to do that.

Getting Tolevi to play along would be useful. It was difficult,
however, to judge exactly what the CIA's attitude toward him
was. They were as cagey as ever, barely admitting that they ran
him, though it was obvious they had sent him to the Ukraine. He
was a black marketer, flouting, if not breaking, U.S. laws on ex-
porting goods to both Russia and the breakaway areas of Crimea
and eastern Ukraine. He had connections to the *mafya*—Johansen
insisted he wasn't a member, though Jenkins was sure he was, even
if it was a few rungs below Medved.

The one good thing about the SVR case—the CIA wouldn't
try to hound in on the glory. In fact, the Agency would stay as
far away publically as possible, fearing they'd get into a tit-for-tat
fight with their Russian rivals. That gave Jenkins's bosses plenty
of room to work with the locals, who of course wanted some
measure of glory for having been lucky enough to be there when
Jenkins's man got Massina down.

Glory all around.

But he still didn't have his brother's murderer.

"I want to call my daughter," said Tolevi.

"You'll call her," said Jenkins. "It's a long ride."

"Am I under arrest here?"

"No. Not at all." Jenkins leaned forward. "If you want to get out, we can stop right here."

They were on the Van Wyck Expressway; traffic was actually moving at a decent clip, unusual even for the middle of the day.

"What exactly do I owe this honor to?" said Tolevi.

"We're all trying to cooperate," said Jenkins. "We picked up a friend of yours, a Mr. Stratowich, who has been giving us a lot of information."

"Stratowich." Tolevi pronounced the name to rhyme with *garbage,* which completely synched with his tone.

"He speaks highly of you," said Jenkins.

"I doubt that. He's talking to you?"

Jenkins shrugged. No, Stratowich was many things, but not a squealer. Still, if you had him, you could get a lot of information, make connections.

"Stratowich is an asshole," Tolevi told them. "I want to talk to my daughter."

"If you're so concerned about Borya," said Jenkins, "why did you set her up to take the fall for your ATM scam?"

"What ATM scam? What is the obsession with ATMs?"

"You had nothing to do with that."

"I don't know what you're talking about. No. Listen, Stratowich is a goon. Strictly low level. He doesn't have the brains to rob a candy store, let alone diddle with banks, if that's what you're getting at."

"A bag guy for Russian intelligence?" asked Jenkins.

Tolevi turned to Johansen. "What's the game here?"

JOHANSEN DIDN'T ANSWER, pretending to stare out the window. Tolevi decided that he could use a little silence himself, so he sat back between them, feeling more than a little cramped in.

Middle seat blues: The theme of the last forty-eight hours.

It wasn't until they were on the New England Thruway nearly a half hour later that Johansen broke the silence.

"So, you could not recover our friend the butcher," said the CIA agent. "Tell me what happened."

Tolevi glanced at Jenkins. Obviously these guys were working together.

"The Russians moved in," Tolevi said. "They were apparently sweeping up the rebels who were corrupt. I got caught in the middle of that. The brother wasn't much help. Nor, frankly, was Dan. I lost track of them."

"How?"

Tolevi described what had happened, leaving out the SVR connection. If Johansen knew about it, he'd bring it up. Otherwise, it would open him up to too many questions, most of which he preferred not to answer.

"The man who cut your ear off is a colonel in the Spetsnaz," Johansen told him. "He has a reputation for being honest. And ruthless."

"I figured he was a colonel. He had that f-u look in his eyes they get when they've been in the army too long."

"Where is your prize now?"

"Still in jail, as far as I know."

"Describe it."

Tolevi slumped back in the seat, trying to force a replay of his visit through his mind. But thoughts of his daughter kept getting in the way.

What am I going to tell her about my ear?

"Oh that . . . cut myself shaving."

And the damn thing was throbbing out of control.

Times like this he really missed his wife. He missed her always, but right now even more. She would have soothed the way somehow, absorbed some of Borya's shock.

The girl will freak. She thinks of me as indestructible. She is such a good kid.

"You're describing an impenetrable fortress," said Jenkins. It was the first sign that he was listening. Johansen shot him a look.

"It's not easy to get into," admitted Tolevi. "But I went through the front door. I would have been able to get him out. The money was all lined up. We need to take care of that."

"The Russian took it over?" asked Johansen.

"It looked that way. There's some sort of power struggle going on. I'd guess the Russians are in the middle of it."

Johansen, satisfied for now, leaned back on the seat.

They really need me, thought Tolevi. *He's playing it too cool.*

But do they need me as a patsy? Or because I'm the only hope they have?

Either way, there wasn't enough in it for him to risk his life going back.

"What was your role in all this?" asked Jenkins. "Why are you involved?"

"Ask Yuri."

"You can tell him," said Johansen. "He knows you work with us."

"I'm just trying to make a living. Sometimes I help an old friend out."

"You make a living by smuggling things."

"It's not necessarily smuggling. I just find a way to get things people need from point A to point B, with a lot of interference in the middle."

"You corrupt people."

"No. I make my living off of other people's greed," said Tolevi. "They're the ones who are corrupt."

"Which explains why you had your daughter rip off those ATM machines."

"You keep talking about ATM machines. I have no idea what you mean."

"You know nothing?"

"Absolutely nothing."

"The night we arrested you—"

"He wasn't technically arrested," interrupted Johansen.

"The night we found you outside the bank with your daughter," said Jenkins, correcting himself. "Why was she there?"

"She found an ATM card. Being a teenager, she wanted to try it. I punished her, don't worry. She knows it was wrong."

"She reprogrammed that ATM card as part of a scam."

"What?"

"She programmed that card so it would put money into her account."

"There's no way my daughter would have done that."

"That's my point," said Jenkins. "No fifteen-year-old girl is doing that. But she confessed. She took the fall for you."

"Are we talking about my daughter?"

"Someone funneled over two hundred thousand dollars from people all across the city. Borya claims it was her."

"Get away."

"You know nothing about that?" asked Johansen.

"Borya did that? No way. She's a good girl. There's no way she did that."

THEY STOPPED FOR a bathroom break and something to eat about two hours out of New York. On the way out of the restroom, Tolevi spotted a pay phone.

"I'm calling my daughter," he told Jenkins.

Tolevi went to the phone and put in a quarter, then all his change to make the call.

He was still twenty-five cents short and had to borrow it from the agent.

He went straight to voice mail.

"Borya, this is your father. What the hell have you been doing with the banks? You are to talk to *no one* until I get there. Do you hear me? No one! And . . . do your damn homework."

He slammed the phone into the receiver.

"Teenagers are tough, huh," said Jenkins.

Tolevi gave him a death stare before starting back toward the car.

"I have a kid about the same age as yours," said Jenkins, trailing along.

"I told her never to lie to me," said Tolevi. "Never. How did she do this?"

"She claims she found some of the information on the Web and adapted the rest."

"Bull. Someone put her up to it."

"Who?"

"I'll break his legs when I find out. I'll feed him his balls. Was it Medved, one of his people? He's a slime."

"Not having your wife is hard, huh? I don't think I could raise my girl on my own. She's not as smart as yours, but she's still a handful."

"Everything is a test," said Tolevi. "Everything."

Johansen was waiting in the parking lot.

"I have to go deal with something," he told Tolevi. "I'll be back in touch."

"When do I get my money?" said Tolevi. "I borrowed money to get the butcher out. It needs to be paid back with interest right away."

"You didn't get the butcher out. There's no payment."

"I need that money."

"Get us the butcher."

"The place is impenetrable," said Tolevi. "You said it yourself."

"Jenkins said it, not me. If you can't do it, that's not a problem. But we're not going to pay you."

"I really need the money."

Johansen stared at him.

"I can't go back to Donetsk," said Tolevi. "Maybe not even Russia. Not for a while."

"Then you have a lot of problems that I can't solve, Gabe." Johansen looked at Jenkins. "I'll be in touch."

82

Massina caught up with Sister Rose Marie as the nun made her way through the children's ward. He watched her from the hall for a moment, talking with the little ones. For a woman who had never had any herself, she certainly seemed to have a way with children. She offered neither toys nor candy, yet the Good Humor ice cream truck couldn't have gotten a brighter response as she walked through the large room, stopping at each bed. Her smile was contagious, but more so was her optimism; she exuded grace, to use the religious term, and the children were eager to soak it up.

As was he.

"I see your secret source of energy," said Massina as she came out of the ward. "This is your fountain of youth."

"It is. The Holy Spirit is strong with them. He always gives me energy."

"What I have to do someday," he told her, "is come up with a computer program that can duplicate your enthusiasm."

She wagged her finger at him. "Computers are not people, Louis. They have no souls."

"Maybe not yet."

"Don't blaspheme. Only God gives souls."

"Why can't God give a soul to a machine?" asked Massina. "Certainly He could. He could do anything."

"You are always provocative, Louis. And maybe you are right. A machine with a human soul."

"Or a machine soul, as God directs."

"Now we are getting into areas that Sister Williams is better at," said the hospital administrator. "Have you had lunch?"

"It's nearly three."

"Have you had lunch?"

"Yes."

"Come with me to the cafeteria anyway. I assume you want to talk."

"Yes."

They walked to the end of the hallway, the Sister waving and nodding to patients and staff alike.

"I had a bad experience the other night," Massina told her in the elevator.

"I saw the news. Someone broke into your building."

"There's a lot more to it than that," said Massina. He had managed to keep much of the story—including the fact that he had escaped to the roof—out of the papers and TV broadcasts. He told her about it now, lowering his voice as they went into the patients' cafeteria. Sister Rose liked to mingle with the families; she had gotten several ideas for improvements simply by overhearing complaints. This had become more difficult over the years, however; few people in town didn't recognize her instantly.

Sister Rose selected a tuna salad from the refrigerated display, along with a water. Massina insisted on paying.

"It sounds like quite an ordeal," said Sister Rose Marie when they sat down.

"It was. There was a moment—I cursed God for putting me up on that roof."

"You climbed there yourself, though."

"True. But I felt as if He wanted me to die. And I didn't want to. I didn't want to follow his will."

"Louis, if you want to make a confession, Father Dalton will surely hear it."

"He'll just give me a couple of Hail Marys and Glory Bes and call it a day," said Massina. "I had my doubts on my roof. I thought I was going to die."

"But you didn't. And so now, what else is it that you're supposed to do?"

"That's a point."

"That's the important point, isn't it? We all have our moments. Peter had his moment of despair. Even Christ on the Cross. *'My God, my God, why have you forsaken me.'* But He wasn't forsaken at all. And neither were you."

"No," agreed Massina.

"So what are you going to do?"

"A lot," said Massina.

"Souls in machines?"

"More than that." He looked around the cafeteria. He'd been so focused on that moment of doubt on the roof, his cursing at God, that he hadn't looked at it as Sister Rose did. And hers was the proper view: It was a moment of affirmation. He was alive. It had to be God's will.

So what was he going to do with that?

"I have a question for you, Sister."

"Yes?"

"What you do—you're obviously a force for good."

"You're very kind."

"I wonder if there are limits to what we can do."

"I can't answer that for you, Louis." She laughed. "You seem to have no limits."

Massina remained serious. "You think it's right to work against evil?"

"Of course. Someone has to. Someone has to fight."

"Yes, we do."

83

Boston—around the same time

Chelsea went to the door of the lab and cleared the lock. The door flew open; Borya and Johnny Givens were standing in the hall.

"Today's supposed to be a study day for you at school," said Chelsea.

"I'm in trouble," said Borya. "Can I come in?"

Inside the lab, Borya played the voice mail her father had left.

"You're going to have to face the music," Chelsea told her. "Even if it's not going to be pleasant."

"Can you be there? You and Johnny?"

Chelsea looked up at Johnny. He looked bemused.

"I'll go for moral support," said Chelsea. "You have to do the talking."

"Can I do it here?"

"I don't know."

"In the lobby. So he sees I'm not lying about the internship. And that I've turned over a new leaf."

"You've turned over a new leaf?" asked Chelsea.

"I work here. That's new."

"Let me check with Mr. Massina to see if it's OK."

JENKINS DIDN'T RECOGNIZE the number on his cell phone, but he decided to answer it anyway.

"This is Jenkins."

"Mr. Jenkins, this is Chelsea Goodman at Smart Metal."

"Ms. Goodman. How are you?"

"I'm fine. I heard that you are bringing Borya Tolevi's father back to Boston."

"I'm giving him a ride, yes."

"His daughter is at our building. She'd like to meet him here. She's interning with us."

"I . . ." He glanced over at Tolevi, who was staring out the window of the SUV. Tolevi had calmed some from earlier, but he was still clearly upset with his daughter. "Why there?"

"It was part of the deal for restitution."

"But why meet there?"

"I think she wants to . . . explain what she did."

"And I can listen?"

"That's up to her. I checked with Lou. He said it's fine. They have to stay in the lobby. No tour."

"All right."

Jenkins hung up, then leaned across the front seat and gave the driver the address.

"We're making a stop before we get to your house," Jenkins told Tolevi.

"Why?"

"To pick up your daughter."

EVERY PART OF Borya's body trembled as she stood in the hallway in front of the reception area. She was relieved that her father was on his way home, and safe.

And petrified at his anger, which came through loud and clear in his voice mail.

Her dad had punished her countless times. But this was going to be different.

At least he was home.

The first man through the door was the FBI agent, Mr. Jenkins. She didn't see her dad.

And then there he was.

Borya forgot her fears and ran to him, throwing herself at his chest. Relieved, crying, joyful to hold him.

TOLEVI HELD HIS daughter for a long moment, unsure what to say. He was extremely angry—so angry that he could feel his face burning.

And yet, how could he be mad at her?

Oh, he was angry. So angry.

PISSED!!!

But damn.

Baby.

"You and I have to talk," he told her.

She clung harder.

"Mr. Tolevi, this is our lawyer," said Chelsea. "He'll explain the legal arrangements. No charges are to be filed. Full restitution is to be made."

"I gave all the money back," sobbed Borya. "I'm working here to pay the rest."

"Maybe we should go someplace where there is more privacy," suggested Chelsea. "There's a space right over there."

IT WASN'T UNTIL Jenkins saw the way Borya clung to her father that he finally accepted that her father had nothing to do with the scheme. He thought of his own daughter, and what he would do if she had pulled a stunt like that.

No way would she ever do it. Not even close.

He should spend more time with her.

"So, let me understand this," Tolevi told Chelsea. "There was a shortfall, and Borya is going to make it up by working here."

"That's right," interrupted the attorney.

"Assuming you agree," said Chelsea.

"I can pay whatever it is."

"Wouldn't it better if she worked it off?" asked Chelsea.

"I agree," said Jenkins. "She's showing some responsibility."

Tolevi shot him a look.

"Just saying."

"Borya," Tolevi asked, "do you want to work here?"

"One hundred percent. You should see the cool stuff they have. Robots, computers—"

"We'll discuss it at home," he told her. "We'll discuss it."

Jenkins didn't have to have a daughter to know that meant yes.

84

"I'd say we're ninety-five percent sure the Russian intelligence service was involved," Jenkins told Massina in his office after Tolevi and his daughter left. "I'd say one hundred percent, but nothing in life is certain."

"They want our plans for the robot. And this Tolevi wasn't involved?"

"No. Although he knows some of the players. The CIA had him under surveillance here. It's Stratowich and this *mafya* chieftain, Medved. Medved has ties to what used to be the KGB. Your plans are worth a fortune. They figured you were an easy mark. Low-hanging fruit."

"Because we don't work on Sunday?"

"They got in. So they weren't that wrong," said Jenkins. "Right now, they're laying low, worried about what Stratowich is telling us. But they'll be back. They don't give up when they want something."

"I don't expect them to." Massina got up from his seat and began pacing around the office. The glass window still hadn't been repaired. "We've had attempts before. All by computer, nothing like this."

"You're going to have to start taking precautions. Personal precautions. A bodyguard. Do you carry a gun?"

"Rarely. Not at work, certainly."

"You might think about it."

Massina walked to the window and looked out. The memory of the other night was going to remain with him for a long time. "This Tolevi—you're sure he had nothing to do with the break-in?"

"I'd love to pin it on him," admitted Jenkins, "but honestly, no. He skirts the line. He's a criminal, if you ask me. But he knows what he can get away with, especially with the CIA backing him."

"He got his ear cut off."

"Maybe it will make him retire."

"I would think it would make him angry," said Massina. "And want revenge."

YES, THOUGHT JENKINS. Massina was right. *Revenge.*

He knew the emotion well. Though for him, it was more a question of justice.

Justice and revenge.

"So, we'll keep in touch on this, right?" he asked Massina. "Share information? Your help on the ATMs was invaluable. I'm sorry I wasn't as frank as I could have been. My hands were tied. I'll try and keep them untied in the future."

"So will I."

85

As tired as he was, Tolevi couldn't sleep. He paced around the apartment, prowling the rooms, pawing the small mementos and household items that reminded him of his daughter and his wife.

He had to be quiet. Borya was down the hall, sleeping in her room. Martyak was in the guest room; he could hear her snore.

He needed a permanent babysitter. That was one mistake. Even though Borya was a teenager now, she still needed someone to watch out for her full-time, if only to tell Tolevi when she was getting into trouble. He'd been far too lax.

She loved him, and he loved her. But that wasn't the issue. She needed more discipline.

You would have thought the damn school would have given more morals. That's what they're there for. You can't find a stricter school in Boston for girls.

Borya was the least of his problems, in the near term, at least.

He owed Medved a lot of money.

Maybe that would go away if the FBI rolled Stratowich.

Couldn't count on that. If anything, that would amp the pressure to get the loan paid quickly.

So. Money . . .

The option for a quick payoff was getting the butcher out. And bribery wasn't going to work, not while the bearded colonel was in Donetsk.

What they needed was someone who could break in and yank him out. If they had their own army.

Smart Metal's robot? The thing Stratowich had videoed going into the building.

Tolevi sat down at the kitchen table and checked the e-mail account where the video had been sent. He recovered the video file (discarded but not erased when the e-mail was checked as "read") and watched it several times, then went to Google Earth, finding a satellite view of the prison where the butcher was.

He worked the idea around in his mind. After an hour, he decided he had nothing to lose.

He got one of his sterile phones from his study. Then he sat down with a bottle of vodka and a large glass, called Johansen's contact number, and waited for his return call.

86

It was the most extraordinary meeting Louis Massina had ever attended, and it took place in a room that had only four simple wooden folding chairs, each padded at their feet. The floor and ceiling were cement, as were the walls. These were isolated from the rest of the building by different layers of material, including a copper envelope that made it impossible to either transmit or receive electronic signals inside. To get here, Massina had submitted to two different searches and been escorted, even inside the men's room.

When he walked in, three men were already waiting. He knew none of them, and they didn't introduce themselves. All wore business suits but no ties. He sat in the open chair, a man on each side, and one across.

"We're very familiar with your work on robots," said the man across from him. "It's quite amazing."

"We try. I have a good team."

"We'd like to enlist your help," continued the man. "We have a situation overseas where we think one or more of your robots would be very useful. We're trying to save the life of someone who might be helpful to the West. He'd be grateful, and so would we."

"Who?" asked Massina.

"We need a commitment from you before we give you any more information," said the man. "As I'm sure you can understand, this is a matter of very high national security. And frankly, if it were known that we wanted to rescue this man, he would most likely be put to death immediately."

"I see."

"You would not be at risk, neither you nor your people. We would take over one of your robots and—"

"Excuse me, but let me understand what we're talking about. If you're looking to buy one of the robots that we sell commercially, that's not a problem. But if you're talking about something else . . ."

The man who had been talking looked at the man on his left. The man reached into his suit jacket and took out a piece of paper.

"This robot. Or something similar."

It was Peter.

"That's an experimental bot. I'm afraid only my people can operate it."

"That might be possible," said the man on Massina's right. "Given the time constraints, it might be the best solution. But there would be a certain danger involved. And I have to emphasize the amount of secrecy involved. We wouldn't want your device falling into the wrong hands."

"I agree."

"If you decided to work with us," said the man across from him, "the government would compensate you fairly. We would have to work out a lot of details, but if there's no interest, or if you think this is not the sort of area you'd prefer to get involved in, then let's all walk out of this room as we came. Friends."

I'm not sure we came as friends, Massina thought.

"Anyone on your staff who was involved would need to pass extensive background checks," said the man on the right. "Of course, we would do everything we could to keep you safe, and your device safe. But there would be no guarantees. We would destroy it if things didn't work right."

Massina decided the seats had been arranged to make him think the man opposite him was in charge, but it seemed more likely it was this man on his right. They were all self-assured, all confident, and they certainly spoke like leaders used to having people agree with them. But the others glanced at this man a certain way.

Do my managers look at me that way?

"Explosives could be rigged in the device," said Massina, "timed to go off unless a command was given. And the programming is already set to erase itself within a certain period of time, as a security precaution; we download it with each use."

A recent innovation, given the Russian interest.

"But my company would have to be adequately compensated for our risk," added Massina.

"We would absolutely agree," said the man across from him. "If you need time to decide, we can give you twelve hours."

Massina looked at the man on his right, the one he thought was really in charge. "Answer one question: Does this involve the Russian intelligence service in any way?"

"It does. Not directly. But if we can rescue the man we're talking about, then they will be harmed severely."

"I'm in," said Massina. "What are the details?"

87

Two weeks after his meeting at CIA headquarters, Louis Massina stood in front of a console in the sub-basement of the Smart Metal building, staring at a hastily erected array of 5K video screens mounted on a partition in front of him. A small, shielded building had been constructed inside Underground Arena One as part of the most important project of Massina's life.

Or his biggest folly.

The miniature building within a building—"the box," they called it—connected Smart Metal and a small, very select group of engineers and scientists, along with a half dozen CIA analysts and specialists, with a covert six-member task force on its way to the Donetsk People's Republic. Besides feeds from Smart Metal's own sensors on the ground, the building within a building was able to receive feeds from the CIA's own covert networks and tie into a limited subset of the spy agency's network. The building and much of its infrastructure were so secret that only a few of Massina's own employees had been involved in its construction; security was provided by the Agency, much to the consternation of Bozzone, who'd had to argue strenuously to even be permitted inside as Massina's personal bodyguard.

Massina had not only learned the identity of the three men he'd met with—Yuri Johansen, a senior officer in charge of the extraction project, Agency Deputy Director Michael Blitz, Johansen's superior and the head of all covert activities at the CIA, and CIA Director James Colby—but he had also had extensive conversations with all three.

If this mission went well, Colby had promised, there would be room for many others in the future.

Massina wasn't sure he wanted that. The next few days might decide.

Johansen stood next to him at the consoles, reviewing recent satellite images of the "target" with someone at Langley. The Russians were still in charge at the prison and apparently at town hall, if the presence of their vehicles was any indication. Dan—the Agency operative who'd worked with Tolevi—had been ordered to stay away as they prepared the mission. That was for his safety as well as security for the mission, but it deprived them of what the spooks called "humanint"—human intelligence, the sort of critical yet often seemingly casual information that only a human being on the spot could gather. It was heresy to the techies, but there were many times when gossip in a bar was far more valuable than the finest-grained image a satellite could provide.

Massina walked back and forth behind the control console, waiting for a connection to the team traveling to the Ukraine. While they could talk at any time over an ultra-secure network, the very fact that there were electronic transmissions could tip off Russian intelligence to the team's presence. Even if this was only a very general threat, Johansen had insisted it be minimized, and until the actual launch of the mission, communications would be strictly limited to times and places that minimized detection.

A clock in the corner of the right-hand screen counted down the time to coms: 00:04:42. Four minutes, forty-two seconds.

Massina began pacing behind the console. Having his bots

on the scene meant he needed to have at least one of his people there.

Chelsea had been the logical person, by far. And if it had been anywhere else, doing anything else, he wouldn't have hesitated.

But . . .

Johansen, of course, had claimed there would be no danger, no exposure—she would be miles away from the prison. If someone was needed for last-minute programming and checks—something he, frankly, wasn't entirely convinced was necessary—then so be it; this would be accomplished in Donetsk. She would be covered there, and with security. She could leave at any point, and nothing would implicate her in the "project."

Completely safe.

Massina wondered if he had said that to Tolevi before he'd had part of his ear cut off.

Reservations aside, Chelsea had been the logical choice. Not only was she the most knowledgeable about Peter, the main bot being used, but she was also extremely familiar with the two other types of robots they were going to employ: Nighthawk, an aerial drone similar to (though larger than) the Hum they had used with the FBI, and Groucho, an off-the-shelf model that was considered disposable, chosen to provide diversion because its technology was not considered that advanced.

More advanced than what the Russians had, probably, but something the Chinese were already busy knocking off.

Chelsea had worked on all of those projects. She was young and athletic. She had already worked with the FBI. His reservations were strictly paternal—he felt very protective. Sexist maybe, because she was a young woman, but most likely he would have felt the same if one of his male engineers had been involved.

In the end, he'd decided to sound her out about it, expecting, knowing, that as soon as she heard of the project, she'd be all for it, regardless of the risks. That was the way she was. That was the way they all were.

Chelsea had all but asked when she could pack her bag.

The CIA had scooped her off for a three-day training session that was basically a mini-version of its SERE programs—the acronym for survival, evasion, resistance, escape, or what a person trapped behind enemy lines was supposed to do to survive.

It was a great course for combat pilots. Did it work for twenty-something computer geniuses? Hopefully they'd never find out.

Massina had had some of Peter's components dumbed down, just in case something went wrong with the fail-safe circuits that would autokill it. Still, the modifications only lessened its value; what was left would spare its captor at least three years of heavy R&D, assuming they were smart enough to use it.

Massina had also insisted on sending one more employee on the team to help Chelsea: Bozzone. His sole responsibility was getting Chelsea back alive.

Period.

And now they were on their way.

You must fight evil. You must do what you can do. Whatever the costs.

Massina walked around to the side of the room. The communications screen announced that "Puppet Master" was ready to receive communications.

Puppet Master—the code name for Smart Metal's "box."

It was Johansen's term. Running robots was a little like running puppets to someone outside the profession.

To Massina, the idea was to create robots that acted on their own. The *opposite* of a puppet master. But you could only explain so much.

Massina paced, trying to turn his thoughts upbeat.

What are the interesting aspects of this project?

An autonomous bot placed in situation where it knows the solution but not the proper steps to arrive at that solution.

Interconnectivity between different bots on a scale and in circumstances never attempted.

The role of sheer chance—unknown unknowns as a major component of the situation.

The last wasn't exactly a plus: not knowing what you didn't know was always a poor starting condition in the field.

"They're on the water, beyond Turkey," declared Johansen. The team had just sent a signal indicating they were en route to Donetsk. "We're under way."

Three minutes early, thought Massina. *I hope that's a good sign.*

88

The Black Sea—roughly the same time

Chelsea Goodman leaned over the gunwale and let loose. Even though she hadn't eaten since lunchtime and it was now well past nightfall, an amazing amount of half-digested food shot from her mouth over the side of the speedboat. Out of all the dangers she'd been warned of, by both her boss and the CIA people, seasickness had never once been mentioned. And in fact, she'd never been seasick before.

Chelsea liked new adventures. Vomiting, unfortunately, wasn't on the list.

Clinging to the side of the boat, she slipped down off her knees, settling onto the deck. She made her breathing more deliberate, trying to relax her stomach. But the hard chop of the boat made that almost impossible, no matter what yoga slogan she repeated to herself. In less than a minute, she was back over the side, spitting and puking some more.

"It'll pass," said Beefy, laying his hand gently on her back.

"Uh-huh," was all Chelsea could manage, leaning her face into the sea's spray.

TOLEVI, STANDING IN the cockpit of the speedboat, fixed his eyes on the light at starboard. It shone from the stern of a small fishing boat anchored off the Crimea Peninsula, maybe a half mile from shore. The boat was owned by one of their contacts; if there were any Russian patrol craft in the area, the light would be joined by another at the bow.

So far, so good. They'd gone nearly one hundred miles in the past three hours, setting off from Sinop, Turkey, a little village on the southern shore of the Black Sea. Tolevi ordinarily didn't ship from there—his wares were too bulky and his shipments too large—but the CIA liked the village for a number of reasons, including its proximity to an airfield. Tolevi suspected the Russians were well aware of this and kept the village and its varied ports under constant surveillance, but he was unable to persuade Johansen. And as in all things, when the Agency decided on something, it simply refused to change its mind.

Agency. It was an immovable entity beyond anyone's ability to control. Pigheaded and obtuse, and full of automatons with far less reasoning power, in Tolevi's opinion, than those packed away in Chelsea's boxes.

He had four of its agents with him, not counting the speedboat "driver," whom Tolevi recognized as a contract worker from an earlier encounter. The man in charge of the CIA contingent—he insisted on being called Paul White, though that wasn't even the name on his phony Turkish passport—was supposed to be taking orders from Tolevi, or at least consulting with him; that was the arrangement, as Johansen had made clear. But from the moment they'd met in Turkey, it was clear that White thought *he* was in charge.

Frankly, Tolevi wouldn't have had him as a driver, let alone a team leader. He was brusque with everyone he met, and while he did speak Russian, he tried to make up with speed what he lacked in pronunciation. This only emphasized how poor his language skills were.

He didn't sound much like a Turk either. Tolevi had no doubt their cover story would sink quickly if they were stopped.

Which was why his heart rate bumped up when a second light appeared on the fishing boat.

"I have Puppet Master," announced White, who was sitting in the cabin just below. "Confirming we're good."

"Turn the god damned radio off!" yelled Tolevi. "We have a Russian patrol boat out there."

"Where?" asked White.

"Why don't you take a better look at the god damned radar and tell me? That's what it's for."

BOZZONE HELPED CHELSEA to the bench in the open area aft of the speedboat's cockpit and cabin. Her stomach was still queasy, but at least it was empty.

"Water?" he asked.

"No. What's going on?"

"There's a patrol boat or something. We got a warning."

"Where?" asked Chelsea.

"Got me. Ukraine's on our left."

"To port."

"Aren't you the sailor," scoffed Bozzone.

"How long?"

"Assuming we get past them and into the Kerch Strait, three more hours. Don't sweat it; these guys probably do this all the time."

TOLEVI SAW THE dark outline of the Russian vessel about ten o'clock to port, long and dark and low against the black shadow of land behind it.

It was a big ship, probably a frigate.

Good thing, he thought. *They won't be interested in us small fry.*

Except they appeared to be. "Picking up speed, coming our

way," said Porter, who was lookout on the port side. He was an ex-SEAL, which Tolevi found reassuring—if the frigate cut them in half, he'd be able to rescue everyone in the water.

Tolevi jammed the throttle, hoping for a few more knots. The choppy water was cutting down on his speed; he was having trouble sustaining fifty knots.

Still, that was good speed, and he was easily outpacing the frigate.

Wasn't going to outrun its radio, though. There would be other patrols up in the straits.

Maybe they'd be interested, maybe not. It wasn't clear that they'd seen them, after all.

"You want to talk to Puppet Master?" asked White.

"No, for crap sake. Tell them we're good and get the hell off the radio. I can tell you work for the government," Tolevi added sarcastically. "You'd never make it in the real world."

89

"Puppet Master, we are five-by. Signing off."

"We copy," said Johansen. He looked up from his station. "They're good. Just coming up to Kerch Strait, between Crimea and Russia. Once they're beyond that, there are very few patrols they have to worry about. Four hours from now, they'll be in Berdyans'k, eastern Ukraine. Or Donetsk Republic, if that's your preference."

"There's a Russian ship nearby," said Massina, looking at the sitrep screen. It was a satellite map that plotted the team's position against a constantly updated grid of military and police assets in the region. Touching the screen delivered specific information about the asset—in this case, the Russian guided missile cruiser *Moskva*. The cruiser was the pride of the Black Sea fleet, its flagship and by far the most powerful craft in the area. Even its smallest gun could blast the speedboat out of the water.

"They know it," said Johansen. "They're avoiding it. There are patrol boats in the strait as well. It's nothing to get too excited about. Tolevi deals with this all the time."

"He told Bozzone he hasn't personally gone with a shipment on the Black Sea since before the war," said Massina pointedly.

"It's like riding a bicycle. You don't forget."

90

Kerch Strait, Black Sea—a short time later

They were past the big Russian ship, but, as Tolevi had expected, there was something else ahead, in the middle of the strait—smaller and quicker. A Rubin-class patrol boat, he suspected, capable of giving them serious problems.

Not as fast as he was, though. And not quite sure where he was yet, anyway.

Tolevi guided his speedboat eastward, heading in the direction of Tuzla Island, a spit of land that jutted out into the strait from Russia. The water there was shallow, not a problem for his craft as long as he was careful about it.

The patrol boat, which would have to be more careful, changed direction as well, heading toward them.

"They're broadcasting to unknown vessel, asking it to identify itself," said the CIA man handling the radios. "Maybe they do know we're here."

"Or maybe it's a bluff," said Tolevi. "We're not helping."

Would have been nice if Puppet Master IDed what we're dealing with, Tolevi thought. *Surely they could have done that. What the hell are they good for?*

"Ignore them," added Tolevi.

"Yeah, I wasn't going to answer."

The strait narrowed beyond the island, to a choke point less than three miles wide. There was a small Russian naval base near it. If the Russians were serious about stopping them, they could scramble boats from there to virtually blockade the strait.

Tolevi checked his gauges. He had enough fuel in the over-sized tanks and auxiliary to get back to Turkey.

Scratch the mission, give it a couple of days before trying again?

Who knew what would happen in the meantime? More than two weeks had passed since he was last in Donetsk. The more time passed . . .

Just get it done.

White poked his head out of the cabin. "What are you doing?"

"Ducking a Russian patrol, what do you think?" spat Tolevi. "I'm going to slide around to the east."

"You're heading right toward their base."

"Relax. We're not worth getting out of bed for."

"They can sink us from shore."

"Unlikely."

Actually, Tolevi had lost a boat to Russian patrols just after the Crimea takeover, probably in circumstances like this. But this wasn't a good time to share that information.

"Everybody just hold on," he announced. "I have to do some maneuvers."

"Depth is getting very shallow."

"I can see that."

He angled closer to the shore, then cut his speed, unsure in the dark what might be ahead. The patrol boat was still coming east, though it was now pointing a little south.

"He can't follow us here," Tolevi told White as he cut the motor almost to idle. "We'll be quiet and slip north."

"Then what?"

"I'll tell you that when I figure it out."

STILL A LITTLE queasy, Chelsea twisted around on the bench to see what they were running from. The Russian patrol boat was playing searchlights across the water less than two miles away.

"They don't have a good idea where we are," said Bozzone. "We're close enough to the shore that they lose us in the clutter. Their radars are not as good as the radars in the West."

Something clunked on the far side of the boat.

"Damn!" cursed Tolevi at the wheel.

The motor revved. They tipped sideways. For a moment, Chelsea thought they were going over. Then the boat suddenly surged ahead, swerving and righting itself.

"We gotta make it in one piece!" shouted Beefy.

"Everybody quiet," responded Tolevi coldly. "Sound carries on the water. Besides, I need to concentrate."

TOLEVI TUCKED BACK toward the deeper water. He had the shadow of land on his left.

The next fifteen minutes were critical. If he could get far enough north before the patrol boat turned, he'd be free—it could never keep up in the shallow water.

On the other hand, if it turned back west and went north now, it could make a race of it. With the island between them, he would have an edge in speed, but it would have a shorter distance.

Fifty-fifty.

Of course, if it turned, it was giving up blocking him from going south. But he'd already discarded that possibility.

A minute passed. Another.

Once past the bottleneck, he'd be good. *Keep going.*

"She's turning off," said Porter.

"Giving up?"

"Moving pretty fast," said the CIA officer. "West, northwest."

"Damn," muttered Tolevi. He slammed the throttle, trying to make the most of his head start.

91

Boston—same time

"There are two more patrol boats coming out in the north," said Johansen, pointing to the sitrep screen.

"Can we warn them?" asked Massina.

"That will tip the Russians off that something's there. Better letting Tolevi handle it."

Massina dropped into his chair, hands behind his head. His artificial limb felt cold.

Helpless.

92

Tolevi cut the engines, listening to the radio chatter. The Russians were definitely looking for them.

He was north of the island, a few hundred yards south of a rocky isthmus that poked down from the Russian side. If it weren't for the naval base directly ahead, he could just slide along the beach in the shallow water. But the radio made it clear that the Russians there were alert and he'd have little chance of getting away without being spotted.

"Let me see your NOD," he told Porter, asking for his night glasses.

The lookout came over with them.

"Take the helm. Just stay on this course, dead ahead, slow, not too much closer to the land."

"No worries there."

Tolevi took the glasses and climbed up onto the forward deck, bracing himself on the rail. He couldn't see the Russian patrol boat that had followed him, or any of the other boats they were talking to.

There was a merchant ship, a smallish cargo carrier, about a mile away in the channel, heading north.

My shadow.

Tolevi scrambled back to the wheel. Revving the motor, he started in a beeline for the cargo ship.

"Keep watching for the patrol boats," he told Porter and the other lookout. "They're going to come right down there. Probably they'll split, one forward, one kind of back up on either side, probably toward land, figuring we're hiding in the shadows. I'm going to swing around that cargo boat and ride near it for a bit."

"That's right in the middle of the channel."

"Yes."

CHELSEA WATCHED THE lights of the cargo vessel grow. It seemed oblivious to them.

"He's using the bigger boat to hide," explained Bozzone. "Old smugglers' trick."

If there were people aboard the cargo vessel—and surely there were—Chelsea couldn't see them. The large, lumbering craft stayed on its course, moving very slowly parallel to the shore, in exactly the direction they were taking.

There were one or two ships beyond, one moving north, one coming south. The speedboat slid around the port side of the cargo vessel, slowing to ride parallel.

"There's the patrol boat," said Beefy, pointing aft.

"It's what's ahead that counts, right?" asked Chelsea. She got up, legs still rubbery, and made her way over to the cockpit area.

"Another patrol boat further north," said White, emerging from below. "They're talking back and forth."

"They see us?"

"No, but I think they may suspect we're near the cargo craft."

"What if you had a diversion?" asked Chelsea. "Make them think we're somewhere else?"

"Brilliant," mocked Tolevi. "You have something like a destroyer handy?"

"How about some flares?"

"That'll show them where we are. Go back to throwing up."
What an asshole.

"If we load some flares on one of the drones and set them off back near the shore," said Chelsea tightly, "maybe they'll think we crashed."

Tolevi didn't answer.

"Well?" she asked.

"If you can do it, sure," he told her, the edge in his voice gone.

Chelsea wobbled back to Bozzone.

"Help me get one of the Nighthawks ready," she told him.

THERE WERE TWO patrol boats north, one right at the choke point and another somewhere farther north, according to the radio steaming toward it. Meanwhile, the craft they had ducked to the south was steaming northward.

Tolevi edged the speedboat so close to the cargo ship that he could just about touch the hull.

One good set of waves and they would be swimming. But at least according to the radio chatter, the Russians still weren't sure where they were. The cargo ship was like a shield, blocking their view.

Not for long. The boat from the south told the others it was heading for it.

"If you're launching that UAV," Tolevi told Chelsea, "do it quick."

CHELSEA INSPECTED THE small, battery-powered UAV as Bozzone pulled it from its case. With a wingspan roughly as wide as a desk, the UAV was designed for slow, silent surveillance. It had two electric engines, one front, one back. Unlike Peter, it was not fully autonomous; it needed to be programmed in advance, or, alternatively, it could follow radio commands.

There was a small payload carriage underneath. She could attach a flare there, but how to ignite it?

"How about we put a flare gun there?" suggested Bozzone. "Rig the payload claws to fire it."

"Yes!"

Chelsea saw it in her head. Rather than firing the flare outward, though, she would fire it at a jug of fuel.

"I need a gas can," she told Bozzone.

"We can't afford to lose any fuel," warned Tolevi.

"We can't afford to get caught," she snapped. "I need some of those straps."

THE CARGO VESSEL slowed, complying with an order from the Russians to heave to. Tolevi decided his best bet was to slip in front and run for it. That would hide him from the craft to the south, probably, but definitely expose him to the ships north.

One problem at a time.

He didn't think Chelsea's diversion was going to work. But at least the girl was trying to do something, unlike White.

"Stand by!" yelled Chelsea behind him.

The drone started up. It sounded like a miniature electric fan, and not a particularly strong one.

"More speed would make it easier to launch," she said.

"That's easy," said Tolevi, reaching for the throttle.

BEFORE THEY'D LEFT, Chelsea had practiced flying the Nighthawks, but launching from a moving platform was always tricky. The aircraft dipped as she revved it off the deck, ducking left and heading for the waves. *Come on, damn you!*

As if hearing her thoughts, the little hawk spurt upward. Chelsea brought the joystick even, leveling off at about a hundred feet. There was just enough light from the deck of the cargo ship to see its outline as she turned it eastward.

The speedboat bounced sharply against the waves as it picked up speed. Chelsea took her hand off the stick, worried she might inadvertently jerk the little UAV into the water.

"It would be great if you could keep the boat smooth!" she shouted.

"It would be even better if we could sprout wings and fly," said Tolevi.

The control panel had a thirteen-inch screen that plotted the aircraft's position via GPS; optical feeds from the UAV could also be selected. Chelsea nudged the plane east in the direction of the shore. It didn't move very fast; at top speed it wouldn't even be able to stay with the speedboat.

It reached 30.3 knots.

"How far is the eastern shore?" she asked.

"A little more than a mile and a half," said Bozzone.

"Do we have that diversion or not?" asked Tolevi.

"I need a minute and a half," said Chelsea.

"Patrol boat is rounding the cargo ship," said Porter. "They'll have a clear view in a few seconds."

Chelsea switched the control pad to cargo mode, which allowed her to manipulate the claws on the underbelly.

She pressed the right claw button.

Nothing happened.

Damn.

THERE WAS ANOTHER harbor to port about a mile ahead. It was primarily for cargo, with a set of slips at the southwest side used by ferries.

Most likely there would be Russians there, or at least some sort of night watch. But going ashore was better than swimming. There was always a chance they could bribe their way past trouble, unlike on the water.

Assuming they made it in one piece. The Russians were broadcasting to the unknown boat again, and they sounded angry.

CHELSEA LOOKED AT the controls. What had she done wrong?

She hit the button again, but nothing happened.

Left, right, port, aft . . .

Oh my God, I wired it upside down.

She hit the button for the other claw.

Red light exploded in the sky nearly two miles away, illuminating the night.

"There's your diversion," she said, quickly releasing the flare and its trigger.

TOLEVI COULD SEE the ferry landing less than a mile away when White yelled from below that the Russians to the north had just spotted the flare.

"They're going to check it out," he yelled from below.

"Porter, where's that patrol boat?" asked Tolevi.

"Just pulling even with the cargo ship. Got their lights on them."

"They coming for us?"

"Can't tell."

Tolevi veered away from the landing, heading north at full speed.

CHELSEA GUIDED THE drone back in their direction, but the speedboat was pulling steadily away.

"You're going to have to slow down so the Nighthawk can catch up," she told Tolevi.

"No way," he answered. "We don't have time to wait for your toy."

"That toy just saved our butts."

"We're not out of trouble yet. I still have a boat north of us."

Chelsea was too busy trying to fly the aircraft to see what was going on around her. The speedboat was moving as quickly as it could, very close to the western shore. She caught a glimpse of searchlights off the starboard side.

"Four miles to open water," said Tolevi. "Push, pray, or get out of the way."

She set the course on auto, which allowed the UAV to continue flying on its own, then selected the infrared image. One of the Russian patrol boats was less than a half mile from the plane, just to the left. She could see two sailors running on the forward deck.

Then it was past.

There was another ahead, this one at about two o'clock.

Painted black and relatively small, the UAV was not only invisible to the radar aboard the patrol boat but difficult for its crew to spot visually as well. And the boat easily drowned out the electric drone of its motor. There was no sign that the boat had spotted the aircraft.

The vessel grew larger. She could see its profile, long and sleek, like a miniature yacht with a deck gun on top.

"That second boat, the one still in front of us, it looks like it's coming in our direction," she told Tolevi.

"No shit."

Something flashed on the deck.

"I think they're firing at us," she said.

TOLEVI'S HEART POUNDED as a geyser erupted a hundred yards away. When was the last time he'd been fired at?

Never by a patrol boat.

Bad time for a first.

"They stopped ordering us to stop," yelled White.

"Get your life jackets on," answered Tolevi. "Pick out a spot on the shore and swim for it if we go down."

AT THIS RATE, there was no way the Nighthawk was going to catch up to the speedboat. But the Russian craft, slowing in its turn, was less than a half mile away.

The bridge was a huge greenhouse atop a sloping superstructure, with large plate-glass windows all around. She could see it plainly in the screen.

Chelsea nudged the stick until the windows were dead on in the screen. She aimed at the one closest to the bow.

Another shell whizzed overhead.

"Typical Russian aim," snickered Tolevi.

Chelsea nudged the stick a little higher. The plate-glass window grew large in the screen.

Then it went black.

SOMETHING FLARED ON the Russian patrol boat. Tolevi glanced in its direction, then continued steering, ducking as close to shore as he dared.

Two more miles. Two more. Then just north.

Porter came over and started to pull a life jacket over Tolevi's head. Tolevi started to resist, then realized what he was doing.

But there were no other shells.

"I got this," he said aloud, sensing they'd made it.

"Russian is dead in the water," said White a moment later. "They claim their bridge was hit by a missile."

Tolevi looked back at Chelsea.

"You hit it with the UAV?"

"Dead on."

"Nice," he told her. "Double ration of vodka at dinner tonight."

"I prefer beer," she told him. "Or better, a Coke."

93

Boston—a short time later

"They're past the Russian ships," said Johansen. "There was an explosion on one of the Russian vessels. Very fortunate."

Massina, greatly relieved, got out of his seat. He doubted luck had anything to do with it—more likely, he guessed, they had used one of the UAVs as a weapon.

Which undoubtedly would have been Chelsea's doing. So she was meant to be on the mission. And she could take care of herself.

"Next coms will be when they land," said Johansen. "There are no Russian vessels between them and the shore. We'll monitor for air traffic, but all the Russian patrols are based far to the southeast, in Russia; they should be OK."

"That's a relief," said Massina. "I'm going to check on things. I'll be back."

"I'll be here."

MASSINA HAD A mental list of improvements he was going to make *if* he continued working with the government: Constant real-time communications that could not be detected. Full coverage of the target area to show where any "obstacles" (such as the Russian ships) were located. Some sort of quick reaction force ready to bail operatives out.

It could all be done with his devices.

Johnny Givens, who had taken over temporarily as his body-guard, was waiting outside the box.

"How'd it go?" asked Johnny.

And that was another thing—his people would have access to the box. Period.

"They have a ways to go," said Massina. "Johnny, you have a clearance from the government, right?"

"There's different levels of clearance. They do background checks—"

"You could pass a CIA clearance check, right?"

"Of course."

"You're with me when I'm inside from now on. Nobody tells you no."

"Great."

Massina made his way across the large room to the elevator.

"You know, I'd rather be out there with them," said Johnny.

"You have a long way to go."

"Next time."

If there is a next time, maybe, thought Massina, but he didn't say it.

BORYA TOLEVI LEANED toward the screen, looking at the string of integers and symbols. She had the entire day off from school, which meant she could work here until early afternoon, when Martyak got back from her classes and would be expecting her.

Borya was working on a defense against application layer attacks similar to what she had used to compromise the ATM networks. In her case, she had used coding that attacked a flaw in a database that left account information intact rather than purging it. The block of instructions in front of her sought to fix that.

She hadn't understood everything involved in her original

attack; mostly, she had followed a script she'd found on the Internet and made some slight adaptations as she'd gone. Now she saw that fixing the problem was somewhat complicated, a puzzle that forced her to think in metaphors as well as code. The instructions were like keys fitting into locks that had to then disappear without a trace.

People didn't do that. Her father was gone, yet so much of him was still present, in her, in others.

"Have you broken the program yet?" asked Louis Massina.

Borya jumped.

"Didn't mean to scare you."

"How's Chelsea?" Borya asked.

"She's fine. So's your dad."

"Where are they?"

"Still can't say. They have you working on the database hacks?"

"I'm looking at it. It's pretty involved," she confessed. "It's like a college class."

"Graduate level," said Massina. "Keep at it."

"Hey, Johnny." Borya waved at the tall former FBI agent. "You hanging with me tonight?"

"If I'm on the schedule." The security people took turns.

"Mary was wondering when you were coming back," said Borya. "You should ask her for a date."

"Can't mix work with pleasure," said Johnny shyly.

"Why not?"

MARTYAK'S BLOND CURLS and ample breasts were a powerful attraction. She was pretty, and before his injury Johnny wouldn't have hesitated asking her out.

Now, though . . .

Johnny followed Massina down the hall to the elevator. Shadowing him inside the building was pretty boring. It did take him everywhere, though; he was really getting to know his way around.

"You're looking a little pale," said Massina as they waited.

"Yeah."

"Tired, too?"

"Time for the meds."

"Go ahead."

"I feel like a junkie."

"If you want privacy . . ."

Massina turned his back to him. Johnny reached into his jacket and took out the syringe set. He pulled up his shirt and injected himself, à la a diabetic, as the elevator arrived.

"Good as new?" asked Massina.

Never as good as new, thought Johnny. But good enough, and sometimes better.

94

In the years immediately following the dissolution of the Soviet Union, there were great plans to turn Berdyans'k—or Бердянськ, as it was styled in Ukrainian—into a major international tourist area. It had many of the necessary ingredients: a nearby airport, a train hub, a willing workforce, and, most importantly, beautiful seaside beaches and relatively accommodating weather.

But neither high hopes nor great assets equated to success, and the city never quite fulfilled its boosters' dreams. Meanwhile, much of the nearby industry, which had scuttled along during the Soviet era, went through hard times, starved of investment.

The civil war further harmed Berdyans'k. Activity at the harbor was a shadow of what it had been even a year before. The cranes along the western stretch of the piers stood idle, almost lonely in the night.

All of this meant opportunity for a smuggler. Fewer prying eyes, more hands eager for handouts. While Tolevi had never done any business here, he scanned the quiet docks and warehouses with knowing eyes as they approached.

Money to be made here. Make a note of it.

Coffee by the boatload, right on that pier.

A green light blinked at the far end of the docks, under one of the large cranes ordinarily used to take cargo containers off a ship. Tolevi cut the engines and drifted, wanting to get a good look before committing to the dock. The Russian forces to the south were on high alert, still not entirely sure what had happened or where their foe was. While the radio traffic did not indicate they were searching this far north, there was always the possibility that some overdiligent junior lieutenant would feel the itch to prove himself by mounting an extra watch.

"That's them," said White after flashing the recognition code back.

"Let's sit here a second and make sure," Tolevi told him. "Porter, we got anything out that way?"

"Only that fishing boat we passed on the way in."

Tolevi stepped over to take the glasses. The small boat anchored about a half mile to the southeast bobbed with the waves, a dim light at the fantail. It could easily be a smuggler's sentry, or just a fisherman who liked spending the night alone on the water.

Money to be made here.

Tolevi then went to the starboard side and scanned the dock area and wharf beyond. Two vans were parked next to a building back by the crane.

His connection.

"All right, let's go in," he said, returning to the helm.

CHELSEA'S STOMACH RILED slightly as she clambered out of the boat to the dock, and she had to step to the side as the others carried the waterproof boxes with the bots and other gear from the cabin to the waiting vans.

Bozzone waited for her to catch her breath, then nudged her gently to walk with him in front of the vans. Tolevi was standing with the man they met on the dock—"Dan"—whom he seemed to know.

Tolevi put up his hand to warn them back, then stepped with Dan a few feet away.

"What are we doing?" Chelsea asked Bozzone.

"No English." His voice was barely audible.

Chelsea rubbed her eyes. Pulling all-nighters in the lab was one thing; pulling them out here was something completely different.

And yet this didn't feel like a place of danger, especially after what they'd just been through. It was too quiet.

They could be back home, or on a vast sound stage, waiting for a movie to be filmed. The sky in the distance, a faint blue between dark black waves and thick clouds, was a painted scrim, shadowed by hidden lights. The sounds of the night—some seabirds, the relentless lapping of water against the docks—were piped in from speakers stashed full circle around the stage.

Tolevi left the other man and walked toward the vans. He yelled something in Russian or Ukrainian—Chelsea had trouble distinguishing the languages—and the men helping them boarded the vans.

Chelsea started for the nearest van, but Tolevi stopped her.

"Our car's up the road," he told her.

"Car?" asked Bozzone.

"Complications. We have to change our plan. This will be safer for both of you."

THE BUTCHER'S BROTHER had kept tabs on Olak Urum's location in the prison with the help of two guards who were close friends of the family, an arrangement the Russian crackdown had failed to end. Earlier in the evening, one of the guards had told him his brother had been moved; Dan had only just been informed before coming to the rendezvous.

The question was where he'd been moved to. The guards didn't know, and while the brother had a few ideas, he hadn't had a chance to check them out.

Given that, Tolevi had opted not to go to Starobeshevskaya, even though that had been the plan. It was too small a place to risk staying for several days, if it came to that. So they were going to a backup south of Donetsk, about a two-hour drive away. There they would split up.

"The gear will be on a farm. We'll stay in a safe house about a mile away," Tolevi told Chelsea and Bozzone. "It's more comfortable, and I can make phone calls from there without attracting attention, and our cover story will make more sense. Plus, there are beds. I'm guessing you don't want to sleep on the floor with the boys."

"Might be interesting," shot back Chelsea.

"Never at a loss for a comeback, huh?"

"Are you?"

"Only when I talk to my daughter." *She's a lot like you,* he thought. *But you're not necessarily as sharp as you think. There's more to the universe than slinging numbers around.*

They drove in silence for the next hour. Chelsea and Bozzone both nodded off. Tolevi turned up the radio, afraid he was going to do the same.

H–20 was the main road north, dividing farm fields and skirting urban areas much like a highway back in the States. Tolevi stayed on it until he was a little more than halfway to his destination. Fearing he might run into a checkpoint as he got closer to Donetsk, he got off near Buhas and began making his way west, using the GPS to guide him, since he had only a vague idea of where he was.

Ordinarily, the back roads were a better bet against checkpoints and patrols. And according to the briefing he'd been given before leaving on the mission, there were almost no more rebel road stoppages in the area.

So when he realized he was heading for one about ten minutes from the farmhouse where he was headed, Tolevi momentarily thought of running through it.

Foolish, foolish.

Unless they've already decided to kill us.

"Up!" he told the others. "Wake up. Remember your cover story. We're being stopped."

An old car had been pushed across the road, blocking off all traffic. There were two pickup trucks on the other side, parked parallel to the road just off the shoulder. A group of men huddled near an oil drum, smoking cigarettes. One of them stepped out, holding up his AK-47 to signal that Tolevi should stop.

As if I have another choice.

Tolevi rolled down the window as he coasted to a stop. He put on his best cheery voice, even though he was tired as hell.

Ukrainians, not Russians.

Good.

Maybe. They'll be more apt to shoot.

"Gentlemen, hello," he said in Ukrainian. "How goes it?"

"Where are you headed?"

"I am taking the model and her photographer to Klaven Farm. I have to be there by dawn for their photo shoot."

The man who'd stopped them leaned over, peering in the back. Chelsea and Bozzone blinked at him.

"Model?" asked the man. He reeked of cigarettes.

"A photo shoot for some fancy French magazine. She is from Africa," added Tolevi. "Somalia."

"Ah, exotic."

"Yes."

"Does she fuck?"

"I don't ask."

They looked disappointed, but not inclined to find out for themselves.

"We have to search the car, comrade. Open the trunk and step out."

"I don't mind you searching," Tolevi said, "but I am late, and if you could hurry it along, it would be appreciated."

The man frowned. Tolevi reached for the trunk latch, then opened the car door. As he did, he palmed a ten-euro note from his pocket.

"If I am late they take it from my pay," he said, producing the bill. "Worse, they don't use me again. Let me help you."

The man grabbed the money, then walked to the back. Two of his companions came over to gawk at Chelsea and Bozzone. There were at least two other irregulars at the side of the road, smoking cigarettes near a rusted oil drum.

"They have papers?" the man asked Tolevi.

"Yes. The company insists on working the right way." Tolevi shrugged, as if he were talking about an affliction. "They're always getting their permits and meeting with the big shots."

"They speak Ukrainian?"

"They don't speak much at all. I don't know. African or something. Maybe English, if you try a bit."

"Where are you from, comrade?" The tone was suddenly suspicious.

"Kiev," Tolevi said proudly. "We got out after the traitors took over. My brother is still there, in jail. Since then, Donetsk. But someday, I will be back. Someday."

The man nodded. He leaned to his left, glancing around the trunk—it was empty—then waved Tolevi away.

"Go. Good luck with your task. She looks pretty, at least. Maybe you will get lucky later."

95

The box—Boston, a short time later

"ISIS is taking credit for the attack on the Russian ship," Johansen told Massina. He'd just sent the order. "A bit of misdirection."

"Will the Russians believe it?"

"Probably just enough to prevent them from looking too thoroughly for our friends," said the CIA officer. "In the meantime, we'll continue looking for the butcher. They can't have taken him far."

"They could have flown him back to Russia," said Massina. "What then?"

"I can't rule it out," admitted Johansen. "If that's what happened, then we pull the plug. We get everyone across the border to Kiev, as planned, and they come home. I doubt that's the story, though. More than likely he is in Donetsk somewhere. Just a question of finding him. These sorts of things are to be expected. They happen. No covert operation ever goes the way you plan. It's not a computer program."

"Those don't always go the way you plan either," said Massina. "How long do we wait?"

"A few days. There's no rush that we know of."

"The fact that they moved the prisoner doesn't mean anything to you?"

"There's nothing we can do about it at this point. We just keep plugging away. Don't worry, Dan's one of the best."

"And Tolevi?"

"He's very good at what he does," allowed Johansen. "As long as his own agenda isn't in conflict with ours, things should go well."

96

South of Donetsk—twelve hours later

Tolevi sat in a small café and sipped his coffee. This was the worst cup yet.

You can make a fortune here! And you don't even have to smuggle it in. Import from Indonesia through Brunei, roast it in one of those empty warehouses down in Berdyans'k.

Cha-ching, cha-ching. Let the cash registers flow.

The bell at the door rang, nearly in time with Tolevi's mental notes. He looked up and saw Dan entering with the butcher's brother. Both looked glum.

They glanced around the place for a moment, then came over to the table and sat.

"So?" asked Tolevi.

The butcher's brother shook his head. "They don't know."

"We have to check the main municipal prison in the city," Dan said. "They reopened it last month. It's the logical place."

"How do we do that?" asked Tolevi.

"I have friends," said the brother. "I'll know by the end of the week."

"That's too long," said Tolevi. "We're taking too much risk as it is."

"It can't go any faster."

Tolevi glanced up at the waitress, who was coming over with menus. Dan waved her off, but the brother ordered *ryba,* fried fish.

"How do we speed it up?" Tolevi asked.

"Any other way is going to be too risky," said Dan, shaking his head. "This guy isn't worth it."

"If he's not worth it, then why are we here?" Tolevi answered.

He glanced at the brother. He was grimacing.

"I'm not saying we don't get him out." Dan backtracked. "I'm just saying we take our time. We have to get him out in one piece. If we rush, they'll kill him."

"And if we wait here too long, we get killed."

TOLEVI THOUGHT ABOUT Dan's reaction as he drove back to the house where Chelsea and Bozzone were holed up. Dan had marked out the boundaries of the risks he was willing to take and trusted the brother more than Tolevi thought warranted. Risk assessment was a matter of perspective: Dan spent a lot of time in the country and could easily fit in, so he didn't see waiting around as dangerous. Whereas Tolevi, who knew that the people he was with stood out like sore thumbs, saw far more danger in waiting.

Whose perspective was right?

Mine.

The whole mission was risky. That's why they were willing to pay so much.

Too much?

The CIA had put an awful lot of energy into getting a rebel out of jail. Maybe he did have information on the Russian "volunteers," but so what? Everybody in the world knew that the Russians were running things; why go to such lengths to prove it?

Of the five CIA officers who'd come with them, four were paramilitary people, covert agents trained in special operations.

From what Tolevi gathered of their backgrounds, all but one were military, the one SEAL and two Rangers. The fourth spoke Russian as well as he did.

White was older than the others, by ten years. He hadn't shared his background with Tolevi—he was way too gruff for that—but it was obvious from the way he carried himself that he was used to being in charge, and Johansen had been noticeably respectful. So figure him for a very senior guy.

It really doesn't matter, does it? Just figure out where the hell he is . . . Damn!

"I know where he is," said Tolevi out loud. He reached for the GPS and zoomed out the map to get his bearings.

THE HOUSE CHELSEA and Bozzone were staying in was an old farmhouse, abandoned for some time. The floors were covered with dust. The few pieces of furniture in the front room—a pair of wooden kitchen tables and three chairs, one of them broken— were well worn and looked as if they dated from the early twentieth century. The mattresses upstairs were new, but they were the exceptions. There was no electricity, and the toilets had to be flushed with water from the jugs stacked along the walls.

Bored, Chelsea reached into her bag and pulled out the paperback of Sudoku puzzles, flipping to the back section where the hardest puzzles were. She'd done most of them on the plane, saving the last two.

They weren't math problems per se, though there were mathematical equations you could use to describe the puzzle and its possible solutions:

$$\text{N combinations for B2} = \sum_{k=0..3} \binom{3}{k}^3$$

"Still doing your puzzles?" asked Bozzone.

"I'd love to take a walk."

"Too dangerous. We don't want to be seen."

"The nearest house is a mile away. No one can see us from the road."

"Didn't you have enough excitement on the water?"

"I sure puked enough." Chelsea went back to the puzzle.

TOLEVI RECOGNIZED THE road even before he saw the Russian military vehicle parked along the side.

There was no question of going inside—the Russian colonel would surely imprison him. But it was the most logical place for them to have brought the butcher.

The question was how to find out if he was there.

Has to be there. The brother would know if he was anywhere else.

Two Russian commandos were standing by the truck. Tolevi drove past, eyes on the road.

Has to be there, he thought. *Now, how do I prove it?*

97

Outside Boston—around the same time

Jenkins took a deep breath, then pushed into the jail's interrogation room. Stratowich sat at the table, stoically erect and staring straight ahead. The room was bare, except for the table, two chairs, and a pair of surveillance cameras in each corner.

"You have a shiner," said Jenkins, sitting across from him. "I heard you were in a fight."

Stratowich didn't acknowledge him.

"There's some pretty serious charges against you," said Jenkins. "Attempted murder. Kidnapping."

"I didn't kidnap anyone."

"I guess the court will decide that." Jenkins reached into his jacket pocket and pulled out a bag of M&Ms. He tossed it across the table. "I heard you had a sweet tooth."

Stratowich continued staring straight ahead.

"Your friends haven't lifted a finger to help you," said Jenkins. "They want you to take the rap for everything."

No answer.

"You know they were Russian agents, right? Spies. Working

with them makes you a traitor. You're an American citizen. How does it feel to betray your country?"

Nothing.

"The thugs you were with, they're talking a lot," continued Jenkins. "Now, it would seem to me, well, you could be in a position to help yourself. And your family. You have two kids, don't you? You'd probably like to see them at some point. Make sure they're OK. I could arrange that."

Stratowich reached for the candy. Jenkins watched as he opened the package, tearing it neatly along the top. He made a very small hole, popping out a candy onto the table. He picked it up deliberately and put it into his mouth, not chewing, letting it melt.

"There are a lot of things you could help with. And if you did, we have a program to protect you. If you help us. Whole new identity, new start on life. People have been placed around the world. It's surprising what they've accomplished as free men."

Another candy, but no words.

He's trying to show me he's disciplined, thought Jenkins. *Well, I'm not impressed.*

"One of the things I'm interested in has to do with the murder of a federal agent," he told the prisoner. "Funny thing is, he has the same last name as I do. In fact, he was my brother. If someone helped me figure out who that was, I would be very grateful. Extremely grateful."

Stratowich raised his eyes to look at him. Jenkins barely managed to duck before a half-melted M&M shot from Stratowich's mouth.

"Think about it," Jenkins told him, getting up. "You can keep the candy."

98

"The only way we can find out is to go in there." Tolevi folded his arms. With all but two of the team inside—the others were standing watch on the road—the tiny front room of the farmhouse felt almost claustrophobic. He could smell Dan's sweat. White paced behind Chelsea, who was sitting in one of the chairs. The rest of the chairs were empty; none of the others wanted to admit they were tired.

"Huge risk," said White. "You go in, there's no guarantee we can get you out."

"We run the same play we were going to run on the prison," said Tolevi. He'd thought about it the entire ride back, pluses and minuses, every contingency. "I spot him, you come in and get us out."

"The robot can only carry one person," said Chelsea. "And it's not armed."

"We don't need the robot," argued Tolevi. "I only need a diversion. You have your little airplane things tell us where people are. We wait until they've gone out on their mission—they go every afternoon and they're away for most of the night?"

"We don't know that for sure," said Dan.

"I do," said Tolevi. "They have a dozen people. Just about everyone goes on a mission—there's only a skeleton crew there. Blow up the front of the building, start a fire. I go out the back with the butcher, grab a vehicle, and we're out."

"Pretty chancy," said White. "I don't like it."

"Then come up with a better plan. Because we can't stay here forever. We don't even have enough food in the house for the rest of the week."

CHELSEA LISTENED AS the debate continued. It reminded her of the single college debate she had witnessed, where both sides made arguments but neither could really make a convincing case. Tolevi said it was their only choice; White said it was too risky. Dan wasn't sure.

Who was right? Impossible to say.

"We could do some reconnaissance," she suggested finally. "Fly one of the drones overhead, see how many people are inside with the infrared. Maybe we can figure out where he is."

"The building is two stories," said White.

"It should be able to pick up heat signatures. It's an old building, right? Minimal insulation. It's worth a try."

"Can it see into the basement?" asked White. "That's where they're likely to be held."

"If the sensors were good enough to see inside the prison building," said Tolevi, "it'll see inside this. It's an old building. Impressive from the outside, but once you look closely you see everything's thin and falling apart. Besides, what's our other option?"

"You're awful damn gung-ho," said White.

"You're awful damn cautious."

"The first goal of any mission is to survive it," said White. "That's all I'm saying."

"Let's try the recon then," said Tolevi. "The alternative is packing it in. Because we're not going to pick up anything on the street. We'd know already. So it's this or we go home."

"When do you check in with the butcher's brother?" asked White.

"An hour. But he would have called if he had something."

"Let's try the drone," said White.

AN HOUR LATER, Chelsea entered the barn where they'd stashed the robots. The two vans were parked in the middle of the open space; the gear boxes were arranged along the side.

The place smelled like cows. Her nose began to itch, and her stomach—still slightly queasy from the night before—growled.

Work to do.

She had the case open before Bozzone and the others were even inside.

"We'll launch from the field at the back," she announced. "You better make sure it's clear."

It'd seemed so easy when she'd said it back at the house. Now she only saw problems: What if she couldn't launch it? What if someone saw them from one of the fields down the road? What if the UAV was spotted? It was black, designed to fly at night. During the day, with the sun fairly bright, it would be a lot more obvious.

Just do it.

"Help me with the wings," she asked Bozzone.

TOLEVI PACED AROUND the barn, waiting as Chelsea got the UAV ready.

He thought of Borya, back home.

Not good—concentrate.

One million bucks. The solution to a lot of problems.

And if this didn't work, then damn it, Johansen was going to pay him something. Half at least. Three-quarters.

I risked my life. You owe me.

Owe you what? Johansen would say.

Hardass.

That was the only way you survived in that job. Tolevi had to admire that; he was a hardass himself.

"Ready to launch," said Chelsea. She looked at him. "Coming?"

THE RUSSIAN BUILDING was some ten miles to the north. Besides the main house and the barnlike garage at the rear Tolevi had seen when he was their prisoner, there were two small sheds on the other side of the copse to the south. There was only one vehicle outside; the unit was obviously out on a mission.

"Let's look inside the house," Tolevi told Chelsea. "Put on the infrared."

"I have to fly right overhead and fly a circuit," she told him. "Those men at the road may be able to see the Nighthawk."

"Chance we take."

Chelsea decided to take the UAV low, hoping that the trees at the front of the property would shield it from view. They would probably hear it, though.

Three passes, she decided. *Three passes and we should have enough.*

She thought of plotting the course and letting the controller fly the aircraft but decided against it. If someone came out of the house, it would be faster to abort if she was at the controls.

Her hand started to tremble as she tucked toward the house on the first pass.

I can do this. Just like dancing.

Not really. But I can do it.

The small aircraft came across the back of the building faster than she thought it would. By the time she had it turning, it was nearly at the tree line. She tightened the turn and banked over the building. The controller was recording the infrared feed; they'd look at it when she was done. She needed her full attention on the ground.

Banking again, she spotted a figure walking near the barn.

Concentrate. One more pass.

Chelsea took the UAV so close to the roof that she nearly hit it. Three turns, done.

She jammed the throttle. The nose of the aircraft pitched up suddenly, starting to stall. Gently she backed off power, managed to catch it, and sailed back over the open field.

"They saw something," said White, who was standing behind her. "I saw the guy at the back look up."

"Did he raise his gun?" asked Dan.

"No."

"Whatever," said Tolevi. "What do we got?"

Chelsea set the plane on a slow course south, then activated the autopilot. She pulled up the infrared screen and reviewed the video over the house.

It was shorter than she'd thought—barely forty-five seconds.

"Two guys there, one there," said White. "That's it?"

Tolevi leaned over the screen. "This is where I was. This looks like a kitchen. Maybe it's the command room or team room. That's why there's two guys there."

"How do you know that's the kitchen?" asked White.

"Look. You can see this is a sink, right? The heat outline? And a stove."

"OK."

"This guy is by himself," said Tolevi, pointing to the other side of the house.

"Prisoner?" asked White. "Or just someone taking a nap?"

Chelsea zeroed in on him, enlarging the image. His hands were together. Possibly tied, maybe not.

"Is that the basement?" White asked.

"It looks like it," said Chelsea. "That's how the computer is interpreting it."

The program wasn't sophisticated enough to make a full 3-D image, but the different angles indicated that the third person was below the others. Which did mean the basement.

"All right, well, with only three people in there, the time to go is now," said Tolevi.

"There are four outside around the property," said Chelsea, zooming back. "Two at the front, two at the garage area."

"Yeah, I got that. Better than twenty." He went over to the case that had their tracking device, which had been engineered to look like a watch. He took out the reader, then tested it by pressing the lower right button twice.

"Make sure this works," he told Porter, who was standing nearby.

"We keep a UAV watching the place," suggested White. "They come back early, we pull the plug."

"Fine," said Tolevi. "I'll be back."

Chelsea went back to the Nighthawk's visual feed. It was flying toward a small hamlet.

Damn.

She banked to the north, pushing it to gain altitude.

"How long before dark?" she asked.

"Two and a half hours before sunset," said White. "People spot it?"

"Not yet."

"Keep it south of the homestead, and watch those roads. This way if they see it, they may not put two and two together."

"Maybe they'll think it's Russian," said Bozzone. "Or a bird."

"Or a psycho ceiling fan with wings," said Chelsea.

For the first time since the mission had begun, everyone laughed.

99

North of Donetsk—an hour later

Here it was, a million dollars. All he had to do was walk in, locate the butcher, send the signal, and let the games begin.

Tolevi did a last-minute com check.

"You guys hearing me?" he asked White, who was with the paras in the trucks a half mile behind him, each pulled off to the side of a different road. Any sign of trouble, and they would pounce.

"Yeah. We're all ready here. Everyone's in place."

"Doin' it," said Tolevi, taking a deep breath as he started his car.

Chelsea and the bots were with White. Assuming Tolevi found the butcher, they'd launch the assault an hour after dusk, when it was plenty dark. If things went south in the meantime, they'd either go in with guns blazing, or . . .

There was no "or." This had to work.

A million dollars. Not as much as I've made in three hours, but up there.

Actually, profitwise, it had to be his best score. Practically no overhead on this mission, assuming you didn't count the abortion of a trip a few weeks before.

That should be counted. R&D.

He made a mental note to do the math on the proceeds per minute.

Focusing on the rewards made the risks seem less imposing. He hated White for playing Mr. Cautious—surely it was an act, because the CIA officer would clearly have been urging something even more reckless if Tolevi hadn't suggested this. He was only playing to the girl, Chelsea.

Who, despite being a bit of a know-it-all, was very pretty.

Only a few years older than Borya.

Probably older than she looks.

"White?" he said. Disguised as a cell phone, the low-probability-of-intercept radio was always on.

"Good coms."

"I'm moving."

Tolevi put the car in gear and drove up the road. The guards were still there, leaning against their truck, blocking the driveway.

"I'm here to see the colonel," Tolevi said in Russian, skidding on the gravel as he stopped.

One of the men threw down his cigarette and came over. Tolevi recognized him as one of the thugs who'd held him two weeks before, but the man didn't seem to remember.

"I have business with the colonel."

"There is no colonel here."

"The hell with you, dog. Moscow sent me. You have a problem with that, you take it up with them."

"Let me see your papers."

"Fuck yourself and your mother's mother. Greshkin in Moscow said he'd sack the whole bunch of you if you gave me shit again."

The name of the head of SVR's Directorate S—the covert unit—apparently didn't mean anything to the man, for he didn't react.

"Are you gonna move?" Tolevi demanded in terse Russian, "or am I going to sit here and insult you until the colonel comes out?"

"The colonel is on a mission," said the other soldier, coming over.

"I'll wait inside. I gotta take a dump. Or maybe I should do it in your truck."

The threat of defecation did the trick. The second soldier pulled the first soldier aside. After a few seconds' consultation, he went to move the truck.

"Driving to the front door," Tolevi said over the radio.

He parked near the door, checked the pistol at his belt, then got out. He'd debated about the gun—they would surely search him when he went in and confiscate it, but since they thought he was working for the intelligence service, the weapon would be more or less expected. It might even enhance his story.

And if they didn't search him, then he'd have a gun. That would make everything easier.

He could hear the thin buzz of the UAV nearby. The soldiers' truck at the front was loud enough to drown it out, but away from other noises you could detect it if you tried hard enough.

"Keep that UAV as high as you can," he told them. "I can hear the buzz."

Knock on the door, or just go in?

Why knock?

But the choice wasn't his to make: the door flew open. One of the colonel's aides stood on the threshold.

"I'm back," Tolevi told him. "I have a message from Moscow, and instructions."

"You are not welcome here." The aide pointed at his ear. "Don't you learn?"

"This is a debt that will be paid in the future." Tolevi pointed at his ear. "Right now we both have orders. You think I wanted to come back? Get the hell out of my way, asshole."

Tough guy had worked outside, but not here. The aide flew out the door at him. Tolevi had been an excellent street fighter in his youth, but his youth was well past. The aide had ten years and a good sixty pounds of muscle on him. He grabbed Tolevi and threw him against the wall, shoved him inside, then picked him up and tossed him to the floor on his back. Before Tolevi could react, the Russian jumped on his chest, pressing his forearm into his neck and his knee into his stomach.

"I'll break you in two, scum," said the aide.

"Fuck you," muttered Tolevi, struggling to breathe.

The aide held him a few more seconds, then got up. Tolevi thought he was starting to pass out. A kick into his ribs sent a wave of pain through his body, and he wished he had lost consciousness.

Another soldier came and hauled him to his feet. Tolevi put up his hands—he'd forgotten about his gun, still in his belt—but couldn't ward off the blow from the side to his damaged ear. As he screamed with pain, the aide snatched the pistol from his belt and smacked him across the chest with it. Then he shoved him to the ground. His radio flew across the floor.

Fortunately, it looked like a cell phone. The soldier couldn't tell the difference when he smashed it with his heel.

"HE'S IN," WHITE said down by the vans. "But they're giving him a hard time. I think we lost the radio."

"Are you going in?" asked Chelsea.

"No," said White. "He knew it would be rough. Hang tight, and keep that UAV overhead."

100

Boston—a little later

Borya looked at the clock on the wall and jumped up.

She'd told Mary Martyak she'd be home an hour ago.

It was hard to keep track of time when you were at Smart Metal.

"I have to go," she told her supervisor. "See you Friday. Regular time."

"Regular time," said Lisa Macklin. "See ya then."

101

North of Donetsk—around the same time

Think about the money. Think about Borya.

Tolevi felt his face swelling, blood rushing to repair the damage done by the Russian commandos' feet. He pushed up to his haunches, sliding back against the wall, dazed but conscious.

No money is worth this. It's not the pain, it's the humiliation. One of them, maybe, but two?

Should have just blown the pricks up and been done with it.

Blown Johansen off.

"Get up, *mafya* shit," yelled the soldier. "You're bloodying the hall."

You'd think they'd at least be a little scared of the damn SVR. If it was still the KGB, they wouldn't pull this shit.

"I'm not *mafya*, asshole." Tolevi winced, expecting to be hit again, but apparently the soldiers were satiated and walked away.

Tolevi took a quick inventory of his teeth—still there, still intact—then attempted to get his bearings.

Three in the house. Two just beat the shit out of me. The other . . . our prize . . . downstairs?

He bent over to the radio and scooped it up. It was smashed and undoubtedly beyond hope. But his watch was intact; it had a signal function that he could use to alert the team. Push the button twice, and they'd move in.

Find the butcher first.

Tolevi staggered into the hall behind the room, heading in the direction of the kitchen. He found his two friends laughing at the table. They had coffee and some sort of goulash, half-finished, on their plates.

"I need water," he told them.

They ignored him. He went to the sink, found a glass.

There was a door to his right. He hoped it was the basement.

"This a closet or the bathroom?" he mumbled.

They didn't answer, which was the response he was hoping for. He walked to the door with an exaggerated stumble, then opened it, intending to go down. Probably they would push him; he braced himself for a tumble.

But it wasn't the basement. It was a bathroom.

Tolevi hesitated.

"Make sure you close the door. We don't want to smell your shit," snarled the soldier who'd done most of the hitting.

CHELSEA PULLED THE radio earbud out and squeezed the plastic, trying to make it more comfortable. Nothing seemed to work; her ears continued to itch.

The screen for the Nighthawks—she now had two in the air—was in front of her on the floor. Peter's controller was to her left; the controls for the Groucho mechs sat on the floor to her right. All three of the ground robots were already positioned in the woods, ready to go.

"Looks like he's in the back with the two soldiers," she told White, who was sitting in the front of the van with Bozzone.

"Move up to the house," White told the paras. "Let's get ready to grab him."

White turned to Bozzone. "I'm going to get in position. You guys OK?"

"We're good," said Bozzone.

"Chelsea?"

"Yeah. Go."

The van rocked as White hopped out. Chelsea checked the UAVs. She had the video divided in half, displaying the visual feeds for both with a small GPS map in each view's right-hand corner.

A warning came up on the screen to the left: the battery for Nighthawk 1, the one they had launched first, was starting to run low; she'd have to recover it soon.

Nighthawk 2 was circling about a half mile south, ready in reserve. She checked it quickly, catching a glimpse of some kids playing soccer. Its vitals were good; she decided she would move it up now, while things were still relatively quiet.

She plotted a new course, then took control from the computer. As she did, she noticed a cloud of dust billowing up in the corner of the forward video image. She banked the bird back south.

"Vehicles," she said over the radio. "I think the Russian commandos are coming back."

102

Boston—about the same time

Massina and Johnny were passing through the hallway when Lisa Macklin ran out of her lab room and nearly knocked them down.

"Whoa, cowboy," said Massina. "Watch where you're driving."

"Trying to catch little Borya. She left this." Macklin held up a backpack.

"I don't see her," said Massina.

"Excuse me." Macklin trotted to the rail, looked over it, then ran to the elevator.

Massina continued down the hall, stopping to check on the 3-D interface unit, which was refining a program that used gestures to command robots. Simple in theory, in practice the need for a complex and deep dictionary of commands made thing vastly complicated. The programming was the easy part; refining the gestures so a wide range of humans could do them unambiguously was proving nearly impossible.

"Put on the glasses and check out our latest iteration," offered the project director.

"I'd love to, but I have some things I have to get to," said Massina apologetically. He was due back in the box. The operation would be starting any minute.

"How we doing, Shadow?" he asked Johnny back in the hall. "How are your legs?"

"Good. Great. How's your arm?"

Massina gave a short, self-deprecating chuckle. "You know, you're the first person that's asked me that all year. Probably since my last checkup."

"How long did it take you to get used to it?"

"I'm not used to it." They stopped in front of the elevator. "You never get used to it. You accept it and move on."

Johnny nodded.

"Eventually it feels more comfortable," said Massina gently. "But there's always loss there. Deep loss."

"Yeah."

The elevator opened. Macklin stepped out. She still had the backpack in her hand.

"Missed her," she said. "I'll have to find somebody to drop it off."

"Why don't you take it, Johnny?" suggested Massina. "I won't need you for a while."

"Sure."

103

North of Donetsk—about the same time

They'd worked out two plans in case the Spetsnaz came back. One was to simply let them; the presence of more bodies complicated matters but didn't make the mission more difficult per se.

The other was to take them out as they pulled up.

It was White's call.

"Set up to intercept the bastards," said White over the team radio. "I don't have coms with Tolevi," he added. "Anybody?"

No one had him.

"What's he doing?" White asked Chelsea.

"He's stopped moving. He's near the first two."

"What about our jackpot?" said White.

"Still prone downstairs."

"Let's take these guys. Chelsea, get the drones moving to the house."

Chelsea turned to the Groucho controls. Both were loaded with explosives. She directed Groucho 1 to head toward the front of the house; Groucho 2 was programmed to move to the garage, where the vehicles would be.

"The trucks are almost past the road," she told Bozzone.

"I'm ready," he said. He raised his rifle, then twisted in the seat so he was facing the intersection where they would pass.

TOLEVI SAT ON the closed toilet, trying to work out where the door to the basement would be.

Front room. Hallway to the left.

Go back there and check it out.

He got up and reached for the door, then realized he'd better flush the toilet, or the two bozos in the kitchen would be suspicious.

As the toilet flushed, he heard the crack of a gunshot outside.

God damn it, White. No way.

There was another bullet, louder, then rounds of automatic fire.

Son of a bitch! White, you asshole!

TWO OF THE paras had set up near the front of the house with scopes, using their MK 17s as light sniper rifles. The shots took down the two men at the road before the three Russian Gazes reached the property. But the gunfire brought one of the men who'd been back by the garage area forward before the CIA paras at the back could get a shot on him, and he began peppering the area in front of the house with covering fire—which would have been a bad thing for his comrades had they still been alive.

More importantly for the CIA team, he radioed the men in the trucks.

The Americans were outnumbered, but they weren't outgunned. Porter aimed a Russian rocket-grenade launcher at the lead truck as it stopped a hundred yards from the property. The grenade hit before more than half of the men could get out; those who weren't hit by shrapnel were burned alive.

TOLEVI YANKED THE door to the bathroom open, expecting to see the others in the kitchen. But they'd already run to the front room.

He ran around the other way, hoping to get to the basement before they cut it off. Bullets shot through the front of the house, tearing up the wood and plaster. He dove to the ground, then scrambled into the room.

The two commandos were at the windows, aiming Minimis—Belgian squad-level machine guns similar to American M249s—out the window.

"What the hell?" Tolevi shouted as the man on the right turned toward him. "Who's attacking?"

"Just stay down, asshole."

"Where the hell is my gun? I'm not going down without a fight!"

"Stay down or I shoot you."

A fusillade of bullets came through the front. Tolevi ducked.

Where the hell did they put my pistol?

He went through to the left. There were two doors. He opened the first. It was a stairway up.

Other one.

As he reached for the door, the front of the house exploded. He fell to the ground, dazed and choking with the smoke.

"WHO FIRED AT the house?" demanded White. "What the hell—was it the robot?"

"The robots are still fifty yards away," said Chelsea.

"A grenade from the Russians," said Porter. "They must have misfired."

"Get these—"

White's voice was drowned out by gunfire. Chelsea lowered her head, as if the bullets were here, not a few hundred yards away. Rattled, she tried to focus on the Nighthawks. That was her job, to spot where the enemy was and tell the others. She flipped on the infrared to make it easier to spot the bodies in the field and woods.

It was starting to get dark.

Eight Russians left fighting.

Another truck coming to the intersection—their intersection.
Turning.

"Beefy, we have another truck."

"Stay here and don't move!" Bozzone told her, bolting out of
the vehicle with his rifle.

TOLEVI GOT TO his knees. The commando nearest him had been
thrown back by the explosion. His Minimi lay on the floor a few
feet away.

Just by coincidence, it was the thug who had taken the first
cuts at him.

Tolevi reached the machine gun just as the commando rose.
The Russian held his hand out for it.

"Here," said Tolevi, leveling it toward the man's stomach and
pressing the trigger. "See you in hell, scumbag."

CHELSEA WATCHED GROUCHO 1 rumble up to the front of the
house. The building was blackened and pockmarked; a grenade
had gone off in the front yard moments before.

The idea had been for Groucho 1 to explode as a diversion,
allowing Tolevi to go out the back; alternatively, it would be used
to clear the way for a frontal assault. Unsure how it could be used
now, she left it parked in ready mode, waiting for instructions.

She looked at Groucho 2, which was sixty seconds from its
assigned position at the back barn. Then she looked back at the
Nighthawk screen, trying to locate the soldiers and radio their
positions to the rest of the team.

Gunfire rattled outside, very close to the van. She ducked
down, folding herself at the waist over the control units.

It's not supposed to go like this.

A sharp rap on the front driver's side door caught her by surprise, and she twisted around, frozen.

A face appeared at the window.

A child's face. One of the kids who'd been playing soccer. Crying.

Oh my God, thought Chelsea, scrambling to unlock the door.

TOLEVI HAD NEVER fired a Minimi before and wasn't used to its heft or kick, both of which affected his aim. But he made up for that with the sheer amount of bullets, cutting the commando nearly in half before letting off of the trigger.

The other man turned, a puzzled look on his face.

Tolevi fired. Two bullets flew from the gun, then nothing. He'd emptied the magazine.

Both bullets missed. The other man, still not entirely comprehending, started to raise his own weapon in defense.

"Damn it!" yelled Tolevi, launching himself toward him.

He swung the machine gun up, using it like a spear as he struck the Russian. They tumbled back against the wall as the Russian's gun began spitting bullets. Tolevi's hand felt as if it was burning—he'd inadvertently touched the barrel—but by this point he was beyond pain, stoked with adrenaline and fear. He wedged the Minimi against the man's throat, violently mashing it downward as the other man began to cough. The Russian let go of his gun and tried to push Tolevi away. But Tolevi had too much leverage now, and all of his viciousness, all of his anger and desperation, went into his hands and arms. He pushed against the man's throat with all his might, awkwardly but effectively, until the man stopped struggling.

One more slam to make sure, then he sprung up, dropping the empty machine gun on the floor. He started to back out, then, realizing a gun would be more than a little useful, he reached down and grabbed the other Minimi.

He looked up.

A man was standing on the other side of the room.

The butcher.

"You really are his brother, aren't you?" said Tolevi, surprised at how similar the men looked in real life. "The pictures don't do you justice."

The butcher shook his head. Tolevi realized he'd been speaking in English.

"I'm here to get you out," he said in Ukrainian. "Your brother sent me."

"My brother?"

"He's outside." A lie, but it was the easiest way to tell Olak that he was on his side. "I'm an American. With the CIA. Working for them. We're here to rescue you."

"What?"

"Come on. We'll get out the back."

THERE WERE TWO kids there, both boys eight or nine years old. Chelsea pulled them inside, hit the lock button, then pushed them down beneath the dashboard in front of the seats.

"Stay down!" she told them in English.

Their confused looks made it clear they didn't understand, but Chelsea didn't have time to try and explain. She went back to the control screens as a fresh volley of gunfire raged nearby.

Beefy!

"Chelsea, we're hearing a lot of gunfire from your area," said White over the radio. "What's going on down there?"

"There's kids, shit," she said.

"What? What are you saying?"

She looked at the screen. Two Russians were running up the side of the road toward the house.

"There are two guys coming up the road, off on the shoulder," she told him.

"OK, OK. Are you all right?"

"There was another truck—Beefy's dealing with it. Beef?"

There was gunfire outside, then silence. Chelsea felt her chest untighten.

There was a knock on the passenger side door.

"Open the door, OK?" Chelsea said to the kids.

They don't speak English!

Chelsea looked at the video screen. Nighthawk 1 was on 10 percent battery. It had to land. She decided instead she would use it as a missile—she zoomed out until she found the truck that had stopped near them, then overrode the safety controls to send it into a crash.

The pounding at the door continued, more desperate, she thought.

"I'm coming, Beef," she said. She left the control unit and scrambled forward. There was no one there.

"Damn," she said. She pushed open the locks, then glanced at the children cowering in the front. "Come in the back with me," she told them. "Come on."

She grabbed hold of both of them, urging and pulling. They had just reached the back of the van when the rear door opened.

"Beefy, I was so wor—"

She stopped midword. A Russian commando was pointing a rifle at her.

104

The box, Boston—about the same time

"They've already started," said Johansen as Massina entered the box.

"You should have called me." Massina stared at the sitrep screen, trying to make out what was going on.

We're going to make some huge improvements, he thought to himself. *I want to see things in real time, up close, and without relying on their satellites and feeds. It's going to be easy to ID our people. We're going to have more bots and devices on the ground. UAVs. It's going to be our operation.*

"Where are they?" he asked Johansen.

"They're at the house." Johansen's tone was even sharper than usual. "Still two or three guerillas to take care of. Then they have to get out."

"Where are Chelsea and Bozzone?"

"They're in their command truck, in the south. It's out of the frame."

"Why?"

"I guess they're concentrating the feed on the house. The vans are too far from the action. Don't worry. Just a few more minutes, and everyone will be fine."

105

North of Donetsk—about the same time

The UAV struck the Spetsnaz truck with a loud crash. The commando at the door of Chelsea's van jerked back, looking to see what had happened. Chelsea reached for Peter's control, hoping to tell the robot to grab the Russian.

The commando got to her first, pulling her out of the vehicle and throwing her on the ground. He yelled at the children, who lay frozen in fear on the floor of the van. Then he pointed his gun at them.

Chelsea jumped up.

"No! No!" she screamed.

He tossed her down again. Then he reached in and dragged out the first child. The other followed meekly. The commando shouted something at them, waving with his hand. He wanted them to move.

Chelsea's body trembled. Her brain froze.

And then her father spoke to her, as he had so often before, voice calm but firm.

Protect the children. Keep your head.

"*Grazhdanskiy,*" she said, trying to tell the soldier they were civilians. But either her pronunciation was so bad he couldn't understand her, or else he was too concerned with getting away from the now smoldering Gaz that he didn't pay any attention. Chelsea grabbed the children to her, shepherding them up the road.

One of the kids smelled; he'd wet himself from fear.

The soldier yelled, then pointed off the road. Chelsea thought of bolting for a moment, then saw that there was another commando sitting on the ground a few yards away. He had a gun cradled in his lap; his pants were red. Obviously he'd been wounded.

Where was Bozzone? Watching, she hoped. Ready to come to their rescue.

Or dead.

There was a building beyond, an outbuilding that belonged to the neighboring farm. The soldier who'd captured them pointed to the building and reeled off a command that could only mean, *Inside!*

Chelsea stooped toward the wounded man, intending to try and help—and maybe get his gun. But the other soldier ran up and pushed her away, shoving her toward the children.

With no other option open, she put a hand on the back of each child and helped them inside the building.

TOLEVI GRABBED THE butcher by the arm and tugged him to the back of the house. The kitchen window had been shattered. Outside, two Russians crouched by the van he'd been in the first night. One was firing into the woodline—aimed shots, so obviously he had at least a vague idea where his target was.

The other was looking back at the house.

"You know how to work this?" Tolevi asked the butcher. "I don't know how many bullets are in the magazine."

"Give me."

"Here. I'm going to see if they have other weapons." Tolevi handed the gun over, then started to leave.

"American!" yelled the butcher.

Tolevi looked back. The bastard was holding the gun on him. "What?"

"Hands up or I fire," said the butcher.

Tolevi started to raise his hands. The butcher pressed the trigger anyway.

BORYA, THOUGHT TOLEVI. *BORYA!*

NOTHING HAPPENED. EITHER Tolevi had picked up the wrong gun in the confusion, or both magazines had been emptied.

I'm nothing if not lucky, thought Tolevi, rushing the butcher.

106

The box—about the same time

The Nighthawk was flying in a circular programmed pattern. The robots were all on standby.

What was going on?

Massina tried to make sense of the confusion on the ground. Where was Chelsea? Why wasn't she moving the mechs toward the knot of enemies on the road? The Grouchos could have taken them out easily.

Chelsea, aren't you seeing this?

Something was very wrong. Massina backed out the image. The control van was empty.

Damn it.

He pulled over the keyboard and began typing the override sequences he'd need to take control of Groucho 1 and 2.

107

North of Donetsk—about the same time

By now, Tolevi was so bashed and bruised that he didn't feel any pain at all as he slammed into the butcher.

"I'm here to rescue you, asshole. God," he said over and over as they rolled on the floor, punching and kicking.

A good three-quarters of the blows by each man missed, but that still meant plenty of punishment for both. They finally fell apart, exhausted. Tolevi jumped to his feet; the butcher slid away, then spun around, revealing a handgun.

"Listen, you idiot," said Tolevi. "I'm here to get you out. I'm taking you to the West."

"I'm not going west," snapped the butcher. "Put your hands up and shut your mouth."

CHELSEA JUMPED AS the door slammed behind her.

Be calm for the kids.

The building was a small shed, barely large enough for a tractor; it was completely empty, save for some empty seed bags on the floor. There were two windows, both partially boarded, one on the left and one at the back.

The children ran to the back window.

"No, no, get away from it," she said, going over to them. "Get back!"

Both boys pointed outside. There was another child outside.

"Is he all right?" she asked the children inside with her. But they didn't understand. She waved her arms at the child outside, trying to get him to duck; he just stared at her, dumbfounded by everything that was happening.

I have to tell the others where I am, she realized. She reached for her radio, then realized that the earbuds weren't there. She'd lost the headset back near the van somewhere; without it, the radio was useless.

Break the window and escape.

It was very narrow, too narrow even for her.

The smaller of the two kids might make it, though, if she broke the glass.

She put her elbow next to the bottom of the pane and smacked it through. The glass was surprisingly thick and stubborn—it took three blows before she broke it.

HANDS UP, TOLEVI moved reluctantly to the door.

"If we go out there now, we'll get caught in the cross fire," he told the butcher. "And we don't want that, right?"

"Open the door and let's go."

CHELSEA BOOSTED THE first boy up. He wiggled into the space, pushing himself back and forth, but he was just too big, and the window was too small. They finally gave up; he slid to the ground.

"We need your friend to go get Peter," she told him. "Just the controls, I mean, I dropped it. Can you tell him?"

The boy gestured apologetically with his hands. He had no

clue what she was saying. She tried miming it out, but that was useless as well.

Translation app, she thought.

Great idea if she had one.

"Video game," she tried. "Control."

The boy hesitated a moment. "*Videohra?*"

Close enough, she decided. "Controls." She gestured with her hands. "Back there."

The boy went to the window and said something to the kid outside. He disappeared for a moment, then reappeared, far too soon to have gotten the controller.

But he passed something inside.

A cell phone.

This is no good to me, Chelsea thought.

Call Smart Metal. Have them get a translator.

She started to dial. How long would it take them?

Borya can speak Ukrainian. And she's a kid; I can give her the phone and have them talk to her.

Chelsea hit the Kill button, then punched the country code for the U.S., hoping she remembered Borya's cell number correctly.

108

Borya looked at her cell phone, vibrating on the kitchen table as she did her homework.

A strange number came up on the ID. It looked very odd.

Probably someone trying to sell her a credit card.

She spun the phone around on the table. Homework sucked. She needed a break.

"Yes?" she said in a funny voice, answering the phone.

"Borya, this is Chelsea. I dropped the controls to Peter by my van, and I need you to tell these kids to get it."

"What? Chelsea? Where are you?"

"I dropped the controls to Peter and need these kids to run and get it," said Chelsea. She was out of breath. "Can you tell them?"

"Um . . . OK."

"You have to do it in Ukrainian."

"OK."

"Do you remember what the controller looked like?"

"I think so."

"Do it! Try! Please!"

MEDVED CHECKED THE address. Tolevi lived in a damn nice house, far nicer than he deserved.

He was a slime. Clearly, Stratowich was right about him squealing to the FBI—that's why Stratowich was in jail right now.

They'd get Stratowich next. The foreign service didn't like to take risks, which was why they used him in the first place.

His car was in the driveway. So he was home.

"Ready?" Medved asked the man alongside him.

"Just about," he said, screwing a silencer onto his gun.

"We get the information first. And my money."

"Talk to him all you want. Just as long as he's mine in the end. No witnesses."

"No shit."

109

The kids thought it was a game.

That was one way to deal with it, thought Chelsea as they giggled, passing the phone back and forth. Then the smaller of the two, the one who'd gotten stuck in the window, tiptoed to it and told his friend outside to go get the controller.

"And tell him not to get caught," said Chelsea.

Outside the house, Tolevi slid to the ground, next to the commando who'd been watching the house. The commando still thought he was on his side.

And apparently he trusted the butcher. None of this was making a lot of sense. Tolevi expected it to implode any minute.

"They're coming in the front," he told the Russian. "Watch this one," he added, pointing to the butcher. "He's nuts."

The commando waved at him, then turned his attention down the hill, firing at something moving in the brush.

Tolevi glanced around, trying to find some sort of weapon.

But it was too late; the butcher dashed across the yard, sliding next to him.

"говно!" yelled the Russian. "Shit, holy shit! What is that?"

It was one of the little bots, the Groucho, walking on six legs toward them.

The commando took aim.

Tolevi jerked around. "Duck!" he yelled to the butcher.

110

The box—that same moment

Massina saw the soldier taking aim at the mech.

"OK, now," he said as he pressed the button, detonating the device at the rear of the robot.

The screen blanked with the explosion. Massina looked over at the sitrep. None of the men near the truck moved.

He directed the UAV to fly closer to the front of the house, then keyed the command for Groucho 1, directing the bot toward the rear of the Russian position there.

"Tell them help is coming," Massina told Johansen.

111

North of Donetsk—simultaneous

The wounded Russian heard the crashing noise at the back of the shed over the din of the gunfire up the hill. It surprised him—he wouldn't have thought a girl and two little boys could break the damn thing down.

He struggled to get to his feet. He was supposed to kill them if they escaped. Truth be told, he didn't want to. But orders were orders.

His legs were wobbly. He'd been struck by two bullets. One had merely squashed itself against his bulletproof vest; it had given him a bruise but not much else. The other had gone into his thigh. He'd lost a decent amount of blood, though the injury didn't figure to be life threatening.

Damn Ukrainian bastards. Damn Putin for sending us here.

An odd contraption turned the corner as he approached. It was metal, alien, something from outer space? It had claws.

The soldier raised his gun and fired. His first bullet missed. His second hit it square in the body.

The thing didn't stop. It sped full into him, claws like spears digging into his chest.

Falling backward, he lost his rifle.

CHELSEA CHARGED AFTER Peter as the bot pushed its "hand" down on the Russian's chest. The kids ran in front of her and started kicking him.

"No, no," said Chelsea, scooping up his rifle. "Leave him. Don't kill him!"

They shouted something at her that sounded like *norham jushua*. She gathered they were saying he was a bad man or evil.

"That's all right. Leave him. He's hurt. Come on."

She started in the direction of the van, following Peter as he headed toward the second Russian.

Someone yelled, and then there was a shot. Chelsea grabbed the children close and pushed them with her to the ground, watching Peter rush forward toward the commotion.

A second later she heard a familiar voice yelling from the woods.

"It's me!" shouted Bozzone. "I know you're here if Peter is. Are you all right?"

Better than all right, ballerina girl, laughed her father in her head.

Chelsea jumped to her feet.

TOLEVI PUSHED HIMSELF up from the dirt. The butcher was still on the ground.

"Asshole," he yelled, stomping his wrist to release the pistol. He grabbed it, then took hold of the back of the butcher's shirt.

Something blew up in the front of the building.

"We're here, we're here!" Tolevi yelled, running around to the side. The last thing he needed was that idiot White shooting him. "The butcher is with me! The butcher is with me!"

112

Boston—about the same time

The doorbell rang.

Borya looked up at Mary Martyak.

"Think we should get it?" asked Martyak.

"Yes, of course," said Borya, putting down her phone. Chelsea had had to hang up but had told her to stand by.

Stand by.

Borya left the phone on the table and ran to the door.

"Who is it?" she asked, pulling it open.

"HEY THERE, BORYA," said Johnny Givens. "You left this at work." He held up the backpack.

"Oh wow, I totally forgot it."

"Hello, Johnny," said Mary Martyak from inside.

"Mary."

"Come on in," said Borya, grabbing Johnny's hand. "I just talked to Chelsea."

"You did?"

ACROSS THE STREET, Medved and the Russian intelligence operative got back into their car.

"We'll come back tomorrow," said Medved. "Stratowich should be able to keep his mouth shut until then."

"He better."

"You're welcome to get rid of him, as far as I'm concerned," said Medved. "Take him and Tolevi out. I'd sleep better."

"What makes you think I'm not going to?"

Medved nodded. There was a little too much menace in his companion's voice, he thought, the sort of tone that hinted he would be next.

"Let's go to my club and have something to drink," Medved said. "Relax with some wine and girls. Tomorrow is another day."

"Tomorrow, yes," said the man. "Tomorrow."

113

The box—around the same time

They were in the trucks, all of them, including Bozzone and Porter, both of whom had been shot.

The butcher's hands and feet were trussed, and Tolevi was not being very gentle with him.

Massina looked over at Johansen.

"They're good," said Johansen. "They'll make it."

"Who is the butcher, really?" said Massina.

"What do you mean?"

"He didn't want to be rescued. He had a gun on Tolevi. You can see it in the videos. And Tolevi tied him up."

"He did want to be rescued. At one point."

"Who was he?"

"The Russian SVR officer who was involved in planning the Ukrainian invasion," confessed Johansen. "The rebels got tired of him and put him in their prison. He sent a message through his brother that he wanted to defect."

"Does anyone else on the team know that?"

"It's need to know. And they didn't."

114

North of Donetsk—about the same time

Tolevi had a strong suspicion about what was up, but there was no way to be sure until it played out. And the only way for that to happen was to pick up the brother as planned, because otherwise they'd never make it through Ukraine. So he drove to an intersection two miles from the compound and waited for the butcher's brother to appear.

It took nearly twenty minutes.

"Hop in," Tolevi said, opening the side door of the van. "We're running a little late."

The butcher's brother climbed in. Tolevi pointed to the lumpy frame under the blanket in the back. "He's unconscious, but OK. We're letting him sleep"

The brother yanked a pistol from his belt. "Bastard," he yelled, shooting at the figure below the blanket.

He got off three shots before Tolevi and one of the CIA paras managed to get the gun away from him. They wrestled him to the side, then searched him for weapons. They found a small 9mm at his back and a radio.

The para tied him up.

"Why?" asked Tolevi.

"He's not my brother. I am working for SBU—*Sluzhba Bezpeky Ukrayiny*." The Ukrainian special service—in effect, their FBI.

"No shit," said Tolevi. "But I will say you guys look a lot alike. You *could* be brothers."

"That's why they sent me, no? I was a colonel in the army. They came to me. We have worked on this six months, more."

"Why?" asked Tolevi.

"He's one of the barbarians who set up the invasion. He was so despicable, even the rebels couldn't deal with him. They put him in the prison to keep him safe. A lot of them wanted to kill him. He was in the house by himself."

"Why didn't you just blow up the prison?"

"We've tried. We couldn't get him ourselves." He spit on the blanket. "We knew the Americans could. I'll help you get across the border. I owe you."

"I hate to tell you this, but this ain't him." Tolevi pulled off the blanket, revealing a pair of duffel bags, a backpack and some rolled towels. "Don't worry, though. He'll pay for his sins many times over."

115

Kiev—six hours later

Getting to the border was easy, even though none of them trusted the directions the butcher's brother had laid out. Dan found a road, and a bribe to the Ukrainian guard saved them the trouble of shooting the poor bastard. Once across, they changed the plates so the vehicles looked like government trucks, and they were left alone.

The "brother" did look an awful lot like Olak Urum, Tolevi thought. But in reality he was a colonel in the Ukrainian intelligence service, which had concocted an elaborate plot to get the butcher killed in revenge for the many deaths he'd caused. Ironically, just like the butcher, he had started his career in the Soviet KGB.

Takes one to know one.

Now the butcher was coming back to the U.S. anyway, where he'd detail Russia's lies for the world.

They drove for several hours before reaching Kiev and the airport. The plane was waiting in the commercial area. The guards there—all CIA—whisked them to the tarmac. Neither the butcher nor his brother, both sleeping with the aid of a heavy dose of propofol, objected at all.

They left the Ukrainian in the back of the van. The butcher was carried onto the plane in a stretcher. It was a 737 registered to a South African airline—according to the papers, at least.

"We got everybody?" asked White as the last para boarded.

Asshole CIA officers, thought Tolevi. *Can't even friggin' count. But they always got to be in charge.*

Screw him.

A million bucks.

I think Johansen owes me a bonus on this one. Call it entertainment tax. How much would one of these planes cost?

CHELSEA STOOD NEXT to Bozzone as he was helped into his seat. He'd taken two slugs, one in the arm and one at the side of his chest, deflected by the ceramic plate in his bulletproof vest. Both he and Porter had been treated by one of the paras; both were going to be fine.

"More than you bargained for, huh?" Bozzone said as he sat down.

"What do you mean?"

"Guns. You didn't expect that, right?"

"No. Not at all."

"They said it would be dangerous. Were you scared?"

She had been scared. Yes.

But . . .

"I was scared," she admitted. "But we made it."

"We did."

The plane began to taxi.

"I'm ready to go home," she confessed.

"Me, too," said Bozzone. "But it's going to be dull after this. Real dull."

"Somehow I don't think so. But I won't mind if it is."

116

Boston, twenty-four hours later

Tolevi had the CIA driver drop him off two blocks from the house, claiming it was a security issue, even as the man protested loudly that they were not being followed.

They were being followed, Tolevi knew—by the FBI, whose motives he was sure had far more to do with nabbing American-based *mafya* connections than protecting him.

How much protection he actually needed, how much the CIA would actually pay him, what he would do next week—these were all unknowable at the moment, and not worth thinking about. What was worth thinking about—though perhaps even harder to contemplate—was what he would say to his daughter.

She needed discipline, that much was clear. If she'd been a boy, he would have sent her—him—to military school straightaway.

But then a boy would never have given him so many problems. A boy . . .

He knew how to deal with boys. He had been a boy. But girls—he'd raised one and loved one and still she was a mystery, a deep, deep mystery.

Chelsea, the robotics girl (as he thought of her), had sung Borya's praises to him on the flight back, calling her a hero and a budding genius, puffing his father's pride. But now that he'd had a little more time to reflect, he'd not only put the young woman's praise in perspective—clearly the robotics girl saw too much of herself in his child—but he'd also thought about the possible implications of what his daughter had done. If the mobsters found out that Borya had actually been involved, she could easily be targeted; a young girl would be easily picked off, and those animals had no scruples, no scruples at all.

Lose Borya? That will be the end. I will kill myself that day.

No, the next day, the day after I have killed the beasts responsible.

So she had to be kept out of harm's way. And he had to discipline her for stealing from the banks . . . as clever as that was. And he had to punish her for breaking curfew and lying. And he had to protect her and nurture, feed this great intellect that apparently she was harboring, because a girl that smart had potential far beyond a normal child, so he owed not just her but probably the race to nurture it properly . . .

He had to do so many things regarding Borya that he couldn't settle on exactly what he should do, either in the short or long term, and certainly not in the two blocks that he walked from the car to the house. He thought of walking around the block a few times, but that would be useless—he wasn't going to get anything settled in his mind out here. He had to go and talk to his daughter, just plunge in, let his gut lead him to where he had to go.

And besides, it was cold.

Shoving his hands in his pockets, Tolevi trotted up the steps. He was surprised to find the door unlocked.

The foyer and front rooms were unlit, and only a dim light came through the hallway.

"Borya?" he asked, biting back his fear.

A second passed before there was an answer; in that moment, he felt ten times the anxiety he'd felt at his worst in the Ukraine.

"In the kitchen, Daddy," she said.

Wary, Tolevi walked to the back of the house, muscles tense. The light flickered—Borya had placed two candles in the middle of the table.

"Ta-dah!" she exclaimed. "Welcome home." She wrapped herself around him, hugging him tight. "I missed you, Daddy."

"I missed you, too, baby."

"Where's your bags?"

"It's a long story," he told her. "But I'm here, safe and sound."

"So am I. I made chicken Marsala."

"Really?" Tolevi glanced at the stove. A covered grill pan sat on the top.

"Have a seat," she insisted. "And there are potatoes."

"Potatoes?" he joked. "I feel like a king. . . . Where's Mary?"

"She went home. I told her I didn't need her."

"*Borya.*"

"Now that I have a job and everything, I'm ready for responsibility."

"What job?"

"Smart Metal."

"I thought that's an internship."

"They can call it what they want. But they're paying. I got you some wine. This is supposed to go with chicken." Borya retrieved a bottle from the refrigerator. It was unopened—a good thing, thought Tolevi.

"I invited Chelsea," added Borya, "but she was too tired. Do you like her?"

"Uh—"

"I'm not trying to set you up," Borya said quickly. "Just, she's really nice. And smart."

"That's good. Not as smart as you," added Tolevi.

"I'm sure she's smarter," said Borya, handing him the wine. "Can you open this?"

In the flickering light, she looked exactly like her mother. Tolevi felt a tear forming at the side of his eye.

"I need a corkscrew," he said quickly, rising so he could brush it away without his daughter seeing.

"We can talk about business tomorrow," announced Borya, her back to him as she opened the stove to retrieve the potatoes. "Tonight, we're celebrating, just me and you."

"Exactly," he managed. "Exactly."